HIS
LAST
SHOT

A NOVEL

ELAINE EVANS

Also by Elaine Evans

- Becoming Mallory

- All In

Cover Design by Get Covers

Illustration by Daniel Evans

Editing by Nevvie Gane

First edition 2025

ISBN 9798218653316

To my dad,
who instilled in me a love for the game of pool.
Even though I'm not that good.

His Last Shot

Elaine Evans

Elaine Evans

"Every shot is a lesson in itself. No matter how much you've practiced, there's always something to learn from each shot."

Willie Mosconi
World Straight Pool Champion

1

Two Ball, Side Pocket

Johnny

I glide my pool cue through my fingers, studying the table. Glossy numbered solid and striped balls sit idly on the green felt, waiting to find their new homes in one of the six pockets of this pool table. A virtual kaleidoscope of angles and possibilities. Flexing at my hip, I line up my shot, resting the shaft on the perfectly formed bridge of my right hand. My left grips the butt of the cue. With laser focus, I zero in on my target.

"Seven ball, corner pocket," I announce, claiming my shot.

I'm in my zone, and I love this exact moment. Right before the tip of the stick contacts the cue ball, the entire world goes silent. The other supposed players on neighboring tables disappear. The lively chatter of this bar/pool hall, Dexter's, fades into the background. Silence falls as my heart stops. It's pure adrenaline and power, all wrapped neatly with a bow.

There's only this table and me. Nothing else exists.

As if it's hanging on a pendulum, my left hand swings the butt of the stick. I hold my breath. The blue tip comes into contact with the white cue ball, which cracks against the solid maroon number seven. I watch with rapt attention as it speeds along the right rail and falls perfectly into the pocket.

I smile.

"Nice shot. How did you do that?" My cousin's question snaps me from the moment, and it's as if someone has turned up the volume in my head. Dexter's comes alive around me.

Scott shakes his head in disbelief. "I have no idea why I come and play with you. Must be a glutton for punishment."

I chalk my cue, carefully eyeing the pool balls, stalking them as if they were my prey. "You have to be here. I need someone to rack for me."

The puff of air filled with annoyance that escapes his lips makes me smirk as I watch him from the corner of my eye. He downs a swig of his beer; his stick hasn't left its resting position next to where he's sitting. The high-top back chair more than likely has his permanent butt print on it.

Because let's face it, that's what anyone who plays against me does. They watch me dominate and rack the balls for my next break.

Yes, I'm that good.

Playing pool has been my thing since I was six years old. I remember listening to my dad practice in our garage in the summer. With my window open, I would fall asleep to pool balls cracking against each other and my dad yelling at himself because he missed a shot.

Then, one day, I asked him to show me how to hold a pool cue and shoot. The smile on his face was one that I will never forget. Man, I wanted to be just like him. Nothing was cooler.

I've never looked back.

The game became my life, my passion. My cousin and best friend Scott was the football and baseball guy in our family. Not me. While he was practicing on the field in high school, I was practicing in my dad's garage. Hour after endless hour, learning this complex game.

Scott stands abruptly, the beer bottle hitting the wooden tabletop with a dull thud. "I'm going to run to the bathroom."

"What the heck, man." I throw my arm in the air because I hate my flow and rhythm being interrupted when I play. "There's only one ball left on the table. You can't hold it?"

He doesn't answer. Just salutes me as I watch him walk away. I know he's doing this on purpose. Hoping that it will disrupt the run of balls I have going.

It won't.

As I wait, I sit on one of the high-top chairs against the wall and survey the other players, shooting around at the neighboring tables.

Out of the corner of my eye, a wave of brunette hair and curves catches my attention. I do a double take, and it's as if a truck has just plowed into me. She emerges out of the shadows of a back hallway that empties behind the bar. Her hips swaying as she pulls her dark hair into a messy bun. Her movements ... angelic.

Suddenly, the world around me comes to a crawl, everything happening in slow motion. My heart stops beating.

With graceful, purposeful movements, she reaches for a bottle of Woodford Reserve from the back display of liquor. She's tall, at least six feet. Before she pulled it up, her hair, a rich dark chocolate brown, fell in heavy, shimmering waves, catching the light. Each wave, silken and dark, begging for my fingers to run through it. She's wearing jeans with holes in all the right places and a black tank top that has Dexter's scrawled across her chest. This bar is too dark, and I'm not close enough yet to take in the color of her eyes. But I have a feeling they are dark.

Which, just punch me now because I am a sucker for a brown-eyed girl.

I can't tear my stare away as she laughs at something a group of three older men say. She plops two ice cubes into a glass and fills a two-finger pour, sliding the drink to one of the older gentlemen.

As she takes an empty glass away, she quickly scans the noisy, dimly lit bar while still talking to the three men.

She stalls, her eyes catching mine briefly before darting away. I stare as a subtle smile plays on her lips, her attention settling back on the older men. Pivoting to another customer, she falters mid-swivel while giving me another lingering look.

She noticed me. Cool. I love it.

My throat is going completely dry, like sandpaper. I swallow hard.

The high-energy atmosphere of the bar dissolves around me, replaced by the heavy pounding of my heart as I watch her. She's the only person I see; her face is the only one I can make out, all else is a blur. I'm disoriented and drunk on attraction as something like fog fills the surrounding air. I watch her effortlessly glide behind the bar, avoiding the two other bartenders as her gaze flicks to me every so often.

Mine? Focused only on her.

"Okay, they killed the design of those bathrooms. They are amazing. And super clean, too." Scott's words cause the buzz of the bar to return, and I shake my head of the lust haze it was just in.

Lord. What just happened?

I clear my throat, trying my best to compose myself. "I wondered what took you so long. Did you reapply your lipstick, too?"

He sits and takes a lazy pull of his beer. "Cute."

Refocusing on the table, I line up my next shot, but not before flicking my gaze to the bar. She's still there. Still cute, still smiling. Taking in a much-needed calming inhale, I refocus my attention on the table and call the last shot of this game. "Two ball, side pocket."

The blue ball glides into the pocket, leaving the eight ball all alone on the table and sealing my cousin's fate. And making him fifty bucks poorer.

He whips out his wallet and fishes out the money, slapping it on the rail. I walk around the table, the scent of stale beer lingering in the air, gathering the last of the balls from the pockets. "Wanna go again?" I ask as I pocket the fifty.

"Are you kidding me? Laura will kill me. I need to get home. She already thinks I'm crazy playing for money against you."

"Your wife has always been smart *and* beautiful."

"As much as I would love to be humiliated again, I need to get home," Scott says as he unscrews his pool cue. He grabs his case, sliding the cue inside while checking his phone. "My Lyft should be here soon." Scott always grabs Lyfts when he plays with me. A few years ago, when his kids were infants, he and I went to a different pool hall with me driving. It was an amazing time, so we stayed and played for three hours longer than he felt was necessary. Needless to say, he wasn't happy, and neither was Laura. So now he finds his own way home.

I'll admit, Scott is a decent player. He can hold his own against guys and gals who believe they know a thing or two about the game.

But he's only beaten me once. A huge chunk of my savings account I owe to him.

Actually, I owe a lot to him. We have been each other's ride-or-die our whole lives. Growing up an only child, I was close with Scott. Everything we did, we did it together. Honestly, now that we are older, nothing has changed. His family is my family.

He finishes his beer, sits it down, and glances around the newest addition to Dexter's. An addition our construction company spearheaded.

Givens Construction.

Scott and I started this company together. It's grown quickly. We have both worked extremely hard at it to become successful. It's supported his family and has given me purpose and something in my life to be proud of.

I slap him on the back. "Thanks for meeting me here to check this place out. It's nice to see it all put together with the tables."

"A far cry from what it looked like before, that's for sure," Scott says with an amused chuckle.

Prior to the renovation, the bar was literally falling apart at the seams. It was last renovated in the seventies, and it showed. Now, the rustic cowboy feel this place has is infectious. The dance floor is bigger, the bar is longer, and the massive new addition houses two rows of pool tables. Ten tables on each side.

When Dexter Jr. approached us about a reno and an addition to this place, we were skeptical. Dexter's dad, Dexter Sr., had a reputation in our area for being a shady businessman. Since this is the most popular bar on this side of town, it makes one wonder what Dex Sr. did with his money because he didn't put it back into this place.

Now, it's the stuff of bar dreams. After his dad's death, Dex Jr. took over, and the rest is history.

We kept it all above books, demanding documentation of everything to cover our own butts. On the outside, Dexter Jr. seems more trustworthy than his dad. But the apple doesn't fall far from the tree.

One of his motivations for the remodel, besides that it desperately needed it, was that Dexter is also the president of the local pool league. The Billiards and Pool Association, or the BPA. Naturally, he wants to have tournaments here.

My first meeting with him was brief. Immediately, I got a vibe that he didn't like me. Spend just five minutes with the guy, and you get a sense that he likes to appear intimidating. And fails at it.

Me? With my height and overall jolly don't-give-a-crap attitude, I've been told I can come across as cocky. Whatever. With Scott being the professional one of our little duo, it makes sense that I would rub Dexter the wrong way. After our initial meeting, Scott even picked up on it.

"Good grief, Johnny. What did you do to piss him off?" he asked once we were back in his truck after leaving Dexter's the day we walked through the place with him.

"Nothing! He's a know-it-all blowhole. You can tell," I retorted. "I hate people like that. You know me."

"Yeah, maybe, but he's a client now, so try to not turn your nose down at him all the time. I mean, seriously, everything he said, you bounced back, correcting him in some way."

"Well, he was wrong. About *everything.* That man hasn't used a hammer his whole life, I guarantee it. Yet, he was talking down to me about the trade I love. I wasn't having it."

"You're right, but just do me a favor and avoid him while on the job. I don't need any issues with this."

So that's what I did. Dexter hovered while the work was being completed, but I kept my distance. Not sure I would have been able to compose myself if he tried to school me on something I was working on.

But now that the job is done, Dexter's no longer our concern.

As Scott texts Laura that he's on his way home, something catches my eye through the bar commotion. A man stumbles out of a back hallway, looking a little worse for the wear. The shiner on his eye is huge, and he's holding a bloody rag over his lip. Two other men follow behind, shoving him out the side door. And then Dexter trails behind all three, looking over his shoulder.

He scans the crowd, probably hoping no one saw the scene that just played out. Briefly, our eyes lock. Then he turns and disappears out the door.

Great.

Ever since the day I met him, I got a bad vibe about this man. Immediately, my gaze roves over the bar, looking for the tall brunette. She's occupied with customers and doesn't see the men leave.

"Anyway, I'm glad the reno is over." Scott's words snap my attention back to him. I nod as he slips on his worn leather coat to leave. I glance at the side door, waiting for any movement, but it remains closed. *Oh well, whatever happened is none of my concern, anyway.*

Scott smiles. "We should do this again soon. This felt like old times."

And by 'old times' he means us partying, being young and crazy. Not sure, at my age, I want that version of 'old times,' but yeah, he and I could use more of this, so I agree, hoping we can make it happen. "It was fun."

"You sticking around?" We both head toward the entrance, passing the packed dance floor. My attention roves to the bar; she's still there, the murmur of conversations surrounding her as she flashes fake smiles to people who probably don't deserve them. As I watch her, a jolt of electricity pierces through me. I've reacted to a beautiful woman before, don't get me wrong. But with her, there is just ... something.

She is stunning.

Scott follows my line of sight. "Ah. I get it." He grins. "Good luck. See you in the morning, and I expect a full report."

My lips curve into an evil grin. "Do I ever strike out?" I don't normally, and when I do, it doesn't matter. But this woman? Well, striking out feels like heartbreak waiting to happen.

He grabs the handle of the door to leave. "Rarely." His light chuckle follows him out into the night.

Nerves erupt in my stomach at the thought of talking to her, and I do not know why. Talking to women, flirting with them, dating them—it's pretty much my specialty. The excitement of the chase is thrilling. Right now, though, I am anything but excited. I am a big goofball, full of nerves. Every time I look at her, and with every step I take, butterflies swarm in my stomach.

Wait ... strike that. Not butterflies. It's more like falcons are flying in there, clawing at my insides with their sharp talons.

With my case in hand, I weave through the remaining crowd toward the bar, my focus only on the tall, statuesque brunette serving up drinks.

She's mesmerizing.

Resting my stick and jacket on the empty seat next to me, and with the scent of alcohol and regret hanging in the air, I settle in.

Sitting, waiting, watching, and drooling.

She slides what appears to be a glass of water over to one of the three older gentlemen, five stools away from me. She leans forward on her elbows. "So Slick, did your grandson graduate school?" she asks him with an ease and familiarity that suggests she knows these guys well.

"He did! Last week, actually. Well on his way to becoming a pilot," Slick answers as he grabs the glass and raises it to his mouth. The man is older than my forty-five years. He's probably pushing seventy and looks weathered with experience. The way life does to a person.

"That's awesome! He will have to take me on a flight sometime." The gorgeous bartender beams.

"Oh, he would love that more than you know," Slick answers with amusement.

Another of the older men, whose leathered face is etched with wrinkles and eyes crinkled at the corners, turns and sees me sitting and waiting. "You better stop talking to us old geezers and wait on your customers, Rachel."

Ah! Rachel. I like it. The name fits.

Rachel flicks her eyes in my direction as I give her a slight nod and wave. But it's the slight double take she gives me, followed by a subtle uptick on her lips, that makes me smile.

Not missing a beat, she retorts, "You telling me how to do my job again, Tiny?" Tiny (who is just that) only grunts. He must be the crabby one of the group.

She taps the slick lacquered bar. "I'll be right back, fellas." She turns, glimpses at me, then reaches for a napkin on the back counter. Her chest rises and falls as if she is preparing herself. I do the same because I know I will not be meeting just another woman.

With bated breath, I observe her approach as her slim waist begs for my hands. She slaps one of her fake smiles, but one thing stands out. A slight gate in her walk. It's not a limp. But she's compensating for something in her strides. Is it pain? Or was it an accident?

Suddenly, I want to know everything about this woman I haven't even met yet.

With a sigh, I push aside all distractions, focusing all my attention on the single piece of information I crave. Her eyes. They are big, round, and—YES!—brown. They lock onto me, bright and swimming with the same attraction coursing through my veins.

I quickly try to regain my composure because now only a shiny new bar separates us.

"What can I get you?" Rachel asks as she sits down the white square napkin. Her fake smile may be bright, but the question came out shaky. She's nervous.

Yeah, me too.

I flash her my warmest smile. "I'll just have a club soda with some lime."

She cocks her head to the side. "Not much of a drinker, huh? Most pool players love their beer."

Interesting. She was watching me.

"I'm not most pool players. My vice is coffee."

"Well, we don't offer coffee," she volleys back.

"That's unfortunate." I lean my elbows on the bar, staring her down.

Her cheeks turn pink under my intense stare with a slight upturn of her lips.

Her lips.

The subtle curve of her top lip, shaped like a perfect little bow, makes them utterly flawless. Her bottom lip is full as they both shine with a pale pink gloss. Gloss that I want to kiss right off.

Geez. Get a hold of yourself, man.

She reaches for a glass and rests it on the napkin. As before, everything happens in slow motion. It's almost as if my brain is searing this meeting into my memory for all eternity, and all she's doing is serving me a drink. I gawk as her slender fingers wrap around the soda gun, and clear carbonated liquid rises to the top. Her eyes, wide and bright, flick to meet mine for a fleeting moment. Then, using some tongs, she plucks a lime wedge and plops it in.

She peers around the bar, checking on the other customers, but stays right in front of me. I marinate in the stillness. She redirects her gaze and, in no rush at all, pans slowly up my torso. Arms, chest, shoulders ... in that order.

If a single look could do me in, this is it.

She coughs while turning her attention to replacing bottles of liquor on the back wall. "I'm usually pretty good at guessing what my customers drink. I never would have pegged you for a coffee or soda water kinda guy."

"Oh, yeah." I raise the glass and take a sip, my gaze locked on her and unwavering.

"Give him your best shot, Rachel!" the third older gentleman hollers out. The outburst jolts me toward the older men, breaking the spine-tingling charged conversation. Each of them is ogling us as if we are their sole means of entertainment for the night. We probably are.

"Cut it out, Randy." Rachel taps back as she plucks a rag hanging from her back pocket and wipes down the bar that's obviously already clean.

"You do it with all the other newbies. Why not him?" Randy smirks.

Huh ... interesting. Now I'm curious.

I drum my fingers on the bar. "What is it you do with the newbies, Rachel?" I ask with a smile, hoping my dimples are popping out.

They must be because she blushes almost immediately.

Just then, the doors to the kitchen swing open on their hinges, and a man whose height rivals mine walks through carrying chili cheese fries. Before he even sets the platter down, the three men are already diving in. "So, Rachel here is an expert at reading people," he interjects into the conversation. "It's a game we like to play. I bet she already has you figured out."

"She does, huh?" I shift in her direction, intrigued.

He smiles warmly at her. A smile she returns.

Dang it. A boyfriend, maybe? My heart sinks.

"Thanks," she mumbles under her breath to the man while giving me a quick glance.

Slick leans forward to address me. "She's never wrong."

Rachel sighs, hesitant. She has now taken up drying glasses. As she pivots to place one along the row of clean ones, a tendril of hair falls from her bun and grazes the smooth tan skin of her neck.

Lord. I'm in trouble.

I lean back on my barstool, resting my forearm along its back, trying to steady myself yet also exuding confidence. Even though I'm feeling anything but around her. "Alright then, try to read me, Rachel. I'm ready."

She sighs, pops out her hip, and rests her hand on it. "Okay, fine."

She's sassy. Add it to the growing list of things that interest me about this woman.

And since we are on the subject, what is it about her? There is an immediate pull, a magnetic force I'm having a hard time ignoring. I have never experienced a connection like this with any other woman. Which is probably why, at forty-five years old, I'm still single.

And naturally, at my age, that lends itself to rumors.

He's a player.

Stay away from that one. He will break your heart.

So, like what? Are you allergic to marriage or something?

Why are you so picky?

Trust me, I've heard them all. And it's not that I haven't wanted to settle down. It's just that this is marriage. A lifelong commitment. I don't take it lightly.

Plus, seeing what my cousin has with his wife, Laura. I want that. He was lucky enough to find an incredible woman. But for me, it just hasn't happened yet. Even though I want it to.

And for that reason, I have had one semi-serious relationship. It lasted six months, and I tried. I really did. I regret breaking her heart, but she wasn't the one. And I have been dating, searching, and longing for the right woman ever since.

Perhaps I just found her.

Rachel gives me a once-over, her gaze holding mine, and for a moment, time suspends as we allow the tension to engulf us. Just as she opens her mouth to speak, a crash comes from the kitchen. Her head whips towards the doors. The tall guy takes off running with Rachel hot on his trail. "Micah, we need to do something about..." The statement fades as soon as she disappears behind the swinging door.

With that interruption, Randy gets out of his stool and slaps two fifties on the bar. Seems like a lot of money for a beer and some fries, but whatever. He faces me and points. "She likes you."

This takes me aback. "What?"

"She is going to murder you, Randy," Tiny speaks up as he rises from his stool and pulls a hundred out of his wallet. *Geez. These guys are generous tippers.*

Randy continues, "Oh, come on, Tiny. She hasn't taken her eyes off of him all night long."

Interesting.

"But you know her policy on dating customers," Tiny interjects.

Even more interesting.

None of this matters, though, if she's taken. "Fellas, look, I don't even know her. And besides, her boyfriend might not like it."

Not ashamed to admit I am fishing for information here.

All three of them burst out into laughter. "Boyfriend? You mean Micah?" Slick asks through his howling while pointing to the kitchen. "Relax, man. That's her brother."

Oh. Well, that explains it. Relief fills my chest.

I wave my hand over the three men who seem very invested in Rachel with the obvious familiarity I picked up on. "Are you guys related to her as well?"

"Nah," Randy answers. "Just regulars who look out for her and Micah."

That's ... considerate.

Randy and Tiny turn to Slick. "We're gonna take off. You staying?" Slick nods.

I watch Randy and Tiny leave out the front door when suddenly, my bladder is screaming at me.

After I take care of business and walk out of the restroom, Micah's behind the bar again, talking to Slick. Rachel is nowhere in sight. Their conversation hits me as I walk past.

"So, Rachel's RA has been acting up again, huh?" Slick asks Micah.

"Yeah." Micah returns. "Not as much as last time, which is good. We are going to see a new rheumatologist next week, though, at the Cleveland Clinic. Hopefully, they can help her more than the quacks around here."

Slick hums. "I sure hope so. She doesn't need to be in that much pain all the time. I hate seeing it. You can tell it's bothering her tonight."

With my head down, I walk back over to the tables, leaving what is an obvious private conversation in the rear-view mirror. Rachel emerges from the kitchen and immediately zeros in on where I was sitting. Her shoulders deflate, but then she scans the bar. Our eyes lock, and a small smile forms on her lips.

Not quite prepared to call it a night, I rack the balls, ready to get some practice in, but curiosity gets the better of me. I pull out my phone, and Google *What is RA?*

Two words stare back at me. Rheumatoid Arthritis.

Empathy rolls over my body as I look over at the bar to find her again. She's attempting to reach for a bottle of booze from the top shelf. She winces. Slick notices, rounds the bar, and retrieves the bottle. As she thanks him, she rubs her elbow, pain etched on her beautiful face.

I click on the first article from the Mayo Clinic and read.

Rheumatoid Arthritis is an autoimmune disease, meaning the body's immune system, which normally protects against foreign invaders, turns against its own tissues. Common symptoms of the disease include joint pain, swelling, stiffness, and fatigue. If left untreated, RA can cause significant joint damage and deformity, leading to bone erosion and spurs. While there is no cure for RA, treatments can help manage symptoms and slow down the progression of the disease.

Shock courses through me. *What? She has this? How is that possible?*

Isn't arthritis a disease a person gets in old age? I mean, I'm pretty sure I have it in my knees. But Rachel looks to be in her thirties or late twenties.

Another quick glimpse, and her distinctive, almost swaying gait is unmistakable even as she focuses on a customer.

It all makes sense now.

My heart swells with compassion, and a need to know everything about this woman consumes me.

Sliding my phone into my pocket, I focus on breaking the balls. With a scrape of chalk on cue, they scatter across the table, the clatter a sharp contrast to the quiet determination in my heart because I'm not leaving until I talk to her again.

Tonight.

2

Closing Time

Rachel

With rapt attention, I watch as this newbie, who is the tallest drink of water I have ever seen, leans over the pool table to take his shot. His shirt stretches across his broad back, his triceps flex with the sway of his arm. His butt is just ... right there.

I have never had a thing for pool players. Maybe if they all looked like him, I would. Most players here are young guys trying to impress girls or older men with beer guts who are super serious about the game. There is no in-between.

Until now.

Okay, I need to stop staring.

Averting my gaze, I glance around, trying to remember what I was doing. Was I drying glasses? Or, wait. I'm so confused. Was I cleaning the ice bin?

I have no clue. My mind has been all over the place since I saw him playing earlier.

Dexter's has cleared out for the night since it's one a.m. Slick took off about an hour ago, and I haven't seen my Uncle Dexter in a few hours. No clue where he disappeared to.

But this dude is still here, glancing my way every so often, flashing me a grin that causes his dimples to appear and makes my already weak legs feel like jelly.

Micah emerges from the kitchen, slinging a rag over his shoulder. "I need to take off. Shelby is waiting for me." He glances over at the pool player. As soon as Micah leaves, it's only going to be me and him. "You gonna be okay here?" His brows furrow, deep in concern.

"I'll be fine. You know me."

"Mm-hmm. That I do." He chuckles, throwing the rag into the dirty laundry bin. "You're going to break that no-customers rule again, aren't you? Is it even a thing at this point?"

Ignoring my brother, I steal a look at the handsome man again. He's tall, very tall. I would put him at six five, I decide right here and now.

I'm embracing this because, as a woman of almost six feet, finding men my height or taller is rare and challenging. So yeah, he is Travis Kelce's level of tall. Dirty blonde hair cut shorter on the sides and slightly longer on top with a natural wave perfectly complements his smooth face. His eyes appeared hazel when we talked earlier. He's dressed casually: jeans and a very fitted T-shirt showcasing his arms and broad shoulders nicely.

It's a whole cool guy vibe. And I like it.

But I can't pinpoint his age. Late thirties, maybe. Which would make him older than my thirty.

The Oldies but Goodies were right. Normally, I'm good at reading people. It's a gift that comes from the countless hours of people-watching I did growing up here with my Uncle Dexter and his dad. I can guess a person's age, job, and background accurately. It is a great icebreaker with the customers.

But for some reason, I can't get a read on this guy. Or maybe I don't want to. Knowing I will like what I see.

Taking his time, he unscrews his pool cue and slips it into his case. He sits on the barstool that rests along the wall next to the tables, finishing his club soda, looking at his phone. Then he runs his fingers through his hair, followed by—

"Um ... earth to Rachel." Micah snaps his fingers in front of my face.

I shake my head, returning my attention to—what exactly? Who am I kidding?

I can't remember my name at this point.

Nope, not gonna happen. I cannot, and will not, get wrapped up in a customer again. The last time I did, it ended in heartbreak and betrayal.

"You have a little drool right there." Micah points to the corner of his mouth with a smirk.

"Stop." I smack his hand away. He laughs, removing his apron and hanging it on the hook next to the kitchen door.

"I'll see you tomorrow." My big brother rounds the bar, gives one last glimpse at this perfect stranger, and leaves out the main door. But not before looking back and making kissing noises like the child he is.

"Closing time!" I holler over the empty bar, hoping he doesn't leave, even though I need him to.

He drains his drink, the ice clinking softly in the glass, then grabs his pool cue and coat and saunters over with a confident swagger. He sits on the same stool he was in earlier. "I never got my read, Rachel."

Refusing to look at him, I continue to stock the beer for tomorrow's shift. "Well,"—I peek at the enormous clock that hangs above the liquor—"we close in five minutes. Not sure there is enough time."

"Do I look that complicated?" he asks, the words smooth as he leans forward. His T-shirt stretches thin across his chest, catching my eye.

Focus, Rachel!

"Considering that your only drink vice is coffee, I would say yes." My grin falters, and I look hurriedly away, overwhelmed by his handsome features.

Suddenly, James Taylor sings out of the stereo, and a soft uptick in his smile appears. "You a James Taylor fan?" I ask, interested, even though I shouldn't be.

His eyes glaze over, a distant stare settling on his face as if the song's words instantly transport him to another time and place. "He's the best. I grew up listening to him and other bands from the sixties and seventies." He leans back in the chair. Easy and carefree. "It's all my dad would listen to when I was younger. James Taylor, Led Zeppelin, Lynyrd Skynyrd, The Who. You name it, it was blaring from the radio in our garage." He leaves the memory as he runs a hand over his smooth jaw. "What about you? What's your music genre of choice, Rachel?"

I lean my elbows against the bar, closer to him, listening to his silky voice. As he talks, it's like velvet courses through my veins, filling me with warmth. He's pulling me in slowly. "Joni Mitchell and, wait. Are you trying to read me now? What's your name, anyway?"

"Johnny."

"Is that short for Jonathan?"

"Nope," he replies, popping the P.

"Really? What's it short for then?"

"I think I need to take you to dinner first before we get that personal."

Phew. Dear Lord.

I am way out of my league with this guy. This conversation is veering into uncomfortable flirty territory, so I need to remove myself before things escalate. Attraction laced with tension builds with every suggestive word. "Nice try. But it's not happening."

Unfortunately for me and him, I ignore my advice and, out of habit, I read this guy. He's confident, that's for sure, but doesn't come across as cocky. Self-assured and a flirt. Plus, he's funny.

My eyes briefly flick at his ring finger. It's bare. Which means nothing in bars like this. Anyone can slip a ring off and tuck it away in a pocket in seconds. Poof! Single for the night.

Some men are pigs. And not only men. Women are just as guilty. And it's disgusting.

But that's not the vibe I'm getting from him. He seems genuine. A family man, perhaps.

He catches me staring at his left hand, then cocks the cockiest of smirks. "Are you reading me, Rachel?"

God, my name rolling off his tongue is doing crazy things to me. And for that reason, I need to get myself in check.

No dating customers, Rachel!

Got it.

Clenching my fists, I push off the bar, rounding my shoulders, needing to steady myself. A swift subject change is in order.

My smile fades, but that zippy current flowing through me refuses to leave. It's sizzling like hot lava, crawling up my throat, ready to burst. "Are you ready to cash out? I need to close down for the night." I can't look at him when I ask this. There is for sure a spark there with this man. But sparks can turn into raging infernos that will blow up your life and cause you unseen misery and pain.

Trust me, I know. And I will never travel that road again.

The bar stool scrapes against the floor. A signal that he's leaving. With my back to him, I work at closing out the register for the night.

"Can I at least get your number?"

I flick the bills in my hand, counting. "Nope."

Way to go, me!

He stands and taps his fingers on the bar. "Well, okay then." I peer over my shoulder and watch as he takes a step, then stops, hesitation gripping him. He runs his palm along his smooth face, then through his hair. Locking eyes with me, he grins as he throws down a twenty. "I guess I'll see you around."

With all the casual, I-don't-care-attitude that I can muster, I grab the money and return to the register. "See ya."

Watching out of the corner of my eye, I see him pick up his pool cue and slip on his coat, heading for the front door. Now that his back is to me, he has my full attention. Naturally, my gaze wanders downward. Good *God*, his butt is phenomenal in those jeans. "*Wow*," I mouth silently.

His whole aura, the way he moves and speaks, has already stolen my heart. He's sharp yet also rugged, seasoned in a way that tells me he has stories to share. Good ones, I'm sure. And I want to know them all.

Plus, he appears older. So that's two rules of mine that he's breaking. Age and being a customer.

The door clicks shut behind him, the sound echoing in the sudden silence, and I exhale, tension leaving my body.

Thoughts and rationalities swirl in my head as I finish behind the bar. I mean, technically, he's leaving, so that means he isn't a customer anymore.

My no-dating-customers rule is in place for a very good reason.

Drew.

My ex-fiance and one huge mistake. Our relationship started off amazingly. As time went on, he was waving red flags back and forth, but I ignored them.

Then there is my RA and my high school boyfriend, Sean. He dumped me on prom night because I was having a flare-up and couldn't dance with him because of the pain. So what did he do? He danced the night away with Brittany Wilson, then told me he was taking her to the after party since I was, and I quote, "too sick to have fun." It was the first time I lost something because of my RA. Ever since, I have kept my diagnosis close to my chest.

So needless to say, my past relationships and heartbreaks have made it difficult to open up my heart again.

I'm jaded now.

I study the door, indecision picking away at the scab left on my heart. Did I just allow the bitter loss of some worthless exes to impede potentially getting to know a good guy?

And the truth of the matter is this: I use the no-dating-customers rule as an excuse to not date. Those two messy break-ups did a number on me, but my RA controls my life. It's embarrassing, and I wonder if anyone will put up with it.

I mean, Sean couldn't.

Chronic illness and dating don't mix well. It takes a really special and understanding person to put up with me. Because it's not just me.

It's me and my RA.

We are a package deal.

And my little friend has been wrecking me lately. Just in the past few years, bone spurs have developed in my elbows, which cause major pain and my joints to lock up. But it's not just my elbows that give me a hard time. My shoulders, knees, and hips will all throw a fit. Like today, for example. When I woke this morning, my right hip was screaming at me. I've tried hard to hide the natural gait that happens when I walk, but it's hard.

All of it is just so damn hard.

Which is why I have sworn off all men ... at least until I can get my health under control. It's hard to grasp that anyone would choose someone defective like me.

But Johnny only asked for my number.

God, this back-and-forth is driving me nuts.

Against the nagging tug of my better judgement, I hurl the rag on the counter, and as fast as my weak hip will take me, I rush toward the entrance. With force, I swing open the door, and I'm instantly hit with the bright lights of his truck and a gust of chilly March air. I squint against the harsh glare, my hand flying up to shield my face from the brightness.

"Wait!" I yell out, as the vapor from the air follows my plea out into the night.

He kills the lights, rolls down the window, and pokes his head out. "Are you okay?"

My breathing hitches, a frantic rhythm against my ribs, as disbelief in my actions washes over me. "I don't date customers," I blurt out.

Smooth, Rachel.

He grins, turns off the engine, and reaches out of the window to open the car door like the cool guy he is. Then he steps out of the massive white Silverado and leans against the door, crossing his arms over his broad chest. "You had to come out here to tell me that?" he says with a chuckle.

Gosh, what am I doing? I curse silently. "Nevermind." I pivot, my hand closing around the cool metal of the entrance handle. "What am I doing?" I mutter, shaking my head in frustration.

Boots stomp on the pavement behind me, and before I can register what is happening, his fingers reach for the handle before mine.

I turn, and this complete stranger I find myself irresistibly drawn to is *right* there. We are standing close. Too close. His eyes come alive as he scans my face. A single look from him is already my undoing.

Running his thumb along his lower lip, he leans in closer. His undivided attention only on me, like a laser beam piercing through the night. A curious glimmer softens his face. "Rachel, I hadn't left yet because I didn't want you to be here alone. I wanted to make sure you locked up and got to your car safely."

Oh, my melting heart.

I swallow hard, and my body sags, turning to dough at his proximity.

"And I'm not asking for anything in return. Just your number and a chance to get to know you. That's all." His gentle tone and soft gaze compel me to pause and reflect.

He waited. Waited to make sure I was safe. This man, who I don't even know, did that.

For me.

A customer not wanting anything is a new concept in my line of work. All men want something. Even your close relatives.

But his calm voice, soft eyes, and all-consuming presence paint a different story. All I see is ...

Honesty.

Trust.

Temptation.

The words threaten to spill out uncontrollably; with a rush of adrenaline, I ask him back inside. "Do you want to come back in? Keep me company while I clean?"

He opens the door wide. "I'll do you one better." He grins. *God, the dimples again.* "I'll help you clean up."

Thirty minutes later, the bar is ready to go for the next day. With Johnny's help, I got done with what normally takes me an hour to do. My joints are thanking him. Especially my hip and elbows.

It was hard to concentrate, though, because I watched Johnny clean, and cover the twenty pool tables as if he was getting paid. You can tell the man loves the game. Plus, closing down those tables at the end of the night is the bane of my existence. I watched as he brushed the tables, each stroke deliberate. With a keen eye, he polished the rails, then covered each one with precision. As if he owned them all individually.

Suddenly, I find myself wanting to know his whole story.

I take off my apron and hang it next to my brother's as Johnny strides over. I check the time on my phone. One forty-five am. *I mean, doesn't he have a job?* I noticed the side of his truck said Givens Construction. That's the company that did the reno of the bar. However, I was out with an extreme flare-up, so I wasn't around much during the renovation. My uncle kept me on light duty, mostly helping him in his office or working from home. Plus, they roped off the construction area, so I didn't see the workers much.

He leans his elbow and back along the bar while not taking his stare off the tables. "I love that you guys used worsted clothes on the tables. It plays faster, less napping, and it will last longer." He turns to me, and I blink once, twice, because I have no clue what he just said.

He lowers his gaze. "Sorry, I'm letting my inner pool nerd show."

I snicker. "It's okay. I'll let my uncle know you approve."

"Is it true that he wants to have tournaments here?"

I nod. "Mm-hmm." Flipping off the lights to the kitchen and bar area, I zip my coat and sling my crossbody purse over my shoulder. "He's the president of the BPA."

"I might love the game, but I don't play in leagues."

This surprises me because my stalking throughout the night revealed he is incredibly good. Like, really good. The other huge specimen of a man he was playing with never took a shot all night.

Walking out the front door, I lock it as my curiosity gets the better of me. "Why don't you play in any leagues?"

"Too much politics. But I love the game. I'm not looking for prestige. I don't need it."

"Why don't you need it?"

A sly smirk plays on his lips. "Because I know I'm great."

A heavy silence settles, broken only by the distant chirp of a cricket, as I wonder what's going to happen next.

"Rachel?" God, I love how he says my name. I focus on him again. "Will you come somewhere with me? I want to show you something?"

I huff out a laugh. *He can't be serious.* "Yeah, okay. I don't even know you."

"I promise you, I am a decent guy."

"Right. That's what all the supposed good guys say. Trust me." Even though I get a good feeling from this man, I still need to be cautious. My heart likes to fall fast. And that fast heart of mine has burned me.

"Fair enough." He reaches into his back pocket. "I tell you what." Sliding his ID out of his wallet, he hands it to me. "Here, take a picture of this and send it to whoever you want. Tell them you are going to Miller's Bluff with me to hang out. Turn on your location so whoever you send this to can track us. We can even drive separate. What do you say?"

I chomp on the inside of my mouth, contemplating. With hesitation and a surge of curiosity, I take his license. *God, what am I doing? I just met this man.*

A sigh of relief and a small satisfied smile graces his smooth, stubble-free face. Refusing to get lost in his stare, I dip my gaze to his mouth, trying to avoid being swallowed whole by his piercing eyes.

Well, that's not any better. So I zero in on his chiseled jaw and the way his Adam's apple rolls when he swallows.

I redirect my attention and snap a pic, texting it to my brother, and giving him Johnny's instructions. His reply comes almost immediately.

> Micah: I KNEW IT! It was the dimples, wasn't it?

> Micah: KIDDING! Be safe. Johnny's company did our reno. Uncle Dexter says they are great guys.

A sense of peace fills my soul when he says this because I trust my brother's judgement.

I hand him back his license, our fingers brushing as our eyes lock. Bravery propels me forward as I smirk. "Johnson Michael Givens huh?"

A chuckle rumbles from his chest as he drinks me in with a glimmer in his roving glare, neither of us letting go of his ID. "You can call my Johnny." His fingertip brushes my knuckle lightly as his words, smooth like silk, fill me from within. Heat flares and whizzes from my hand, up my arm, and straight to my cheeks. I let go of his ID and as I watch him pocket it, I immediately realize I didn't look at his date of birth to get his age.

Dang it!

I blink before dipping my chin and huffing out a laugh of utter disbelief in myself and my poor decision-making. "Okay. I'll follow you there."

At this point, I will follow him anywhere.

3

You Know Where to Find Me

Rachel

Before I know it, we are lying in the bed of his truck on some blankets, gazing at the most beautiful brilliant sky I have ever seen. It's a perfectly clear night, and I swear every star ever created shines in the sky.

It's breathtaking, and I get why he brought me here.

My big coat and his hot body help with the frosty night air.

We lie here, stargazing as we talk, with him pointing out a shooting star every so often. Never have I had a conversation flow the way that it is with him. It's as if we have known each other for fifteen years and not fifteen minutes.

It's refreshing, easy. And scary.

The temperature takes a nosedive as a cool breeze brushes across my body, and I know this will wreak my joints. It already is. My elbow is stiff and resists bending, while a dull ache throbs in my knees.

The night air is seeping into my bones, causing me to shiver. Johnny turns, noticing. "Are you cold?"

"A little."

"Okay, stay right here." As if I'm going anywhere, he jumps to his feet, causing the truck to rock some as he opens the back window and heaves out a huge wool blanket. He returns and, with extra care, covers my body, the warmth of the wool already taking the chill away.

Gratitude fills my heart. "Thank you."

He nestles back down and adjusts the blanket to cover both of us. He stretches his arm behind his head, staring at the heavens. "Okay. I'm ready."

My eyes grow wide. "Ready for what, exactly?" Because if he thinks THAT'S happening, he's crazy.

"For you to read me. You've had enough time." His gaze never leaves the expansive sky as he wiggles his body and settles in. "Hit me."

Well, okay then. This I can handle. I flip on my side and tuck my arm under my head. A sharp pain shoots through my elbow with every bend, but I hide my grimace and push through the discomfort, not wanting to raise any alarms. Which would cause him to ask questions. And I'm not ready for questions.

I stare at him for a long minute. He gives me a side eye, and the corner of his mouth ticks upward playfully. "Is gawking at me part of the process?"

I chuckle. "It is."

"Do you like what you see?"

Yes. Yes, I do. But I don't say that out loud.

"Okay. I'm guessing you are in your mid to late thirties. You've never been married, and construction has been your only serious job. You use humor to cover up whatever pain you might have buried." I pause as he swallows hard, his Adam's apple bobbing. "No kids, but my guess is that with the right woman, that option isn't off the table. I can't figure out the coffee obsession, but I'm guessing alcohol isn't your thing." I lift the blanket to peek at his clothes again. "Your clothes are perfect. Too perfect. I don't know any single guy that irons his clothes, but it's obvious you do. So you are neat but yet also messy." He grins. "Am I getting close?"

He pivots and sets his head on his hand, his elbow resting on the blanket, our faces inches apart. "You are about ninety-nine percent correct."

"Ah, man. Do I get to learn about the other one percent?" Somehow, we've ventured even closer, his body heat surrounding me.

"Well, to start, my dad passed away when I was sixteen. Tragic car accident. I grew up in a not-so-great part of town. Scott—my best friend, cousin, and business partner—on the other hand, lived only four streets from me in a totally different, fancier neighborhood. Train tracks separated both sides of town, so yes. I literally grew up on the wrong side of the tracks."

I swirl a small circle on the blanket as I take in his story. "Is Scott the guy you were with tonight?"

"So you noticed me?" he asks with a playful grin, pleased that I asked because yes, Johnny, I did notice you.

I roll my eyes, ignoring his question. "Keep talking."

"Hmmm, the lady is still interested." He smirks, obviously pleased, then continues. "The street I grew up on was small, a major truck route that was busy yet full of families. On one end of the street was an old bar/pool hall called The Parlor. Like clockwork, I would get woken up at two am, closing time, to drunk people walking past my house after a night of debauchery. To this day, I still wake up in the middle of the night.

"On the other end was a huge factory. And sandwiched in between were fourteen houses, seven on each side. So, I'm grateful my dad taught me the game. Pool was my outlet and a way to stay out of trouble. It was where I came to grieve and heal after his passing. The focus that this game takes would push aside my anger and grief." He inches closer to me. "It's been healing me ever since."

"Sounds like an interesting childhood."

He sighs. "It was. But regarding your first assessment of me, I am single and have no kids. I never thought at forty-five I would be wifeless and childless."

My heart plummets to my stomach. Forty-five! It's worse than I imagined. When I got in the car, after sending the photo of his ID to my brother, I looked at it to get his age. Of course, I didn't pay attention and cut off the most important part. His birthdate. It's not my fault. He's so dang distracting! But yeah. Fifteen years my senior is a no-go.

And I was right, he's older. And masculine in that hardened way. The way I like. The way that always gets me in trouble.

I sigh, the sound heavy in the surrounding peacefulness of the night, and I plop onto my back.

"What?" His curious eyes pin me in place.

I continue to have a staring contest with the stars. "You're ... forty-five?" I choke on the number.

"I am. Why? Is that not okay?" he asks with a chuckle. "I mean, I feel like I'm twenty-five, but some days my knees—"

"I don't date customers." Yep, I am putting a nail in this coffin right away, refusing to look at him as I deliver my final blow. "Or older men." I need to hear the words leave my lips; I need to say that out loud. To reaffirm it to myself.

"So you've thought about dating me? Interesting." He chuckles, completely unfazed by my coffin nailing. I won't peer over at him. I can't. It weakens my resolve. A lot.

Hell, looking at him is what got me here in the first place.

Only crickets and the light breeze fill the surrounding air. Now it's his turn to sigh. His shoulders sag as he plops back onto his back. "How old are you, Rachel?"

I let out a long, shaky exhale before I answer. The quiet amplifies the potential death blow of my age, which threatens to extinguish a flame that had yet to be fully lit. But feels like maybe, just maybe, it would have sparked and burned through my life. "Thirty."

He completely ignores my age confession as we continue to stare at the universe.

Lacing his fingers together, he rests them on his stomach. "I come here a lot," he starts, "to clear my head of all the chaos that can exist in my thoughts. When you look up there"—he points to the night sky—"it helps with any pain we carry around." He pauses. "There is always a certain quote I recite when I'm here. *Only by contending with challenges that seem to be beyond your strength to handle at the moment can you grow more surely toward the stars.*"

His words float over me like a dream. I try to blink back the sting of tears as my chest flutters. Because I have no strength. I am weak. Body and mind both.

He regards me. "Who hurt you, Rachel? Or what?"

My head whips around, our eyes meeting with an intensity that stills my breathing. "How can you tell I've been hurt?"

"It's in your eyes. You are closed off, afraid to open up to anyone. I'm guessing either someone hurt you or something else is going on. A secret that you hold close to your chest."

He's right. On both accounts. But I'm not about to tell this stranger about my RA. So, I guess I'll tell him about Sean and Drew.

"Two people, actually. My high school boyfriend dumped me. He was a loser, obviously. But then there was Drew, and we were engaged. I met him at the bar, and he was ten years older than me. He decided, out of the blue, that I wasn't the girl for him. So, he let me know this by cheating on me. End of story."

His jaw tenses as his nostrils flare. "What a spineless jerk."

"My uncle pushes me to reconcile with him. I know that's what Drew wants." I shrug, void of all hope. Those words sealing my fate.

"Would you? Go back to him?" I'm staring above. He's staring at me.

"No, never. But it's hard, sometimes, to say no to my uncle." And it is. It always is. He has this control that looms large over me. I owe him a debt.

"What about your parents? What do they think of Drew?"

"My parents died in a house fire when I was nine." The confession tumbles out, a torrent of words I can't believe I'm unleashing.

"Jesus." A crease forms on his brow as he stares at me, completely engrossed. Somehow, our feet brush under the blanket, stealing my breath.

I pause before I continue. "Uncle Dexter was my mom's brother. He took in both my brother and me and raised us. I grew up at the bar. It's all I've ever known."

"You've never wanted to do anything else? I mean, if bartending is your thing, more power to ya. But if I'm reading *you* right"—I bristle at his assessment, full of truth—"then I'm guessing bartending isn't what you want to do with the rest of your life."

"You don't know me," defiance fills my reply.

"You're right, I don't. But if tending bar was your dream, your face would light up when you mention it. And it doesn't."

He's right. And since I am here now, under the stars with a perfect stranger, I should just be honest. I have no idea if I will ever see him again, so confiding in him is easy.

My hidden secret spills out. "I've always wanted to be a nurse."

"There ya go!" He nudges me in the ribs with his elbow, making me chuckle. "My cousin's wife is a nurse. She loves it. Why not pursue it? You're young. It's never too late to go to school."

"It's not that easy."

"Why can't it be?"

I sigh. "My uncle needs me."

"Oh, come on. I was there for the reno. I know what he put down on that place. And with the tournaments that he wants to host, he is making money. He can hire anyone to fill whiskey glasses and hand out bottlenecks."

"He likes for me to be close."

He pauses, confused. "That's ... odd." He's right, it is odd. My uncle keeps tabs on me, and he cares, in his own weird way.

"Maybe. But he trusts Micah and me. Family means everything to him. Plus, he takes care of me." I have no clue why I'm defending him. My uncle pays for everything when it comes to my RA. All my meds, the doctor's visits, the therapy. All of it. It's like I'm a slave to him and Dexter's.

Suddenly, anger flares in my chest at the reminder that my life isn't really mine, and now this conversation is pissing me off. So I need to redirect this off of me ... like, now. "What about you?"

"What about me?"

"Have you always wanted to hammer in nails while drinking coffee?"

He laughs. "Well, the no alcohol thing is because of a minor incident in Daytona in my twenties that I never speak of. So coffee became my addiction. The more sugar and fancier the coffee is the better. And as for building things ... well, I love it. I'll build anything. I built my home, my pool table, the swing that hangs on my front porch. Give me a hammer and some nails, and I am a happy man."

I smile. "Your face lit up when you said all of that."

"I guess I was right then. So tell me, why do you want to be a nurse?"

I can't tell him the full reason. But I will tell him enough. "I want to help people. And I know that's a generic answer, but it's true. When people are sick, they need comfort, hope, and compassion. Healthcare workers are some of the best. It's people, selflessly helping people. We don't have enough of that in the world today, ya know?" Excitement is building in my chest as I continue, and the words spill out in rapid succession. "I want to provide support to someone when they are in their darkest hour. Give them just a glimmer of hope or comfort. Plus, I love medicine. I love it so much that I'm willing to pay someone to teach it to me. Like, how crazy is that? Late night study projects, cramming for tests, then taking care of my patients with integrity. It all sounds so ... exhilarating." I stop, catching my breath.

His dimples pop as he studies me. "What?"

"Your face lit up."

"Oh, my gosh." I cover my face with my hands, embarrassed. Or hide the enormous blush that I'm sure is creeping on my cheeks. Rough, warm hands, calloused from years of hard work, close over mine, their unexpected gentleness a stark contrast to their texture. His pressure is soft but firm, guiding my hands downward.

I'm forced to once again gaze into his hazel eyes. "Plus, you were rambling. Do you do that a lot?"

I chew on my cheek. "I tend to ... when I get nervous or excited about something."

During our conversation, we have inched dangerously close to one another. His eyes dart back and forth between mine, full of a mix of temptation and uncertainty. Deliberately, he raises our hands to his mouth, his breath misting in the chilly air as he blows on them. The hot mist seeps into my skin, and a shiver runs down my spine because, *oh, my God.* "Your hands are cold," he whispers, his words ghosting across my skin as he blows on our hands again.

Well, that is literally the only cold thing on me right now because a fever is permeating through my whole body. Our fingers interlace, the warmth of our skin a comforting contrast to the cool air as our faces inch closer, anticipation thrumming between us. "I really want to see you again, Rachel," he confesses. My skin itches with uncertainty.

"You know where to find me." The mutual vapor from our breathing dances and intertwines as his eyes briefly land on my mouth. Closer, closer, closer still. "What are we doing?" I ask, even though I know what's going to happen. And I'm powerless to stop it.

"I don't know."

He knows.

On instinct, our eyes close, and the featherlight touch of his lips reaches mine. It's brief, passionate, and oh, so intoxicating. I know this is a terrible idea, but my body didn't get the memo. Every nerve is humming, coming alive with only a brush of his lips. Everything is reacting as if this is the most epic kiss in all of human history. My breathing stutters in my lungs, my stomach bottoms out, and my head becomes an inferno.

Pretty sure this is the best peck of my whole life.

God, what am I doing?

That thought is exactly what I need to break this spell. I gasp as I jerk back, my heart hammering in my chest. *I can't do this to myself again.*

His eyes pop open at the broken connection. "Rachel, what's wro—"

"I'm sorry, I need to leave," I mumble, shrinking away, my eyes darting from his, his cologne suddenly too strong. The confusion I sense from him hangs heavy in the air, a palpable tension. I attempt to stand, my movements jerky as my joints scream in protest, my body a stiff, weathered wooden board.

He immediately follows and stands way faster than me, offering me his hand. I take it as he wraps his fingers around my wrist. Wincing as he tugs me upward, I try hard to not let the pain show on my face. He's observing me like I'm a wounded, scared animal. "Rachel, I'm sorry, did I do something?"

With a dismissive wave of my hand, I lower my head to the truck bed. "No, no. I'm sorry. I just need to go." The memory of his lips against mine, soft and firm, floods my brain. I press my fingertips to my mouth, desperately trying to wipe away the lingering sensation. With a sharp shake of my head, I need to banish the moment to the recesses of my mind. A long shot, a Hail Mary pass—an attempt that probably won't work. "It's late, and you probably have to get to work tomorrow. It's already"—I glance at my watch—"oh, geez ... three in the morning."

His eyes brim with such sadness that my heart aches just looking at him. "I meant what I said. I would love to see you again." His offer is right there, so tempting. But I can't, so I state the obvious. To both of us.

"Johnny, we are fifteen years apart."

He shrugs carelessly. "It's just a number."

With a soft sigh, the blanket slides from my shoulder, the coolness of the air replacing its warmth. "Not to me," I admit. Gingerly, he pulls the heavy wool back up. The tenderness of this loving gesture is making what I must do incredibly hard. The possibility of starting something with Johnny is a mountain reaching to the clouds. Out of reach and too difficult to climb. "I can't, Johnny. I'm sorry."

He lets out a slow puff of air and nods. "Okay, fair enough. I will respect that."

With little to no difficulty, he hops out of the truck. Lowering my body, I sit on the edge of the hatch, his hands wrapping around my waist, the cool metal scratching lightly against my clothes as I slide down.

He doesn't let go, and we stand motionless. Close. Our eyes lock. "Let me walk you to your car," he whispers, releasing his hold on me while securing the blanket in place, his arm slung around my shoulder.

A gesture full of concern.

Ten whole steps are all it takes to reach my car. With a gentle click, he opens the door, the quiet hum of the night buzzing along. With a hushed "thank you," I slip the worn blanket from my shoulders and hand it to him, the familiar texture comforting even as I let go. Casually, he slings it over his arm as I slide in and start the car.

"I'm going to follow you to the highway to make sure you at least get that far safely. You can't tell me no."

I chuckle. "Okay. Thank you. And I'm so sorry." But I'm not remorseful. It's regret.

"No need to apologize. I had a very unexpected but lovely evening. Drive safely, Rachel." He shuts the door, then steps away, walking backward toward his truck, but not before making a signal with his hand for me to roll down my window. I do.

"You know what? I suddenly have a desire to join a pool league. Looks like we are going to be seeing more of each other, after all."

He winks. He freaking winks. Then he slithers into his truck, leaving me gobsmacked.

What a little stinker.

As I pull out onto the road with his truck lights behind me, giddiness fills my heart at the thought of seeing him again. Soon. Plus, I can't erase an image from my head.

His face lit up when he said it.

4

So What You're Saying Is ... Be Careful

Johnny

"Welcome to Starbucks. How can I help you?"

"Yes, I would like a grande dark roast, black. And a venti hot white mocha, with blonde espresso oat milk, vanilla sweet cream cold foam, and caramel drizzle."

One thing is for certain, I need a huge sugary coffee this morning to wake myself up. By the time I got home from one of the best nights of my life, it was almost four am. I'm running on an hour and a half of sleep, so I'm hoping this coffee, with the bonus of all the added sugar, will do what it's supposed to do.

Last night was amazing. I never thought, in a million years, that I would meet someone randomly at a bar and that she would be fifteen years younger than me. Not that age matters. It doesn't. But for whatever reason, it does to her, so I need to proceed with caution. I want her to recognize me as the stand-up guy I am. Which is why, after her freak out, I made sure she was comfortable. I wanted to send the message that her withdrawing her consent was fine.

It's always fine.

A goofy grin spreads across my face while I wait at this drive-through, tapping my fingers to the radio at the thought of running into her. Granted, Dexter's is clear across town. It's not remotely close. There are plenty of bars and pool halls near me I can frequent. But for starters, I am not a bar guy. Not anymore, anyway. Also, when it comes to the game of pool, I am an introvert. Shooting around in the solace of my garage, alone with my thoughts and my music, is where I thrive.

But now, I have every reason to drive forty-five minutes across town to play. And probably join a God-forsaken pool league. All to win over the tall brunette with the most captivating eyes.

Though I'd only slept for ninety minutes, the haunting memory of those eyes lingered in my dreams.

Last night, being with her felt as effortless and natural as breathing. I could tell she felt it as well.

With steaming coffees in hand, I drive to the job site, her face still vivid in my mind, the aroma of dark roast filling the car. Concern seizes my heart, mirroring my feelings from last night. The cold air made me anxious about how it was affecting her joints. I don't know enough about RA, but I know that when you have arthritis, cold temps can make them stiff. So, when I held onto her hands, and the chill reached my fingers, I did the only thing I could think of. I blew on them to warm them up.

That simple gesture was possibly one of the single best moments of my life.

Then we kissed. It was featherlight and brief. Our lips met in a fleeting, barely there brush of our lips, yet somehow, it was the best kiss I've ever experienced. How that is even possible, no clue.

Her bolting right after just reaffirms my suspicions that she has some pretty thick walls built up. But I need to know her story. My gut tells me that there is more to everything. Her uncle, the ex-boyfriend, her RA. All of it.

So, for now, I will respect the boundaries that she has put up, never pressuring her into doing or saying anything that might make her uneasy.

But I will make darn sure she doesn't forget me.

My truck tires crunch along the gravel as I pull into the makeshift driveway that leads to the apartment complex our construction company is building.

I need to talk to Scott about all of this. He's my go-to guy for everything. Somehow, after working together every day for over a decade, we haven't killed each other.

I park right next to him, resting my head against the car seat back. Squeezing my eyes shut, I try to shake off the pure exhaustion coursing through my body.

Breathe in. Breathe out. Breathe in ...

Tap. Tap. Tap.

My head tilts toward the windshield, and I squint one eye shut. There stands Scott. His eyebrow arches. I must have dozed off for just a second because I didn't hear him get out of his truck. A rush of fresh, cool air sweeps through as I roll down the window.

"Hey," I greet him, my voice hoarse.

"Hey there yourself, lover boy." He lets out a chuckle. God, he knows me so well. "I knew you would talk to her. What time did you get in?"

Reaching out the window, I hand him his coffee. He immediately takes a sip. My gargantuan size cup meets my lips, and I gulp. "God, that tastes good." I raise my fist to my mouth. "Ahem! Four am."

Scott takes a step back as I open the door and pour out of my truck, rounding to the back to retrieve my tool belt. While I cinch it around my waist, I glance at the bed, and the whole evening crashes into my memory. I smirk, then unleash an enormous yawn as I stretch, twisting my arms overhead, my back cracking with each movement.

Scott whistles softly. "You up for this today?"

"Sure. I'm tired, but I'll deal." A grin spreads across my face uncontrollably. "Adrenaline coupled with this"—I hold up my coffee—"is the fuel that's driving me forward right now."

"Mmm ... adrenaline, huh? Is that what we are calling it these days?" he asks through a laugh.

We begin our walk toward the row of duplexes that are being built, designed especially for senior citizens and the disabled. "Shut up," I mumble while also stifling a smile.

"So tell me about it," he implores as we step onto the porch of the build.

I fill him in on the details of most of the night. How I helped her clean up, then convinced her to go to Miller's Bluff to stargaze. How we talked and talked until she ended things.

He chimes in with a grunt every so often as we work.

But there is a truth I keep to myself. Her RA. It's not my place to divulge that information. That's Rachel's business and something I found out purely by accident. It's her secret, therefore it's mine.

He's examining the work that was done on the porch railings as soon as I finish. "So you like her?"

"I do. A lot, actually. She's different. And young."

His focus abruptly shifts back to me. "How young?"

I take a sip of my coffee, letting the warmth of it coat my throat before I continue. "Thirty."

"Geez, you scared me for a minute. When you said young, I thought like in her early twenties." He crouches down, studying the base of the railing. "This edge right here needs to be closer to the house. Make a note to tell Richard."

I grab my phone from my back pocket, open my notes, and type, then continue. "So you don't feel like age is a factor."

"No. Why would it? As long as it isn't for you guys, why would it matter? You are both legal adults and then some."

With the toe of my boot, I kick a piece of gravel and watch as it skitters across the ground. "Well, I have a feeling it matters to her. Unfortunately."

He lets out a soft sigh as we step into the entryway of the duplex. "Well, to be truthful, I feel like age is the least of your issues. It's her family I worry about. Especially her uncle."

"You mean Dexter Jr.? The know-it-all we did business with?"

"One and the same." As I walk into the kitchen, I sit my coffee on the concrete countertop, checking if the right cabinets were delivered while I wait for him to say more. He's in the adjoining bathroom, fiddling with the toilet, more than likely.

I keep working and waiting, not so patiently, as each clank, bang, and flush is adding to my anxiety.

For a beat or two, I hesitate, waiting, but he says nothing else. "Okay, you're killing me. Care to elaborate?" I interject. "I mean, we had our suspicions when we took the job, but is there more?"

He meets me in the kitchen, studying me as I read the purchase order and check it against the boxes. "Just be careful." He sucks in a long inhale. "I heard he's someone not to be trusted, and he's involved in some pretty shady stuff."

"Who did you hear that from?" I feel like now would probably be a good time to tell him what I saw at the bar last night.

"One of the other subcontractors. He said that Dexter is possibly into heavy illegal gambling with a little bit of tax evasion thrown in. Crazy stuff. It made me nervous, so I went over our contract with a fine-toothed comb. I even had our lawyer give it a once-over. Thankfully, everything is good. But I doubt we should take on any work from him again."

"Why didn't you tell me this?" I ask, a tad annoyed. We are partners, after all.

"I was. I am ... now."

"So what you're saying is ... be careful."

He nods. "Be careful."

I chew on my bottom lip as I watch him kneel, turning his attention to the subfloor. Then, I blurt it out. "Well, I probably shouldn't tell you I'm going to join his pool league. Plus, I saw him and some really big dudes escort a man who looked pretty roughed up out of the bar."

He drops his tape measure and rotates his face up to meet mine. "Are you kidding me right now?"

I take a sip of my coffee. "Nope. Dead serious."

"Did you not hear me? Illegal gambling. If it's true, what game do you think his ring is involved in?"

"Probably my favorite game. Pool."

"There's no 'probably.'" He reaches for the tape measure again with a little too much force. He continues without acknowledging me. "Is the guy you saw okay?"

"I have no idea."

"Well, count me out of all of it. I don't want anything to do with that man. Have fun in the league, but don't invite me to join. I got too much going on."

I scoff. "I wasn't going to anyway."

"Good," he grumbles.

Look, I know he's right about Dexter. Rachel's description of her uncle left me with a deeply unsettling knot in my gut. Add in the lousy first impression I had of the guy, then the dude at the bar, and now what Scott's heard, I don't like him.

After our initial meeting and Scott's warning to stay away from him during the reno, Scott and our lawyers dealt with him during the bar's remodel. And I trust Scott's judgement. He wouldn't repeat these accusations unless he had hard facts that were true and came from a trusted source.

"I'll be careful," I reiterate to put his mind at ease. But he knows me. I tend to jump into things, feet first, blindly.

"Scott, there is just something about Rachel." He faces me, brow furrowed. "I can't put my finger on it. It's just ... something."

This brings a smile to his face. "I get it. Laura has the something."

And for years, I have wanted what my cousin has with his wife. They have been married for over twenty years, and they still look at each other the way they did when they were dating.

You know what I mean.

Like a couple who are in that can't-keep-your-eyes-off-each-other phase. The way you miss her when you aren't together. How you find yourself reaching out to touch her whenever she's near, and you believe the moon rises and falls because of her.

That's Scott and Laura.

I want that.

I deserve that.

I need that.

My plea for his understanding continues. "It's unlike anything I've ever felt for a woman before, so I have to get to know her better. Even if that means driving clear across town to play a game that I can play on my table in my garage."

"And in a pool league. Which you hate."

"Which I hate." My gut twists in excitement just thinking about seeing her again, and my cheeks are on fire.

Scott's laugh echoes in the empty space as he points to me. "You're blushing."

I'm not sure I have ever blushed in my whole life.

I guess I do now.

Because of Rachel.

5

Family Sticks Together as One

Rachel

"Okay, Rachel, are all your medications still the same?"

"Yes."

"How about your pain on a scale from one to ten? Are you in any pain today, and if so, where is it located?"

My inner eye roll is huge with this question. And not that nurse Renee isn't sweet and understanding. I get she is just doing her job, but yeah. I am in pain.

Like all the time.

"Yes. I would say it's a seven. My elbows are really bothering me today."

Empathy stretches across her face, adding another brow crease to the three already there, hitting her salt-and-pepper hairline.

During the nurse's typical assessment of me, I casually survey the room. The office has stayed the same ever since I started coming here at ten years old, following my RA diagnosis. Mauve and sea-foam-green-painted walls surround us. The border, adorned with tiny seashells, runs along the top of the wall, peeling slightly in the corner. Ripped and stained vinyl chairs rest along a scuffed wall.

I like to call it retro chic, but really, it's tacky 1990s Bill Clinton era decor.

When my Uncle Dexter became our guardian, this is where he said I had to go after my diagnosis. And I've been here ever since. Plus, it helps that my uncle takes care of the cost.

I have my suspicions about how the doctor gets paid. I've never seen a bill, but I have noticed the doctor's name among a list of others titled *THEY OWE ME* in my uncle's office.

I don't know what it means, and honestly, I don't want to.

Truth be told, I had an appointment at the Cleveland Clinic this week, but I canceled it. This office, although I'm not sure I'm getting the best care, is comforting to me. The nurses here are like friends. I can't leave them. My brother will be livid when he finds out I canceled it. He wants me out of this place and somewhere else. Somewhere 'more world-renowned,' as he calls it.

I get it. He loves me and cares. But they won't be able to help me, I know it. I'm stuck with this disease with no way out, so why even try?

Also, it's here that I decided I wanted to be a nurse. Every single nurse that has treated me has been amazing. I want to impart that same kindness and understanding to others who suffer like me.

But I can't do it. My RA always gets in the way.

I mean, how can I work for someone else other than my uncle? How can I put in the time at school? If I were to have a flare-up, would anyone be understanding? They can come on without warning. I can't be calling off all the time.

But also, I always wonder, could this be possible for me? Why can't I do it? The job at the bar isn't easy at times. It can be physically demanding, yet I push through and do it.

And then, seeing Johnny's excitement when I told him has forced me to reevaluate some things. To have a man I hardly know express such enthusiasm for my dreams was unlike anything I've had in my life. Drew showed no interest in me unless it had to do with my body.

I distinctly remember the day I told Drew I was contemplating pursuing nursing. His exact words were, "Heck, yeah! You would look so hot in scrubs."

That was it. That's all I got.

So, having a man cheer me on is ... exhilarating. Plus, Micah supports me with this, so maybe, just maybe, my uncle will, too. I know he loves me and wants the best for me.

A sudden rush of ideas floods my mind, grinding and churning their gears as I watch the nurse with her orthopedic shoes enter my info into the computer. Renee has been here since I was young. We have a nice dynamic, so I muster up enough bravery to get her thoughts. "Can I ask you something, Renee?"

She continues to concentrate on the computer screen. "Sure, sweetie. What's up?" Her nails *tap-tap-tap* on the keyboard as she adjusts her reading glasses on her nose.

"How long have you been a nurse?" She boops her name badge on the computer screen, pushes away the keyboard, and gives me her full attention.

She swoops her glasses onto her head while glancing at the ceiling. "Let's see." She pauses as she contemplates her answer. "I would say around thirty-five years now."

"Wow! And you've always loved it?"

"I have. I mean, every job has its moments, of course, but yes. It has been very fulfilling." She tilts her head in curiosity. "Why are you asking me this? Are you thinking about going to school?"

I sigh in response, take a moment to gather my thoughts, and decide to confide in her. Also, she will be only the fourth person I have ever confessed this to. The first being my brother. The second being my cheating ex, and then the too-hot-for-his-own-good stranger who took my breath away and I kissed under the stars.

Wringing my hands in my lap, I rhythmically swing my legs back and forth over the edge of the exam table. "I have thought about it before. I've always wanted to be a nurse. To help people. But it's out of my reach." I shrug and sheepishly turn my face away. "You know, with my RA and all."

A wide grin stretches across her features. "Well, don't let that stop you!"

Regarding her again, I let out an exasperated sigh. "Oh, come on, Renee. With my flare-ups and chronic pain, how could I ever do"—I wave my hand over her—"what you do? And then there's the schooling. My body won't allow for it."

With a deliberate step, she walks over and places her weathered hand on my knee. "I am a type 1 diabetic."

My mouth drops open. "You're kidding me?"

She shakes her head. "No, ma'am. And the other nurse, Bobby, he has MS." She squeezes my knee. "Then there's Chrissy; well, that poor dear deals with Crohn's disease." Determination fills her expression, raising her chin in the air. "Let *nothing* stop you from doing the things you want to do. There are nurses who work through cancer. Some have personal family problems; others take care of their aging parents." She raises her hand and then points to herself.

"You can totally do this. You are smart, capable, and have an enormous heart. That's all the makings of an incredible nurse. And you're still young." She lets out a heavy sigh, then smiles sweetly. "You can accomplish big things, young lady." She gently shakes my knee, then leans forward. "Do the big things," she whispers, then releases her hand. "The doctor will be in soon."

After she exits the exam room, soft pop music creates a calming atmosphere, leaving me to contemplate my life in peace.

Hearing her words creates a swell of excitement in my chest. *Could I do this? Do I want this?* The thought of going to school is daunting for sure, yet very exhilarating. And the cost wouldn't be an issue. The OBGs have been very generous tippers over the years. They will nurse one seven-dollar beer for hours, then slap a hundred on the bar. I've tried and failed to reject the kind gesture. It brings them joy, so I let them. But because of their generosity, I now have a modest savings account that is more than enough to pay for the schooling.

And money that I keep hidden.

Suddenly, the ache in my elbow is gone since all I can think about is a brighter future.

But first, I need to talk this over with my uncle.

Knock, knock, knock.

I'm standing outside my uncle's office, wringing my hands to release some of this tension building.

"Come on in." His muffled reply sails from the other side of the door.

With a deep inhale, I puff out my chest and slowly turn the knob. As soon as the door opens, I'm met with the smell of cigar smoke and fresh paint from the remodel and his kind eyes.

"Hey, Rach." A genuine smile reaches his ears.

Uncle Dexter did not receive the height of our family. I tower over him, and he definitely suffers from short-man syndrome, that's for sure. It can be a blow to the ego when your niece, who is only twelve, surpasses you. I was five six back then. He's five five.

In order to make up for his lack of height, he always walks fast, head back, arms swinging with purpose. He ensures he commands attention and respect in any room he walks into by projecting an aura of importance. With each passing day, his receding hairline inches back further while he carries extra weight around his midsection. He's never been married, yet always has a woman on his arm.

Uncle Dexter loves Micah and me as if we are his own. After my parents passed away, he and his father took us in and raised us. He has been there for me through so much.

And, I know it's weird for me—a thirty-year-old woman—to ask him for permission to attend nursing school, but there is this debt I feel I owe him. He employs me here and pays my way more than he should; he takes care of my medical bills, and he's family. The only family Micah and I have right now.

Plus, he relies on me to run this bar. Micah and I handle just about everything, so in order for me to go to nursing school, I will need to cut back on my hours. And Johnny was right. He may need to hire someone to fill in.

Suddenly, the thought of Johnny and maybe seeing him again soon is making my cheeks pink.

My uncle notices.

"You okay today?" he asks as he rises from his chair behind his desk, abandoning whatever work he was doing to give me his full attention.

I shove aside my thoughts of Johnny. "Sure. Why?" I answer, attempting to look all unbothered, although I am anything but when it comes to thinking about that man.

"You're flushed. I was hoping you weren't sick."

With a shake of my head, I try to reassure him. "I'm fine."

He grabs my head, pulls it toward him, and kisses my forehead the way he always has. "Good. What brings you by?"

"I'm so sorry to bother you. I know you're busy today."

He waves his hand in the air. "Nonsense. You know I always make time for you." He casually leans against the front of his desk, crossing his ankles. The arms follow, resting on his protruding belly.

I take a deep breath in for courage and spit it out. "I am going to have to cut back some of my hours here at the bar."

His eyebrows raise. "Why is that? Have you been having some flare-ups?"

"No, no. That's been fine. Well, not fine, but not getting any worse, which is good."

The words explode from my mouth, a chaotic jumble of emotions and confessions. "I want to go to nursing school," I blurt out. "Nursing has always been my passion, and I think it's about time that I find work that will be more stable." My hands are gesturing and flaying as I talk. "I can go to school in the morning, study, then come here to bar tend if you need it. Then, of course, you know I would always be here on the weekends to help, so don't worry about that. I know it's not convenient, but I really want this. I've always wanted it. And then..."

With a dismissive flick of his wrist, his hand shoots up, cutting me off. "Rachel, slow down. You're rambling again." He uncrosses his arms and grips the desk, letting out a heavy sigh. "You know I'm starting pool tournaments here, right? Like next week. I'm going to need you here to help with that."

"You could hire someone." My voice rises as I offer this as a solution quicker than I should.

"Hmmm." He takes a stroll around the room before sitting behind his desk again, pen in hand, continuing the task that held his attention before my arrival. "How long have you been thinking about this?"

"A while now. I've always been interested in it." He continues to write, head down, as if now, since I need something for me, this conversation is a waste of his precious time.

"And you think with your RA you can do this?" he asks, squinting at me. "Come on, Rachel." A condescending tone laces his words. "How would this work? What if you have a flare-up? Will the instructors be as understanding as I am if you need time off? Or if you get a job. Will you call off all the time? No boss, other than me, can help you. You know that, right?"

Disappointment quivers across my lip and plummets straight to my heart.

My shoulders droop because ...

He's right.

Every doubt I had I heard in his reasonings. No one will hire me if I'm defective. How could I put in the time for school? Is it feasible for me to pursue a career in nursing, given the physical demands of being on your feet constantly? The answers are as clear as a sunny day with no clouds in sight. None of this is possible.

A pipe dream.

So stupid, Rachel.

"Yes," I agree while lowering my gaze to the floor, silently chiding myself for ever considering that this was a possibility for me.

Turning to leave his office, he calls my name. "Rachel?" My hand trembles on the doorknob as I pivot to meet his gaze. "I can't run this place without you. We are a family. And family"—we both say in unison—"sticks together as one."

He nods, a triumphant smirk crossing his lips, and raises his eyebrow as if to say, '*See, I'm always right!*' "You got it."

He's satisfied, because he won. Again.

I respond with a smile, forced and tense.

That mantra we recited on repeat after my parents passed was comforting. It was nice to know that despite losing our parents in one of the most tragic of ways, we still had family that cared for us and had our backs. Anytime some sort of adversity would attack us, we would all repeat in unison, 'We are family. And family sticks together as one.'

That chant helped me in more ways than one. But now, as a thirty-year-old woman, this family and those words are like a prison.

"Oh, yeah, one more thing, since we are on the topic of your health." I have no idea what he's going to say next. "How is your physical therapy going? Is it helping?"

"Um ... Okay, I guess." My therapist is currently an hour's drive away. Even though there are PT facilities in this area, it's hard to find a physical therapist that specializes in therapy for those with RA.

"I wonder if it would be better for you to just do the exercises at home. I really need you here at the bar." The intensity of his stare makes it impossible to refuse. My uncle doesn't take no for an answer. Ever.

"Okay, yeah, sure. I can do that." To be fair, those long drives twice a week felt like such a chore, especially since my presence was constantly required here at the bar.

"Perfect." He settles in his big leather chair. "Shut the door on your way out, will ya?"

I know when I'm being dismissed. I walk out of his office and click the door shut behind me.

On heavy legs (both literally and figuratively), I walk down the hallway and out into the bar area. The hurt and burning in my knees reminds me that my uncle is right. This job is hard enough. Nursing? Forget about it.

But that doesn't mean it's not heartbreaking all the same.

And therapy? I guess that isn't happening anymore. It was too far away, anyhow.

Nothing in my life is working.

The Oldies but Goodies are here for their nightly drink together, and as soon as I enter their line of sight, they all light up. I love these three men. They have been a presence in my life since I was a teenager. Countless times they have given me advice, fought off handsy customers, and made me feel like one of their own.

The three of them started coming in for their evening meet-up about fifteen years ago. Slick was the sole reason I passed math in tenth through twelve grades. One of my favorite things growing up was coming here to the bar after school and hanging out in the office until dinner. It was Micah who gave them the nickname Oldies but Goodies, and they loved it because they loved us. They range in age from sixty-five to seventy.

And since they know me so well, they immediately can sense my sour mood.

"What's up, Rachel? Everything okay?" Slick asks first as he takes a sip of his beer.

I shrug as I go about my pre-shift ritual. Stocking glasses, making sure the ice maker is full, garnishes, mixers, and syrups are all lined up and ready to go. "I don't want to talk about it."

Tiny chimes in next. "Dexter giving you a hard time?"

"What did he do now?" Randy joins in as Micah walks out of the kitchen holding clean white plates he stacks neatly behind the bar.

"What did who do?" Micah asks.

"Stop it, guys. It's nothing. Really," I retort, needing to put the whole thing behind me.

"Yeah, right!" Slick exclaims. "As soon as you left Dexter's office, you looked like someone killed your pet puppy. Now spill."

I meet Micah's gaze, and his furrowed brow tells me everything I need to know—he's worried. "Rach? What's going on?"

I study each of the four men carefully. Men who would move hell or high water to protect me. Men who treat me with respect, dignity, and pride. Why shouldn't I tell them what I asked Uncle Dexter about? I know they would support me and be understanding of a dream that will never come true. So what's the harm in telling them? Plus, maybe, if I let more people in, talk about this out loud, it won't feel like such a long shot anymore. And these guys know how to extract information out of me. It's an art form at this point.

I let out a long exhale. "I told Uncle Dexter that I want to go to nursing school."

"Heck ya!—That's incredible!—Nice going kiddo!" The OBGs all cry out at once.

Micah runs a tired hand over his stubbled face, his eyes heavy-lidded as I regard him. He knows but asks anyway, "How did he take it?"

"As good as to be expected."

"What's that supposed to mean?" Tiny asks. "He's happy for you, right?" Anxiety etches itself on all three of their faces.

"Not necessarily. He just reminded me how hard it would be with my RA and that he needs me here since we are starting the tournaments soon." I keep my head down, busy filling the sliced limes. "I mean, he's right. How could I possibly go to school and work in a demanding job like nursing with me being me?"

Tiny's eyebrows lower and pinch together. "That's such bull—"

"Language!" Slick and Randy yell out.

The OBGs have been watching their cussing lately. There's no swear jar. They only yell at each other as a reminder. It's funny to watch them school each other when one slips. Despite my sour mood, this whole exchange forces me to smile.

Tiny flips his hand dismissively. "Whatever. Anyway, that's so ridiculous. Don't let his small opinion of you and his laziness in hiring any help around here stop you!"

"He's right, Rach," Randy chimes in. "You are totally capable."

All three nod before sipping their beers. It doesn't escape my notice that my brother has been awful quiet throughout this entire conversation. "What do you think, Micah?"

He studies me as he pulls his apron over his head, getting ready to start his shift as head of the kitchen. Micah has big dreams, as well. He wants to go to culinary school and someday become a chef and own his own restaurant. But just like me, he's trapped.

"Tiny's right." Tiny sits a little taller in his chair, something he does any chance he gets. "But maybe you should wait just a little longer, you know, until these tournaments get started. Hopefully, Uncle Dexter will see that we need help, and that might be the right time to bring it up again." He rests his hand on my shoulder and squeezes gently, then makes his way to the kitchen.

As the OBGs delve into a political discussion, I refocus on preparing for my shift while trying to forget about my shattered dream.

The events of these last few hours whirl around in my head. The talk with nurse Renee, the renewed sense of purpose I had after, then the crushing defeat once I talked to Uncle Dexter. How the OBGs were supportive, as usual. How my brother knew my uncle's reaction, even though he wasn't in the room with us.

A stray tear tracks over my cheek when a voice cuts through the noise in my head.

"What's wrong?" My gaze shoots up, and standing in front of me … is Johnny. His nostrils flare. "Who made you cry?"

6

Watch and Learn

Johnny

Her head snaps up, eyes widening in surprise as the question hangs in the air. She gently brushes away the stray tear.

I've dated countless women over my forty-five years, yet the profound sense of protectiveness I have towards Rachel is unparalleled. I don't know what it is, considering that I just met her. But her being upset right now, while she's at work no less, I need to know what happened.

And how I can make it better.

Was it a customer who got too close and thought he had the right to touch her without permission? Is she sick? Did she get bad news at the doctor's appointment I heard her brother mention to ... I think it was Slick. Or maybe she's just hormonal and emotional, like we all get sometimes.

I don't care what the reason is. I just want to help and comfort her. And punch someone if need be.

After her initial shock wears off, her shoulders square, and she stands a little straighter, trying to compose herself and not show any emotion. The mask she wears is back on. "I'm fine, Johnny." Her bartender persona takes over as she flashes me a smile, and a napkin appears in front of me. The small, strained smile that graces her lips is devoid of its characteristic brightness; it's forced and stiff. "What can I get you?"

If she assumes I'm letting this go, she's crazy. I perch myself on the barstool, the smooth wood cool beneath me, my pool cue resting beside my hand as I keep my attention glued to her. The rhythmic crack of pool balls mixes with Blake Shelton's twangy voice bouncing off the walls as I study her. "Club soda with lime." I peer around her as I remove my coat. "Unless you've installed an espresso machine back there since last week, then I'll take a mocha with a double shot of espresso and vanilla sweet cream."

This makes her chuckle. Good. Mission accomplished. I've lightened her mood.

She fills my glass and plops the lime inside. "You really love coffee, don't you?"

"The sweeter, the better. Plus, it beats this garbage." A broad grin stretches across my face as I tilt the glass, the crisp, clean fizz of the club soda exploding on my tongue.

With a slight head shake, an inaudible tone eludes her lips before she resumes meticulously wiping the bar. I love that I have an effect on her. "Back again so soon?" she inquires while trying to hold back a grin.

"I am." A subtle upturn of her lips tells me she's glad I came. "For a few reasons." Turning, I watch the other players, their movements jerky and awkward, each missed shot accompanied by the pungent smell of desperation. "I told you I was going to join the pool league," I explain, itching to hold the smooth pool cue in my hand. I take another sip as I observe some scrawny kid trying to make the nine ball in the corner pocket. He misses … by a mile. His stance is all wrong. His legs are too close together, his bridge isn't tight enough, and his aim's bad.

Lord help me if this amateur is going to be playing with me. I'm going to be carrying this team on my back. I may need to step in and teach these boys a thing or two.

Her sweet voice pulls me from my thoughts. "You here to audition?"

What? Audition? This redirects my attention to her, away from the unpleasant scene unfolding at the tables.

When I checked out the BPA website, it listed the locations that house tournaments. Dexter's wasn't the closest, but I didn't care. My goal with this whole thing hasn't changed. Sign up for the league, and I get to see Rachel more.

But there was nowhere on the site to register as a player. The instructions gave dates and times to show up if you were interested. It never stated that you had to audition. Granted, I'm not in the pool league circuit. But I have buddies who are and never have I heard of people auditioning. It's strange, to say the least.

But let's be real. If they need people to audition, I'm a shoo-in.

"Maybe. But first, you need to tell me why you were upset."

She leans on the work station behind the bar, rows of liquor line the wall behind her. Thankfully, it's Tuesday, and this place just opened, so it's a ghost town right now. In about an hour, people will fill this joint after a hard day's work, ready to cut loose with some alcohol. But right now, I have her undivided attention, which I love.

With a long sigh, she steps closer and rests her elbows on the bar, her tank top leaving nothing to the imagination. In order to avoid staring like a perv, I avert my gawking and focus on the big brown eyes I could get lost in. "Why am I telling you this?" she asks herself, then pauses. Her gaze darts aross the room as if to make sure no one is around to hear this. "I want to apply to nursing school," she declares in a low voice.

A wave of pride, warm and undeniable, swells in my chest. During our night under the stars last week, she shared her dream of becoming a nurse. Despite my attempts to encourage her, her voice still carried a tone of doubt and uncertainty. Who knows, I could have planted a seed.

Her telling me this feels like a secret shared between just the two of us. "Your face lit up when you said that." Grinning at the memory, she tucks a piece of hair behind her ear.

Gosh, she's adorable.

A sudden, intense need to touch her, a primal urge, overwhelms me. Gingerly, I reach out and place my palm on her forearm. Her skin is just as soft and warm as I remember. Internally, I sigh in relief because she doesn't resist or pull away. Instead, a tense breath leaves her lips, the air charged with unspoken energy between us. This slight connection is like color filling my black-and-white world. Heat fills the tips of my fingers, sparking as the electricity sizzles between us.

I inhale deeply and refocus on the conversation. "Rachel, that's incredible. So what's the problem?"

With an even shake of her head, her concentration is glued to my hand on her arm. A worried frown creases her brow as she nibbles on her bottom lip. I can practically hear the gears turning in her head as she tries to decide whether to trust me with this personal side of her life. The confident woman that Rachel puts out there with her customers is not the same woman that stands here behind this bar, full of fear.

And I want to strangle the person who makes her feel this way; my hand is clenching into a fist just thinking about it.

She remains quiet, so I push ... a little more. "Why would pursuing your dream make you cry? A dream should make your heart soar. You deserve to soar. And shine." On instinct, my thumb glides over her soft skin to add comfort.

"It's a long story," she starts, so low that I can hardly hear her. "But it's my unc—"

"Rachel?" A voice comes from behind me and interrupts our moment. A short, pudgy man glares at me; his eyes are burning coals.

It's dear ole Dexter.

Instantly, his presence causes the surrounding air to crackle with unspoken hostility. His focus zeroes in on my hand resting on Rachel's forearm.

Rachel's back goes ramrod straight as if she was just caught making out with me in the alley behind the bar.

If only.

She yanks her arm away, breaking our connection. A heavy loss washes over me at the release of her touch. She grabs the rag she abandoned, folding it into a perfectly neat square. "Hey, Uncle Dexter."

Between our initial meeting, what Rachel told me, and Scott's revelations, this man is no good.

Standing at my full height, a good foot taller than him, I maintain eye contact as I loom over him.

"Sorry to interrupt time with your friend here," Dexter says, trying his hardest to appear intimidating and scary.

He's failing.

"He's not my friend," Rachel quips back.

My head whips around, the sharp movement causing my neck to pinch as her eyes flick to meet me for only a millisecond.

Is she ... scared of him?

I thought our connection was real. I would definitely say we are 'friendly' if nothing else. A strange stillness settles between us at her hesitation to introduce me or even acknowledge me to her uncle. Each passing second amplifies my discomfort.

Something is itching at me. And it's telling me that this man is controlling and a bully.

I'm going to make it my aim to find out.

With my usual charming smile fixed in place, I extend my hand to the puny man. "Nice to see you again, Dexter. It's been a while."

He sneers at my outstretched hand with disgust for a beat or two before reluctantly offering me his.

"You as well." He squints as recognition fills his expression, then points at me. "Didn't I see you in here playing about a week ago with your cousin Scott? He was great to work with. Nice guy."

"I tend to agree," I answer, completely ignoring the question about him seeing me here last week. I'd rather not bring up the unsettling scene I witnessed; it's best he's not reminded.

"How come I never had time to talk to you during the reno?"

Because you're an obvious narcissist, so I avoided you like the plague. But I don't say that.

"Scott handles the contracts and blueprints. I just enjoy getting my hands dirty. Give me some two-by-fours with a tape measure, and I'm a happy guy. I guess I was just busy."

"So, a simple man, then?" If he feels this insult is going to hit, he's mistaken. I've heard it all before.

"Or just someone who knows his worth and what he's capable of."

He glances away, jaw tightening, obviously annoyed with me. "Well, sorry, I didn't have time to talk to you when you were working here."

I take a sip of my drink. "Yep, I never saw you around, come to think of it. You must be quite the busy guy." Busy doing what? I have no idea. And it's better that I don't.

"What brings you by?" He tilts his chin up in order to make eye contact with me.

Rachel gives me a quick side eye before heading to the kitchen. Probably smart.

"I would like to join the BPA. The website said to show up, so here I am. Rachel mentioned auditioning?"

"You play?" he probes, ignoring my question as he pulls over a barstool, and with a grunt, he hoists himself onto the seat, huffing and puffing.

"Since I was a kid," I answer as I sit with ease across from him.

"So you're not just looking to get into my niece's pants?" He raises an eyebrow.

Come again?

I grit my teeth, a vein throbbing in my temple, trying to stay calm. It's taking every ounce of willpower I have in me to keep my cool. This guy is unbelievable, and I've only talked to him for five minutes. Which is five minutes too long. I wonder if he would have asked this crass question if she was here. Doubtful. This man has coward written all over him. "You wouldn't be the first man to show his face here, hoping to hook up with her."

Does he hear himself right now?

Would I love to see Rachel again outside of this place? Absolutely.

Am I hoping to get to know her better and use the pool league as an excuse to spend time with her? You bet.

Is this about sex? No.

I want to get to know Rachel as a person. Dig deep into who she is and what she can offer the world. Her uncle's belief that men are only interested in her body is sickening.

And I get it; maybe he is just being protective. He raised her. It's only natural to worry. But he could be more respectful about asking and not degrading his niece.

"I'm just here to play. And show you what you would gain by having me on your team."

He clicks his tongue. "I'll be the judge of that."

I find myself unable to contain a snort of amusement. He has no idea the spectacle that is superior pool playing he is about to witness.

With a confident grip, I grab the handle of my case and face him. "What's the next step?" This guy is testing my patience, and I'm one wrong word away from a regrettable outburst; I need to leave now.

"Head on over to that small desk in the corner. Irene will set you up." I glance across the room, noting the newly installed pool tables gleaming under the lights, their felt surfaces smooth and inviting. A woman, who I assume is Irene, sits there. I noticed her earlier. An older lady with gray hair and reading glasses perched on top of her head, looking like she just stepped out of an episode of *The Golden Girls*. "There's a fifty-dollar audition fee. Cash only."

I sharply redirect my gaze towards Dexter. His eyes narrow, a sinister smirk playing on his lips as he taps his finger on the bar top. I know there isn't an audition fee. Funny how the website neglected to mention the audition or the surprisingly hefty fee. And no one has paid Miss Irene a dime.

His behavior is quite telling, so I know what he's doing. He is just trying to get a rise out of me. Or trying to steer me away from Rachel and from joining the team. Scare me off, perhaps.

Won't work.

Sitting my pool cue on the bar, I fish out my wallet and dig out four fifties. "I'll do you one better." I slap them on the bar. "Here's two hundred."

"You're that cocky, huh?" He jams his finger into the bills and swipes them off the slick surface, not even offering to mention that I have given him too much. Or to pay Irene and not him.

I grab my cue, walking backward toward my happy place, smiling like a fool. "Like I said, I know my worth. Watch and learn ... *Dex.*"

"It's Dexter."

I salute him. "I know." Before I head towards the tables, Rachel emerges from the kitchen, and her eyes immediately meet mine. Her gaze darts to her uncle, then back to me, as a flicker of uncertainty spreads across her face. With each backward step, we hold our stare, a silent magnetic current flowing between us.

The weight of Dexter's disapproval, heavy in his scrowl, swings back and forth between his niece and me.

He sees it. He knows.

But just to drive home the point, I give her a playful wink, which causes her eye to crinkle when she grins at my flirtation.

As the tables get closer with each step, a sudden clarity washes over me. I should expect a long, hard road ahead; nothing about being here at Dexter's will be simple or straightforward.

But I am up for the challenge.

For the pool.

To keep an eye on sleezy Dexter.

And for *her.*

7

Are You a Serial Killer?

Rachel

"There's one!" Johnny's arm shoots up to the twinkling sky, his finger pointing to the shooting star that just streaked across the black void. He turns his head to me, his eyes bright and full of excitement. "Did you see it?"

A wide smile stretches across my face as I nod, the sound of my happy sigh filling the air. "I did! That was beautiful!"

We both settle back under the thick wool blanket covering our bodies as we lie on an air mattress in the bed of his truck and stargaze. It's a chilly April night, but the bed of the Silverado is full of nothing but warmth. It's like I'm being swallowed by blankets and pillows, and the low hum of the small space heater is doing little to drown out the beating of my heart.

He does everything to make this time together comfortable.

These little truck outings (they are not dates; I refuse to call them dates) have been a frequent part of my life since I met Johnny one month ago.

The last four weeks have been a whirlwind of joy and pain, the best and worst of my entire life. And that's because of the gigantic tree of a man lying next to me, who shows up to win pool tournaments for my uncle.

Watching him play is quickly becoming my favorite pastime. And my number one distraction as I try to do my job. I've broken almost two glasses a shift as I drool over Johnny like a lovesick schoolgirl.

He is impossible not to notice, and that's part of the problem.

And it's not just the man's looks. Which, I mean, come on. He's Glen Powell and Justin Hartley rolled into one. He's not playing fair. No other men stand a chance when he's in the room. Every woman who enters fixates on him. And every time one of their claws tries to touch him, a wave of nausea and bitter jealousy washes over me.

And it shouldn't. Johnny can date whomever he wants. I have no claim to him whatsoever. We aren't dating. We aren't a couple. And that is by choice.

My choice.

I've kept him at arm's length, and he's respected my decision, even if he doesn't understand it. Which makes him even more desirable.

Every time, though, a woman tries to flirt with him, Johnny's eyes always find mine, lingering for a moment before he glances away with a slight smile. He refuses them with a polite but definite no. It's like he's waiting.

For me.

And that's an insane thought. No one wants to be with me. Even a man who had me willingly found someone better. Prettier. Less arthritisy.

And to make matters worse, his gentlemanly actions are becoming increasingly obvious, making it even harder to cope with my feelings. Johnny has taken the time to get to know the OBGs and has even managed to get grumpy Tiny to like him.

Recently, Slick needed a ride since his car died while he was at the bar. Johnny arranged the tow truck and made sure Slick got home safely. Rumor has it he paid for the tow and Slick's repairs, but neither of them is talking. Micah spilled the beans when I threatened him.

Then it's what he does for me. He stays every night I'm working, after hours, to help me. He takes the time to clean and close the tables—my least favorite chore because of my joints.

And even though we have spent all this time together, he hasn't made one move on me. There have been accidental touches and soft hand grazes, all of which send my nerve endings on fire. But nothing other than that. Which, if I'm being honest, leaves me somewhat disappointed. But at the same time, it's refreshing. It's almost as if he cares more about my mind than my looks. The men who come through the doors of the bar can be forward and downright disgusting with their comments and innuendos.

But not Johnny.

Maybe it's his age. And with age comes experience. Or his parents raised him that way. Whatever the reason, the man is kindness personified.

And the age gap, a worry that initially had me spiraling, surprisingly feels nonexistent now. Yes, he was a freshman in high school when I was born. Yes, when he was starting his business with his cousin, I was still in elementary school. But when we are together, under these stars, the years melt away and don't feel like years.

It shouldn't be this good. Should it?

Which is the part that makes me sad. Johnny is the perfect man, the kind of man who makes you believe in fairy tales, and I'm like a broken toy next to him. And besides, he'll find out, eventually, about my RA; the moment he does, his interest will get tossed right out the window. So why get my hopes up?

Taking his eyes off of the stars, he scans the surroundings of our little comfy bubble, then glances at me. His eyes narrow slightly as a flicker of concern flashes across his features. "Are you warm enough?"

My body is chilled and aching as it usually is, but it's his question, laced with nothing but concern, that warms me.

But it's also the five hundredth time he's asked.

"Johnny, I'm fine. I told you."

He sighs, directing his attention back to the heavens above us. "Sorry, I just want you to be comfortable."

"I am. I'll tell you if I'm not, okay?" I promise him as I nudge my knee to his under the blanket.

With a grin, he playfully nudges me back, his touch feather-light, but also not pulling away.

Oh, God. Now we are touching. And why does that excite me like I'm still a teenager?

He seriously wants to know if I'm cold. No, Johnny, I'm not cold since now I'm burning up because our knees are touching. And barely.

This is insane.

We lie in comfortable silence when a wave of bravery washes over me.

Throughout our evenings together, the conversation always flows. It's as if we have known each other for decades and not just one month. It's so easy and stimulating. We talk about our lives, funny stories from the bar, our likes and dislikes. Gradually, through his words and stories, he is becoming one of my closest friends.

Some topics are off-limits for me, though. My RA being one of them and then my ex, Drew. The way things ended with Drew made me feel like a fool. I don't want him to know about any of it. On our first night together, in this very spot, I briefly mentioned my biggest heartbreak. But I'm not quite ready to tell him the full story.

Not yet anyway.

But his dating history ... well, I want every detail. I know it might not be fair, but for whatever reason, I have to find out why this man is still single.

I bite my lower lip as my stomach somersaults with nerves. Interlacing my fingers and laying them over my stomach, I turn to take in his beautiful face. "Johnny, can I ask you something?"

"Of course." He stares at the stars above.

"Are you a serial killer?"

His head whips to mine as a huge grin graces his perfect lips, and a chuckle vibrates through him. "What?"

"I mean, come on. That has to be the reason a woman hasn't snatched you up yet. Have you seen you?"

He shrugs. "I thought the man staring back at me in the mirror tonight before I left the house looked pretty good."

Now it's my turn to laugh. "You know what I mean. I've seen how women flock to you at the bar." He arches one eyebrow. "Do you have a secret wife and kids, a third nipple like Chandler on *Friends*, or do you catfish people on the internet?" I gasp mockingly. "Are you a closeted cat lady?" His billowing laugh fills the night air. "I'm serious."

"I promise you, I am none of those things."

"Then how come you're still single? Have you even tried looking, or are you happy being alone? You are quite the catch, in case you didn't know."

His brow relaxes as his eyes soften. "And somehow, I can't catch you."

Whoa.

My eyes burn, and something thick lodges in my throat at his honest retort. I push it down, redirecting my attention back to the sky.

Why did I start this conversation?

After a few tense passing minutes, he shifts to his side on the mattress, facing me. "I never found the right woman." It's my turn to shift and face him as I tuck my arm under my head, settling in to receive the answers I asked for. "I guess you could say I have a reputation for being a serial dater, not a killer. A reputation I've leaned into. And I've played the part well, even though it's not really who I am."

The night air picks up, and a piece of his dark blonde hair falls on his forehead. My hand has a mind of its own. It reaches out and swipes it away. "Why would you play into that?"

His eyes search my face. "It's a defense mechanism, I think. But the constant chasing and dating, at my age, is getting old. I've always wanted to settle down, have a wife and a family. That's why I tried so hard with Julie."

Julie? I already hate her. "Who's Julie?" I ask with a thinning breath.

He turns onto his back, tucking his arm behind his head while running his tongue over his top teeth. "I met her through mutual friends, and we hit it off right away. She was gorgeous. Huge green eyes with fiery red hair. She had a nose dotted with freckles and beautifully pale skin. It would always turn pink when she was in the sun for longer than five minutes. She was gorg—"

"You already said that. I get it. She's pretty. Move on, please."

The scowl on my face must be pretty big, because he flicks his eyes at me briefly and smirks. "The lady doth protest too much."

"Funny." I tuck my arm closer to my chest for warmth. Or maybe a shield.

He shifts slightly as his socked foot drifts toward my feet in a slow slide against the mattress. It brushes against mine. My breath hitches. A single touch from him pulls me from the cold water my thoughts were in, and it's as if I'm encased in his arms. And only our toes are touching.

He continues. "At first, the relationship was going well. We were having fun. My family loved her. My mom loved her. She was great. We were great together."

"So, what was the problem?"

"After a few months, I slowly realized that she just wasn't the woman for me. And that made me sad, you know?"

"Because you would have to break her heart."

He lets out a long, weary sigh. "Yeah."

"How did she take it?" My head is buzzing with anticipation, wanting to know how this ends.

His focus never leaves the full moon. "I didn't break it off right away."

"You led her on!?" I smack him in the chest, but before I can pull my hand away, he snatches it and covers it with his own, resting them on his chest. His thumb begins to rub small circles on my flesh. Goosebumps erupt up my arm.

"I know it sounds that way. But I wanted to try. She checked off every single box. It should have been working. Eventually though"—he squeezes my hand—"after being together for six months, I broke it off. She was devastated and told me that I was the love of her life. She begged me to not give up on us. I didn't have the heart to tell her that all I was doing was trying." He sighs. "That was a hard day."

"I'm sorry."

He finally turns to face me, still grasping my hand as he grins. "Don't be. I'm not."

"Do you still talk to her?" *Please say no. Please say no.*

"No. Not for a long time. I ran into her a couple of years after we broke up at the movies, of all places. She was with a date. A date who is now her husband. They have two kids. So it all worked out in the end."

"It worked out for her. But you're still single."

Not removing his eyes from mine, slowly, he drags our hands up to his mouth and tenderly kisses my knuckles. Once, twice, three times.

I'm melting.

"Thank God for that."

After a few more, far less serious conversations, we part ways.

And on the ride home, I secretly thank Julie for not being the one.

8

It Could Never Happen, Slick

Rachel

Another month and four truck dates later, I'm still obsessed with the man currently bending over the table to take his final shot. And winning another pool game for my uncle. And getting his team one step closer to the tournament.

How do I know I'm obsessed? Because I can't stop staring at him in those jeans. It's pure torture. I'm falling headfirst into a sinkhole I can't crawl out of.

I avert my ogling ... for the hundredth time tonight.

Okay. One more peek. *Dear Lord, he's beautiful.*

The bar has died down, with a lot of the tournament guys leaving for the night, which gives me a chance to start my closing duties. With a final stocking of beer for the next day, I close the cooler and immediately find Johnny again. Like I always do. He's showing another member of his team a few tips and tricks.

Slick follows my line of sight. He swivels back in his chair with a smirk on his face, lets out a low chuckle, and shakes his head.

With his subtle shift in posture and the amusing twitch of his lips, I'm pretty sure I know what's going through his head. "What's so funny?"

Sighing wearily, Slick slowly lifts the glass of water to his lips, the ice clinking softly, and takes a long swig. "When are you going to get out of your own head and ask him out?"

I almost drop yet another glass, juggling it in my hands, shocked at his question. "What? Me?" Slick shrugs, with a '*Why not*' expression on his face. "Maybe I'm waiting for him to ask me out."

"Yeah, right." He lets out a puff of air. "That man is waiting for you to make a move."

Curiosity gets the better of me as I lean on the bar to get closer to Slick. "How do you know that?"

"He told me that night he drove me home. Which was out of his way, by the way."

"Out of his way? How?"

He points in Johnny's direction. "He lives forty-five minutes north of here."

My jaw drops in surprise. *How did I not know that?* "Are there no other bars around closer to him that have tables? I mean, why would he drive all this way? He doesn't even like pool tournaments."

Slick chortles and stands, throwing three fifties on the bar, even though he's only been sipping water all night. "Oh, I'm sure there is. But, Rachel, we both know why he drives all the way here to Dexter's. And if you don't know, then you're blind."

I do know. But still...

I shake his absurd assumption out of my head as I refill the straws and napkin holders. Johnny comes here for me ... I know it's true. But that doesn't change anything. "It could never happen, Slick. As soon as he found out about me, that would be it. There's no point even dwelling on it."

Slick's old and weathered hand lands on top of mine, stopping it. I drag my gaze to meet his. A stark line etches across his forehead. "Don't take away his right to choose if that would be a problem. You are deciding for him, and that's not fair. That man has showed up here almost every night to see you. Sure, he plays incredible pool, but that's just an excuse, and you know it." He squeezes my hand. "He could very possibly be exactly what you deserve in your life. Don't let your insecurities get in the way of a lifetime of happiness." He gives me a final tap of his hand, grabs his jacket, and walks out the door, leaving me alone with my thoughts.

His words give me pause. Is he right? Am I sabotaging a possible good thing with my own hang-ups and insecurities? Johnny is a good guy. No, strike that, he is a *GREAT* guy. Hope swells in my chest as I build up enough nerve to ask him out tonight.

Can I do this?

Heavy footfalls come from the hallway beside the bar, and that can only mean one thing: My uncle is leaving for the night. All hopeful thoughts of Johnny get tossed out the window as he makes his approach.

"How were sales tonight, Rachel?" he asks as he swivels a bar stool and sits.

"I haven't closed out the register yet, but good. We were busy. Word is getting out about that one"—I point to Johnny—"and people want to come and try to beat him."

He turns, the sharp crack of another pool ball breaking echoes in the otherwise silent bar, to watch Johnny shoot. He observes him land four balls in a row with little effort. "Huh. He's that good?"

"No one can beat him. Basically, they are just showing up to rack. So yeah, he's that good." My uncle's attempts at conversation are lame. He knows about the gambling that goes on around these tournaments. Gambling that I am sure isn't one hundred percent legal. Needless to say, Johnny has made him a lot of money these last two months.

My uncle assumes that Micah and I are ignorant to what happens behind the scenes at this place. Illegal gambling and tax evasion are the two that we know of. Which is another reason I want to go to nursing school and get out of here before it all catches up to him.

And it will catch up to him.

It's just a matter of time. And I don't want to be here for the fallout. Whether it's from the cops or someone he's wronged, count me out of all of it.

Micah, too.

I need a conversation change because there is no way I want my uncle to figure out that I may or may not have feelings for Johnny.

Okay, fine. I have feelings. Lots and lots of feelings that I need to squash.

Pronto.

I clear my throat as I cover the lime and lemon wedges. "Have you picked up your tux for the wedding yet?" This weekend, my brother and his lovely fiancée, Shelby, will be tying the knot. It's been a long time coming, and I'm excited.

"Not yet."

I roll my eyes. "You realize you need to do that by tomorrow, right?" The wedding is in two days, and my uncle is the biggest procrastinator.

He waves me off, not even glancing at me as he studies Johnny. "I will. Don't worry."

Johnny unscrews his cue and puts it away, grabbing it, and heading in our direction.

"Crap," I mutter under my breath. I do not want Johnny anywhere near me when Uncle Dexter is around. I don't trust my natural reactions to his presence.

My uncle whips his head around. "What?"

Before I know it, Johnny is right in front of me. His enormous, muscular tree trunk legs carried him over here faster than the average person could. He sits his pool case down and leans forward, his forearms resting on the bar, flashing me his famous smile.

God, those stupid dimples! I just want to stick my finger in them, then kiss them.

Okay, Rachel ... not now.

He's wearing his signature dark denim jeans that are tight but not too tight and a gray Henley that hugs his broad shoulders and chest. His hair is styled to perfection as usual, and the way he smells is simply divine. Cedarwood mixed with vanilla. His face is smooth and clean-shaven. There has been no stubble on this man's face. Ever. And all I want to do is run my fingers over his jaw to know if it's as velvety smooth as it looks.

It probably is.

I sigh internally. He's perfect.

"Hey, Rachel." His deep, smooth voice instantly churns my insides to goo. "Let me know when you want me to start shutting down the tables."

This catches my uncle's attention. He immediately sits straighter, his piercing gray eyes pin me in place. His accusatory expression is full of questions I don't want to answer.

With clenched fists, his attention focuses on the object of my affection. "You've been staying to help Rachel close up?" He raises his voice slightly, being dramatic as usual.

Johnny pivots effortlessly, unfazed by my uncle's aggressive stance and booming voice. "Oh, hey there, Dex. Didn't see you sitting there."

I snort out a laugh at Johnny's obnoxiously cheerful tone. Oh, he saw him, alright. No one has ever made such an effort to make my uncle appear unimportant. I like it and fear it, all in equal measure.

"It's Dexter," my uncle retorts, his grip tightening around the stool handle.

Ignoring the correction, Johnny continues. "Yep, I've been staying and helping Rachel with the tables at the end of the night when I'm here." Johnny turns, scanning the worn green felt of the pool tables, and lets out a long, low whistle that echoes slightly in the dimly lit room. "I mean, that's a lot of tables to clean," he states, addressing my uncle again, "especially on tourny nights. As a man, it would be unkind and rude of me to leave her here to fend for herself." He regards my uncle again and cocks his head to the side. "Wouldn't you agree, Dex?"

The accusation hangs heavy in the air. Johnny has seen Dexter leave night after night. Leaving me here to close on my own, not once offering to help, knowing I did it all by myself before Johnny waltzed into my life.

Uncle Dexter, never one to look like the bad guy, changes his mood. He smiles. But it's his fake one. The one he wears when he's about to destroy someone. "Your mom must have raised you right."

Johnny smirks. "She sure did."

Now they are having a full-on shoot-out-at-the-OK-Corral kinda stare down. Johnny's shoulders are tense. Uncle Dexter clenches his fists, his knuckles bone-white with anger.

Dear Lord, this is ridiculous. My head pings back and forth between the two of them as if I'm at a tennis match, not knowing what to do.

Uncle Dexter breaks eye contact first. He stands and yanks the keys out of his suit pocket. "You feel okay and safe here with him?"

Oh, please. Now he's concerned? It only shows how little he pays attention. I have been alone here in this bar with him for the past two months. His head would explode if he knew how alone we are in the back of Johnny's truck.

"Of course. Johnny has helped a lot recently and has been nothing but kind. I'll be fine."

His downcast eyes, the way he lingers, and the slight tremble in his hands tells me he is reluctant to leave; my uncle, who knows me better than anyone, can see I like this guy. And that he likes me.

My breakup with Drew utterly devastated my uncle. They are close, and he has tried and failed to get me to reconcile with him. And in the meantime, he blocks any guy that has tried to ask me out. Uncle Dexter is all about control. Everything and everyone around him. And that includes me. But I can tell Johnny is different. He is bringing in a lot of money for Uncle Dexter. Therefore, he will put up with him pursuing me.

But for how long is the question?

Johnny addresses my uncle. "I'll make sure she's safe"—he turns to me and grins —"like I always do."

My heart explodes. *God, this man.*

Uncle Dexter wiggles out of the barstool and faces me, done with Johnny. And, per usual, he has to have the last word. "Remember Drew is picking you up for the wedding Saturday at noon? Be ready. He'll be excited to see you."

Shoot me now. He knows what he's doing. Tossing Drew's name out there as if we are a couple to throw Johnny off. My eyes dart to the object of my desire. His shoulders sag in defeat. I only agreed to go with Drew to, again, keep the peace with my uncle.

Uncle Dexter lets out a huff and waddles out of the bar, humming, satisfied with himself.

There's a churning deep in my gut, wondering what's going through Johnny's head. His retreating form, fading footsteps, and head hanging low cause my chest to pinch. He probably thinks Drew and I are back together. Panic creeps up my neck.

I need to do some damage control, pronto.

9

See Any Shots Worth Taking?

Johnny

I grab the brush off the top shelf and sweep the first table. I needed to get away from Dexter as quickly as possible. Every flashing alarm bell goes off in my head when he's around. I don't trust him.

And to make matters worse, Drew and Rachel are going to her brother's wedding as a couple, obviously. My heart dropped.

Rachel has mentioned her uncle wants her to get back together with her ex. And that she has a hard time saying no to him, so maybe he wore her down. Or, it could be that Rachel has forgiven Drew, and she wants to give the relationship a go.

Which, if that's the case, why spend evenings with me stargazing, talking, getting to know each other? Did none of that time we spent together mean anything to her?

I take a lot of pride in my self-confidence, but right now, I am feeling anything but.

Whatever. It's none of my business. Even though I desperately want it to be my business.

All I want to do is leave this place, but I won't do that before I help her first. As I brush the table, footsteps approach from behind me.

"I'm not dating Drew," she blurts out. Before I know it, she's standing on the opposite end of the table, waiting for me to respond, her eyes pinching with concern.

Why does she care? Why is she standing here telling me this, as if it matters?

For the last two months, I have tried to get this incredible woman to notice me. Yet, trying not to pressure her. We have spent so much time together here at Dexter's while closing the bar. And nothing beats the time spent in my truck over the past few weeks, talking and stargazing. I see the heated stares, the way her cheeks blush when I wink at her from across the bar, how her breathing increases when I help her out of the truck.

Every time I touch her, there's a current of desire that fills my bones. It's maddening. Granted, I have felt attracted to women before. But this ... this urge I get when I'm with her, it's unlike anything I have ever experienced.

I know this isn't one-sided. Yet, she is keeping me at arm's length. So, it must be this Drew guy. They may not be dating, but something is going on. And she never mentions him when we are in the truck. I've brought his name up a time or two, hoping it will prompt her to talk about him, but she always redirects the conversation.

The rhythmic scrape of the brush against the table is all I attempt to concentrate on; I don't look up. "It's none of my business who you date, Rachel. Drew or otherwise," I state without emotion. Because it's true. As much as I want to care, and do care, Rachel can date whomever she wants.

She slowly saunters over closer to me, running her fingertips along the side rail until she is right next to me, leaning against the table. "Maybe I want it to be your business," she purrs.

Well, well, well.

Finally, she is showing some interest!

I chuck the brush onto the table and round the side, standing right in front of her. She steps back, resting her backside and hands on the table, taking me in. I lean forward; my hands land on either side of her, caging her in. "Is that so?"

She nods. Our eyes lock. The air crackles with anticipation as we stare, the electric current in the room so strong, my skin comes alive. With our faces millimeters apart and her warm breath skating over my skin, I zero in on her lips. The desire I have to pull them to mine washes over me like a waterfall.

"Why did you feel the need to tell me that?"

She lifts her chin in defiance. "Tell you what?"

"That you and Drew aren't a thing."

She shrugs, unblinking.

The weight of her stare, how close we are standing and yet not touching, and just ... *her*. All of it is causing me to lose my freaking mind.

I'm about to snap. In a good way. The best way.

Even though my heart is ready to explode out of my chest, something is gnawing at me, and it's this ... I can't rush anything with her.

For one thing, she's special. For another, I am putting the ball squarely in her court. I mean, great, we've established that it isn't Drew holding her back.

Thank the good Lord.

Then that leaves her R.A. I am about ninety-nine percent sure her reluctance is due to that and what it does to her self-confidence. And for that reason alone, I will wait for her to make the first move.

Which means, right now, I need to create some distance, because ... *GOD. This is intense.* A swift subject change is in order. And there's no better subject than my favorite. Pool.

But I don't back away. Not yet. "Do you play?" She answers with a slight shake of her head, our noses grazing slightly. "Wanna learn?"

"Will you teach me?" she whispers and arches her back slightly.

I grin. "Gladly." Pushing off the table, I grab the brush and place it back on the shelf. Rachel takes a few deep breaths to compose herself before heading to the door. She flips the lock, and it clicks into place, echoing throughout the empty bar. She glances at me as I take her in. No one, and I mean no one, makes jeans and a tank top look as good as she does. Mesmerized, I watch as she effortlessly piles her hair atop her head before making her way to the jukebox; the rhythmic clinking of her bracelets shoots straight through me.

I'm staring.

And ogling.

I have no shame at this point.

I'm like an out-of-control teenager when I'm with her.

"Do you want a drink?" she asks as she studies the jukebox, then punches in some numbers. Teddy Swims serenades us.

This is what Dexter's does best. It mixes the old with the new. Vintage mirroring modern. An old-fashioned jukebox playing recent hits. New pool tables alongside old coin-operated ones. Weathered booths line the walls, mixed with new shiny fancy bar stools.

And maybe that's why Rachel and I work. Me, old and vintage. Her, new, younger, and shiny. We mesh well.

"I'm good," I say as I reach for the box of pool balls and the rack. She comes back to the table, me on one end, her on the other. Separated by felt and slate.

A divide. A barrier.

Literally and figuratively.

The weight of her stare burns into me, a heavy, silent pressure as I meticulously arrange the smooth, polished balls in the varnished triangle of wood. I shake them back and forth along the green felt.

Clack, clack, clack.

"You've done that before," she says with a smirk.

I peer at her from the corner of my eye, noticing a subtle smile playing on her lips. "Once or twice." Flinging the rack in the air, I step forward, catching it behind my back. She giggles. Freaking giggles. It's so dang cute.

Having put my cue away for the night, I grab two sticks from the cue rack. I walk over and hand one to her, our fingers brushing slightly as I do. "I'll break, and then I can show you a couple of things."

"Okay." Her hand settles on the sturdy rail.

As I slide the wood stick through my fingers, a confession blurts out of my mouth. "I've always wanted to teach pool." I have never admitted this to anyone, not even Scott. For some reason, this woman brings out everything in me. Even my secrets.

Intrigued, her head tilts to the side, curious. "Why haven't you?"

I shrug. "I don't know. No time, I guess. It's always been something I have thought about but never followed through on. The game is life-changing, and I would love to show others how amazing it is."

She pushes off the table and smirks while adding chalk to her own cue. "Well, let's see how this lesson goes first."

Oh, I'm sure it's going to be just fine.

I bend at the hip, lining up my shot, but not before giving her one last glance. Breaking the pool balls when I play is by far my favorite part. The virtual unknowns, mentally preparing for whatever lies ahead, thinking on my feet as I watch the balls scatter across the table. The whole thing lasts only seconds, and it's one of the biggest adrenaline rushes.

Well, that and the beautiful woman standing only inches from me. Her scent engulfing me, her presence igniting a fire in my belly.

With force, I slam my stick into the cue ball, sending it careening down the table. Rachel jumps and lets out a yelp, followed by a laugh. With rapt attention, I watch as the cue ball strikes the triangle of multi-colored balls, creating a resounding clack and sending them scattering across the table. Three of the pool balls find their homes in the pockets.

Once the balls settle, I look at her. "See any shots worth taking?" She glances at the table and begins to circle it, trying to decide. Me, I already know how this whole table is going to play out.

She uses her cue to point. "Two ball, corner pocket," she announces proudly. I knew she would pick that one. It's the obvious choice, but not the best one.

I wiggle my finger at her. "You would think. But if you take that shot, the cue ball will rest here"—I point to the spot with my cue—"behind the twelve and three, with no shot available. Try again."

She frowns and examines the table again, and I watch her every move. Her shoulders, tan and smooth, reflect off of the light overhead, the Dexter's tank top clinging to her body in all the right places. Her eyes, big, brown, and bright, study the table. All she's doing is focusing on pool balls, and I am completely taken by how magnificent she is.

She points to the seven ball. "Seven, corner pocket."

I grin because it's the perfect shot for her to learn with. "Alright, line it up and shoot."

She bends at the waist and stretches over the table, but it's all wrong. Her legs are way too far apart, her hips aren't square, and she's too high.

Darn. I guess that means I am going to have to touch her.

Before she pulls back her arm, I grab her forearm to stop the momentum. "Whoa, whoa, whoa," I say as I slide my hand over to her delicate wrist.

She spins around. "What?"

"Your stance is all wrong. If you hit the cue ball standing like that, you'll send it flying across the room." With hesitation, I step toward her. "Line up the shot again." She smirks at me and bends over the pool table, as Teddy Swims crooning voice fills the void. And, hopefully, masks my pounding heart.

I squeeze my eyes shut. A feeble attempt at trying to center myself. Stepping behind her, I hover my hands over her hips. With hope skating up my chest, I ask permission. "May I?" She nods. Nerves explode straight to my fingertips as I rest my hands on her hips. God, how do they fit so perfectly in my hands? I swallow hard.

A piece of dark hair curls at the nape of her neck as she glances over her shoulder, silent desire passing between us.

We don't smile.

We don't blink.

We only stare.

Slowly, she lets out a long, low breath and turns back around.

Man, did I feel that.

I shake my head, trying to get my mind under control, then shift her hips so that they are square to the table. "Now, bring your feet closer together. They are too far apart." She does as instructed. "Okay, now bend your knee that's closest to the table."

"Like this?" she asks, but the question comes out squeaky.

I glimpse her feet, trying hard to avert my gaze from landing on her backside in those jeans.

Who am I kidding? I looked.

"Okay, great. Now, lower your back arm." My fingers brush lightly against her skin as I place my hand on her upper arm. I give myself permission to let it linger there for a moment and then carefully lower it, lightly dragging my thumb along her smooth flesh. "You're holding the cue too high."

I study her bridge hand, and it's good, but then she switches it. "How about my bridge? Does it need work?"

What a little sneaky thing she is. I smirk because her bridge was perfectly fine. Which means she wants me closer. A wave of happiness at the fact she isn't pushing me away explodes in my chest. Instead, she's initiating this whole thing.

Leaning over the table, I press my chest against her back as I trail my hand slowly down her arm. My body pressed close, my arm brushing hers, fingers tracing the delicate curve of her arm.

I'm in heaven.

Goosebumps erupt all over her skin at my nearness, the air catching in her throat, her skin tingling under my touch. Her face is right there. The scent of *her*, a light and airy coconut fragrance, washes over me as I lean. It's making me unsteady on my feet.

She's close. So close.

I whisper in her ear. "Your bridge was perfect the first time." The fine hairs on the back of her neck rise.

"Was it?" she teases while changing her bridge back. I release my hand from her hip and tickle her waist. She wiggles away as she squeals.

We readjust our stance, hand on hip, chest to back, arm brushing against arm, cheek to cheek, you know. All the good stuff. "Now, line up the shot," I instruct, redirecting our attention to the task at hand. Learning to play pool.

Sure. Let's call it that.

"You want your tip to hit the cue"—I point to the center of the cue ball—"right there."

"Got it."

"Now, don't hit it too hard. Just gentle enough to contact the seven ball."

"No pressure, huh?" She grins.

"You got this," I whisper back, my breath warm on her skin. Her eyes flutter close. Then I watch them zap open with intensity, focused, determined. She pulls back her arm and hits the cue ball dead center. It rolls down the table and connects with the seven ball. As my hand tightens around her hip, we both watch as the maroon ball rolls along the green felt and lands in the pocket.

Clank.

She squeals and jumps with excitement. "I did it!!" I scoop her up, twirling her above the floor as our joyful shrieks fill the quiet space of the bar.

With both of us panting and with hearts pounding, I gently sit her on the table. Our eyes lock once again in an intense, silent stare. All playful laughing now replaced with yearning. Longing.

Her legs dangle off the edge as I swipe a piece of hair off her forehead. I inch forward, tossing my cue on the table, standing between her legs, and resting both of my hands on either side of her hips against the rails. Her gaze trails down my face, stopping at my lips; a spark ignites in those chocolate browns.

I remain still, not even a muscle twitching as the seconds pass. I white knuckle the rail to stop my hands from shooting up and grabbing that tiny waist again and pulling her to me. Teddy isn't singing, and the silence is heavy, thick, and unsettling, broken only by our steady breaths.

A soft sigh passes her lips as she arches her back, angles her chin, and closes her eyes. Her lips part slightly and graze mine. Feather-light and perfect. I don't move, letting her take the lead. She hesitates, contemplating, pulling back just an inch, then her lips brush mine again. A whisper of a kiss.

A frantic rhythm thuds in my chest, and instantly, one hand lets go and finds its way to her waist, pulling her into my embrace. Her hesitancy vanishes at my touch. She tilts her head, and our lips meet in an all-consuming kiss as I suck in a breath. Saying what we are both feeling, yet saying nothing at all.

Yes! She's surrendering to this.

Releasing my other hand from the rail, I rest it on her hip, where it fits like a glove. Our lips stay locked, moving with ease yet overwhelming every single one of my senses.

She scoots closer to me, which only spurs me on further, and I'm happy to oblige. My grip tightens around her waist, tucking her closer as she sinks into my touch, and my other hand squeezes her hip. Then —

"AH!" With a sharp cry, her head snaps back, her stick flying from her grasp and clattering onto the floor. Her hand instinctively shoots to her hip, her face contorting in a mask of pain.

Oh, my God. I hurt her.

A wave of guilt settles in my gut. Our connection shatters, leaving a ringing lull in my ears. And it's all my fault.

She quickly glances off to the side as her fingers skim her lips. Her other hand leaves her hip and rests on the table, leaning back, trying to get as far away from me as possible. With a soft thud, she slides off the table, and I quickly step out of her way. The room is silent, and the air between us that was full of explosive electricity is now thick with tension.

I have to *do* something. Say ... *something.*

"You should leave." But she beats me to it. Her words hit me hard, like a punch that takes the air out of your lungs. I choke on the emptiness.

"Rachel, please. Is it me?" I plead as I bend and pick up the cue, handing it to her.

This hurts. So much.

With a frustrated shake of her head and a sigh, she walks over and carefully places her pool cue back in its rack. "No. It's not you."

"Then what? Is it Drew?" Because Lord help me if so.

An amused chuckle rumbles from her chest. "God, no. It's definitely not Drew."

As I approach, my hands settle on her waist, gently. She flinches, probably afraid I'll hurt her again.

The fever of her skin through her shirt is a welcome sensation against mine. Her hands rest on my chest, our bodies close. Yet so far away. "Then tell me, Rachel. Tell me what I need to do to make you comfortable. Because I will do it. Anything you need." The quiet is suffocating as she gazes at the floor, avoiding my pleading stare; the thick tension coiling between us. Without saying the actual words, I'm begging her to open up to me.

Please, just tell me.

She raises her head, and we connect. For a millisecond, there's a glimmer of hope in her stare. She may say yes.

She might give us a chance.

Give *me* a chance.

But then, her shoulders sag, and her hands push back against my shirt.

I step back, giving her the space she is asking for without words.

A tear, slow and silent, tracks a path down her tan cheek. She whisks it away. "I can't. I'm sorry, Johnny."

With a silent nod, I make my way to the pool table, the click of my shoes on the floor echoing softly, to retrieve the brush and ball box. We finish closing, neither of us saying a word. And as we lock the door and stand face to face at the entrance, the world spins and blurs, a dizzying rush of emotions overwhelming me.

All I want to do is hold her close and whisper assurances I'll carry whatever weight she's bearing, freeing her from all the burdens she has.

But it's all just a fantasy. One that will never come to fruition. The more time I spend with Rachel, the more she feels unattainable, like a rare, amazing dream you don't want to wake up from. One that's so real and colorful when you're in the thick of it. But as soon as you wake, the beauty of it is over. The sooner I realize how make-believe this is, the less it will hurt each time I'm with her.

I reach out and tilt her chin upward, our eyes locking with unspoken words. My hand lingers on her chin, holding onto the dream just a little longer. I don't want to wake up. "Please text me and let me know you made it home safe, okay?" I implore her.

She only nods and steps away. As she climbs into her car, hesitation stalls her for a moment; she pivots and grins. "You should do it. Teach pool. You're really good at it." The car door clicks shut, and she pulls away from the curb, ready to leave me behind. But not before pausing, peering at me one last time, a silent farewell heavy in the air. A grimace contorts her features, a landscape of pain, sorrow, and regret. I give her a slight wave goodbye.

Twenty minutes later, as I careen along the highway, my phone dings. As soon as I stop at a red light, I pull it out.

> Rachel: I'm home.

> Rachel: Please forgive me.

I don't reply. I can't.

But also, there is nothing to forgive.

10

You're Kinda Creepy

Johnny

Four days have come and gone since Rachel's pool lesson. And we haven't spoken.

There has been no communication, and I'm surprised how unsettling that feels. These past two months, her voice has become a familiar comfort, a rhythm in my daily life. But now, nothing.

Also, the wedding was two days ago.

Maybe she and Drew reconnected and got back together.

My knuckles whiten as my grip tightens around the smooth, cool pool stick.

I aim my cue at the white ball on the table in my garage.

They probably danced the night away in each other's arms, then kissed as they said goodnight. Or they didn't say goodnight.

With anger, I hit the white ball, miss the twelve I was aiming for, and scratch.

God, my mind is all over the place. I'm obsessing over this woman like I'm a lovesick freshman in high school.

I try to shake my head of these jealous thoughts piercing through me because this is so unlike me.

But at the end of the day, I worry about her. Like yesterday, for example. It was a tournament night at the bar, and she wasn't there. Randy told me she called off.

Did she call off because of her RA? Is she having a flare-up? Or is she avoiding me?

None of those reasons puts my mind at ease.

I wonder if she is working tonight. Although it was difficult, I decided to stay home rather than drive over there to help her. I'm sure she's anxious and questioning my whereabouts; the truth is, I desperately need some solitude to gather my thoughts.

With my next shot in focus, I strike. The one ball bounces off the corner of the pocket, and the cue ball goes in instead.

Another scratch.

I rest my forehead on my hand as it grips my cue. I'm mentally checked out, lost in thought, and unengaged with the game tonight. And this is my happy place. After a day of work and then some dinner, you can find me out here shooting around with my coffee. Just me, my thoughts, and the table.

Lately, all I can think about is that tall brunette with her dark silky hair and eyes so intense they burn into my soul. I'm not even in a relationship with her, and yet I know I could fall in love with her.

Hell, maybe I already am.

It's a dream. A fantasy, I remind myself.

I round the table, removing all the balls from the pockets, when footsteps mix with the classic rock playing from my phone. My spider sense tingles as my head whips up. It's late, ten o'clock, so to say that it's unusual that someone is at my home is an understatement.

A shadowy figure materializes, its outline indistinct against the dim light, and I can't discern who it is. My shoulders tense, muscles bunching like coiled springs, as a wave of unease washes over me.

Shielding the glare from the blinding garage light, I focus on the growing sound of approaching footsteps.

"Nice house you have here, Johnny. The construction business must be booming."

Even before I can process the words, his voice—a familiar blend of rasp and danger—gave away exactly who this is.

It's Dexter. Or Dex. Maybe it's DJ. I don't give a crap what this weasel's name is. All I know is that I do not want him at my house at ten pm.

What in the heck does he want?

I lean against my table, crossing my arms over my chest. "To what do I owe the pleasure of this visit?"

Uninvited, he waltzes into my garage. The scent of his aftershave hangs in the air as he scans his surroundings. Including my table. I watch him intently, my gaze never leaving him, like a hawk circling its prey.

He lets out a low whistle. "Nice table."

"Thank you. Built it with my own two hands."

He runs his hand along the nap of the blue felt, then picks up the eight ball, tossing it once in his hand. "Centennial balls, I see. The best."

"Absolutely." I clear my throat. "What can I help you with ... *Dex*?"

A flinch and a slight frown showcase his dislike for the nickname, his shoulders visibly tense. Therefore, it is the only name I will address him as.

"It's Dexter, and I was wondering what your intentions were with my niece," he commands and then clicks his tongue.

Haven't we already had this conversation?

He pulls a cigarette out and places it between his lips. On impulse, I reach out and grab it out of his mouth. "Don't smoke in my house."

He puts his hands up in surrender. "Sorry about that." He steps into my space, chest puffed out, a silent taunt in the air as he tries to appear taller and more important.

It's not working.

"You didn't answer my question," he challenges.

My head shakes as a soft chuckle rumbles in my chest, a quiet sound in the otherwise still air. The gall of this man to just show up here and demand to know what my feelings are for his niece. A grown woman who is capable of making her own decisions.

In no way, shape, or form does he deserve any explanation from me. But I want to keep the peace on some level. So, I answer him. "Not that it's any of your business, but I like her. I want to date her. I'm sure you are aware of how amazing she is."

His nostrils flare, not happy with my reply. "She's seeing someone. His name is Drew." Dear Lord, he didn't even agree with me about Rachel.

Chuckling, I gather the pool balls, their smooth surfaces cool against my fingertips, helping me with my rising anger toward this idiot. "Funny, that is not what she told me just a few nights ago at the bar. Run that little scenario past her. Oh, and she told me *all* about Drew. He's a real stand-up guy."

With a determined step towards me, he's obviously not happy with my statements. Too bad. His feeble attempts to get in my face are comical, to say the least. He steadies himself and stops. A long pause follows as he wipes his hand down his face. "You should probably know ... Rachel is disabled. She has RA. You know, Rheumatoid Arthritis?" He allows me a second to take this not-new-to-me information. I remain unreadable. He coughs. "Anyway, the last thing she needs is someone trying to date her. She should be with people who know her and can give her what she needs."

I'm shook.

Speechless, I stare at him, my mind reeling from the incredibly private information he had no business sharing. He has no right to tell anyone about Rachel's medical history. Let alone someone he barely knows. The nerve of this guy. But I'm not about to let him know I know.

"And by this little showy display and unexpected visit, I'm assuming you think the only man worthy of the job is you. Or maybe Drew. But the way I see it ... Rachel doesn't need a man to take care of her. Just stand by her side."

"I'm her family."

"You don't say."

"And Micah. Plus, Drew. We are all that she needs."

God, the nerve. I click my tongue. "I hate to be the one to tell you this. But you're kinda creepy." I shrug. "I've never been one to shy away from the truth, and I will not start today, so do you know what I see when I look at you ... *Dex?*" I step into his space. "An insecure man-child who loves control. He enjoys watching people he claims to love suffer because it makes him feel better about himself."

"How dare you," he seethes at me through gritted teeth. "You have been a thorn in my side since the day I met you! The only reason I am putting up with you is because of the amount of money you are making me. Word is getting out about your skill level, and people are coming in droves to watch you and bet on you."

In a mock gesture, I place my hand over my heart. "I'm flattered. Truly. And you're welcome."

He grunts and turns to leave my garage but stops abruptly, pivoting towards me, his face splitting into the widest, most predatory grin I've ever witnessed. "I will tolerate your relationship with Rachel as long as you keep showing your face at the bar, playing and winning money for me."

Frustration bubbling over, I let out a huff. *He'll tolerate it?* Whatever. This man has no control over me, and he can't keep me from his niece.

He has no power.

But still, he continues. "Just know that I own you now," he pauses, "Johnson Michael Givens. Born January 25th, 1971." My back snaps straight as a rod, a shiver tracing its icy path down my spine. "Parents Cynthia and Michael Givens. Family Scott, his wife and their kids, Jake and Mallory. You own Givens Construction with your cousin, but he has majority stake. You have a surprisingly squeaky-clean record ... well, except for that speeding ticket you got last year and that incident in Daytona Beach when you were in your twenties. Now, *that* sounded like a good time." His amusement at my expense is clear as his lips crinkle into a snide smile.

"Last night, in fact, you ate dinner at your cousin's. Isn't that right? Did you have a nice time?"

What the...? He's following me.

"They look like a sweet family. And that wife of your cousin's. What's her name?" He snaps his fingers as if he suddenly remembered. "Laura. That's right!" He lets out a low whistle. "Now, that is one hot piece of—"

I charge for him, baring my teeth like an animal. He steps back, hands up.

"Whoa, whoa, whoa. No need for that. Just making an observation. Plus, you can't tell me you've never looked."

Lord help him if Scott was here.

Despite the rising anxiety, I remind myself to stay calm. I can't give this guy any reason to retaliate despite my simmering anger. His veiled threats have targeted my family, instilling a sense of unease and fear straight to my heart.

"Like I said, I own you. Therefore, I can destroy you. Fall in line, play pool, win me some money, and I promise to not interfere with you and Rachel ... deal?"

I'm trapped.

But I will do this ... for Rachel. Because now, a sudden force and urge to protect her from this sick SOB wash over me.

I nod, sealing my fate. "Now, get the hell off of my property. You aren't welcome here."

"Careful, Givens ..." He takes a once-over of my house. "I may own this someday, too. And don't force my hand and cause me to visit again. I'll bring friends next time. And you won't be standing."

With that, he taps the button to the garage door and walks away as he whistles. Freaking whistles.

As the door creaks and descends, suddenly, my sanctuary feels like a tomb. I brace myself against the pool table and lower my head. A deep, sickening intuition washes over me as I realize I've stepped into something. Something huge.

And the only thing I know for sure is that I need to go along with this. For Rachel.

She deserves better.

And I'm going to give it to her.

11

Did You Dance with Him?

Rachel

The bar has emptied on this dreary night, which I'm fine with. Well, except for Sam, Ricky, and Big C. Three regulars who have been coming to Dexter's forever. It's eleven, and the sweeping of my workstation is the only sound breaking the room's lack of bar commotion. With my brother and Shelby on their honeymoon and the other bartenders gone for the night, it's just little ole me here to fend for myself. Eva, the bar waitress, is still here, but I'll send her home shortly since it's slowing down.

Then, there is one other thing. Johnny didn't come tonight.

I can't help but wonder why, although I know the reason.

Me, I'm the reason. I pushed him away ... again.

Plus, he knows I went to the wedding with Drew, so I'm sure that is weighing heavily on his mind.

But what I wasn't expecting was how much I would miss having him here with me. Knowing that last night was a tourney night, I cowardly called off, not wanting to face him. But then soon after regretted it.

Add it to the long list of regrets I have with that man.

"Hey, Rachel!" I turn to the sound of Ricky's voice and him waving me over. Ricky and I exchanged phone numbers when I met him here a little while ago when the remodel was almost done. We talked some here and there. He's a great guy, just not the guy for me. We have struck up a nice friendship, though, so I always make time for him and his friends when they come in.

"What's going on, fellas?" I ask, leaning in as Ricky's eyes rove over my chest. We may not be dating, but he's still Ricky. Always a flirt and quintessential ladies' man.

He smirks, addressing me. "Our friend Sam here is driving us nuts."

Sam rolls his eyes while taking a slow pull of his Heineken. "I don't need any additional relationship advice, Ricky."

Big C lets out a huge belly laugh, one that matches his hulking frame. "Yeah, you do."

Ricky turns back to me. "You see, Rachel, Sam here is dating a woman named Cara." He shrugs. "She's okay." I glance at Big C; his moan, as he rolls his head back with a low, guttural sound, makes me chuckle. *These guys are too much.* Sam sits and stares straight ahead, completely annoyed. "And he's obviously still in love with his ex-slash-love-of-his-life. Her name is Maria. She's *amazing*."

Sam's head whips in Ricky's direction. "I am not still in love with Maria. I love Cara. How many times do I have to tell you that?"

"No. You need to keep telling *yourself* that."

Sam and Ricky continue to argue as I fill Big C's Ginger Ale. He must be the DD tonight. "These two always like this?"

"Worse actually." The glass rises to his mouth while laughing at his two buddies going toe to toe right beside him.

"I'll leave you to it. But you should start charging a referee fee."

He lifts his glass to me. "No lie there."

I open my mouth to continue my conversation with Big C, when the door creaks open, bringing with it the chill of the night air and the faint scent of rain. Johnny enters, and his commanding presence fills the bar as he zeros in on me. A surge of energy courses through me as his determined strides propel him in my direction. But as he nears, the raw terror etched on his face is unmistakable.

What in the heck is going on?

His eyes dart around, searching through the few patrons that remain.

Tracking his every move, I watch him round the bar. This is odd since he always stays on the other side, never stepping into my work space unless it's closing time.

"Johnny, hey. What are you—"

"Did Dexter come back tonight? Is he here?" he asks with urgency.

It's an odd question. I chuckle at him, trying to lighten the mood. "You're not even going to say hi?"

"Is he here?" he asks again through gritted teeth.

What is going on right now? I can't tell if he's angry. Or scared? "Johnny, I'm confused. What is—" Something dawns on me. "Wait, how do you know he left?"

"This guy bothering you, Rachel?" Big C interrupts, already beginning to rise from his stool while Sam and Ricky continue to bicker.

Not turning to acknowledge him, I wave my hand dismissively behind me. "No, no, it's fine."

Johnny's eyes flicker to Big C, then his worried gaze, intense and unwavering, burns into mine. "He came to my house."

Okay, that's confusing. I take him by the arm and steer him away from the three men, out of earshot. "Why?"

"Is there somewhere we can talk? Privately."

"Um, sure." I untie the apron from my waist, the knot tight like my stomach, and place it on the counter below the bar. "Let me just get Eva to cover." Thankfully, she agrees when I ask.

Grabbing Johnny by the arm, I lead him to the kitchen, glancing around to make sure that we are alone. "What do you mean, he came to your house?"

"He came to ask me what my intentions are toward you."

I chuckle. "Oh, that's no big deal. He has done that with every guy that has ever liked me."

"No, Rachel. This was different." He stops as he rubs the back of his neck, taking a moment to gather his thoughts. My amused chuckle dies in my throat with his noticeable distress.

Something's wrong.

He turns to face me, his Adam's apple bobbing, then hesitates, his mouth clamping shut. It's almost as if he's holding back. His voice, cracking slightly, breaks the silence. "He said that you and Drew were back together and that only Drew and him could take care of you."

Oh, God! Did he tell Johnny about my RA?

"What else did he say?" I'm practically choking on the fear.

"He had me followed."

Oh, thank God he didn't—"Wait, what?" Uncle Dexter had him followed?

"He knew I spent time at my cousin's last night and had dinner with them. Plus, he did a small background check on me. He knows my date of birth, my parents' names. Obviously, he knows where I live." One by one, he's ticking off the accusations on his fingers. "Hell, he even knows about the incident in Daytona Beach."

"You still never told me what happened in Daytona."

He throws his hands in the air, exasperated. "That's not the point!"

"Sorry." I lower my head. But also make a mental note to circle back to that one. "So, what? He had you investigated? Why would he do that?"

He takes a deep breath and steps closer to me. "He said that he owns me. Because I am bringing in so much money for him."

Now, don't get me wrong. I'm not naïve. I know my uncle is ... well, shady. "Did he threaten you?"

"I mean no, not in so many words, but he knows about Scott, Laura, and the kids, Rachel! He even made a lewd comment about Laura."

Well, that doesn't surprise me.

He rests his hands on my shoulders, his voice softer, etched with the same concern that matches his face. "I am really worried about you. Forget about me. I can take care of myself, but he is weirdly protective and controlling of you." He exhales. "I'm scared. For your safety."

A feeling of defensiveness breathes fire into me. There are so many men in my life trying to tell me what's best for me. I don't need another one. No matter how hot he is.

I shove his arms off my shoulders. "Well, don't be, okay? I can take care of myself. And Uncle Dexter would *never* hurt me." His eyes snap open, startled by my outburst.

Sometimes I get so sick and tired of people trying to protect me. And maybe I'm overreacting because, deep down, I know Johnny is right. Uncle Dexter is controlling and manipulative. He always has been with me. Plus, I have seen and heard how he can treat people who cross him. *But me? Is he capable of hurting me?*

"I know you can," he says, his voice tight with a mixture of worry and barely suppressed anger.

He crosses his arms defensively over his chest, his posture stiff. "Your uncle seems to think Drew, that steady and reliable chap, is more than capable of taking care of you. Tell me, is that what you want?" This unexpected question pierces me with a jolt of adrenaline.

No. That's not what I want. Not at all. What I want is this beautiful man standing right in front of me. But I can't have him. He *thinks* he wants me now. But as soon as he finds out about my RA, he will run.

With a tilt of his head, Johnny continues his questioning, each query sharper than the last. "How was the wedding? You and Drew have a nice time?" I'm smacked out of my self-loathing.

I step back. *Maybe this is the way out.* The lie is easy, a simple fabrication to give him the false hope he's asking for. Then avoiding the inevitable heartbreak when he discovers my secret and runs away.

Because he would. They all do. And it would hurt. So much.

No other option is on the table. Because there is no doubt that I am falling for this man. Fast and hard.

I need to do this. Pushing him away is the only route, so I puff my chest out in mock confidence in this crazy idea as I lie to him. "It was amazing. Drew and I had a great time."

Yep. Solid plan!

"Huh." He takes one swift stride toward me. "Did you dance with him?" he asks, a hint of challenge in his tone as I take a quick step back. The question hangs heavy in the air, his voice a dark, velvety murmur that steals my breath.

Another step, closer to me.

Keep it together, Rachel!

"Yep. Lots and lots of dancing. Loads of dancing. Slow, fast, you name it." The lie comes out shaky, my stiff joints making even the thought of dancing laughable. The reception comes flooding back. Drew gave me the same look of disgust Sean did when I couldn't dance at prom. And for that reason, Drew and I only danced once. And it was oh so awkward. His hands on my body felt foreign and made my skin crawl.

On the ride back to my place, he apologized over and over for his, as he called it, "error in judgement." Then, to top the night off with a cherry on melted ice cream, he tried to kiss me. He left with my palm print on his cheek, but not before calling me a tease as he stormed off. That's it, full stop.

Johnny stalks two more steps closer.

He moves toward me, determined.

Two steps away.

With a thud, my back hits the refrigerator door. Johnny is standing centimeters from me now, his breath warm on my face as he peers down. And, dear Lord, his scent—something undeniably him—engulfs me. His eyes land on my lips. "Did you kiss him?"

I can't form words as his hand skates up my bare arm. My lids flutter close. "Mm-hmm."

His lips are *right there*, warm and close, as his hand, rough against my skin, rakes my arm. Up and down. Up and down. Up and—I'm not breathing.

"I don't believe you," he whispers. "Want to know what I think?"

My eyes fly open. We stare. The zippy knot in my chest isn't moving. It crackles and sizzles like a campfire. Each touch from him a log being tossed at it, igniting it more. I nod involuntarily. His lips tick slightly. He knows what he's doing right now. "The only thing on your mind that night was me."

God, he's so right.

A searing heat from that darn campfire now radiates through my head with each word he speaks. "As he stood beside you in his cheap rented Men's Warehouse tux, you ached for me. When he pulled up in his Kia Soul, you wanted more than anything to be sitting in the passenger seat of my truck, with me in the driver's seat."

My whole body comes alive as he reads me like a book. His voice is low, and God help me, nothing but ... all man ... as his truthful words roll off his tongue. This pent-up chemistry I have for him vibrates within me, a frantic hum, and I swallow hard, trying to push it away.

It doesn't work.

"And when his hand landed on your lower back while you were dancing"—his large palm spreads across my back, tugging me to him—"you wanted it to be mine."

Plan? What plan? I had a plan?

"And when his lips touched yours, it was my face that you saw. My lips that you felt." His mouth inches closer. "Tell me you feel what I feel when I'm with you. Tell me."

I'm pretty sure I am having an out-of-body experience at this point. My eyes close. "I feel it."

"What do you feel?"

"Alive."

And that's exactly how my body reacts as his mouth lightly grazes mine in yet another feather-light kiss.

It comes alive.

He's tentative at first as his mouth glides over mine softly, waiting for me to kiss him back. But this time, I don't pull away as I did before.

My hand skates around his waist as I pull him closer and press my mouth against his. It's all the signal he needs. He intensifies the kiss as a satisfied moan vibrates from deep within his chest.

God, his lips are divine. Soft yet powerful. Smooth yet demanding.

This is our most intense kiss yet, and it's perfection. His hand lands on my waist and squeezes as he pulls my chest flush against him while his other hand slams on the stainless steel behind me.

And that's when I snap out of it.

Again.

I can't do this. Because what happens next, after this world-altering kiss, is him leaving me as soon as he finds out about my RA.

A sharp intake of breath escapes my lips as the weight of this realization settles, severing our connection. His head whips back, eyes wide as he searches my face. Both of us are panting and out of breath. I avert my gaze to the floor.

"God," he mutters as he pushes off the refrigerator door and takes steps backward. It's as if someone has flipped a switch on all my senses because the noise of the bar fills the air. His kiss lingers on my lips as my tongue darts over my bottom lip, getting one last taste.

The chemistry and energy that were coursing through the air only moments ago are painted with uneasiness and tension. Seconds crawl by as I muster enough nerve to take him in. Johnny is having a staring contest with ceiling tiles. "I'm so sorry. I shouldn't have allowed that." I blurt out, but don't mean it.

He groans, the sound heavy with frustration, with hands planted firmly on his hips, his gaze remains fixed on the drop ceiling. I wait for him to do something. Say anything. But he just stands there, trying to find answers in the air above his head, his chest rising and falling. He releases a long, weary sigh, the sound deafening in the quiet kitchen, before walking past me to leave. Without sparing a glance, he pauses at the threshold.

What have I done? He can't even look at me.

He doesn't turn around, his back a rigid, unyielding wall of muscle, but glances slightly to the right. "Please be careful, Rachel. Dexter is a bad guy. If you need any help at all, you can call me anytime." Pausing, his back heaving, the unspoken words a heavy weight, he continues with a strained voice. "And just so you know, when I'm with you, I feel more alive than I have in my whole life."

With that, he pushes the swinging door open, and he's gone.

My hand shoots to my mouth, unable to stop the raw, guttural sob that bursts forth.

What is wrong with me?

My back slides down the refrigerator door, and I lose it, not knowing how my stiff joints will get me back up again.

Maybe I deserve to be at the bottom, feeling anything but alive now that he's gone.

12

Drew Who?

Johnny

Three weeks.

That's how long it's been since I've spoken to Rachel. Twenty-one days since the best kiss of my life—the pressure of her lips, the taste of her skin, the exhilaration of the moment. It's branded into my brain and on my heart for all eternity.

I still show on tournament nights for my team, but I haven't come in just because.

Just for her.

I can't.

Being around her now is uncomfortable and as awkward as a cold weight that hangs heavy. One kiss, plus another rejection, and the world shifted from a blissful heaven to a fiery hell in her presence.

That kiss was my come-to-Jesus moment, let me tell ya.

And then, obviously, when I'm here, I help her at closing, of course. I'm not callous. I know she needs the help, and I will always be there for her.

Always.

But the ease we once had is gone. We barely speak, and I miss the intimate talks and time spent sharing a blanket beneath a star-filled sky in the bed of my truck.

I miss *her*.

But there is still this magnetic pull when we are together. Somehow, we always find ourselves making contact. A shoulder brush here or a finger graze there. We mutter our apologies to each other awkwardly. But somehow it happens again, and the electricity that courses through us has nowhere to go. Eventually, though, this current will ignite.

She's insecure and scared, for good reason. I could tell after our conversation and mind-blowing kiss in the kitchen that she was lying about Drew. Because there is no way she would kiss me like that if she were dating him. Rachel is too good of a person to cross that line. Period.

But also, I want her to trust me with this deeply personal part of her life. I pray that day will come sooner rather than later.

With that thought hanging in the air, I hit the nine ball into the corner pocket, giving our team the win.

Everyone celebrates with whoops and hollers, followed by high fives all around. We all make our way over to the bar to get a quick drink before the next team arrives. My teammates are already making small talk with the other bartenders. Rachel notices me approaching and quickly fills a glass with club soda and plops a lime wedge inside. She places it in front of me, the tension thick between us.

The OBGs observe us with their wise, knowing scrutiny.

"Thank you," I say as she gives me a small, pursed smile. I take a quick sip.

"Welcome." Her monotone response is like a knife to the heart.

A long silence follows.

"Brrrr," Tiny says through a pretend shiver. Slick elbows him in the side. "What?" he asks. "These two went from sizzling-Miami-hot to Iceland-cold in just weeks." He turns to address us. "What happened to you two?"

Randy chimes in next. "Tiny, leave them alone." He leans over the bar to get a better view of us. "Unless you want to tell us what happened. Then we are all ears." All three of them nod in agreement.

With a dramatic eye roll, Rachel turns her attention back to me, ignoring them.

"How's play going tonight?" she inquires as she tidies her work station. I stare at her for a beat, blinking, because she's attempting to make conversation. It's a start, I guess.

"You know me ... mopping the floor with these losers." She chuckles, which sounds like a song as she rests her forearms on the bar, leaning in low, her voice barely above a whisper.

"Look, Johnny, there's something you need to know about the next team coming in."

"Uh-oh," Tiny murmurs as he focuses on his drink.

My attention flashes to him momentarily, then back to the subject of all my dreams. "Oh, yeah? What's going on?"

Just as she opens her mouth to enlighten me, the bar door opens, and a group of men walk in like they own the place. A skinny bald guy, his shiny head held high as he leads the pack, surveys the tables and dance floor until his watchful eyes land immediately on the bar. It only takes him a few seconds to locate her, finding Rachel amidst the crowd, and he grins warmly, followed by a silent 'Hi.'

My stomach bottoms out.

"Who's that?" I ask, my usual confidence betraying me. Did she meet someone else? Is that why she has been distant?

"That's what I was going to tell you. The new team coming to play. Drew is on the team."

Fantastic.

"I didn't know he played." My words are tight with uncontrolled irritation.

Scattered empty glasses litter the bar. She gathers them up, placing them in the sink behind her, crashing and clanking. She continues. "He does casually. But this is his first time playing in a league."

I give Rachel a pointed look. "Come on. You can't tell me the timing is a coincidence. I'm sure Dexter persuaded him. His pockets will be padded by the time everything is said and done."

"Got that right—No doubt—For sure," Tiny, Slick and Randy all proclaim in unison.

She lets out a deep sigh, surrendering to my line of reasoning and the OBGs confirmation. We are right, and she knows it. "Drew always loved fancy things, and if my uncle offered him a cut of the dirty money that comes through these doors, then I am sure he jumped at the opportunity. So, you're probably right."

A sly smirk, hinting at mischief, plays on my lips. "I'm always right."

She throws her rag at me, which I catch. "Oh, my God." She snickers. I laugh, thrilled she's joking with me again. A sure sign that things are getting back on track. "You're so humble, aren't you?"

"It's one of my better qualities, yes."

Slick chuckles and wags his finger between us. "Now, that's more like it, you two."

There's no doubt that these three fine gentlemen are rooting for us.

I knew I always liked them.

Just then, Rachel stands straighter, her shoulders becoming stiff as she glances up. "Great."

"What?" I follow whatever it is that catches her attention.

"He's coming over here."

I slowly turn my head, taking in the sight of this pathetic loser.

It's Drew Foster—yes, I Googled him when Rachel first mentioned him—in the flesh.

The All-American guy who was the star quarterback in high school and also a womanizing loser. He saunters over to us, his posse right behind him, taking his time surveying the bar and probably still waiting for the applause he always got back in the day.

He'll be waiting a while.

Rachel said he's ten years older than her, which makes him forty. I glance at his bald head, which he obviously shaves because he's losing his hair. Relief washes over me; I'm suddenly thankful that gene skipped my family.

I run my fingers through my thick mop as he strides over, locking eyes with me, trying his best to be intimidating.

The OBGs pierce him three distinct glares of disgust, each one more pronounced than the last. Rachel keeps shifting her feet as she tries to decide what to do with her hands, her unease speaking volumes.

The OBGs all whip out their payment and hefty tips, slamming them on the wooden bar. With that, they make their exit, muttering goodbyes on their rushed exit out the door.

Apparently, they find him as repulsive as I do.

As for me? This guy hurt the amazing woman standing in front of me. Therefore, the only thing he will get from me is a small greeting and a beat down on the pool table.

This should be fun.

He stands next to me, his stare unwavering, concentrating completely on Rachel.

"Hey, Rach. You look amazing tonight."

Rachel ignores the compliment and folds the rag she was holding with aggression. "What can I get you, Drew?"

"The usual, baby."

"I'm not your baby." She grabs a bottle of scotch from behind the bar, and the fact that she knows what his usual is spikes a surge of jealousy in me I don't like.

This is a new emotion for me. I've never been serious enough about a woman to experience jealousy. And that includes Julie. Which only tells me how special Rachel is to me. And how much I wish I meant the same to her.

Without so much as a word or a smile, she places the drink in front of him, and he takes a sip. Slowly, he turns to me.

"So, you must be the legendary Johnny Givens."

"Nice. Glad to know people have their facts straight." I extend my hand. "You must be Drew."

With an actual snarl on his lips, he glares at my hand but doesn't offer his own. Shaking my head in disbelief, I retreat mine, then reach for my drink, my fingers brushing against the cool glass. "You ready to play?" I'm cutting right to the chase because there is no way I am exchanging pleasantries with this guy.

He doesn't answer me. Only grabs his cue and speaks to Rachel. "You didn't call me after the wedding."

No wonder Dexter likes this dude. He's manipulative, just like his mentor. I'm sure Dexter has told him about me. And not just my pool skills, but also that there is something brewing between Rachel and me. So, obviously, he's peeing all over his territory.

Good luck, man.

"I never said that I would," Rachel claps back, and a small snicker comes out of me. Drew's head snaps in my direction as I take a sip. She continues. "You didn't get the message I sent you after you tried to kiss me?" She cocks her head to the side. "Tell me, does your cheek still sting?"

I choke on my club soda, coughing through my laughter. Drew drops his head as waves of anger roll off of him. It's almost as if he's shocked that Rachel—or any woman, for that matter—isn't falling to his feet.

And I'm not blind; he's a good-looking guy. I'm sure he was told his whole life how amazing and handsome he is. His mom likely reassured him that everyone envied him and he was never in the wrong.

Which is why he is the narcissist he is. He gives off a whole Lex Luthor, master of the universe kinda vibe.

His stare, narrow and blazing with disgust, zeroes in on Rachel as he takes a step in her direction. On instinct, I rise from my chair because there is no way I am going to allow this small man to insult her in any way, shape, or form. My sudden movement gets the reaction I want out of him, and he redirects his attention back to me. Rachel raises her eyebrows, wondering what's about to happen next.

"Something I can help you with?" Drew snides. Our faces are inches apart as we stand off against each other.

He's toast.

"There he is!" Dexter's booming voice echoes throughout the bar as he saunters over to us. I've never been happier to see the guy as I take a step back from Drew. Dexter waltzes out of the back hallway, his beaming face thrilled his favorite person is here. They give each other one of those obnoxious bro hugs. "Mind if I steal your man away for a minute?" he asks Rachel.

God, these two are completely delusional.

Rachel goes about her job, not acknowledging either of them. "I don't have a man here, so do what you want with him."

I have to admit, this comment makes me equal parts proud and bummed. Proud that she isn't going along with the little fairy tale these two men devised. And bummed that I'm not her man.

Not yet, anyway.

Dexter and his obvious apprentice walk back to his office as Drew's friends make their way to the tables. And now, it's just Rachel and me again.

With a deliberate spin on the barstool, I give her a pointed stare, raising an eyebrow, my expression hard and questioning. "What?" she asks.

"Please explain to me what in the world you saw in that guy." Because other than her one and only mention of him the first night we met, she hasn't spoken of him since. I had a sense that the topic was off-limits. But now that he's front and center, I'm asking.

She lets out a long sigh. "He wasn't always like this. When we first met, here actually, and started dating, he was sweet and caring. A really nice guy. Like I told you before, he's ten years older than me, which wasn't an issue for either of us. Plus, he's easy on the eyes." Her gaze meets mine, shy and hesitant, anticipating my reaction, but I keep my face impassable.

She continues. "After we dated for a little while, he asked me to marry him, and I accepted, even though my head was screaming at me to run."

"Did you love him?" It's a simple question. The anticipation of her response is agonizing, but the sickening thought of her being in love with him turns my stomach.

She shrugs. "Yes and no. I think I was in love with the idea of what he was promising me. A home, kids, a future family, you know, a life."

"And is that what you want? A family, a life with a good man?"

"It is."

Adding that to my list of goals I want to accomplish with this woman. Because that is what I have always wanted. And maybe, just maybe, I can break through her walls and make her see me. Maybe we can build that future ... together.

"Anyway, things changed after he became close with my uncle. He gradually pulled away from me, and that's around the time the love bombing started. I mean, before this, he would buy me gifts and do sweet things, but out of nowhere, it grew into enormous bouquets of flowers and expensive jewelry. It was constant and overwhelming. I felt smothered even though he was distant."

"You aren't a jewelry girl," I interject. How I know this, I have no clue.

I just know.

A fleeting smile dances across her lips, confirming my assumption, before fading as quickly as it appeared. She opens up some more. "Well, it turns out all the gifts were just him feeling guilty because that's when I found him with one of the bar waitresses"—she pauses as if this memory is painful to relive—"in my bed."

My jaw drops. "Whoa, whoa, whoa. You found him with another woman, in *your* home and in *your* bed?"

"Yep."

"Good grief. What a pig. Rachel, I am so sorry that happened to you. I can't imagine how devastating that must have been." And I mean it. No one deserves that. Especially not someone who brings such light into the world. Into my world. Without even trying. "I bet you let him have it, huh?" I grin as images of Rachel losing it and dumping him right there on the spot seep into my thoughts.

She sheepishly tucks a piece of hair behind her ear. "Umm ... no, actually, I didn't. I just texted him that night and told him it was over and that I knew about the waitress. He tried to lie about it, but it was over."

I tilt my head in confusion. Rachel is sassy, at least she plays the part of the sassy bartender. But the more I get to know her, the more something or someone dulls her light. Whatever it is or was has completely eroded her self-confidence, which I know she has deep inside. And it's not just Drew. It's her uncle, too.

Because why in the world would Dexter push her to reconcile with someone that hurt her so badly? He raised her, for crying out loud. Wouldn't he want her to be happy with a partner who treats her with respect and love? Mallory and Jake aren't even my kids, and I want the world for them.

None of it makes sense.

She squares her shoulders and lifts her head, flashing me the biggest smile, signaling that she's done reminiscing. "So, that's the story of the one serious relationship in my life. I've sworn off all men since. At least for a while. Especially anyone older."

Those last three words, spoken with such conviction, resonate in the air, leaving an almost tangible wave of energy in their wake. She's making a point. Whether it's to me or herself, I'm not sure.

A heavy stillness presses down around us. "Don't let him make you think all men are the same, Rachel. There are some good guys out there." Like me.

She shrugs, and a visible tremor runs through her chin, betraying her inner turmoil. She's trying to pretend like this experience hasn't had a profound effect on her. Plus, I wonder what details she's leaving out. Like how her health factored into everything. I'm sure Drew knew.

"Well, from my experience, they are. Except for Micah, of course. And the OBG's." A hint of a smile shines through at the mention of them.

Just then, two of the smallest men who ever lived emerge from the back offices. Dexter has his arm slung over Drew's shoulder as they laugh and carry on. Suddenly, a new nickname for this worthless piece of garbage flashes in my head.

The murmur of their conversation fades as they walk past me, heading to the tables. A flicker of something—curiosity, perhaps—passes across Dexter's face as he glances back at me. More than likely wanting to know what Rachel and I were discussing. "Come on, Givens. You and your team are up."

With a swift movement, I snatch my cue, its weight reassuring in my hand as it always is. Ice cubes clink in my glass as I toss back the rest of my drink. I place the glass on the bar with a little too much force, trying to keep my anger about this man in check. Rachel studies my every move, and somehow, her stare calms me. "Are you ready to watch Drew Who? get the beating of his life?" I ask her, giving her a playful wink.

Her brow furrows as confusion washes over her face. "Wait ... Drew Who?"

I smirk, waiting for her to get the joke. "Exactly."

She gasps, her eyes widening as she snorts. She claps her hand over her mouth. "That's good," she says, understanding that Drew Who? deserves to be a question mark and an afterthought in her life.

I don't turn my back until her gaze meets mine, making sure I have her full attention. "It's time you have a new experience with a good and decent man, Rachel." With a smile, I walk towards the table, her gaze burning into my back the entire way.

13

A Promising Touch

Johnny

Three hours later, we lie under a blanket, beneath the stars, silent. I didn't invite her to come tonight, but somehow, she knew I would be here, waiting for her.

When she arrived, she said nothing. Only slid under the blanket and watched the sky.

Earlier at Dexter's, once play started and for the next hour and a half, Drew Who? did nothing but rack the balls for me and my team, his anger blazing with every loss. Dexter observed the whole match and never looked disappointed, which tells me he knows better than to bet against me.

Turning my head to study her profile, I silently hope Rachel will bet on us.

And her deciding to come here tonight ... well ... it's a start.

A shooting star zooms across the sky above, capturing my attention as her finger lightly grazes mine under the blanket.

My heart stops.

For the next hour, we lie side-by-side, our hands brushing occasionally as we gaze at the glittering stars, the night air a silent witness to our unspoken connection.

And a surprise touch that feels more promising than any that came before.

14

You Belong with Me

Rachel

"**M**icah, what am I supposed to do? I can't get a hold of Uncle Dexter, and I have to be there in"—I look at my watch—"like forty-five minutes."

"I'm sorry, sis, but the food delivery is late, and who else is going to stay and inventory?"

Weighing my options, I pace the living room floor. "No, no, you're right."

My follow-up doctor's appointment to discuss my latest blood work is today, and I'm a little anxious to hear the results. Every three months, I need to get my inflammatory markers checked, and lately, my RA has been angry, so I know the news isn't going to be great.

And, of course, to add to my anxiety, my car is currently in the shop. And now, my one and only ride can't take me. A Lyft isn't an option, since they won't be here in time, and I'll miss my appointment.

He pauses on the other end of the phone. "Now, I'm going to throw a harebrained idea out here, so don't bite my head off, okay?"

"Don't say it!" Because I know exactly who he is going to suggest.

"Oh, come on! You know he will drop whatever he is doing and come running. Let that man prove to you what you mean to him. Stop pushing him away."

Thanks to me having one too many a few nights ago, I told Micah everything about Johnny. My tipsy, wagging tongue spilled all my secrets. He says I'm nuts to *not* dive headfirst into a relationship with him. But Micah doesn't get it. He doesn't understand the deep-seated insecurities that gnaw at me or the constant fear that grips my heart.

Plus, Johnny has been keeping his distance. After rejecting him again in the kitchen, then me confessing about Drew, followed by a silent truck date, things have been awkward between us.

"What about Shelby? Is she available?"

"Nope. Parent-teacher conferences tonight."

I collapse onto the couch, the cushions sinking beneath my weight as I surrender to my one and only option.

"Ugh! Fine ... I'll text Johnny."

"Maybe you should give him a nice big hug and a kiss as a thank you."

I pull the phone away from my ear, still talking. "Thanks for nothing. Gotta go ... bye!"

Slamming the red button, I toss my phone onto the sofa and take a few minutes to regain my composure.

I should just cancel and catch up on *The Bachelor*. I'm already three episodes behind, and snuggling on this couch with my favorite blanket and some wine is a much better idea than the doctor's.

But I can't do that.

Micah's right. I should text Johnny. He will help me. I know he will. But after everything, the possibility of him being done with me feels real, like a cold, sharp knife twisting in my gut.

I guess there is only one way to find out.

With a resounding sigh, I reach for my phone, open to messages, find his name, and type.

Me: Hey. Sorry to bother you. Are you busy right now?

Johnny: Leaving work and picking up Mallory from school. Why? Are you ok?

Of course he asks if I'm okay. He cares. He always cares.

> Me: Oh ok. You're busy. Nevermind.

> Johnny: What's going on? Don't make me beg because I will. On my knees … the whole nine yards.

What a sight that would be. My mouth goes dry as I bite my lower lip. *Focus, Rachel!*

> Me: So I have a doctor appointment in like forty minutes and my car is in the shop. Micah can't take me, I can't get a hold of my uncle, and no ride share will be here in time. You are my last resort.

> Johnny: Ouch. I'll pretend that didn't hurt.

> Me: I hate to ask. But can you pick me up and take me?

> Johnny: I'll be there. Text me your address.

> Johnny: And explain again why I've never been to your house yet?

There are so many reasons for that, Johnny. I chuckle as I text him my address.

> Me: Thank you.

> Johnny: No thanks necessary. Be there soon.

Nerves erupt in my gut as I take in what I'm wearing. *Well, this won't work.* Just because there is a distance between us doesn't mean I can't bring it when I'm with him.

I race to my bedroom and replace my leggings with my favorite dark denim ripped jeans. Whipping off my Ohio State t-shirt onto my bed, I run to my closet and grab my favorite vintage Aerosmith t-shirt. The one that is V-necked and hugs my body like a second skin.

Heart pounding, I race to the mirror, turning side to side, checking every angle. I smile. *Yep, this is the one.* With only a few minutes left, I hurriedly apply a little more mascara and blush, then finish with a quick swipe of eyeshadow and lip gloss. Now I have to do something with my unwashed hair.

With no time to spare, I throw my hair into a super cute Pinterest-worthy high ponytail. One last once-over in the mirror, and I have to admit, I look decent. And kinda pretty.

I rub my sweaty palms over my jeans when the doorbell rings.

My nerves are shot as I grab my crossbody bag and throw it over my shoulder. Before I open the door, I inhale deeply to steady myself.

How this man affects me is unreal.

You're only going to the doctor's, Rachel. He's basically your Lyft.

A hot Lyft driver, but whatever.

And who knows? We could get some dinner after. If he's up for it because I need to apologize for everything. It's a long shot, but worth a try.

With a wide smile, I swing the door open, and the balmy early June air smacks me in the face as my eyes immediately find him. Smiling and looking incredible, as usual.

And holding the hand of the cutest girl I have ever seen.

Not gonna lie. I'm mildly disappointed here.

From our texts, I assumed that he would have already dropped off Mallory at home before coming to get me. Wrongly assumed, because here she is. Holding her cousin's hand, scared to death.

And now I feel terrible because I'm pretty sure I have messed up their routine.

My attention darts from him to Mallory. "Oh, hi."

"Hey, Rachel. I didn't have time to drop Mallory off. I hope that's okay," he says with a hint of remorse.

Dismissively, I wave my hand in the air. "No. No. It's fine. I'm the one interrupting your day."

A tight knot forms in my gut as I realize I should introduce myself to Mallory, so I extend my hand. Are you supposed to shake hands with kids? I have no clue. "Hey, Mallory. My name is Rachel."

Her eyes immediately avert away from mine as if looking at me makes her uncomfortable. She takes a step closer to Johnny, not taking my hand, and instead grabs his. "Hi," she replies, the greeting soft and sweet.

I lower my hand. "I hope it's okay with you that Cousin Johnny helps me out."

She looks up at Johnny with a wide, concerned expression. "I don't have to go into the doctor's, do I?"

He rubs a soft, tender hand down her head, his voice sweeter and calmer than I have ever heard it. "No. Of course not. Remember, we talked about this in the truck."

Huh. She's shy. Plus, this tender, fatherly vibe Johnny is sporting right now ... well, I like it very much.

Pretty sure my ovaries just exploded.

He turns his attention back to me. "You ready?"

"I am." I'm not, but I slip on my sandals anyway and lock the door behind me.

"Mallory, go ahead and get in the truck, sweetie." She takes off like a rocket.

As I follow, I'm startled by a huge, calloused hand seizing my wrist, gently pulling me back. His touch ... still burns, still ignites me, still leaves me breathless.

I shift, and Johnny intently watches as Mallory hops in the truck, waiting until she is out of earshot. "She has autism."

"Ah," I reply. "Well, that explains the no eye contact and hand shake rejection."

With slow and easy steps, he walks to the truck. I follow. "I just wanted you to know. She doesn't like crowds or new unfamiliar places, so that's why she looked so fearful about going into the doctor's office. Also, she doesn't like to be touched by people she doesn't know."

"It's no problem. I get it."

"On days that Laura works at the hospital, Scott likes to leave work early to pick up Mallory, but today, he was stuck with one of the sub-contractors. There was a huge screw-up that he had to handle. So he asked me to get her." He lets out an amused chuckle. "Which Mallory *loves* because I always get her ice cream."

Okay, it's official, a new favorite Johnny feature has been unlocked. He's obviously a huge family man. And, my Lord, does my heart explode with equal parts want and fear. "It's fine, Johnny, really. I'm just grateful you could do this."

One more thing that I find striking about this situation is … Johnny has never asked why I need to go to the doctor's. He isn't prying, giving me space and privacy. Which I appreciate more than he could ever know.

We reach the truck. He halts and inhales deeply as he skims me over from head to toe, a silent assessment passing between us. "You … you, um … you look really nice." His eyes darken, and he swallows.

I internally high five myself at the choice to glam up because the way he is taking me in right now is telling me it was the right decision. Fire creeps up my neck at his compliment. "Thank you," I mutter. Our eyes lock, unmoving, as something like a current in the ocean pulls us together.

He quickly glances away, not wanting to prolong the moment any longer than needed. More than anything, though, I want these little moments to last. But because of me, they are fleeting. I can't be upset about it. He's being a gentleman.

We make to his truck, and he opens the door for me. I climb in.

As soon as he settles in the driver's seat, Mallory speaks up. "Your hair looks soft."

Out of the blue, but okay. After what Johnny revealed about her, I go with it.

I swivel in my seat to take her in, noticing the way she's concentrating on the squirrel outside her window. "Well, thank you."

"I like to touch soft things," she replies, her attention laser-focused on the squirrel.

Johnny gives her a stern warning. "Mallory, remember, boundaries." She crosses her arms over her chest and pouts as she never breaks eye contact with the woodland creature.

"Soft things make me less nervous," she admits so quietly I barely heard her.

Oh, my heart. I have a feeling I've really disrupted this girl's day, so I need to remedy this.

"I'm sorry," Johnny mouths to me.

"It's okay," I mouth back.

I shift in my seat. "Mallory, you can play with my hair if you want to. I don't mind. Truthfully, it might calm me down and make me less nervous for my appointment. We could help each other that way."

Her eyes light up as she looks at Johnny for permission.

He chuckles. "You heard her."

Mallory scoots forward in her seat as far as the seatbelt will allow. I fan my ponytail out on the back of the seat, and immediately, her fingers glide through the strands.

An awkwardness hangs in the air as Mallory's delicate fingers stroke my hair, and honestly, it's quite relaxing. This unexpected turn of events has somehow eased my anxiety about my appointment. And to make it better, Johnny's gaze is on me every time we stop at a red light or a stop sign.

Then Mallory breaks the palpable tension. "Cousin Johnny talks about you all the time."

Johnny coughs out a laugh, which makes me chuckle. "Oh, he does now, does he? What does he say about me, Mallory?"

"That you're really nice and pretty." A small, satisfied smile crosses my lips. "And I'm not supposed to listen to other people's conversations. Mom says it's rude, but I heard him tell Daddy one day that your butt looks—"

"Okay. That's enough of this conversation," Johnny says sternly. "How about some Taylor Swift?" he begs Mallory while he addresses her through the rearview mirror.

Gosh, I wish he hadn't cut Mallory off. I glance over at Johnny, and I kid you not, the man is blushing. Pink cheeks as far as the eye can see. He gives me a fleeting glance, and I can't help but snicker.

"Yes please. But not too loud." The playful lilt in her voice heightens my curiosity.

Before Johnny takes off from the stop sign we idle at, he starts Spotify. I peek at his phone, and he has a playlist named *Mallory's music.*

Now my heart is officially melting.

Seriously, how has no woman snatched him up yet and made him their baby daddy? Because I know this man would make an amazing father.

Before Johnny hits play, he addresses Mallory. "Are we going to whisper-sing and dance?"

She giggles. "You bet!"

"Whisper sing?" I probe.

With a glint in his eye, he looks like he is about to describe his favorite thing in the universe. Heck, it might be. "Well, Mallory doesn't like loud noises."

"It hurts my ears," Mallory adds.

"So instead of singing loud, we whisper-sing. And we dance," he says with pride as he warmly smiles at Mallory. "You ready?" he eagerly asks her.

"Ready!" she squeals.

Johnny puts the car in drive and starts down the road while hitting play. "You Belong With Me" begins at a low volume, and sure enough, as soon as Taylor's voice fills the truck, Johnny and Mallory whisper-sing the lyrics.

The smile on my face is so wide at the sight unfolding in this truck, I'm pretty sure it's reaching my ears. Johnny is bouncing, swaying, singing, and pointing to himself when the lyrics call for it ... like he is the main attraction.

I mean, he kinda is at this point.

Mallory belts out the lyrics in her own way, singing her little heart out even though it's soft and whispery. This girl is having the time of her life. Arms are flailing all over, disregarding my hair, as she dances in the back seat in her own little world. Her own smile ... huge and infectious, full of nothing but joy.

Johnny did that for her. He put that smile there.

There go my ovaries again.

Glancing over at me in between beats, he slaps my arm, probing me. "Come on, Rachel! Join us!"

So I do.

Verse two begins, and the three of us are singing, dancing, laughing as if we don't have a care in the world.

It's freeing. Despite my stiff joints, I do the best I can. I'm shaking my head, causing my hair to fly all over the place. My hands wave back and forth in the air. Right here, right now, is probably the most fun I have ever had in my whole life.

The truck comes to a stop at a red light as the song is about to end. Johnny turns, and our eyes lock, hard and firm, as he mouths the last words. Directly to me. Their meaning ... loud and clear.

"You belong with me."

The music fades away, leaving a heavy stillness in the truck as we stare at each other, my chest still heaving from the dancing and singing ... and other feelings.

I know what he wants. And he has been so patient with me. So kind. So perfect. So Johnny.

His right hand instinctively leaves the steering wheel and moves across the console, his fingers crawling against the cool leather. My hand creeps to meet his. The moment our fingertips touch, there's a sense of undeniable connection, our skin grazing, our eyes searching.

Every time he looks at me, I'm weightless, as if I'm floating. The way he finds me from across the bar while cleaning sends shivers of ecstasy along my spine. And how his eyes meet mine before he takes a shot on tournament nights fulfills me. Or the way he always searches for me when the bar is wall-to-wall bodies gives me purpose. And the way he's pinning me with a stare right now. Like to him, no one else matters. I'm the only woman in his whole orbit.

HONK!

We both jump and jerk our hands back. The sudden, jarring blare of a car horn behind us breaks the spell.

"Johnny, the light is green," Mallory chimes in from the back seat.

He shifts in his seat and refocuses on the road as he rolls the truck forward. "Thanks, Mal Pal."

I smooth my ponytail down, attempting to clear my head of the lingering effects of too much Johnny, his touch still clinging to me like a second skin.

How does this man have such a powerful hold over me? The question stirs up a mixture of confusion, fascination, and curiosity.

I turn back around to address Mallory, hoping she will help ground me back to reality. "Mal Pal, huh? Is that your nickname?"

"Yep!" she exclaims proudly. "My Daddy calls me that. And so does Cousin Johnny, but only them, so you can call me Mallory."

Of course, he's the only one with an adorable nickname for her. So much for the redirection.

"I like you," she says matter-of-factly. "Can you and Johnny get married?"

I giggle.

Johnny groans.

Well, I was right. The doctor delivered some pretty crappy news. My blood work is a mess, and now he wants to prescribe a steroid to help with my inflammation.

Fantastic.

Something inside gnaws at me. There has to be better care out there, right? My brother keeps urging me to check out the Cleveland Clinic, so maybe it's time.

All of this weighs heavily on my mind as Johnny pulls into his cousin's driveway and kills the engine. I scoop the last of my ice cream into my spoon and shove it into my mouth, the coolness helping with my nerves. Because also, once Mallory is gone, it's only going to be me and Johnny.

Alone in his truck.

Which is causing way more anxiety than my health.

Mallory jumps out, ice cream cone in hand, without a second to spare.

"Mallory, wait!" Johnny hollers as he bolts out of the truck, and she stops halfway up the walk to meet him. With a gentle hold, he places his hand on her shoulder and squats to get to her eye level. He's talking to her in a calm, soothing voice, a low murmur that barely carries as she glances my way, her tongue swiping across the sweet, cold treat.

She nods in agreement as Johnny rises, and she takes his hand, heading in my direction, her mouth still working on the cone.

He opens my door, and I have no idea what is about to happen. "Go ahead, Mal Pal."

"I forgot to say bye to you, Rachel. I'm sorry." She makes eye contact with me. Surprise flashes across Johnny's face. "I hope your doctor appointment went well," she says with a small, shy smile.

God, she is adorable.

My heart melts, and I can't help but smile back. I may be halfway in love with Johnny, but I've already fallen in love with Mallory. "It was nice to meet you today, Mallory. I hope I see you again soon."

Johnny whips his eyes to me, his smile almost painful in its eagerness at the mention of me seeing his family again. There was something underlying in my words.

Hope.

"Can I go inside now?" she impeaches Johnny. You can tell she is done with this whole excursion.

"Sure."

Mallory takes off like a rocket and disappears into the house as Johnny turns to me. A thoughtful expression crosses his features. Hopeful and unsure. "Would you like to come and meet my family?" he invites. "They know about you, as Mallory so kindly confirmed in the truck earlier." He blushes. God, I love it when that happens.

The fact he has told his family about me gives me pause. It's heartwarming, but I don't think I am ready to take that step yet since I have no clue what we are to each other.

"Thanks, but I'll wait here. Take your time, though."

His shoulders sag. He's slightly dejected, yet trying not to let it show.

Which I have been making him feel a lot lately. And the thought of that fills me with a heavy, aching sadness.

"I'll be back in a minute." He winks, then smirks. "Don't miss me too much."

"I'll do my best." His gaze holds mine, unwavering, as the door clicks shut, leaving me alone to grapple with the jumble of emotions swirling within me.

Today, his tender treatment of Mallory gave me a moment of clarity.

If Johnny can handle a twelve-year-old with autism so effortlessly, why wouldn't he be able to handle my issues? And I know these two conditions aren't the same, but ... it's still compassion. For some people, this comes naturally. And Johnny is one of those people.

While I waited for the doctor today, I tallied all that he has done for me these past few months.

He helps me at closing, even though the bar is out of his way. When we stargaze, he encourages me to pursue my dream of nursing. He knows Dexter is an issue and promised to be there for me if I ever feel in danger. And he stood up to Drew for me.

Then, there's his patience. I have pushed him away three times while our lips were literally locked together. Never demanding an apology, only giving me understanding and grace.

Alone with my thoughts, there is only one thing that I need to do before he takes me home. Agree to go out with him on a date.

If he even still wants to.

And also tell him about my RA. Slick is right. I am taking away Johnny's choice, and that's unfair to him. Maybe it won't be a big deal for him. Maybe it will be. Either way, I am putting the ball in his court and letting him choose whether he wants to be with me.

And I am ready to face whatever it is he decides.

Out of extreme nervousness, I pick a nonexistent spot on my shirt when I hear laughter coming from the front porch. A man just as big as Johnny emerges from the house, and I recognize him from the first night I met Johnny. It's Scott.

He peers in my direction and gives me a slight wave and a smile. Returning the greeting, I sit back and wonder what on earth they fed these boys in childhood? Whatever it was, it worked because those are two incredibly handsome men.

Mallory peaks her head out from around Scott's legs. "Bye again, Rachel! Marry Johnny! He loves you!" she yells.

A deep, resonating laugh from Scott shakes the air, easily heard down the street as Johnny playfully chases Mallory. "Get back here, you little stinker!" She squeals and runs into the house.

I chuckle at the scene as sadness pinches through my heart. They are a family. A close-knit, there-for-each-other family. The type of family I have always yearned and longed for. One that I still want.

After a quick goodbye between Scott and Johnny, I watch as Johnny walks back toward the truck, his hands shoved deep into his pockets. His strides, heavy, slow and uneven.

It's almost as if Mallory was his safety net, and now he's forced to be alone with me. And that makes him uncomfortable, which ultimately, is all my fault. A pain of guilt creeps into my chest.

He climbs into the driver's seat, and I giggle as he smirks and shakes his head in disbelief. "I can't believe she said that."

"It was cute. She's adorable."

He smiles as he turns the key, and the engine rumbles to life. "That she is."

A rush of bravery zips through me, pushing away my fear. "So you like my butt, huh?"

He glares at me with some serious side eye. "I don't think we are at that place in our relationship for me to address that one, darling."

Well, darn. *Who's fault is that, Rachel?*

He backs out of the drive and honks his horn as we drive past the house. A few minutes of agonizing quiet stretches, thick and suffocating, before he breaks the tension. "She must really like you. We are working on her social cues, which is why I had her come back and say bye to you." His glance shifts my way. "She looked you in the eye."

Joy spreads over my heart. "I'm honored. I mean, I noticed earlier, but is that hard for her?"

He nods. "Absolutely. Among other things. Scott and Laura are working so hard to provide her with all the tools she needs to succeed and someday become an independent adult. It's amazing to watch."

"Sounds to me she has more than just her parents and brother in her corner."

"I would move heaven and earth for her. She has me wrapped around her finger."

"It was very..." My voice trails off as I weigh the impact of my words. "Sweet. And fatherly."

A lazy smile stretches across his lips.

Johnny as a father? Yes, please. It's decided. I want lots of his dimple-faced babies.

A heavy stillness falls over the truck as we get closer to my house. The Who sings out from the stereo as a sudden realization strikes me.

It's obvious that Johnny is waiting for me to make the next move. I already know he's on my side; his loyalty is clear. So it's time to show him I'm ready for more. He said so himself in the kitchen that day.

I need to swallow my pride and let him take center stage and shine.

Shine for me.

Okay, here goes nothing. I bite my lower lip. "Johnny?"

"Hmm?" His right arm casually drapes over the steering wheel, his focus on the road.

"Will you go out with me?"

His arm drops in surprise, the sudden movement catching on the steering wheel, sending the truck swerving sharply to the right. "Whoa!"

He gains control and then pulls over to the side of the road. I'm laughing uncontrollably as he puts the car in park, rests his arm on the seat, and turns to face me. His eyes are wide. "What did you just ask me?"

"I said, would you like to go out with me?"

"It was the father energy I was putting out there, wasn't it? You liked it, didn't you?"

I playfully smack his arm as laughter bubbles out of me. "No!"

Yes.

I mean, it was the whole daddy vibe, but I won't tell him that.

He laughs right along with me, and once we get ourselves under control, he gives me a pointed stare. "What made you change your mind?"

"Just you. Being you." I shrug. "I guess I'm ready for more."

"And I have been ready, for so long, to show you more." I shyly avert his gaze. He reaches out, his fingers twisting a strand of my ponytail. "Saturday night?" he asks.

I meet his burning stare, the heat of his gaze palpable against my skin. "That sounds good."

Abandoning my hair, he cups my face as his thumb tenderly traces slow circles on my skin. "I can't wait."

My eyes slide shut as I sit and soak up this moment. Because, right here, right now, somehow, I have fallen even harder for this man.

He drops his hand and puts the truck in gear, pulling back out onto the street.

"Me too," I reply with a mischievous glint in my eye, "Daddy."

His big, booming laugh fills the truck.

And my heart.

15

She Deserves the Sun

Johnny

"Johnny!" My name being called from across the noisy bar snatches my attention. "Get over here and talk to us!" Turning, I see Slick beckoning me toward the usual perch of the OBGs, their laughter already audible.

Anticipation grows in my chest at the prospect of spending some time with these men. My plan is to tell them I have a date with Rachel and see if they have any useful advice to hand out. Rachel knows and loves them like family, so I want to pick their brain some.

Because I have waited three long months for this day. Needless to say, I don't want to screw it up. I mean, I talk about her so much that Scott already believes we are a couple. I've corrected him too many times to count, but he just shrugs and says, "Whatever, dude. You two are a thing."

I hope to make whatever this thing is between us official soon.

Before departing, I shake hands with my team, all of us happy for yet another win. With an eager stride, I grab my cue and head to the bar. It's Thursday, and Rachel is off today. Which also means this is my least favorite day to play.

With a sigh of contentment, I set my cue on the empty stool next to me, while Micah places my drink—the usual club soda with lime—within easy reach.

"How's play tonight?" Slick starts the conversation.

"Good." I take a quick sip. "The guys on the team are improving with the few lessons we have had after play." I watch my four teammates shoot around as pride swells in my chest.

"Ever consider teaching lessons? Like as a side gig?" Tiny asks. "Because I would be interested."

"No kidding." He nods in agreement. "I've thought about it. Honestly, it's my favorite thing to do. Teach people the game. It's incredible watching them catch on and improve."

"You should think about it," Randy chimes in.

"Thanks. I might." I pause before I continue. "Actually, if you all have a second, I wanted to talk to you guys about something."

They all peer over at me. Nerves erupt in my gut. It feels like I'm about to ask her father for her hand in marriage instead of asking three bar regulars for advice. "So, Rachel and I—"

"Are going out on a date. Yeah, she told us," Slick finishes my thought for me. "It's about time. You better do good by her."

Three pairs of very stern eyes stare back at me, shooting their warning.

Happiness fills my soul for her because I have a sense that their love is pure and unconditional. Unlike her uncle's.

However, their pointed stares are sending quite the message.

Hurt her and you will have to answer to us.

Got it, fellas! Message sent and received.

Still, their devotion to her brings me such joy that I can't help but smile. "That's my plan." All three of them offer me happy grins, but it's the one man here who is her blood I really want to talk to. I regard Micah. "You're her brother. Care to offer a nervous man any advice? I'll take whatever you got."

Micah leans forward on the bar, his voice firm. "Look, Johnny, Rachel is loyal to people who treat her with love and respect. So do that for her. Give her that with all of your heart, and I guarantee she will return it right back to you. A hundred times over. That's how much she cares about people she's closest to."

All three of the OBGs nod in agreement.

Okay, cool. I can do that. I already respect the hell out of her. And I'm pretty sure I'm already halfway aboard the love train.

Randy is next to offer his advice. "Rachel will be the best woman to enter your life, hands down. So, if you are lucky enough to be the one she lets in, take it. Let her in and make her feel safe. Give her security and a soft place to land when she needs it. Because you have no idea how badly she will need it."

Not a problem. My arms will always be her safe space if that's what she wants. Always.

Also, I'm pretty sure he is referring to her RA. And unlike her uncle, he respected her privacy and revealed nothing to me.

Point Randy.

Next is Tiny. "I see how you look at her. As if the sun rises and falls in her presence. If this continues into a life together, never stop looking at her that way. She deserves the sun."

Tiny is a man of few words, but when he chooses them ... man! He's one hundred percent right. Rachel deserves not only the sun, but the moon, stars, the whole freaking galaxy. And I plan on expending all of my energies to give her that.

Slick rolls his glass of water in his hand, pondering his pearls of wisdom. "Got any advice for me, Slick?" I ask as I watch him intently. Rachel and Slick share a deep bond, making his opinion incredibly important to me.

He brings the glass to his lips, the cool water sliding down his throat as he finishes it. With a sigh, he sets the glass on the bar, the weight of his thoughts pressing on me as I wait. Micah refills it, giving him time to gather his thoughts. He breathes in slowly, his eyes narrowing as he regards me, his expression thoughtful. "I've watched Rachel grow up, and it was a sight to behold. She's like the daughter I never had. I want her to be happy because God knows she deserves it." He rests his hand on my shoulder. "So make her happy. Make her smile, not frown. Make her laugh, not cry. Let her love you, and don't give her any reason to hate you. Ever. And please"—he pauses—"take care of her. All I want, more than anything, is for her to be happy."

In reality, all I expected out of this conversation was some timely advice about a first date. But these men are giving me life advice. It's almost as if they know that whatever this is between Rachel and me will become something permanent. And the love they have for her is indescribable. The three of them aren't even her relatives. No blood relation. But sometimes, family isn't always blood. It can be the people in your life who want nothing but the best for you. They cheer you on and love you in the process.

That's the OBGs.

Tiny chimes back in. "Oh, and kiss the shi—"

"Language!" Slick and Randy yell out in unison.

"Gross," Micah chides and disappears into the kitchen. A wave of laughter washes over us four.

"What?" Tiny asks while also rolling his eyes. "Every woman loves to be kissed within an inch of her life."

Hopefully, on Saturday, I will get to do just that.

16

I Have to Wash My Hair

Rachel

The bar commotion, muffled and low, fills my ears as I count the cases of beer in the back room. It's a typical Saturday here at Dexter's. There's no pool league play tonight, but that doesn't mean people aren't here to blow off steam after a long week of work.

Saturdays are usually nothing but chaos.

Normally, on our busiest day of the week, you can find me and Micah filling beers from the tap, tossing out glasses of whiskey, and making Long Islands (which are half off on Saturdays) with the other bartenders. All while attempting to keep the customers happy and the bar neat and tidy. It's exhausting. Especially for someone like me.

But thankfully, I have the night off because of my date with Johnny.

Butterflies erupt in my stomach as I count and write totals on our inventory sheet. I hoped that coming in to do weekly counts would help keep my mind busy, but I was mistaken. This date and my nervousness have taken over my thoughts. But most importantly, how anxious I am to tell Johnny about my RA.

It's time. If I want to pursue any kind of relationship with this man, I need to be honest and tell him about this deeply personal struggle.

And believe me, I have an entire speech planned. It's epic and one I have practiced since I asked him out in his truck. For the last three days, I have stood in front of the mirror in my bedroom, rehearsing my words while imagining him scooping me up in his arms and reassuring me he doesn't care.

Out of habit, I rub the stiff spot on my elbow because, of course, my joints are especially angry with me today. It's just plain old-fashioned stress.

This morning, I woke up with extreme soreness and my elbows seizing, the pain a sharp reminder of how my body works against me. Despite taking my usual dose of Tylenol, the throbbing ache won't stop. My movements have been stiff and jerky all day, like a malfunctioning machine. So, as usual, I try my best to hide it. A truth I keep hidden to avoid judgement from others.

And obviously, being nervous about this date and the terror of talking to Johnny about everything are causing me not only to lose sleep but also to not eat. Which is a huge recipe for disaster.

Thankfully, I washed my hair last night, so I don't need to worry about that. For most people, when they get into the shower, washing their hair is a task they don't give a second thought to. They wash, rinse, and repeat, just like the shampoo bottle instructs.

But for me, when I'm having a flare-up, well, washing my hair is the largest task in the universe. It's painful and borderline impossible, so there's no repeating. If I manage one wash, I'm a happy girl.

Both Micah and Shelby help me wash it in the kitchen sink when they can. But tonight, Micah is here, and Shelby is visiting her family out of town. So, Smart Rachel thought ahead, and thankfully, I won't have to worry about it tonight. I'll just add some soft waves that, hopefully, Johnny will run his fingers through at some point.

A small smile plays across my lips because if Johnny is accepting of everything, it will be nice to not have to hide my pain around him anymore.

Will he, though? Accept me for ... me. RA and all?

With a sigh and a determined set of my jaw, I try my hardest to shake the doubts and anxious thoughts that plague me and swarm into my head like wasps. Getting back to why I'm here in the first place, I count the cases of alcohol.

"Twenty-two, twenty-three, twenty-seven, twenty-nine ... wait. Crap!" Ugh! I can't do this. I toss the clipboard onto a carton of whiskey as footsteps approach from behind me.

"Can't concentrate, huh?" Micah asks with amusement in his tone. He easily lifts a case of a local IPA, one that has been popular with the regulars. When I see how simple tasks like that are for him and others, jealousy shoots straight to my chest. Reminders like that surround me every day.

I pinch the bridge of my nose. "No." I sigh and draw my eyes to meet my brother's. "What if he can't handle it?"

Micah sits the case on the ground and rests his warm palm lovingly on my forearm. "Then you saved yourself a lot of time, and you know he isn't the guy for you. But you wanna know what I think?"

"Even if I didn't, you're gonna tell me, anyway."

"That man is over-the-moon, move-hell-or-high-water crazy about you. Everyone here knows it. There is no way something like a chronic illness is going to keep him away." He bends and heaves up the case onto his shoulders. "Trust me. Have I ever lied to you?"

I smile. "No. You haven't."

He takes a few steps back toward the bar but stops and kisses me on the cheek. "Love ya, sis."

"Love you too." The door clicks shut behind him. Of course, Micah is right. If Johnny isn't on board, I've saved myself a lot of time and heartache. But if he's accepting, I could be jumping into the greatest adventure of my whole life.

With a sigh and a yank of the clipboard, I complete the inventory with just enough time to leave. After locking up the cooler and importing the numbers, I grab my purse and walk down the hall, heading to the bar to let Micah know I'm leaving.

With anxiety coursing through my veins, I round the corner and survey Dexter's.

It's a madhouse.

Patrons fill every stool; the air is thick with the smell of alcohol and anticipation as they wait for their drinks. The bartenders spin and move around each other with professional ease. Dancers sway to the pulsing beat on a packed dance floor, a sweaty mess of bodies; meanwhile, the rhythmic clack of pool balls echoes from the lively tables.

But I don't notice Micah, who I know is behind this bar somewhere. "Micah, I'm taking off! Inventory is all done!" I call out, hoping my voice will carry and cause him to pop up from somewhere.

With the rowdiness of the crowd at an all-time high ... he doesn't.

My fingers dig into my purse, searching for my keys amidst a chaotic mix of lip gloss, receipts, and loose change. Finally, I find them, and as I jerk them out, I lose my grip, and they clank onto the floor. I bend to pick them up while Micah approaches with a pitcher of beer and three brimming glasses.

WHAM! Our bodies collide.

"OH MY GOD!" Micah exclaims.

Glass shatters onto the floor, and as for the beer? Well, it's now dripping down my hair and clothes, puddling onto the new LVT floor.

Utterly speechless, I stand, stunned, my arms spread wide, a tremor of shock running through me. "Rachel, are you okay?" He immediately notices my hair. "Oh, no." His voice trembles, the words barely audible, knowing the impact this will have on me. "Your hair." His gaze, brimming with remorse, locks with mine; the weight of his regret is heavy.

I choke back the tears because now I am going to have to go home and attempt to wash my hair. And I can barely lift my arms over my head, let alone bend my elbows.

"I am so sorry, sis," he whispers.

Within seconds, a flurry of activity happens. A bartender and a waitress run over as Slick jumps up. "I'll get the broom."

How does he even know where the broom is? He doesn't. Helping me is his knee-jerk reaction.

My mind is a whirlwind of thoughts, and I'm stuck, motionless, standing in a puddle of Bud Light.

Micah shakes my shoulder, drawing me from the inner freak-out I'm now having. "Rachel, go. We got this."

Zombie-like, I walk out of the bar, leaving the chaos behind. Someone yells my name, but it doesn't register through the fog of my shock. I open my car door, get in, and stare as person after person files in and out of the bar. And I bet none of them have trouble washing their hair.

No! I am not going to let this get the best of me!

I pull down my visor and wipe away the tears streaming from my cheeks. Droplets of beer fall from my soaked hair onto my jeans.

There is no way my RA is going to keep me from this date with Johnny. I am going to find a way to go home, wash this beer off my body and hair, and get ready for what is going to be the best time of my life.

I start my car, pull it out onto the street, and hit the gas. Determination coursing through my veins.

I got this.

"I totally don't got this," I say to absolutely no one as warm water cascades down my naked body, masking the tears that are already there.

Because of my bone spurs, no matter how many times I try to lift my arms to my head, my elbows lock, and pain shoots into the joint. I even attempted to bend over to see if that position would be easier. It wasn't. So now, I've been standing here for so long that the shower is running cold.

The coolness of the water is giving me the shivers, and without finishing a simple task like washing my hair, I know I need to leave this bathroom and cancel my date.

With slow, robotic motions, I grab the nozzle and turn it, leaving me even colder than I was before. Before getting out, I run my hands through my wet hair, which still reeks of beer. Now, I'm stuck waiting for my brother to come home and help me. The frustrating drip, drip, drip of the water only amplifies the headache forming behind my eyes.

Reaching for my towel, I dry off my body the best way I can, drudge down the hall to my room, and slip on some comfortable clothes. Shorts and a baggy zip-up hoodie are my only choice since I can't lift my arms over my head. Shivering, I yank on my warmest, fluffiest socks.

I'm beyond crying at this point. The tears have dried on my cheeks as I fish my phone out of my purse and settle on the couch. My favorite fuzzy blanket rests beside me, so I yank it over my exposed legs.

The time on my phone catches my eye before I open my messages, the digital glow momentarily blinding as I inhale deeply, resting my head back on the couch.

Crap. He's probably already on his way here.

I type anyway.

> **Me: Are you on your way?**

> **Johnny: Of course. Driving cow. Can't wait to glee you.**

> **Johnny: Driving now. See you.**

> **Johnny: Stupid talk to text.**

I let out an amused chuckle. Ugh! He's making this even harder. Time to rip off the band-aid.

> **Me: I'm so sorry, but I have to cancel.**

Three dots appear, then disappear. Then reappear again.

> **Johnny: Are you ok?**

Even though it will sound like a lie and beyond ridiculous, I decide to be honest and tell him the truth.

> **Me: I have to wash my hair later.**

There's nothing for a few more minutes. Restless, I wait, my leg frantically bouncing against the blanket.

> Johnny: I had to pull over. Are you serious?

> Me: Yes. Please go home. I can't do this.

Suddenly, my phone lights up in my hand. He's calling. I'm sure he wants answers. Answers that I can't give him. Because now, after what just happened in the shower, there is no way I can tell him about my RA. I mean, come on, what kind of woman can't even wash her own hair?

A weak one, that's who.

I feel so helpless, like a child that needs her mother. Not a strong grown woman that this amazing man deserves.

I'm not the person for him.

I hit the red button, sending him to voicemail. Then I throw my phone on the coffee table in front of me and stew in my self-loathing. The remote catches my eye, and I decide to watch *The Bachelor* as I wait for Micah. It will be a nice distraction, and I might as well watch other people fall in love since it's obviously not in the cards for me.

It's better this way. He deserves to be with someone who is perfect.

And I am anything but.

17

I Know

Johnny

"**Y**ou have reached Rachel. Sorry, I can't come to the phone—"

Frustrated, I jam the end button and throw my phone into the car's console.

She didn't seriously just use the oldest excuse in the book to cancel this date. A date I have waited months for. A date I knew I wanted from the first time I laid eyes on her at Dexter's.

I shake my head and yank the truck into drive. *Nope. Not happening.* I am going to do whatever it takes to get her to talk to me.

Before I know it, my truck is steering its way to her house. There is no way that one, I believe her lame excuse, or two, she gets to shut me out.

I'm going over there to find out what's going on.

Ten minutes later, the bright lights from my truck illuminate her street as I make my way to her house, my hands tightening around the steering wheel. Feeling overwhelmed and scattered, I remind myself to keep my composure and give her the benefit of the doubt because this might not be about me at all. Something could be really wrong.

Her dimly lit house comes into view as I pull into the driveway. Warm light spills out from the living room window, so I know she's here.

Throwing the gear shift into park and killing the engine, I hop out as my boots crunch and stomp on the driveway. With determination, I walk to her front door, ready for answers. My mind is blank, fueled only by adrenaline, as I stand here with no idea what to say. I raise my hand to knock on the bright blue door—

"Go away, Johnny." Her meek words jolt straight through me as my hand freezes mid-knock. Then, I hear a muffled sniffle. I was right, something's wrong, and I am not okay with her not being okay. Suddenly, my nerve endings are firing away.

"Rachel, talk to me, please. What's wrong?" I plead as I lay my hand on the cold aluminum, ears open wide, waiting for her answer.

"I can't let you see me like this." Another sniffle. Confusion rings out in my head.

"Like what? Rachel, please. If you need help, let me help you." *God, why won't she just open the door?!* She lets out a long, weary sigh, barely audible due to this enormous slab of metal locked and separating us.

"Johnny, I need to tell you something." Her voice, weak and shaking, rips me in two, and the terror in her words carries. She wants to tell me about her RA, I know it. All I want to do is wrap her in my arms and tell her it's going to be okay. That I don't care. That her RA is only something she has. It's not who she is.

"Okay. Sure. Open the door and we can talk," I implore.

Nothing.

A few very long moments pass, and I wish her reply would replace the constant hum of the crickets. The slight chill in the air does nothing to settle the dread in the pit of my stomach. She coughs, then ... "I changed my mind. Go away, Johnny, please."

Nope, not happening.

Ever since I saw her behind the bar that first day, my whole world tilted on its axis. I want this woman in my life. I need her in my life. If she believes I'm walking away this easily, she's sadly mistaken.

There have been so many women in my past, and not one of them measure up to Rachel. All of them have been steps leading me here. And she needs to know that I am on her side.

It's her news, her life, so I was waiting for her to tell me. But for whatever reason, a nervous energy churns beneath my skin, urging me forward. She needs to know that I have been there for her these last few months. That I asked her out, multiple times, even knowing.

I rest my forehead on the cool metal and anchor myself. I have no idea if this is going to upset her. But it's a chance I'm willing to take. "Rachel"—I steady myself—"I know."

Silence. Well, except for the dang crickets.

Seconds pass, and it's like hours as I wait for her to respond. *Maybe she didn't hear me.*

"Rachel?" I lift my head, staring at the blue door. "Are you still there? I said I know about—"

A sharp click of the lock echoes in the night's stillness, and I take a step back to watch the doorknob turn. Slowly, the door creaks open but just a sliver, only enough for her eye to peak through the slit. "What do you mean? You know?" she demands in a hush whisper, her lip is trembling.

"I know about your RA."

She sucks in a breath. "What? H ... How? I don't understand."

The moment has arrived; it's time to tell her, though a knot of anxiety tightens in my chest at her reaction.

"The day I met you at the bar. Remember?" She nods and glances at her socked feet, a slight blush grazing her cheeks at the memory. "I overheard your brother talking to the Oldies but Goodies. It wasn't my intent to eavesdrop, I swear. I was coming out of the restroom and heard your brother telling them you had a doctor's appointment with a new rheumatologist and how nervous you were. Then Slick asked if your RA was acting up. I walked away after that because I recognized it for what it was ... a private conversation."

She's still staring at her big fluffy socks, taking this in. A single tear drops and hits the hardwood floor. She swipes another from her cheek and looks at me again, contemplating. Processing. "I don't understand. You knew and yet you asked me out, anyway? Like, you kept asking."

"I did."

"And you kissed me. Three times."

"Best kisses of my life."

"Why, though? I'm damaged. My body works against me and literally hates me. And you're"—the door opens a tad wider as she waves a hand over my body—"you. You could have anyone. Why me?"

Motivated by nothing but love, I step to get closer to her. All I want to do is push wide open this huge blue door and encase her in my arms. But I won't invade her space until she invites me in. Nervous tension rises in my stomach. "You really want to know why?" She shrugs, her eyes back on her socks again.

God, I hate what this disease has done to her self-esteem. It's time to let her know why I'm here on her doorstep, the weight of my feelings for her heavy on my chest. "Because you're you." I tilt my head to the sky, trying to collect my thoughts. Everything I've felt about this woman is bubbling to the surface. "When you smile, there is nothing simple about the movement of your lips. Your grin travels clear to your eyes, making them shine. It changes the color of your cheeks, and the laugh that usually follows causes your nose to crinkle. The whole thing is a marvel to watch, and it is so genuine. Yet, I know every person who is fortunate enough to get a smile from you deserves it because nothing about you is fake."

I inch forward some more, and she opens the door wider, gradually letting me in. Physically and emotionally. Quickly, I scan her body. She couldn't look more adorable if she tried. An oversized zip-up Pittsburgh sweatshirt with shorts and socks. Reaching through the crack in the door and placing my finger beneath her chin, I gently lift her face towards mine, her skin soft. I need her eyes on me while I describe the incredible woman standing in front of me. Because I'm not sure any man ever has.

Their loss is hopefully my gain.

Our eyes lock. The tranquility of the night suspends, breathing, flowing. "You are so much more than a pretty face." She shakes her head and tries to break away again, but I hold firm. "I'm serious. I have never met a woman as cool as you." A mock chuckle erupts from her like, *'Yeah, okay.'*

I continue. "It's true. You have substance and a story, one I hope you will share with me some day. You are so strong. I can't imagine what you have gone through. You show up every day for your uncle, who I'm not sure even deserves it." I pause as her expression goes flat with this statement, yet she studies me, taking in my entire face. "You are smart. So smart. The medical field is lacking at the moment because you aren't in it. And if you ever decide to go to nursing school, I will cheer you on every step of the way. Hell, I'll even wear a uniform with a skirt if that will help change your mind."

The smile I love so much appears. It's small but pure as her eyes shine slightly. "Will you have pom-poms?" she asks.

"Obviously."

"I'm going to hold you to that."

"Good. So, is that a bet?"

"Yes, that is most definitely a bet." And this is a bet I'm happy to lose.

The door swings fully open, revealing her inches from me, yet I hesitate on the porch, silently requesting her permission to enter. As I wait, I take in more of her appearance. Her face is free of makeup, and she's been crying. Hard. Blotchy face, puffy eyes; dried tears stain her cheeks. It's obvious she was crying *way* before I got here. Yet, she's never been more beautiful.

It's her hair, though, that I zero in on. Wet, shiny strands hang limply from her shoulders. That's when it hits me. She really was washing her hair. But why cancel our date for that?

I reach out and slide my fingers under a wet strand. "Rachel, I could go on and on about how wonderful you are, but ... I need to know. Why did you cancel our date? Please, be honest with me. Now that the truth is out there, you can tell me anything. No judgement."

Gradually, she steps out of the way and motions for me to come inside.

Thank goodness!

She shuts the door, taking a second to compose herself. "I wasn't lying when I said I needed to wash my hair. I collided with my brother at work. He was holding a pitcher of beer, and it went everywhere. My hair was down, and so it took the brunt of it, together with my clothes. I didn't want to show for our date smelling like Bud Light. But also, I'm having a flare-up today. When that happens"—her left hand goes straight to her right elbow and rubs—"I have a very hard time raising my shoulders and bending my elbows. Which makes it hard—"

"To wash your hair," I finish for her. My gut clenches with the rising tide of guilt as I berate myself for having any sort of anger toward her for canceling. I peer at the floor, taking in this new and private side of her life.

"My brother will do it for me when he's here. But he's working, and my sister-in-law is out of town. I thought I could do it myself, but as you can see"—she points to her head—"I failed."

An idea strikes me like a lightning bolt. "Let me wash your hair for you."

She jolts back in shock. "What?"

"My mom was a hairdresser, and I used to help during summer break. I would wash her clients' hair. The older ladies loved me."

She laughs, followed by a small snort as her hand flies to her mouth. "What's so funny?" I ask.

"I'm sorry," she apologizes, still giggling. "A vision of a younger Johnny working in a hair salon just popped into my head, and, well, it's a vision, that's for sure."

After we both calm down, I plead with her. "I promise to tell you all about it, but please, Rachel. Let me help you."

"I don't know..." She turns away, wrapping her arms around her body. She's still so guarded. It's heartbreaking.

"I've been told that I do a mean scalp massage."

This catches her attention, and I'm met with a smile. This one changing the color of her cheeks.

"Okay."

18

Consume Me

Rachel

Before I can even register what's happening, I'm sitting on one of my bar stools, with my head tilted back over my farmhouse-style sink, a towel under my neck for comfort, and Johnny is using the sprayer to wet my hair.

How is this my life right now?

"Is the temperature okay?" he asks. The water hits my head, warm and comforting.

"Mmm...hmm," I murmur as my eyes flutter close because I can't form words at the moment.

My head is a chaotic mess of thoughts, swirling and colliding like cars in a pile-up as I try to make sense of the last twenty minutes.

Johnny knows about my RA. He has known since the day he met me. And he doesn't care. Ever since his confession, this same thought keeps running through my head in a loop. It's almost too good to be true.

He knew.

He always knew.

"Oh, wait, hold on a sec," he says as he turns off the faucet. "I need to roll my sleeves up."

On instinct, I watch as he unbuttons his wrist collar on the navy blue button-down shirt he is wearing and rolls the fabric up his toned forearms.

Well, well, well, it looks like construction does a body good because, oh, my God, hello, forearms!

Holy crap on a cracker.

The whole thing is happening at a crawl, and I can't stop staring, unblinking. His brawny hands tug and pull on the fabric as, inch by inch, his smooth, tan skin is being exposed. Blue veins snake along the underside of his arm as my mouth goes completely dry. A flush rises in my cheeks, hot and fiery. I probably look like a tomato.

He finishes the second sleeve and catches me gawking.

Busted!

I quickly jerk my eyes away and squeeze them shut, my cheeks burning with embarrassment. Awesome. He caught me staring and drooling.

"You okay? Your cheeks are a little pink there, Rach," he asks, and I can tell he's smirking that sexy smirk he always has.

"I'm fine. Yep ... totally fine." It comes out all hoarse.

He chortles as he goes about what he was doing. Which was what exactly?

Oh yeah, washing my hair. *Geez, concentrate, Rachel!*

He must grab the shampoo bottle because I hear it click open, followed by a squirt. He dispenses it into his hand.

As he gently massages the shampoo into my strands, the aroma of papaya and mango wafts through the kitchen. His fingertips massage my scalp, the pressure soothing and expert. He wasn't kidding.

"Dear Lord, you are really good at this." I try not to sound like I'm panting.

Give the man a gold medal in hair washing. Throw in a silver and bronze, too.

He chuckles as he continues to work the suds in. "Yeah. My mom was desperate for a hair washer one summer when I was sixteen. So she showed me how. I thought it was going to be a great way to meet and flirt with some girls." He huffs out a laugh. "Little did I know that all my mom's clients were over the age of sixty. But it worked out in my favor because they loved me. I turned on the charm, and the tips followed."

The mental image of Johnny, a gangly teenager, delicately washing the hair of all the older women cracks me up; it was utterly ridiculous.

The kitchen gets silent as he rinses out the suds, only to apply some more shampoo, and I am entirely too excited that I'm getting the wash and repeat.

The pressure of his fingers around the base of my scalp sends waves of relaxation through my body. He tenderly lifts my head, his firm hands kneading the knots in my neck due to all the stress I've had.

God, this feels fantastic.

Without any conscious thought, a moan of pure satisfaction slips past my lips. "Mmm..."

Johnny's hands go still.

"Sorry." Embarrassment courses through me as I silently scold myself. *Good job making it awkward.*

He remains motionless. Not moving. What is he doing? I can hear his heavy, ragged breathing, and his hands are still resting on my neck.

Don't open your eyes, Rachel! Don't do it. Do not —

I open my eyes. He's staring at me, his gaze intense and unwavering. His brow pinches together, and the temperature in this room suddenly rises about twenty degrees. The chemistry that has ebbed and flowed these last few months is ready to explode. His chest heaves, each rise and fall a visible struggle. As if he is in pain.

He shakes his head, lets out a low exhale, and his hands work once again.

Johnny continues, not uttering a sound. Which is a good thing because my mouth can't form any words at the moment. I close my eyes, gluing them shut.

The man is all round me. He's everywhere. His smell, his strength. When he bends over to gather my hair, his hot breath skates across my face. He stands over me, tall, evoking a sense of security, protectiveness, and an intense attraction.

Like he has since the day we met.

Before long, he's spraying the shampoo out, followed by the conditioner, a final rinse and squeeze of any excess water out of my strands, and we are all done.

Phew. Full disclosure here. *That* was one of the best experiences of my whole life.

But what now? He is going to leave? Are we going to talk about everything?

He turns off the faucet. "Okay ... all done. Just let me wrap your hair." Before I realize it, he's skillfully wrapping my hair in a towel, forming a flawless turban.

I make a move to sit up and hiss, wincing from the pain. He grips my shoulder, stopping me in my tracks. "Wait, let me help you."

He noticed.

I'm swooning.

Johnny's powerful hand is now resting on the base of my skull as he gently lifts my head and helps me into a standing position. The turban almost slips off with the movement, but before I can react, he's right there adjusting it. "Here, I got it."

He's there.

He's always there.

For me.

"Thank you." The two grateful words come out raspy and strained as I attempt to be cool. And I'm failing, obviously.

Without warning, we are inches apart. Neither of us say a word. We just stand in my kitchen, our bodies pulsing in each other's presence. Every fiber of my being is reaching out to him. Begging to hold him.

His gaze lingers on my lips for a moment, igniting a spark inside me. A single bead of water trails my cheek as I stare into his piercing hazel eyes, trying to remember how to breathe. He swipes the droplet with his thumb and slowly grazes my neck as goosebumps erupt all over my body. And I mean everywhere. Who knew you could get goosebumps on your toes? Well, I'm here to tell you it's possible.

He removes the towel draped over my shoulders and cocks his head toward the living room. "Why don't you sit in front of that chair over there?" He points to my favorite huge, comfy chair that rests in the corner of the living room. "Are you able to do that?" I nod, still unable to form words. A virtual mute at this point. "I'll clean this up. Where do you keep your hairbrush?"

My heart catches, surprise shooting through me. "You're going to brush my hair, too?" He doesn't answer. We stare. Our silent communication is loud and clear. "You don't have to."

"I want to, Rachel. Now, where's your hairbrush?"

"It's in the top drawer in the bathroom. Down the hall, first door on the left."

He cups both sides of my face, gently pulls my head forward, and kisses my forehead. His round, plump lips rest there briefly before he pulls away. "Go relax. I'll be right back."

I watch his back recede down the hallway. He looks good at my house. He looks good, period.

But mostly, he's just Johnny.

Before I know it, I'm sitting with my legs outstretched in front of me. My back is against the chair, and Johnny is sitting behind me. Both of his thick thighs rest on either side of my body, and I'm pretty sure this is the best almost-non-date of my life.

The brush glides through my wet hair even though I'm sure it's completely tangle-free at this point, yet neither of us wants this to end.

He lets out a contented sigh. "I love your hair," he confesses.

"My hair, huh? That's what you love about me?"

Wait! What am I saying? Shut up, Rachel!

He chuckles, unfazed by basically telling him he's in love with me, as the brush makes another pass along the side of my scalp. "Let me rephrase that. It's one of my favorite things. I love everything about you. Everything. Even your flaws."

Okay, wow.

Did he just admit to loving me? I can't go there right now. Not yet.

He continues. "You're perfect. And if people don't know that about you, well, then they are missing out. Because I see it. Every time I'm with you."

Those words, so raw and unexpected, resonate with a depth I'd never encountered. My skin prickles with excitement. Not even Drew said those things to me, and we were engaged to be married. He would only talk about my body as if it was an object. A possession. His attraction to me was always surface-level.

But Johnny? He sees me. All of me. Inside and out.

Johnny must be thinking about Drew as well because he has questions.

"Did Drew know about your RA?"

If there is one conversation I hate more than anything, it's talking about Drew. Telling Johnny about him that day in the bar was necessary. Little by little, I was letting Johnny in, but now, he deserves to know all of it. Even if it brings up painful memories I want to forget.

The words catch on my tongue, but then somehow, they release. "He did," I answer as another pass of the brush runs through my tresses.

"How did he handle it?" he volleys back.

Another swipe.

"I wouldn't know. He never talked about it with me."

The brush glides through again.

"What do you mean?" he inquires.

Bristles massage my head.

"I told him about it pretty early in the relationship. Of course, he said he was fine with it and never acted like it was a big deal. Which, at first, I thought, 'Wow. This is awesome. It doesn't even faze him.'" I huff at how naïve I was. "But sometimes, when my flare-ups were hitting hard, I would need him. Some compassion might have been nice, ya know. Instead, I always got, 'Suck it up!' or 'It's not that big of a deal.' And my personal favorite, 'This is all just in your head.'"

The brushing stops. "He actually said those things to you?" I can hear his teeth grinding together.

"Yes. All the time. Which made me second-guess myself. Like maybe he's right. This could all just be in my head, and I'm being overly dramatic." I sigh. "For the whole time we were together, I always doubted myself. And in the end, he eventually ended up choosing someone else. Someone who wasn't broken. Which is why I didn't bother getting upset. He did what he did because of me and my RA."

"No, Rachel. He did what he did because he is a selfish SOB that didn't love you enough. No one deserves what happened to you."

He continues brushing as I let his reassuring words wash over me. "Maybe. But I guess I'll never know. He was older, so he probably didn't care enough. I was just his young and dumb fiancé who was overly paranoid about her chronic illness."

Carefully, he sets the brush on the table next to the chair, its bristles softly scraping against the surface. "Is that why you are so guarded and afraid of men older than you?"

"And customers, since that's how I met him. So, yeah. My guard is up now."

"Is your guard up with me?"

There it is. The million-dollar question.

Silence fills the room as I decide how to answer. My heart pounds.

I nod.

The weight of my reply is almost unbearable; I'm so completely torn right now. I need Johnny more than I need air. But the walls I've built around my heart are still there. And I fear they always will be. And yes, I agreed to this date. But now that the truth is out there, how will things be? Will he tip-toe around me? Treat me like a porcelain doll? I don't want that.

But I want him. So bad. Sometimes, I hate myself and these doubts.

He places his hands on my shoulders and gives them a slight squeeze as he kisses the top of my head. "I better go," he whispers.

My quiet admission is all the answer he needs to know where my head is at. He swings his leg up and over my head with such ease it's like he's a freaking ballet dancer. I watch as he plants his feet directly in front of me, extending his hand. I grip it, and the effort to stand causes a sharp, agonizing protest from my bones as my grunts and groans fill the air. Before I know it, we are face to face.

"Unless you don't want me to?" he asks.

Yes, no. Yes, no. Yes, no. Each option swirls in my head like a tornado.

"I don't know what I want." And that's the honest-to-God truth. Him being here feels so right. Letting him leave feels so wrong. But there is still so much hurt in my heart. Every one of my insecurities flashes like neon signs.

His hands envelop my face, a comforting touch amidst the uncontrollable thoughts. Unconsciously, I step closer, the scent of him filling me as my hands instinctively find their way around his waist.

Our mouths inch closer with every passing second. I want this. I want this so bad. More than I have ever wanted anything in my whole life.

Slowly, our lips brush as ragged breaths catch, and a current surges through me, making my skin burst.

Once again, jolting me to my senses.

I jerk back, a strangled noise catching in my throat, the air thick with the scent of fear. Dejected, Johnny's shoulders slump, his head hangs low, and his arms fall limply at his sides, a picture of utter defeat. With a determined set to his jaw, he takes a step back.

My skin, still tingling from the memory of his hands on me, quickly grows cold, a stark contrast to the lingering eagerness in my heart.

"I'm so sorry," I whisper as I wrap my arms around myself. "I don't know what's wrong with me."

This guy, this incredible, amazing man, is ready. He is ready for me.

"I can't keep doing this, Rachel." The confession hits me like a physical blow.

No! No, no, no. This can't be happening.

He stops, his gaze unwavering on the floor, a palpable tension in the air while I wait patiently to hear the words that I know are coming. "I can't keep kissing you. It's happened four times now, and I can't be the one that keeps starting this."

"What do you mean?"

"It means just that, Rachel. For whatever reason, you are afraid. Are you afraid of us? Afraid of me? Afraid of what?"

He lifts his face, and it's like I've slapped him. "I have never been more sure of anything in my whole life. But this constant back and forth. This feeling of rejection I get every time we are together and you push me away. I can't do it anymore. And I just don't—"

Whatever he was going to say stops on his tongue. He pivots to leave, walking to the door and grasping the handle. He pauses, not turning to look at me. His back rises and falls with each shallow breath, his rigid stance noticeable as he lingers.

His silence screams more than words ever could; I know he wants to say more, so I stand here paralyzed, a cold sweat prickling my skin.

Then, he speaks. "I desire to be consumed by you."

Whoa.

He continues, still facing the door. "I want you to overwhelm, complicate, and burn through my life and everything in it. My thoughts, my future ... everything. Nothing has ever compared to you."

Perhaps for the last time, he shifts to look at me. "When you're ready to be consumed by me, let me know. Because you're it for me, Rachel. You and your illness. I want it all."

Then he delivers his final knock-out punch. "But ..." He pauses. "I won't wait forever. The choice is yours." He's still not leaving. I wait. I breathe. "Choose yourself. Choose us. *Please.*"

The knob turns and clicks, slicing through the thick silent tension in the room. As the door creaks open, he cautiously takes one, two, three steps out, and suddenly, something snaps deep inside of me.

What am I doing? I can't let this man walk out of my life. The one and only man that has truly looked at me and saw me. Saw past my RA. My demon that holds me hostage. He will fight this battle with me, shoulder to shoulder. We can walk through anything together.

If I let him get in his truck and leave, he won't be back. I've made this too hard.

Sheer panic at the sight of him walking out of my life—literally—filters through every nerve ending in my body, and before I can stop it, I call out to him. "Johnny!" It's as if my feet have turned to stone, rendering me immobile and unable to move. Frozen in place, my arms hang, dangling by my side.

I'm afraid. But I'm pushing. Pushing past the fear and self-loathing.

And pulling love in.

He comes to an abrupt halt, takes a moment to collect himself, and then turns towards me with a deep frown.

As I wipe away the single tear of joy that slides down my cheek, I can't help but smile. "Consume me."

In a split second, he's back in my living room, forcefully closing the door, the jarring force shaking the walls. He stops just inches in front of me.

His chest heaves with each labored breath, rising and falling.

His eyes, sharp and bright, lock with mine as I tilt my head back; a silent challenge passes between us.

"Are you sure?" he rasps out.

Lord help me.

"Please," I whisper my plea. "Make me feel alive."

In one fell swoop, he snakes his arm around my waist and draws me flush to his body, pressing me firmly against his chest as his mouth crashes into mine. I'm breathless. The world falls away.

And I surrender.

The brick walls I built like a fortress around my heart come crashing down around me. With every pass of his mouth, the bricks fall at my feet. Every doubt, insecurity, and fear I had crumbles to the ground.

I'm free.

I'm alive.

On instinct, I snake my arms around his broad back, pulling him closer to me, our lips moving as if we have done this a thousand times before. His other hand lands on the back of my head as he weaves his fingers through my wet hair, pulling me to him. The speed of our kiss intensifies, and something akin to fireworks explodes throughout my whole body. My hands clutch onto his back with purpose, wanting more of him. Needing more of him.

But he doesn't take more. Out of nowhere, he softens the kiss. As my lips yield to his, a lightness fills the air. Johnny's lips are undeniably meant for kissing. I've decided that kissing him every chance I get is my new goal in life.

How is this man so perfect?

I'm sure I'll get my answers later, but right now, I mold my mouth to his, yearning for more as my pulse races. This kiss, this perfect kiss, is warm, sweet, and full of passion. My mind is clear of all that troubles me. For the first time in my whole adult life, my RA isn't front and center in my mind. It's only Johnny, this moment, and his mouth. The world and all of my fears melt away.

Taking his time, he pulls away, breaking our connection yet leaving behind a soft, lingering peck, while his hands gently cup my neck. As I let out a satisfied sigh, I muster the strength to open my eyes, instantly connecting with his longing gaze. Nothing compares to this.

This feeling.

I'm falling.

My hand journeys up his chest and rests on his shoulder. A sly smile forms on his face, and his heart thumps beneath his shirt, quickening with anticipation. My lips part, and he captures the tiny whimper with his mouth, consuming me. Another kiss follows, then another, each one deeper than the last.

After an eternity, we break apart. His calloused fingers gently caress my face, then he plants a light peck on my nose before pulling me into a tight embrace; his arms encircle me in a comforting hug. Wrapping me up in his orbit.

A wave of safety, love, and anticipation flows through my soul, soothing it. Passion courses through my veins as I bury my face in his chest, sucking in a deep breath, taking in his scent of forest trees and vanilla.

"Are you ready for what happens next?" He exhales.

I pull my head away to look at him, curiosity and anticipation filling my heart. "So what's next?"

"Our forever."

"I've never wanted anything more."

I'm ready. For us.

Neither of us wants to let go. Neither wants this night to end. So, for God knows how long, we stand locked in an embrace in the middle of my living room, our bodies pressed together, our breaths syncing.

This man, this all-consuming man, is claiming me and our life together.

And I'm here for every second.

"God, I can't wait to start this new chapter with you. I'm going to show you everything." He cups my face again as that sly smile I love so much makes an appearance. My favorite dimple follows. "Are you ready for that? Ready for us?"

"I'm ready."

His lips meet mine again, and I know without a shadow of a doubt that my life has just begun.

19

That's Very High School of You

Rachel

With a wineglass in hand, I leisurely sway back and forth on the swing on Johnny's front porch. Laura, Shelby, and I just finished cleaning up after a picnic Johnny hosted. Micah, Shelby, Scott, Johnny, Jake, and the OBGs are playing a small game of football on the front lawn. Mallory is in the house, coloring and taking a much-needed social break.

Laura had to take off and go to work, so it's just me, my wine, and my heart.

And that heart of mine is so completely in love with the man currently in a huddle with Scott, Jake, and Micah. I can't help but smile as he's being all Daddy Johnny again.

This time it's with Jake.

Before the game started, he was showing Jake the proper techniques for throwing and catching a football. And it was by far one of the cutest and sweetest things I have ever seen.

After kissing me to high heaven in my living room and committing ourselves to each other one month ago, Johnny and I have been inseparable. There are days when I sit back and wonder how I got so lucky. How Johnny treats me is what I have always wanted and desired from a man.

He pushes me yet doesn't hold me back. He cheers me on with passion, which is truly motivating. When I'm having a flare-up, he cherishes me and takes care of me in a way that can only mean one thing.

He loves me.

And my feelings are bubbling to the surface, ready to burst open.

After that night in my living room, we ordered some pizza and talked for hours. Once the truth was out in the open, I felt safe enough to share with him my deepest desires. My voice shined with newfound freedom as I told him everything. About my diagnosis, my treatment, my fears. All of it. Each passing minute, each confession, was another brick of that wall I built around my heart tumbling down.

Rarely spending a day apart has been nothing short of amazing. I have no idea how I have lived for thirty years without him.

Practically every night, he's at the bar, and no matter where I'm at in the room, he finds me with only a soft smile and his presence. And on days I'm off work, and it's a tournament night, I'm still there, sitting and cheering him on. I love it so much.

Then, on clear nights, nestled under a thick warm blanket in the bed of his truck at Miller's Bluff, we'll watch the stars, share quiet words and kisses as we fall in love. One shooting star at a time.

Thinking back to all of it causes me to smile as I take a sip of my cabernet, watching Jake throw the ball. It spirals through the air, and Scott catches it, giving their little team the win.

Everyone reacts. Scott, Johnny and Micah scream in celebration. The OBGs and Shelby all moan in defeat.

"Oh, you have got to be kidding me!" Tiny yells as Scott and Johnny run over to Jake. "No one stands a chance up against you, Givens boys."

I smile as Johnny scoops up Jake, beaming with pride. "That was awesome, kiddo!"

"I can't believe I threw that so well," Jake exclaims, full of shock in his natural abilities. He is a Givens, after all.

"I think we just found Pittsburgh's future QB!" Scott proclaims, beaming with pride.

"Whoa, whoa, whoa!" Randy's head draws back quickly as he points to Scott and Johnny. "You guys are Pittsburgh fans?"

"Uh-oh," Slick murmurs, lowering and shaking his head as he laughs under his breath.

"I mean, obviously," Scott retorts, kind of like, *Who isn't?* "Aren't you?"

"We would no sooner die," Tiny deadpans back.

"Looks like we have a situation on our hands, fellas," I holler from my perch on the swing, already knowing who Randy, Tiny, and Slick root for.

Scott looks over at me. "Please tell me it's not Cleveland."

"Worse, actually." Laughter rings out through my response.

Jake finally puts the pieces together. "No way! You guys are Baltimore fans?!" The OBGs all answer at once. "Absolutely!"—"Heck ya!"—"Play like a—"

"Get off my property," Johnny interrupts and points to the street.

It's strange, actually. We live in Ohio, a town right on the border of Pennsylvania, yet we are all Pittsburgh fans. Well, except the OBGs.

Everyone breaks out into laughter, and I have a feeling football season is going to be a lot more interesting this coming year.

The entire gang heads to the backyard, laughing, joking, and having fun. As friends and family do. "Who wants a beer?" Scott asks.

Everyone takes him up on his offer, except for one. "Count me out. I'm going to hang out up here on this swing with my girlfriend," Johnny replies as he jogs in my direction. His smile touches his ears as he takes the three steps up onto the front porch.

Heading straight for me.

I peer up at him, his shadow looming large as he stands over me. "Your girlfriend, huh? That's very high school of you."

He sits, and I scoot closer, feeling the warmth of his body beside me as he settles in. "I can't help it," he lifts me onto his lap. "I feel like a high schooler when I'm with you."

His palm lands on my knee as I snake my hand behind his head. Running my fingers through his hair, I tug his head toward mine, and he kisses me like he always does. Gentle, yet with a possessive firmness that I love.

We break apart, and a soft smile tilts his lips. We stare at each other for a few seconds, my pulse pitter-pattering the way it always does when I'm this close to him.

His thumb brushes my cheek. "Having fun?" he asks softly against the summer breeze.

"The best time. Thank you for this. It was nice having everyone together, getting to know each other."

He smiles, peering out over the front yard as he rubs small circles over my thigh and boisterous laughter rings out from the backyard. He turns his attention back to me, a subtle shift in his posture indicating a change in focus. "Rachel, there is something that I need to say to you. Something I have been wanting to express since that first night in the truck."

Our eyes lock, an almost unbearable intensity passing between us. My heart pounds in my chest as I wait, his confession hanging in the air.

"I love you," he chokes out, emotion catching and seizing.

I gape at him as my heart fills to the brim with those three syllables. The lump in my throat tightens, threatening to burst into sobs as he continues. "I love you fiercely, and more than I ever thought I could love anyone." He rests his hand on my chest. I cover it with mine. "I love your perfect heart and the strength it gives you. I love your soul and how you make everyone that is around you happy. I just love"—his eyes brim with tears—"everything."

So this is it. This is love. This is the feeling they write songs over and make movies about. It's what has brought down empires and shaken up the world.

And it's ours.

We own it. Our love belongs to us. And no one can take it away.

Taking his face into my hands, his skin butter soft as I utter the three easiest words I have said to anyone.

Ever.

Because let's face it, I have been feeling this for a lot longer than I would like to admit.

"I love you too."

He wraps his arms around my waist and pulls me to him as our lips meet again.

This is *the* kiss. The one that seals our feelings together after our confession. The one that tells the other, 'Yeah, I feel it too.' The one that has a future after it. The one that means more than the ones before it.

The one after the 'I love you.'

"So gross!" Jake's sudden appearance and words startle us apart. "They are kissing again!" he hollers to the backyard.

We can't help but laugh, and I'm pretty sure my cheeks are turning every shade of pink after being busted by a teenager ... making out *like a teenager*. Johnny clears his throat as his hand finds my thigh again. "What's up, Jake?"

"Before mom left for work, she told me to take pictures of everyone, so that's what I'm doing." He steps up onto the porch, holding up his phone. "She'll be mad if I don't get you guys."

I lean my head on Johnny's shoulder, and both of his hands rest on my legs.

"Okay. Now smile!"

We smile.

Jake snaps.

My life is complete.

20

Nothing We Can Do in Public

Johnny

I glide my hand into Rachel's under the table of our favorite restaurant, Fire & Embers. It's a hopping Friday night. Patrons occupy every table at this retro eatery, chatting, eating, and enjoying life. Clanking forks and plates mixed in with chatter and a low hum of indie rock fills my ears. But the only presence I want and need is Rachel's.

As her fingers intertwine into mine, a contentment spreads through me, a silent acknowledgment of a connection deeper than words. A connection that has only grown stronger in the three months that we have been together.

And they have been the most glorious three months of my whole life.

We complete each other in a way that I never thought was possible. The time we spend together is effortless, easy, and everything I never knew I needed in my life.

One of my favorite things is at Dexter's. I love to grab her by the waist and pull her into the kitchen or back office while she's working when the bar isn't busy. We are all lips and limbs.

And thankfully, Dexter hasn't been an issue. He's cordial, but every time my hand snakes around Rachel's waist, the muscles in his jaw tighten. And I always make sure I'm touching her when he's around. That freak show needs to know that I'm the only man Rachel needs in her life.

Now, we are on a dinner date with Scott and Laura. Rachel and Laura have become fast friends, and as I sit here, watching the three of them talk about Mallory and Jake, visions of future family dinners are dancing in my head. Maybe even family vacations on the beach.

Rachel in a bathing suit? Tell me when and where, and I'll show up. My life is in clear focus, and it's as if I'm seeing my future through my reading glasses.

God, that makes me sound old.

I've been so lost in thought that I have totally missed whatever has the three of them cracking up.

"And then," Scott continues through gasps of laughter, "Johnny's eyes got as big as saucers when the cops showed up. He was so busted."

Oh geez, they are talking about Daytona. Scott *loves* to talk about that night. Leaving out the most important details, of course. "Hold on. I thought we were talking about Jake and Mallory."

Rachel turns to me. "Quick subject change. I would have loved to have seen that, babe."

I groan out. "Scott, please tell me you didn't tell her the entire story."

"Johnny, I *still* don't know the whole story," Laura confesses, laughing so hard she can barely get the words out.

Rachel whips to Laura in surprise. "Wait"—she waves her finger between Scott and me—"you haven't even told Laura what happened?"

Scott shakes his head, then takes a sip of his bourbon. "Nope. Johnny and I made a pact that night to tell no one what happened in Daytona."

"It's that embarrassing?" Rachel asks through a disbelieving smile.

Scott chimes in. "Johnny would move heaven and earth to keep that secret buried."

I sneer as I take a sip of my coffee, yet my insides twist, knowing that Dexter is the only other person who knows.

As if on cue and saving me from any further embarrassment, the waiter approaches to take our orders. Soon after, Scott gets a work call, and Laura excuses herself to use the restroom. Leaving me and the most beautiful woman on the planet alone at the table.

She releases my hand, squeezes my thigh, and faces me. "So what do I need to do to get that story out of you?" she purrs.

Our faces are so close she can probably smell the coffee on my breath. "Nothing we can do in public."

"So, later than?" she inches closer, mocking me by batting her eyelashes playfully.

"Your womanly wiles won't work on me." She pouts her bottom lip out. "That means I would have to break a pact that I made with Scott. I love you, Rach, but the secrets of that night are pretty sacred."

And, *God,* I love this woman.

The way she makes me so happy and complete is like sunshine on a winter day: warm, bright, and full of life. When we're not together, a heavyweight settles on my chest—that's how deeply I love her.

I promised myself that night in her living room that I would take things slow, and I meant it. It took a lot of work for me to break through her barriers.

But I did.

I lean in, cup her cheek, just like she loves, and whisper the easiest three words that I have ever had to string together. "I love you."

Her lips tick up in a ghost of a smile as she replies the only way her heart allows. "I love you too. So much."

The noise of the restaurant fades into the background; I don't even care that we are in a public place. Pulling her mouth to mine, I seal our confession with a deep and lingering kiss.

"Ahem!" The rude interruption forces us to break apart. Without removing my palm from her cheek, I turn to regard the person who inserted themselves into our private moment. And who it is doesn't surprise me. His looming presence is always unmistakable.

It's Dexter and Drew Who.

Casually, I drape my arm over Rachel's shoulder while she shyly turns her face to her water glass and takes a quick sip. "Dex. Drew." My greeting is flat, void of any emotion.

Drew's bald head is especially shiny tonight. It looks like he's greased the thing. He probably did. And Dexter, of course, is wearing one of his obnoxious three-piece suits. His pot belly sticking out like a sore thumb. Staring at him reminds me of a character from a movie or TV show. But I can't place who.

Shaking the thought from my head, I turn to Drew Who. He fixes his narrow, angry eyes, blazing with fury, directly at me.

I meet his fiery gaze, smirk, and lightly squeeze Rachel's shoulder.

Drew and I still play each other on tourney nights. And I beat him. Every single time. I will, however, give credit where credit is due. His play has improved. A lot since we met at the table a little over three months ago.

When we play, I can't help but notice the disdain on his face every time he sees Rachel and me together. I'm sure it drives him mad when my arms snake around her waist from behind and I kiss her shoulder (she loves it). Or when we sneak in little pecks on the lips or cheek every chance we get.

Hey, if he was a better human, this could have been him sitting here with her. His loss equals my gain.

Rachel's relationship with Dexter has changed as well. I've stayed out of it, since it's something she has to work through on her own terms. But gradually, the hold and control he has over her is slipping through his fingers. Now that her life is moving forward with me, she is realizing how she can have happiness and freedom. Plus, she's even mentioned nursing school from time to time. My girl is ready to shine like the star she is.

And I can't wait to witness all of it.

Thankfully, Drew hasn't tried to interfere in our relationship. He knows better than to attempt any conversation with her. But it's pretty obvious the man is still in love with her.

Which does not sit well with me and another reason I like to be at her side whenever I can. I don't trust these two.

But since we are in a public place, and I don't want to appear rude, I will be cordial.

Reluctantly.

Dexter decides to open his mouth. "Rachel. Johnny. I hope you are having a lovely dinner tonight?"

"We are, thank you," Rachel answers. Her voice is small. Like it always is when she's with her uncle.

"Rachel," Drew calls to her. She glances at him. "I've missed you. How have you been?"

My back stiffens as I recoil my arm from Rachel's shoulder, and immediately, my defenses are up. "Are you kidding me right now?" I challenge through gritted teeth. Rachel's palm finds my thigh and squeezes. I'm not sure if she's trying to calm me down, or she's uncomfortable and is grounding herself to me. Probably a little of both.

"Johnny. Don't. Please," she pleads with me in a low voice.

"Now, now. Rachel's right. There's no need to get worked up. Drew here was just stating the obvious," Dexter comes to his buddy's defense.

"The only obvious thing I know is that"—I look Drew squarely in the eye—"you have no right to miss her after the way you treated her."

A small smile creeps across Rachel's lips. I continue. "If she doesn't want to speak to you or have a relationship with you, that's on—"

"I can speak for myself, Johnny," Rachel chimes in.

My gaze whips from Drew and locks on her; I can't deny the truth in her words. Rachel can speak for herself.

So she does.

Her shoulders square back as her chin jets out. Narrowed eyes land on him as she exudes nothing but calm and focus. I sit back, giving her this moment.

I grin. *Let him have it, my love.*

"Drew, don't talk to me. *Ever* again. The day you slept with someone else, in *my* home and in *my* bed, is the day you lost all rights to miss me. Because I'm pretty sure when I saw you with her, you weren't missing *me.* Were you?" Drew's lips form a fine line. He is not enjoying being put in his place.

She continues. "As you clearly saw just a second ago, I'm happy. The happiest I have ever been in my whole life." She snickers. "Do you know how wonderful it is to feel valued, heard, and loved? I mean, *you* would, since that's what I gave you. But for me, this is a first."

My hand finds her knee. I will love and value her until the day I die.

But she isn't finished. "Don't speak to me, don't even look at me. You are insignificant. Nothing. A nobody. I would say have a nice life, but I don't even wish that for you."

As Drew's face continues to grow redder by the second, Dexter intervenes. "Rachel, you need to control—"

"Control what, Dexter?" Her glare is now directed at her uncle.

"It's Uncle Dexter."

"I prefer *Dex,* actually," I argue with an amused smirk as I sling my arm around Rachel's shoulder. She shimmies closer to me.

A voice comes from behind me. "Weird. I thought it was DJ?" Scott appears, done with his phone conversation. Dexter's and Drew's attention snaps from me to Scott. "Is there a problem here?" he asks, making his voice deeper. I love it when he does this. It has solved many confrontations on the job over the years.

Dexter raises his hands. "No problem at all. Drew and I here were just stopping over to say hi to my niece and her date." He extends his hand. "Scott, nice to see you again."

Scott takes it and does his famous squeeze. Dexter tries to pull away, but Scott's grip only tightens. He's letting this small man know, right here in this crowded restaurant, who has the upper hand and that he isn't welcome. "You as well. I hope the remodel is still holding up."

Scott releases his grip as Dexter flips his hand. Probably from the pain.

But he keeps his cool. "It is. The compliments we get on the daily are always glowing. I might call you to do an addition on my house. I was thinking—"

"We're booked," Scott deadpans as he relaxes back in his chair, sending a message. *'We will not be working with you again.'*

Dexter clicks his tongue. "Fair enough. Glad to hear business is booming." An awkwardness hangs over us, filled only with the buzz of a busy restaurant. You would think the two of them would take that as their cue to leave, yet here they stand. Looking over my shoulder, I glance at the restroom, hoping Laura doesn't emerge. Dexter's lewd comment about her that day in my garage ... well, let's just say, I don't want his eyes on her. At all. When I refocus, Drew Who's stare is solely on Rachel.

However, only I have my girl's attention. She lets out a low exhale of relief, and briefly, her lids flutter close. When those beautiful chestnut browns reopen, she sees only me. I'm sure this whole little exchange was hard on her, even though she did what I'm sure she needed to do. But now, with the unspoken emotion, you could almost taste the tension.

This little meet and greet needs to end. "Well, if you fellas don't mind, we would like to continue our evening." In other words, 'Bye.'

"I guess that's our cue to leave." Dexter takes the hint while grabbing his keys from his pocket. "Enjoy the rest of your dinner."

Dexter turns to leave, but Drew lingers. "Bye, Rachel," he says with a flicker of hope in his voice and sadness in his eyes.

She doesn't respond. Instead, she leans toward me and kisses me on the cheek. She wasn't kidding.

Insignificant.

With her lips still on my skin, I glance at where he was standing, but all I see is him retreating. Hopefully, disappearing into the hole he crawled out of.

"Mind telling me what in the hell that was all about?" Scott commands once they are out of earshot. "Geez, Johnny, I leave you for a minute."

Just then, Laura returns to the table. She pulls out her chair and sits, scooting herself back in. "So, what did I miss?"

"That's it!" I snap my fingers. Everyone's eyes dart to me, a sudden hush falling over our table. The image of who Dexter reminds me of pops into my head.

"What's it?" Rachel asks in confusion as she takes a sip of her water.

"Dex reminds me of the dad from Family Guy! Peter Griffin, only meaner and gruffer."

Water sprays from Rachel's mouth, a sudden geyser that soaks the table as we all lurch backward, chairs scraping against the floor. Then, the joke hits. A burst of laughter from Rachel, Scott, and me fill our corner of the restaurant, drawing the attention—and stares—of nearby patrons.

"Come on. Tell me you don't see it?" I ask through laughter.

"You're right," Rachel says, tears spilling over from the amusement, the air hitching with ragged gasps. "He totally does!"

"Seriously?" Laura asks in confusion while wiping down her shirt. "What in the heck did I miss?"

The headlights of my truck cast a bright beam, illuminating her driveway as I pull onto the hard concrete. With a final click, I kill the engine. The smell of exhaust lingers in the air, as I twist my body towards her. She's fidgeting with her cuticles, her sign that she's nervous.

"Wanna talk about it?" I plead, reaching over and tucking a piece of hair behind her ear. I rest my hand gently on her shoulder, rubbing small circles into her soft, silky skin, the subtle rise and fall of her breathing evident under my fingertips.

She glances out the window, then turns to me, sighs, and grins.

She's hesitant, so I lean over the worn leather of the middle console and gently kiss her perfect lips. "No matter what it is, remember that I love you."

"I love you too," she murmurs between kisses, her lips lingering on mine.

We break away, our breaths mingling as our faces are inches apart. "What's bothering you?"

"How do you know me so well already?" She slides back over to her side of the truck.

"I can read you."

"Now, who's reading who?" She laughs.

Then her expression becomes serious, so I stretch my arm over the seat. My fingers play with the silky strands of her hair. "Saying that to Drew felt so good. So empowering. Even when I saw him"—she pauses, probably because that image is burned into her brain for all eternity—"with her, I really didn't tell him what I wanted to. What I needed to. I was scared. Not brave enough, ya know?" She looks over at me.

I nod, giving her the validation she needs and deserves while rubbing small circles on her shoulder.

"But God." She smiles and lets out a long, shaky breath. "Saying that to him felt *so* good."

"I was so proud of you." I lean in and give her a peck on the shoulder.

Her cheeks blush from the compliment. One that I'm not so sure she received enough of in the past.

"Thank you." She peers at her house through the windshield, pondering. "But I worry about the repercussions."

This makes me snap my head back as my skin tingles with unease. "Repercussions?" I probe. "Like what?" She pauses, rolling her bottom lip between her teeth. "Rachel, what aren't you telling me?"

My gut clenches as a heaviness settles. She's keeping something from me. Something huge and possibly dangerous.

She starts. "Well, you know about the gambling." I nod, anticipating. "And that it's illegal."

"I suspected as much."

"Well, I'm pretty sure Uncle Dexter is grooming Drew to take over. Or just bring him into the fold. I don't know. It's just a hunch. He and Drew have been having a lot of secret meetings in Dexter's office lately." She pauses. "But also, people have 'disappeared.'" She uses air quotes for that last word. "People who have worked with or crossed my uncle."

Kinda like the guy I saw Dexter and his men escort out of the bar that day. "So, are you talking like murder?"

She shrugs. "They disappear. That's all I know."

"And you're what? Worried about Drew, of all people?" I mean, I'm not going to lie here. A tinge of jealousy pinches at my heart. *I hate this feeling.*

Her hand stretches over to mine. "Johnny, he hurt me, yes. But I don't want something like that to happen to him. Or anyone, for that matter. But it's more than Drew." She focuses on me, her posture goes rigid. "It's you. I'm worried about you."

"Me?" I laugh at the thought. "I can handle myself, Rachel."

Her brows knit together while she wrings her hands in her lap. "I'm sure those other men thought the same thing."

"Come here," I command, waving her over. A tight, nervous smile crosses her lips as she shimmies across the truck and crawls into my lap, wincing slightly along the way because of her joints.

This is one of our favorite things. Her sitting in my lap anywhere, really. In the truck, on the couch, in a chair. Doesn't matter. She loves it because she feels cherished, which she has never felt before. Me, I just love having her in my arms. But, right now, she needs to be reassured that everything will be okay.

On instinct, I plant a kiss on her lips, then a small peck on the end of her perfectly sloped nose. "I'll be fine, my love. But now that you've told me all of this, I will be more cautious."

"I can't lose you," she whispers while her palm rests on my heart and her forehead against mine.

"You won't. I promise."

"You can't make that kind of promise."

I let out a long sigh. "Okay ... how about this? I promise to never *intentionally* leave you."

A low chuckle rumbles in her chest. "That's just a fancy way of saying it."

"But it's one hundred percent the truth." I grab her waist and pull her even tighter against me.

"Please, just promise me you will be careful. I highly doubt he would do anything to you since he knows how much that would hurt me. But I don't trust him, Johnny. Power and control. He loves it."

I snake my fingers through her hair and pull her face closer. Perfect lips hover over mine. "I promise." I seal my words with a searing kiss.

On my drive home, I replay the conversation in my head. Both from dinner and in my truck. A spark of unease gnaws at me. I've never trusted Dexter. Even when Scott accepted the remodel, something didn't sit right with me. He oozes shady and untrustworthy.

But Rachel's revelation is causing me some anxiety, I admit. I rest my elbow on the door as I run my thumb over my lip, trying to calm my nerves. Other than illegal gambling, what is this guy involved in? And how is Drew in on it all?

And how can I protect Rachel from them?

21

What Do You Want From Me?

Rachel

With music streaming throughout the bar and the liquor stocked, I flip the lock on Dexter's door.

It's three pm. Opening time. Which means I'm all alone until four, since that's when the rest of the staff arrives and the kitchen opens. Around that time, our regulars, including the OBGs, amble in. When they are here, it gives this place a familiar, comforting atmosphere.

My other true north and calming presence is spending the evening with his family. Scott gave him grief the other day, saying he's never around anymore since he met me. I mean, he's not wrong. But then Scott went for the jugular and told Johnny that Mallory missed him.

That was all it took.

But it's fine. It's Sunday, our slowest day of the week, which also means we close a few hours early. I'll meet Johnny at his place when I get off. My body tingles at the thought.

As I head back to the bar, Dexter emerges from the hole that is his office. Immediately, my shoulders tense. Our relationship has changed as of late. He planted this seed of resentment when he shut down my nursing school ambitions, stifling my hopes and leaving me unheard.

It was a turning point for me. It took time, but ultimately, I realized he has no interest in helping me grow as a person. He likes me here in this bar, slinging bottle necks with hurting joints, dating Drew, and controlling my life. Something I let him get away with for far too long.

But then Johnny entered the picture. Because of him, I feel special, valued, and like I deserve to have what I want in life. Like I can achieve anything. I'm a woman of beauty and strength, and I'm desired.

My hands cover my cheeks as they pink with thoughts of Johnny. Dexter pulls up a bar stool and sits. "It was nice running into you and Johnny last night."

"It was," I lie.

"But you really hurt Drew."

Rolling my eyes, I huff out a small chuckle as I grab myself a water from the cooler under the bar. I unscrew the cap and take a quick sip; the coolness doing little to calm my nerves. "Nope"—I screw the cap back on—"he hurt himself when he cheated on me."

"Come on, Rachel, we both know he messed up and wants to fix this. He still loves you."

"He told you that?"

"He did. Last night, after we left."

With a shake of my head and a sigh, my disbelief hangs heavy in the surrounding air. "Okay, I am not cool with you talking about our past relationship with him. It's none of your business."

"I just want you to be happy."

Oh, please. He just wants to keep us all under this roof to control us.

"Well then, you should be thrilled because I am with a man who is making me the happiest I have been my whole life."

He clicks his tongue. "Johnny isn't the right man for you. You'll see."

I shrug. "I guess we will."

"He's going to disappoint you. Drew and I—"

I'm done.

I slam my hands on the bar. "What do you want from me, Dexter?!" He flinches, and his eyes widen. It's rare for me to react this way around him. Normally, I would cower and conform to whatever he wants from me.

But that was me then.

Not anymore.

"If you claim to love me like you say you do, then act like it. If you preach, and I quote, 'we are family, and family stick together as one,' then stick by me and support me! And stop trying to control my life, derail me from going to nursing school, and push a man on me that I don't love or want to be with. JUST STOP!!"

Lost in the heat of my plea, I didn't even notice Micah enter the bar. He's at my side faster than I realize. "Hey, hey! What is going on?"

"Get your sister under control, Micah."

I rear my head back. "Excuse me? No man controls me! Not anymore! Are you kidding me right now? Did you not hear anything I just said to you?!" My head is burning, a searing heat spreading through my scalp. My tense, rigid stance causes my elbows to lock. Out of habit, my left hand rubs my right elbow.

Dexter only stares at me, and I study his face. It's void of any affection. No empathy or understanding. I see nothing.

Which causes an enormous hole to open in my heart. Uncle Dexter raised us. He was a good provider. And I know he loves me. But he changed when his dad died, and he took over Dexter's. The love of power and money clouded all of his judgement. His heart then grew cold, and a craving for control overtook him. Even control over me and Micah.

I will admit, I miss the Dexter of old. Honestly, the reason for his change doesn't matter to me anymore. I'm not his therapist. All I know is I am a thirty-year-old woman who is ready to live her life with the man she loves. A man who loves her unconditionally. A man who supports her, cheers her on, and wants the best for her.

Johnny is it for me.

And now, all of Johnny's warnings about this man are playing in my head on a loop. He knew from day one that Dexter was trouble. On so many occasions, he tried to warn me. Telling me to be careful.

Dexter is my family. Other than Micah, he is my only family. I just want us to … stick together as one.

That hope is long gone.

I turn to Micah. "Will you be okay for like an hour?"

"Where are you going, Rachel?" Dexter asks.

With my back to him, I ignore his question and address my brother. "I just need some air. I'll be back in an hour."

Micah's eyes flick to Dexter briefly before landing on me. "Take as much time as you need. And tell him I said hi." He knows where I'm going.

As I'm undoing my apron from my waist, Dexter protests. "Rachel, I am your boss, and I did not give you permission to leave." No longer acknowledging him, I grab my purse from under the bar and sling it around my shoulder.

I waltz past him with my head held high. He's practically foaming from the mouth, spitting as he rants. "Rachel, if you walk out that door—"

I turn on my heels. "You'll what? Fire me? Go right ahead. I couldn't care less," I spat at him.

We stand off, his chest heaving and his breath coming in short, sharp gasps. A thick tension engulfs us. He knows I'm not backing down, so his shoulders slump, surrendering. "You have one hour," he says through gritted teeth as he gets out his phone, texts someone, and waltzes back to his office.

I'll take two.

Me: Hey, are you still at Scott and Laura's?

I toss my phone into the console, waiting for Johnny's reply, my leg shaking with anxiety. After that heated exchange with Dexter, I need him. My phone pings almost immediately.

Johnny: I'm here. We are ordering pizza soon. Everything OK?

Me: I just need to see you.

> Johnny: Wait. Aren't you working today?

> Me: I am. I was. I'm not. I don't know.

> Me: It's a long story.

> Johnny: Of course, love. We are all here.

> Me: Ok thanks. Love you.

> Johnny: Love you more.

I don't doubt that last text.

Thirty minutes later, I pull into Scott and Laura's driveway, and Johnny greets me at the door. I jump out and practically run to him. "Hey, sweetie, what is—" I crash into hard muscle and wrap my arms around his waist. "Well, this is a surprise," he says through a chuckle that rumbles through his chest and encases me in his secure arms.

I angle my head up and peer into his deep eyes, full of concern. "What's going on?" His voice softens as he smooths his hand down my head.

"I got into a massive fight with my uncle," I choke out, trying to contain my tears.

"Wanna talk about it?"

"Yeah." He releases me, wrapping his calloused hand around my wrist and leading me to the swing on the front porch. We both sit, and I rest my legs over his. He immediately skims his fingers along my thigh.

I rapidly word-vomit out the entire argument between my uncle and me, trying to catch my breath between sentences. He listens.

As soon as I finish, I exhale and rest my temple on his arm that's stretched out behind me. His feet continue to rock the swing. The faint sound of laughter coming from the living room behind us fills the outside air. The chains squeak.

Back and forth.

Back and forth.

Back and forth.

"What are you going to do?" he asks.

"I was hoping you could tell me that." We both chuckle, the laughter warm and comforting.

Back and forth. More squeaking.

"I can't tell you what kind of relationship to have with your uncle, Rach. That's your decision to make. But I will tell you this." I regard him, anticipating. "Live your life. Do what makes you happy, and don't let anyone tell you what that is. Not even me. You are a strong, independent, sexy woman."

"What does being sexy have to do with anything?" I ask through a giggle and pink cheeks.

"I just like to throw that into random sentences here and there to remind myself that I have been lucky enough to land you. Kinda like, 'Hey Rachel, wanna go catch a movie? You are a strong, independent, sexy woman.' Or 'Rachel, need help cleaning up tonight? By the way, you are a strong, independent, sexy woman.'"

I playfully slap him on the chest through my giggles. "You make me happy. The happiest I have ever been in my whole life," he declares, then leans forward and kisses me softly.

"Ugh!" I dramatically exclaim as I roll my head back. "I don't want to go back to the bar tonight." I shimmy closer and snuggle into him, his scent warming me from the inside out.

"Then don't. Stay here with us. Mallory would have an aneurysm if you stayed."

Chewing on my bottom lip, I consider his offer. It is Sunday, so Micah and the other bar waitresses could handle it. Suddenly, staying here with this family—people who are slowly burrowing their way into my heart—seems a lot more enjoyable.

"Okay ... I'll stay."

Johnny's head recoils. "Really?" I nod in agreement. His fist bumps into the air. "Yes! Best Sunday ever!"

I shoot a text to Micah.

Me: I'm staying.

Micah: I figured. Have fun, sis. Love ya. We can handle this.

Johnny swings my legs off of him and stands in front of me, extending his hand. I glide my palm over his, and he helps me up, then leads me to the door.

"Hey guys! Guess who's coming to dinner?!" he shouts into the living room as we enter. Mallory's head whips around. We make eye contact, and the biggest smile I have ever seen stretches across her face. She sprints off of the couch and launches herself into my arms. Simultaneously, four sets of eyes widen upon the contact.

Because of her autism, Mallory doesn't like touch of any kind. She has what she likes to call a Hug List. A list of people that she gives hugs to. It's small and elite and only family.

And I think I just made the cut.

22

A Loving Nudge

Johnny & Rachel

Johnny

*H**ow is this my life right now?*

This thought runs through my head a lot. I have no clue how everything is so unbelievably perfect.

For starters, I've fallen in love with the most incredible woman.

Then, in a total plot twist, I'm actually enjoying being in a God-forsaken pool league.

And as an added bonus, I've started teaching the game a little on the side.

My family is happy and healthy, business is booming.

Life is freaking fantastic!

And every time I'm with Rachel, my future is always front and center. Visions of babies, changing diapers, school drop-offs, T-ball games, and growing old together play on a constant loop in my head.

Hell, most men my age have grown kids heading off to college. Me? I'm just getting started.

What can I say? I've always been a late bloomer.

A goofy grin crosses my lips as I pull into Rachel's drive. Today, I'm picking her up for our date, and I have something different planned. She won't be expecting it, *and* I hope she doesn't get mad at me.

Also, Rachel is a huge baseball fan, so I was able to snag some tickets for the Pittsburgh/Chicago game next week from Slick. Turns out he has a nephew that works for the team, and he needs some work done at his house. It was time to barter. So in exchange for tickets right behind home plate, I'm going to do an addition on his nephew's garage. Total win-win.

When Rachel asked what to wear today, I told her to dress casually and to bring her ID. Which she found strange, to say the least.

Before I can get out of the car, she hops out of the house and walks towards my truck, looking radiant as always. It's a balmy August afternoon, and the breeze picks up slightly, causing her loose, flowing shirt to blow in the breeze. She's wearing the cutest short shorts that are frayed on the ends. Her hair is falling around her shoulders, catching the sunlight as she strides toward me, being adorable. I notice, however, that her slight limp is back today. Her hips must be bothering her.

Before she can reach me, I slam shut the truck door behind me as I scoop her into my arms, and she yelps slightly. The smell of *her,* coconut and summer, fills the surrounding air as we kiss.

Reluctantly, I lower her back to the ground. "Wow. What was that for?" she asks, trying to catch her breath.

"For being you." I kiss the top of her nose, then walk around to the passenger side of my truck to hold the door open for her.

She climbs in, nervous energy bouncing off of her in waves. "Are you going to tell me where we are going?"

"You'll know when we get there." She rolls her eyes at my retort.

"I hate surprises, you know."

I smirk at her because, yeah, I know.

We drive the twenty minutes to our destination while she plays twenty questions, trying to get the information out of me. She won't.

"We are almost there," I promise as I kiss her knuckles, and nerves swim in my gut. Where I'm taking her is an enormous risk. It's a little trick I learned from observing Laura and Scott with Mallory.

Given Mallory's disabilities, she can lack bravery with trying new things. So at times, Laura and Scott give her what I like to call a 'loving nudge.' A little push in the right direction. And every single time, it has worked out.

Not that Mallory and Rachel are similar with their disabilities, but Rachel lacks self-confidence, just like Mallory does.

So today, I am going to give Rachel a loving nudge.

We make the turn onto One University Drive, the main campus road of Ohio Northeastern University.

I glance at Rachel; her gaze is unwavering, and a sudden stillness falls over her, the silence heavy with unspoken fear. "Johnny, why are we at ONU?"

"You'll see."

She cranes her neck, taking in the sights of the vast campus. I approach a bend that leads straight to a building I'm taking Rachel to. The sign out front is hard to miss.

ONU DEPARTMENT OF NURSING ADMISSIONS OFFICE

I pull my truck into a parking spot and kill the engine as I turn to face her. She's stoic, still staring straight ahead.

Her hand shakes slightly as I interlace our fingers together. "So, look, don't be mad," I begin.

"I'm not mad," she counters. Staring. Only staring.

"I just wanted to bring you here and talk about this. We don't even have to go inside today. But if you want to, I will go with you. And if you say you can't, that's okay, too."

She nods, never veering her gaze off of the two-story building.

"Rachel, I know this is what you want. Your face always lights up when you and Laura talk about her job. You get practically giddy when she tells you about a patient case or talks about a surgery she assisted with." She continues to stare. "I never thought hearing about heart surgery could make someone giddy, but somehow, it does with you."

"It truly is fascinating." A lazy smile settles on her lips.

"Rachel." She faces me, unreadable. "There is nothing I want more in this life than to see you happy and thriving. Doing something that you love, something that brings you joy. This is it." I point to the building. "And I promise to help you in any way that I can. I'll help you study, I'll drive you to class, I'll pump you full of coffee to help you cram for an exam. Whatever it takes. I'll even pay for—"

"Nothing," she interrupts me. "You'll pay for nothing. I have the money."

My heart stops. *Is she seriously going to do this?*

"Are you upset I brought you here?"

Her gaze locks onto our interlocked fingers, and she shakes her head. "No. I'm not upset." She lifts her head, her bright eyes meeting mine, a slow smile spreading across her face, crinkling the corners of her eyes. "No one has ever believed in me as much as you have. I didn't think it was possible, but I love you more now than I did five minutes ago."

Okay, there's no way that *doesn't get acknowledged.* I tug her toward me and pull her close, her hair soft as silk between my fingers as my lips meet hers in a sweet kiss.

She looks back at the building, rolling her bottom lip into her mouth. As she contemplates, I attempt to put her mind at ease. "Like I said, you don't have to do this today. I just wanted you to know that you have my full support."

"I want to." Determined and so sure. "I want to register."

"Yes!" I exclaim as I clap my hands. "That's my girl!" I grasp the handle to open the door. "Let's go then."

She reaches out and catches my arm, stopping me. "Wait." I pivot to face her, curious about her sudden reluctance. "I want to do this by myself." She takes in the building again. "I can't explain it, but I want to stand on my own when I say to whoever is in there, 'I'm here to register for nursing school.'" She redirects her attention to me. "Does that make sense?"

I sigh in relief that she's not backing out. And I'm proud. Oh, so proud. "It makes so much sense. But I'll be right here, waiting for you when you're done."

"Thank you. Thank you for bringing me here and pushing me."

"Always."

Rachel

I'm standing at the receptionist desk, one hundred percent questioning this decision.

I rub my elbow. *What am I doing?*

I should have had Johnny come in here with me because without his 'Go Rachel!' enthusiasm, I've reverted to 'I can't do this.'

The sign at the desk reads, "Be back in 10 minutes," and I decide that this is my out. As I stand here, staring at the sign, my heart pounding, all of my typical self-loathing doubts bubble to the surface, tasting bitter as usual.

I'm too broken.

Definitely not smart enough.

My RA will get in the way.

You're no good, Rachel.

Defeat settles in my heart as I let out an enormous sigh. "What am I doing?"

As I turn on my heels to leave, footsteps pounding hardwood come from behind me. "Hello, can I help you?"

Darnit. Didn't make my hasty exit fast enough, apparently. Now I'm going to have to talk to a person.

"Um ... no, that's okay." I stumble over my words. "I was just leaving," I say as I reach for the door handle.

"Are you Rachel Garcia?" the older woman asks.

How in the world does she know my name?

I turn. The woman appears to be in her sixties with reading glasses perched on her smooth, gray hair, styled in a blunt bob, her eyes reflecting a lifetime of experience. She appears kind, her smile is soft, and her words come out sweet. I decide I like her right away. "He said you were tall and beautiful and that you might bolt. He wasn't wrong." Her chair scrapes across the floor as she sits and brings the glasses low on her nose.

Please speak English, lady. I shake my head at all the confusing words spilling out of her mouth. "I'm sorry. What?"

"Well, yesterday, a tall drink of water walked in here and told me you might change your mind once you entered." She fans herself with her hand. "Hubba hubba. He's a handsome fella, that's for sure. You are one lucky lady."

"Johnny was here?" Nothing is making sense.

"Sure was. He came and told me he was going to bring you and that you had some doubts about going to nursing school." She points her finger at me, glaring from above her glasses. "We will circle back to that, by the way."

I nod sharply. "Got it."

"After that, he proceeded to tell me how extraordinary you are. He actually made me late for a meeting because he wouldn't stop. Rachel this and Rachel that. That man is over the moon for you, little missy." My cheeks pink as my gaze lands on the floor. "I tell ya, if my ex had spoken about me the way that man praised you, we would still be married.

"Then, about an hour ago, he came back again and handed me this." She grabs a long white envelope from the corner of her desk and extends it out to me. "He gave me very strict instructions to give this to you if you wanted to bail. Which I'm guessing you were considering. Am I right?" I nod. "He flashed me the most amazing dimples I have ever seen. How could I resist?"

I laugh out loud. "I tried. It doesn't work."

"Anyway, said that I was to tell you to read that before you left." She stands from her chair and pulls out a box of chocolate-covered strawberries from the bottom drawer. "To sweeten the deal, he gifted me these." Her eyes light up with excitement. "I'll be right in the next room enjoying my treat and give you some privacy." She exits out the same door she entered through.

Reluctantly, and with my stomach in knots, I sit in a chair that lines the wall behind me. With shaking hands, I run my finger over the words he has written on the front.

My Love.

Paper ripping echoes through the small office space as I pull out a hand-written letter.

From Johnny.

Rachel,

If you are reading this, then I know that my new friend Cindy came through for me. I knew I could count on her! I also know that you are scared. And that's ok. It's ok to be fearful of the big things. The things that will afford a change in our lives. I know this because you scared me.

That day I walked into Dexter's and saw you behind that bar, my world turned upside down. Talking to beautiful women always came easy for me my whole life. But you ... talking to you scared me. But I did. And man, am I glad I got out of my own head. You changed my life, Rachel. For the better.

Now please, let this opportunity change yours. Do you remember our first night under the stars when you told me you always wanted to be a nurse? Your face was brighter than the moon above us that night.

That's what I want for you. To see you pursue this and shine like the stars. So this letter is my last loving push. Don't do it for anyone else but yourself. Just know that you deserve this. You are smart and so capable. And tell those self-loathing thoughts in your head right now to take a hike. Let your actions today become louder and more powerful than those voices that are lying to you.

I love you, and I am rooting for you. No matter what you decide, I will forever be by your side.

Love,

Johnny

P.S. Oh, and one more thing. I have two more surprises for you. One is included in this letter. The other is for when you walk out of that building registered. You'll love it, I promise.

I reach inside the envelope and pull out four tickets. For the Pittsburgh/Chicago baseball game. And the seats are right behind home plate. I smile. He knows me so well.

With tears streaking my cheeks, I fold the letter and hold it to my chest. How did I get so lucky? This man, this huge force of a man, loves me and believes in me. It's time I believe in myself for once.

As determination swells inside of me, Cindy walks back into the room, full of smiles and hope. "So ... what's the verdict?" she asks as she laces her fingers in front of her, waiting for my answer.

As I wipe away my tears, I stand with conviction. "Hi, Cindy. My name is Rachel, and I am here to register for nursing school."

Cindy grins. "Well, alright then."

Thirty minutes later, I am walking out of the registration building with an ONU tote bag full of goodies and a brighter future. Cindy and I became fast friends as she told me all about her nursing journey. As I open the exit doors, with Johnny's letter tucked in my hands and Cindy's stories fresh on my mind, I know I am making the right decision.

I have never been more proud of myself. I'm strong, confident, in control of my life for the first time, and ready for this next chapter.

As I walk down the steps, Johnny's truck idles, still parked in the same spot. Another sign that he will never leave me alone. He's sitting in the driver's seat, scrolling on his phone.

He must sense my presence because his head pops up. A huge smile follows. As I get closer, he rolls down the window. "Wait right there," he commands, halting me in my tracks. Which disappoints me some because all I want to do is hug the man. His arm dangles out of the window, and I notice that it's bare. Which is odd since he was wearing a short-sleeved dress shirt when we got here. "How did it go?"

"You are looking at the newest student of the ONU nursing program!" I say, as I jut out my chin, and puff out my chest with pride.

He slams his palm onto the side of the truck door. "Yes! I am so proud of you!"

"Well, I have to take some pre-req classes first and pass an entrance exam, but if that all goes well, then it's official."

"You will. No doubt." Pride fills his response.

"So what's my surprise?"

"I'm so glad you asked," he says with a smirk.

He opens his truck door from the outside as he always does and tumbles out. That's when the most ridiculous thing I have ever seen assaults my eyes.

Something I can never unsee.

Johnny is standing ten feet in front of me, in a red and blue cheerleading uniform. Holding pom-poms.

Let me tell you, the gasp that I gasp. My hand flies to my mouth, and the biggest laugh erupts from my gut. "Oh, my God!"

"I told you that if you signed up for school, I would wear a cheerleading uniform." He poses, popping out his hip and resting a pom-pom-filled hand on it. "How do I look?"

Adorable. Ridiculous. Goofy.

My Johnny.

I approach him, stunned. "I didn't think you were serious. Where did you get that?" The uniform is clearly way too small for his six-foot-five frame. His hairy, tree-trunk legs are on full display beneath the flared skirt. The cut-off top of the uniform reveals his toned abs. But the best part is that he is still wearing his casual shoes. The whole thing is off the charts absurd and incredibly endearing.

"Online. I got the largest size, and it's still too small." He reaches behind his back and pulls out a wedgie, making me laugh even more. I approach him and wrap my arms around his middle, taking in this man. My very own life-size cheerleader. He peers down at me. "I always keep my promises."

"That you do." He kisses me, and how this looks to passersby is no doubt questionable.

But I don't care.

"I am so proud of you," he whispers.

"Thanks. I am pretty proud of myself, too." He grins, and I place a finger into one of his dimples. "And thank you for my letter. And the tickets."

"I thought you would need one last loving push."

"I did."

We stand there, arms wrapped around each other, taking in the moment for what it is. The beginning of our life together. New directions, new beginnings. New everything.

"I have a cheer ready." Instantly, I'm broken from my thoughts.

No way. I back away from him, laughing. "Don't you dare," I warn. A wicked smile crosses his lips. "Johnny ... what are you about to do?"

He throws his hands in the air, shaking the pom-poms. I try to stop him. "No, no, no..."

"Gimme an R!"

23

The Choice Is Yours

Johnny

It's been a wild week!

Everything started on Monday with the quarterfinals. My team and I sailed through those with flying colors. But once we made it to the semis, several of the guys tripped up. Nerves got the best of them, and it came down to the wire for two games. I was a nervous wreck the whole time. Because somehow, along the way, winning this whole thing became important to me. And it's not just for me, it's for them. I've been teaching these guys the game, and I want their hard work to pay off.

With tournament play, our plan of attack has always been the same. Win and get me to the last match. I guess you can compare me to the anchor leg of a swim team. Kinda like Michael Phelps.

And I never lose. Kinda like Michael Phelps.

Thankfully, we made it to the finals, which is tomorrow, and if we win, we earn a trip to Vegas for the national title.

I mean, let's face it, we are shoo-ins.

Which is why I'm here early at the bar, shooting around, getting in some practice on the table that will be the center showcase of the tournament.

Rachel isn't here yet. She had a checkup at her doctor's this afternoon. So it's just me, the music, and ... Dexter, apparently.

Because here he comes, approaching me as I lean over the table, ready to take my next shot. With shoulders back and head held high, arms swaying with each step, he appears to be on a mission. His eyes, intense and unwavering, lock on me. I abandon the shot I had in my sights and stand, leaning my weight on my pool cue, the table separating us.

"*Dex*. What can I do for you?"

"It's Dexter," he replies through gritted teeth. I grin. "Actually, yes. There is something I need you to do for me."

Dear Lord. A favor? He can't be serious.

"I'm pretty sure I'm doing a lot for you as of late. Loving your niece being at the top of that list."

God, I love throwing that jab out there and reminding him he no longer controls her.

He clicks his tongue. "It's true. I've never seen her happier."

"You're welcome." I lean down and take the shot that was ready and waiting for me. The three ball careens along the green felt, but Dexter's meaty paw stops it.

"I need you to throw the final match tomorrow," he deadpans. As if he said a statement so mundane, instead of something that is entirely out of the realm of possibility for me.

Standing abruptly, I huff out a laugh. "You can't be serious?"

"I'm very serious."

"And let me guess. If our team loses, you get a nice hefty payout, am I right?"

"I always knew you were smart."

I grab the blue cube of chalk and rub it over the tip of my cue, not sparing him a glance as I examine the table. "Absolutely not."

He doesn't take my dismissal of his plan as his cue to leave. He continues to stand and watch me play as patrons wander into the bar, oblivious to our standoff.

"I don't think you understand. I'm not asking."

"No, I don't think *you* understand." I round the table to get closer to him. "I have never lost a match on purpose in my life, and I don't plan on starting now. What happened, Dex? Short on funds, so you need people to bet on me, then when I lose on purpose, your purse becomes heavier? Not happening. I will not rig this match for you. Your poor and shady bookkeeping isn't my concern. Find a new lackey to do your bidding because you're barking up the wrong tree. Maybe Drew is available."

"I don't like to call it rigged. It's more of striking a balance," he taunts.

I wave my hand at him dismissively. "Call it whatever you want. Keep me out of it."

He's silent for a few beats as I continue to shoot. He won't go, his gaze never leaving me, full of tension, analyzing. He has more blows to hit me with; I know it.

Within a single beat, he does. "Now, now, Johnny. Shutting me out isn't in your *or* your family's best interest."

This grabs my attention. My back goes ramrod straight as the hair on the back of my neck stands on end. The anger builds. I throw my cue on the table, storm toward him, and stand over this puny excuse of a man. "What did you just say? Are you threatening my family?" My blood is boiling, hot as lava.

"Throw the match, and your family will be just fine. If you choose not to"—he shrugs—"well, you won't want to know what happens."

I see red.

With little effort, I grab onto his suit lapel, pick him up, and slam him onto the table. As his back hits the rails, a loud thud echoes throughout the bar, catching the attention of the handful of people that are here. Their yelps of surprise fill the bar. Leaning over him, my face inches from his, I issue my warning. "Stay. Away. From. My. Family." The words come out full of venom. Spit flies out with each word, coating his face.

He laughs. Actually laughs. "The choice is yours," he taunts.

Rage is pulsing through my head, beating in my ears. All of my focus is on Dexter, which is why I don't hear her.

"JOHNNY!" Her voice, shrill, raw, and urgent, slices through the anger clouding my mind, snapping me back to reality. She's running toward me, her face a mask of terror, eyes wide with fear, and hair flying behind her.

With a shove, I let go of Dexter and step away, observing his panting from what just transpired. He stands, tugging hard on his suit jacket and meticulously smoothing out the front. The rustle of the fabric a contrast to the nervous beat of my heart. Rachel reaches us, out of breath from her sprint. I can't imagine how that must have looked. Suddenly, disbelief at my reaction sinks into my gut, weighing me down.

She grabs my arm. "Are you okay?" I nod, lying. Her attention pings to her uncle, searching for answers. "What is going on?"

"Ask lover boy," Dexter answers as he walks past her, confusion painting her features. He takes a determined step toward me. "You know what to do."

With his same overconfident swagger, he waltzes out of the bar, patrons gawking, leaving behind the scent of his cheap aftershave.

I grab Rachel's wrist and practically drag her to the back of the bar, where the tables remain covered, and the light is dim, shrouding us in darkness.

Tugging at my hair from its roots, I pace. My lungs can barely keep up with my labored breaths. Rachel just stands and watches me. "Johnny ... what's going on?"

I plant my hands firmly on my hips, the weight of what I need to tell her pressing in on me. "Your uncle wants me to throw the final match tomorrow."

"What?!" she screeches out, then glances around, realizing how loud she was. She lowers her voice. "But that makes little sense."

"Think about it, Rach," I implore. "He knows everyone will bet on me. I'm the sure thing. Then, when I lose, on purpose, he—"

"Walks away big," she says, realizing the situation for what it is. "Why would he do that?"

With a frustrated sigh, I cycle through the possible reasons. "I have no clue. Greed, financial troubles, power, control, take your pick." She stares at me, her frown tight. "But that's not the worst part."

"What? What's the worst part?"

The words catch on my tongue because I'm still in shock myself, my senses still dull from what happened. "He ... he threatened my family if I didn't do it."

A strangled gasp breaks out while she wraps her arms around her body. "Do you think he would actually follow through on that threat?"

I throw my arms in the air, a silent scream building in my chest, then smack them on my legs in frustrated defeat. "I don't know, Rachel!" I rub my hand down my face, wishing for any sort of escape from this madness. "You're the one who told me people disappear with Dexter. So, yeah ... I kinda believe him. I have never thrown a match."

With determination, she stalks over to me and cups my face. Her touch is already doing wonders, bringing down my blood pressure. She's my center. My north star. "Win. Do you hear me?" I scan her face, her eyes focused yet stern. "Win. I am *done* letting that man have an ounce of control over us. He's trying to intimidate you, control you. Don't let him. There is no way he would hurt anyone that I love. He's full of empty threats."

She's right. I know she's right.

But... "You have said yourself that people who have crossed him have disappeared. What if—"

"Shh," she whispers as she places her index finger on my lips, the smell of her lotion wrapping around me like a warm blanket. Suddenly, my shoulders relax, my thoughts come into clearer focus.

My arms coil around her waist, and I pull her into me. "Okay. I'll win. For us."

"For us."

24

It Will Make Beating You That Much More Fun

Johnny

It's the day of the final.

I'm in my truck, the engine humming beneath me, on my way to Dexter's, as a thousand and one thoughts race through my mind like a runaway train. The sheer number of them overwhelms me; I can't keep them all straight.

My pool cue rests beside me on the passenger seat, and as much as this stick of maple has been my constant companion for most of my life, I wish it was Rachel sitting next to me right now.

She was beside me last night, though. After Dexter's, she came back to my place, and we snuggled on the couch, talking through what might happen today.

I actually contemplated throwing the match, just to keep my family safe. But she wouldn't allow for it. Her exact words were, "If you throw this match, I will never speak to you again."

Well, that was that. Because not speaking to Rachel again is an option that is never on the table.

Having her in my arms made everything better. She eventually dozed off, looking like an angel. It was in that moment that I knew I was going to ask her to be my wife. I have no clue when it's going to happen. But the thought of waking her so she can go home was tearing me in two.

Because I want it.

The life.

I want to see her, a vision in white, walking down the aisle. I want to feel the weight of her gaze as she approaches me, like the goddess she is. I want to wake up next to her every morning, the warmth of her skin against mine, for the rest of our lives. I want to see her, fresh from a shower, her skin glowing, still damp, and smelling faintly of her body wash. I want to watch her with our children, holding their tiny hands as infants, then chasing them as giggling toddlers. I want her hand in mine, sitting close, while our daughter says "I do." I want us to create beautiful memories with our grandchildren together. Then, as the years turn us old and gray, I want to sit with her on that porch swing outside, our wrinkled hands clasped, sharing memories of our wonderful life.

I want it all.

When I kissed her goodnight, I was already making plans to buy a ring this weekend. The sooner, the better, if you ask me.

At the light right before the block where Dexter's sits, I shoot out a text to her.

> Me: Almost here

> Rachel: Can't wait to see you. <heart emoji>

Nerves twisting in my stomach, I pull my truck into a parking spot, the tires crunching on the gravel. And, look, I am a guy that never gets nervous. Well, except when I wanted to talk to Rachel for the first time. Other than that, I am calm and collected in just about any situation.

A final exam that I have to pass in order to graduate? No big deal.

A first date with a beautiful woman? Easy.

Waiting in a jail cell in Daytona Beach for my cousin to bail me out? Cool as a cucumber.

Throwing my life savings at a new construction business with no idea if it will be a success or failure? Whatever.

Getting ready to play in a pool tournament final I have to throw or the pool league's owner may or may not do God knows what to my family? Yep. That will do it.

The smell of exhaust mingles with the night air as I sit in my truck. The flickering neon sign of Dexter's casts an eerie light, and I wonder what awaits me on the other side of that door.

Killing the engine, the sudden ping of my phone notification slices my thoughts. A nervous smile touches my lips as I reach for the phone, half-expecting to see Rachel's name again.

It's not.

> Unknown Number: Remember our deal.

Yeah, thanks for the little reminder, Dex.

A reminder that I don't need or want. But he knows what he's trying to do here. Intimidate me into throwing this match.

But I'm calling his bluff.

And, man, am I glad Scott isn't coming tonight. He knows it's the finals; I didn't offer for him to come and watch, and he hasn't expressed any interest. After everything that has transpired since I first joined the league, it's better that he's in the dark about it all.

With a deep inhale for courage, I grab my cue, shoving my phone with Dexter's text—unanswered—into my back pocket, and walk inside.

A flurry of activity smacks me in the face as soon as I open the door.

Geez. This place is packed!

Country music blares from the speakers. Dexter has transformed the dance floor into a sitting area for spectators to watch the match with portable stadium seating for everyone. It's wall-to-wall people. Some I recognize as players from other teams, here to watch the finals. Some are patrons I've never noticed here before. The OBGs are on their usual perches at the end of the bar, waiting for the action to start. Irene is off in the corner, taking bets.

But none of them are the one person I need more than anyone.

With a sense of urgency, I scan the bar, searching for Rachel. As I do, I zero in on a group of men emerging from Dexter's back office. Impeccably dressed in suits, all of them laughing and chatting with Dexter himself. My grip tightens around the handle of my cue.

I can't let him notice me. Not before I see Rachel.

Arms snaking around my waist bring me back. My shoulders relax at the familiar contact. Her comforting scent, which is literally summertime, envelops me.

Calming.

Soothing.

Loving.

Her.

The gentle weight of her fingers on my abdomen triggers a primal response; my hands shoot out, gripping her wrists as I whip around to face her. *She. Is. Gorgeous.* "Hey, handsome. Are you new here? I don't think I have ever seen you before," she says with a playful look in her eye. She's being cheeky. More than likely trying to put me at ease.

It's working.

How does she know exactly what I need when I need it?

And, my God, she's a vision. Her long, silky chestnut hair is cascading over her shoulders, smooth and sleek. She's wearing her usual work attire. Ripped jeans, a Dexter's tank top; this one is green, my favorite color. Her long eyelashes flutter over her brown eyes, and the pink lip gloss on her lips is an invitation for a kiss.

So I oblige.

Softly, my mouth floats over hers, and she returns the affection, letting me know she is with me. Present. As she always is.

I pull back, a sticky, sweet smear of pink lip gloss now all over my mouth. "Is this the greeting you give all new customers because, if so, this is my new favorite bar?" She grins at my teasing.

She runs her hand down the buttons of my maroon untucked shirt. Pressed to perfection, as always. "Are you here with anyone?" she purrs, still playing make-believe.

"I am now." I flash my dimples as she wraps her hand around my neck and draws me in for another kiss. Any and all nerves I had are now gone. Swept away by Rachel and her presence.

We break apart. "How are you feeling today?" I ask, my concern for her health trumping anything else.

"The usual. Achy all over, my elbows are on fire, and my hips are locking up. But nothing four Tylenol can't handle."

I run my hand over the side of her neck, empathy and sadness filling my chest and squeezing. "I'm sorry, love." If I could, I would take this burden from her and transfer it to me. In a second. No questions asked.

She shrugs as if her pain is no big deal. "It's fine, and I'm used to it. Besides, I wouldn't have missed this for the world."

I pull her in for another kiss, the taste of her lipstick still lingering. A thank you for always being there for me, cheering me on. As our lips stay locked, a presence looms near us. Watching.

"Johnny," the voice starts, "nice of you to show."

With a jolt, Rachel and I separate, our gazes instantly drawn to the source of the interruption.

It's Drew Who.

My opponent for this final match, my girlfriend's ex and all-around nemesis. I loathe the man.

His eyes narrow into slits, the muscles around them tightening with irritation. He's more than likely drunk on jealousy; you can practically smell the fumes of resentment rolling off him. Good. I hope he vomits, passes out, and wakes up with a hangover.

He tries to continue the conversation I didn't ask for. "Are you ready to—"

My finger shoots up, a quick, sharp motion, to cut him off. "One second." Turning to Rachel, I run my thumb across her mouth, the slightly sticky, sweet residue of the gloss coming away. A wicked grin stretches across her lips.

"You have a little right here," she says, her fingers brushing lightly against my lips, wiping away the glossy shine. "I'll make sure to add more later," she whispers with a knowing smirk.

Oh, she better.

We know what we are doing. And we don't care.

We both pivot back to Drew as I wrap my arm around her waist and tug slightly.

He clears his throat, and if I'm not mistaken—and I rarely am—fear flashes across his features. It's fleeting, but I saw it. "As I was saying, are you ready to get beaten?"

He can't be serious.

It appears again. The fear. Small beads of sweat form along his upper lip. He's trying so hard to appear calm and in control. But he's failing. Miserably.

And I have no idea what kind of pressure Dexter has him under. But I am one hundred percent sure that Drew Who is in on this little scheme. Does he want to be? Don't know. And frankly, it's none of my business. The only thing I'm focused on is mopping the floor with this guy.

Standing in front of him, I cast aside any doubts about throwing this match.

Recoiling my arm from Rachel's waist, I step forward. Despite Rachel attempting to pull me back, I am determined to send a message to this guy.

Standing almost eye to eye with him, he recoils and flinches just an inch. I scan his face, pausing before I deliver my question. "You aren't afraid to play me, are you?"

Trying to gather himself together, he scoffs and shoves his hands into his pockets. "Nope," he replies sharply.

Love that. Because I know he's lying.

"Good," I answer. With a firm grip on Rachel's hand, I pull her swiftly past him. His narrowed gaze follows. But before we disappear into the recesses of the bar, I stop one last time, meeting his stare. We stand locked in a standoff, the air thick and intense, punctuated only by the clinking glasses and the commotion of conversation. "I enjoy looking my opponent in the eye and *not* seeing fear. It will make beating you that much more fun."

Let the games begin.

The finals game of choice: nine ball.

To win: best out of seven.

And it's all tied up.

We are down to the final match. Whoever wins this game wins the tournament. Each team has four players, and of course, both Drew's team and mine have chosen us to play this game head-to-head. Which means I am now staring at Drew while I rack the balls. I've observed him these last few months, and he has improved ... a lot.

Is he up to my level of play? Nope.

Is it necessary for me to stay focused and not provide him with any openings? Absolutely.

He's chalking his cue and adjusting his glove, talking to one of his teammates. The five rows of seats taking over the dance floor are full. People have squeezed themselves together, sitting shoulder to shoulder. The rest of the bar is standing room only. The hum of the crowd is full of anticipation. I have never played in front of this many people before. A sense of anxiety is weaving into my stomach, a kind of alert pressure. I feel good, tense, but good.

And it's more than just winning a free trip to Vegas. It's Dexter. It's his threats. It's my family's safety.

I glance at my watch—play begins in five minutes.

And that gives me five minutes with Rachel. She is exactly what I need to calm down.

She's sitting in the front row of the viewing area, sandwiched in between Slick and Micah. Randy and Tiny are right behind them. Glancing off to the far corner, I spot Dexter. He's watching and nods.

I know what he's expecting of me. Mistakenly, he assumes I'm going to throw this match.

He's wrong.

I grab my cue and march over to the most beautiful woman in the room. Her face breaks into a wide, radiant grin, eyes crinkling at the corners.

"You ready for this big guy?" Slick asks.

"As ready as I'll ever be," I answer and glance at Rachel, her smile now gone as she plays with a string hanging off one of the holes in her jeans.

Nerves are rolling off of her body.

"He's really improved," Tiny adds, pointing to Drew.

"I'll give the loser credit. He has gotten better." I look over, and Dexter has abandoned his perch and is now talking to Drew in low hushed voices. Both of them glance in my direction. "But not great."

"That's the spirit!" Randy yells out.

Rachel stands and places her hand on my shoulder, forcing me to face her. "You okay?" she asks.

I smile, trying not to let my anxiety show. "I'll be fine. But I need a kiss, for good luck."

She places her hand on my chest. "You don't need any luck. I will give you a kiss, though." A feather-light kiss grazes my mouth. She pulls back and gives my chest a slight shove, then smacks my butt. "Now go win."

I smirk and tip my imaginary hat. "Yes, ma'am."

Drew won the coin toss for the break, so he is up, ready to start. Sliding his cue through his gloved hand once, twice, three, then four times, he readies himself to slam the cue into nine balls, neatly arranged in a diamond at the opposite end of the table. A heavy stillness descends on the crowd, broken only by the soft hum of the light above, its warm glow a stark contrast to the tense atmosphere at the table.

Sitting in a high-back chair, off to the side, buying my time, I swallow hard as Drew bends over the table, bridges his hand, and aims. This break means everything. If the nine ball pockets on the break, the match is over. Drew's team would win.

The crowd is dead silent as his left hand holds the butt of his cue gently. Just as a violinist holds their bow, steady and with confidence. He strikes, and the white cue careens down the table and collides with the nine balls. The crack is deafening, scattering the colored balls across the table. I zero in on the yellow-striped nine ball.

The break is good. But not perfect.

Plop.

Plop.

The one and five balls find homes in the pockets. The nine ball rests on the side rail.

I sigh in relief.

In nine ball, the shooter has to hit the balls in numerical order. Which means, since the one ball is already in the pocket, he needs to start with number two.

I examine the table, taking in the positions of all the balls, already knowing how the whole game will play out. Drew is doing the same. He chalks his cue, looks me square in the eye, and smirks. "Two ball, side pocket," he proclaims. As he bends, for a fraction of a second, his eyes dart to Dexter. I glance over, and Dexter grins.

A silent communication between the two. A conversation only they are in on.

And they are secretly talking about me.

The shot on the table for the two ball is one of the easiest in all of pool. A ten-year-old, picking up a cue for the first time, could make it.

And that's when I know he will miss it.

On purpose.

The blue ball rests on the edge of the side pocket. The cue ball? A good foot in front of it, lined up perfectly. If Drew hits it right, the two would fall in the pocket, and the cue would rest directly behind the three, positioned to land in the corner pocket.

As predicted, Drew hits the cue way too wide. The ball creeps along the nap of the green felt and misses the two while hitting the rail and bounces back. The crowd gasps. Dexter smiles.

Drew pushes himself up and backs away from the table, mock disappointment written all over his face. "Well, damn. That's too bad." He waltzes around the table to sit on his stool next to mine, separated by a standing table. "You're up, Givens," he says with entirely too much ease and calm for a man who has seen me play. He knows what I'm capable of. He knows this is a piece of cake for me.

Which means he knows what Dexter expects of me.

But what he doesn't know is that I am going to mop the floor with him.

Because I'm Johnny Givens.

My fingers embrace the polished shaft of my cue, the softness of the felt always ready. My life is this rectangle of wood and slate covered in green or blue. Colored balls, solid and striped, spin and roll at my command.

It's the color and shape of my world.

And I'm about to crush Drew's world. And Dexter's.

Without saying a word, I rise from the chair and grab the cube of chalk, rubbing it across the tip. "Two ball, side pocket." Leaning over the table, I line up my shot. With the perfect amount of English, the two ball falls.

Plop.

With no hesitation, I walk to the opposite side of the table and take my next position. "Three ball, corner."

Clank.

The cue rolls back and comes to a dead stop behind the four. "Four ball, corner pocket."

Clink.

"Six ball, side pocket."

SMACK!

UGH! I hit this one too hard. The six ball lands violently in the side pocket, the cue banks off of the side rail, resting way out of position for the seven ball, derailing my entire plan of attack.

Adrenaline and nerves got the best of me. Murmurs from the crowd fill my ears.

Come on!

Like the bloodhound he is, Drew sniffs out my tension at seeing my predicament.

And he pounces.

"I thought you were better than that, Givens." Ignoring him, I round the table, studying it, deciding on my next move. I lean over, meticulously tracing imaginary lines and angles in my head, the way a golfer carefully studies his putt, visualizing the perfect arc.

He continues his taunts, but this time, his objective is clear. He wants to get in my head.

And under my skin.

"Rachel is a great kisser, isn't she?" My grip on my cue tightens as the temperature in my head rises. "Does she still like it when you nibble on her ear?" My breathing grows ragged as I clench my teeth and circle the table, running my fingertips along the wooden rail. Doing my best to allow this table's energy to ground me.

A low chuckle rumbles in his chest. "You know, she told me once, and I still remember the way she said it, all low and raspy, that nobody's kiss ever felt as perfect as mine." This stops me cold.

Why am I letting this guy get to me?

While I'm leaning over the table, I focus on Rachel.

A playful grin spreads across her face as she rolls her eyes, clearly amused and unfazed by his ridiculous words. Then she opens her mouth, inserts her finger, and makes a fake gagging face. Slick chortles next to her.

I hold my stance over the table but lower my head in amusement. It's the exact playful banter I need to get my head on straight and finish this guy. His words are meaningless.

He's meaningless.

With a playful wink thrown in her direction, I straighten as the chalk squeaks against the worn leather tip of my cue. I'm ready to end this. "Well, Drew, I'll be sure to ask her tonight if that's still the case." I bend over the table, my cue in hand, ready to strike. "When we are back at my place. Celebrating." Before I hit the white cue, I glance back at Rachel. "Alone." She gives me an air kiss.

"Seven ball, side pocket."

The cue ball curves around the eight, hitting the seven and sending it down to the side pocket.

Clack.

"Eight ball, side pocket."

Plop.

Drew squirms in his seat as he grabs his drink, taking a sip. Because this is it. The moment of truth.

I could do it. Right here, right now. I could throw the match, miss the nine ball, and give Dexter what he wants. But I know that won't be the end. Dexter would own me. He would have this one secret and hold it over me and use it to get what he wants or needs. Who knows for how long? By throwing this match, I am no better than Dexter. I would be a cheat and a liar. There is no way I could live with myself.

That's not the man Rachel fell in love with. That's not the man I want to be for her.

I have no clue what happens next or what the consequences will be.

I only know that I have to do the right thing.

The temperature in this bar just rose about twenty degrees. A collective stillness hovers over the crowd, broken only by the occasional nervous cough as they anticipate, watching.

Watching me.

I stand over the table, resting my hand on the cool wood of the rail. I squeeze my eyes shut, letting myself live in a world where Rachel is mine. She belongs to me. We belong to each other. A world before Dexter threatened me and my family. A world where I walk into a bar my company remodeled and see her for the first time. A world where I'm washing her hair, then kissing her. A world where I'm wearing a cheerleading uniform, cheering for her success. Literally. A world where we are in my family's living room, sharing pizza, laughing, being a family.

A world that includes us.

Because as soon as I sink this nine ball, our world will be different. I don't know how or why.

But different.

I open my eyes and look at Drew. He smirks.

I turn and take in Rachel. She mouths, 'I love you.'

Leaning over this table for the last time, I bridge my hand, hold my cue, and line up. But before I pull back, I make eye contact with Dexter.

He shakes his head in warning.

"Nine ball, corner pocket."

I hit the white, chalk-smudged ball. It connects with the nine ball … perfectly.

The crowd gasps.

Number nine rolls with a gentle, satisfying hum along the rail. It catches the corner of the side pocket, oscillates, then it stills as it teeters on the edge. A hush falls over the bar as everyone holds their breath, leaning forward, anticipating. Some in the bleachers stand to get a better look. Then…

Plop.

Dexter drops his head as the crowd erupts in hysterics.

Rachel's squeals are all I hear as I throw my cue onto the table and run straight for my love. I reach her, lift her up, and spin her around, peppering her face with kisses. My team rushes over, and the entire bar is now encircling us.

Spectator after spectator offers their congratulations.

My arm never leaves Rachel's shoulder as I glance one last time over at Dexter.

But he's gone.

25

That Was a Little Overdramatic

Johnny

P ulling into my driveway, I can't erase the massive grin on my face. It's been there ever since the yellow-striped ball did its job landing in the pocket, and I scooped Rachel in my arms.

The celebration didn't stop after.

There was the trophy presentation, then pictures, then the usual recounting with my team of the whole match. We made plans for Vegas. For a few hours, we felt like kings, basking in the glory of our imaginary kingdom, recounting tales of our conquests.

It was incredible.

I left roughly an hour ago, just to come home and shower. Then, I'll head back to help her close up so we can celebrate alone. A sense of urgency propels me to hurry because that is something I am really looking forward to.

Mostly, I can't wait to prove Drew wrong and show her who really is the best kisser.

Is it petty? Sure. But it will be fun showing her who the better man is.

As I get out of my truck, my world is free, complete, and full of hope, and—
SNAP!

My head whips around toward the noise, my ears straining to pinpoint the source.

What was that? An animal? I scan the area around my truck and home, but nothing is amiss.

Just me, the crickets, and passing cars.

Whipping my keys around my finger, I shut the door and head to the garage. I lift the keypad panel and type in my code. Rachel's birthday. With a slow drag, my garage door opens as my pool table greets me. I swear she smiles. This beautiful rectangle has meant more to me than—

SNAP!

What the?

Once again, a sharp sound slices through my thoughts, making me jump. My yard and house are silent, each glance raising my heart rate, a rising tide of fear threatening to overwhelm me.

"Hello?" My voice strains against the black void.

Nothing.

With a tad bit of unease swirling in my gut, I hit the button to shut the garage. The huge white door starts its descent as I retreat into my sanctuary.

Creak, creak, creak, creak....

I take one, two, three steps, and that's when two things happen at once. A shadow moves in my peripheral vision as a crushing blow to my back slams me to my knees. The garage door starts an unexpected upward crawl. The jarring impact echoes in my ears alongside the grinding metal of the door.

The pain is blinding. I grab onto the rail of my table for balance.

Footsteps, lots of them, fill my ears, each one a sharp reminder of my precarious position as I attempt to stand. And that's when I hear him.

"Johnny, Johnny, Johnny," he clicks his tongue. "I warned you, didn't I?" His voice, menacing and scary, rasps like sandpaper, each word a threat. I stumble as I attempt to stand. "Get him up," he commands to whoever is behind me and trespassing on my property.

"Shut the door," he bites out his next demand. The weight of two men on either side of me is immense, their arms heavy around mine as they haul me to my feet. Their colognes overpower my nostrils. A searing, sharp pain shoots down my back. Pure white agony forces me to gasp at the jolt.

As the door descends, a metallic groan echoes in the confined space, closing us in. The burly men roughly turn me, revealing Dexter and two others besides the two gripping my arms. The smell of stale sweat and fear hangs heavy.

Now, look, I'm a big guy. Bigger than most. But these four goons are *enormous*, each nearly as large as the wrestler The Undertaker, and they fill my garage with their presence.

I'm guessing they haven't come for coffee and a quick game.

One is holding a cold, heavy metal bat, the weight of which I can still feel on my back. The other man casually rests a sledgehammer on his shoulder, the metal gleaming faintly in the dim light. And I recognize both of them. They were the ones I saw that very first night at Dexter's. Shoving that beaten-up man out the side door.

A shiver, like ice water, runs along my spine, raising goosebumps on my arms.

Rachel flashes in my head. She's with me, nestled against me in my truck, watching the stars twinkle above. The memory of her laughter, the way her eyes crinkle when she smiles—I hold on to that vision because it might be the last time I see her.

"You didn't throw the match." Dexter has a habit of pointing out the obvious.

I lift my head. The room sways slightly, as I struggle to focus on him through the haze of the earlier blow; a ringing in my ears adds to the disorientation. But I have to keep my cool. "Well, no one can say you aren't both smart and observant, Dex."

He squints at the guy branding the bat and flicks his head in my direction.

The big guy steps forward and...

"Oomph!" The bat slams into my stomach, a sharp grunt forcing its way out of me while also taking the air from my lungs. My knees buckle, but my new friends on either side of me hold me up like I weigh next to nothing. On instinct, I bend at the waist as the pain, both searing and blinding, washes over me like a white-hot wave, leaving me breathless.

I cough. Once, twice, three times. "That was a little overdramatic, wasn't it?"

"Oh, you ain't seen nothing yet," he says with a smirk. "Let him go."

Both men shove me forward at their master's bidding. When they release their grips, I yank my arms away and clutch my stomach, trying hard to hold back the vomit threatening to surface. Swaying like a drunk, I try to stand upright.

Big guy number one, who's guarding the garage door and holding the bat, reaches into the back waistband of his jeans and pulls out a manilla folder. He hands it to Dexter.

"Remember, this is all your fault. Oh, and Drew is going to Vegas in your place." With that friendly reminder, he tosses the envelope onto my table. "Open it. And don't try anything, friend."

I don't give a crap about Vegas. Drew can have the time of his life for all I care. But this envelope is taunting me. With hesitancy, I reach for the folder and unclasp the wire brad holding the flap closed. "Oh, so we are friends now, huh?" Shoving my hand inside, my fingers graze the contents, and I slide them out. *Don't try anything? What does that mea—?*

My brain short-circuits when my eyes focus on a black-and-white photo of Mallory playing in her backyard. The next picture ... Scott and me on the job. I flip to Laura, clocking in at work. Jake getting off the school bus is next.

A rising anger pulses through me, making my hands shake uncontrollably as my head throbs. Dozens of photographs of my family, of me, and of Rachel stare back at me one by one as I frantically shuffle through them.

My flipping holts because now I'm looking at our text messages. I fan through them. Months' worth of our intimate conversations. Molten hot rage courses through my veins.

My eyes land on the last photo. A grainy picture of Rachel and me in my truck, stargazing. The knowledge that our private moments were being watched, read, every kiss, every hushed word, every touch, fuels the blinding anger inside of me.

The pictures fan out onto the table as I toss them and charge Dexter like a bull to the slaughter. "You slimy, sick son of a—" The words stop on my tongue as big guy number two punches his fist into my already damaged stomach. Once again, the contact and searing pain send me to my knees.

Slamming my palm on the table, a feeble attempt to redirect the pain, I try to stand. "If you lay one hand on Rachel, so help me God, I'll—"

"You'll what?" he interrupts with a laugh. "You look pretty helpless right now, Givens." I stand as he runs his hand down his oversized belly. "Give me some credit. I would do *nothing* to hurt Rachel. I'm not a monster, for God's sake. Everything that I am doing right now and with my business is to help her and Micah. You aren't the right man for her. Drew and I will take care of her. I can promise you that."

"And like I said," he charges toward me. "You did this!" he points his finger at me. "All you had to do was miss that nine ball. That's it."

Finally, I'm able to get my bearings and stand. Even hunched over from the pain, I still tower over him. I clutch my stomach. "Oh, please. We both know that wouldn't have been the end."

If he believes a few pictures and a baseball bat to my torso will compel me to do anything for him, he must be out of his mind. Besides, he has made his point with this little sideshow. He's punishing me for winning, which has caused him to lose money.

Fine. I took it.

But right now, I need these five whack jobs to get out of my house so I can formulate some sort of plan to get Rachel and me away from this guy.

I stare directly into his eyes. "You've made your point. Now get off of my property." I pivot back to the table, and my hand stretches towards the pictures, then stops; a small, shiny object, reflecting the light, rests on the blue felt. With trepidation, I reach for it.

A flash drive.

"What the heck is this?" I study it. A knot of uncertainty tightens in my stomach as I wonder where this is now leading.

"Call it insurance."

"I'm sorry ... what?" I whip back around to face him; my sudden movement stabs my ribs, which I'm sure are broken.

"That drive"—he points to the shiny silver object resting in my palm—"contains falsified documents that implicates you in illegal gambling and tax evasion."

Okay, this is bad. Really bad.

"And I'm sure you realize that's not the only copy."

"So, what? You're blackmailing me?" This went from a lot to OH, MY GOD in seconds.

He cocks his head left then right while blinking at the ceiling, faking uncertainty. "Well ... yes and no."

With a sharp intake of breath, I pinch the bridge of my nose, the anger a tight fist in my chest. "What do you want from me, Dexter?"

He laughs with unearned confidence. "It's simple, really. Break up with Rachel, cut all ties with her, or these four fellas will pay a visit to your family." He pauses. "Let's just say I have a way of dealing with these types of ... situations."

Now the vomit is right there.

He snaps his fingers. "Oh, yeah! I almost forgot. The documents on that flash drive will be sent straight to the authorities. So not only would you lose your family and Rachel, but everything you have ever worked for will be gone."

He crosses his arms over his chest. "You see, your little stunt tonight cost me about a hundred grand. And I'm not happy. Now, I know you probably don't have that kind of money."

"I do," I answer, the words spilling out. Because I will give every red cent I have to this man in order to protect my family.

Mockingly, he nods. "Impressive. But that's not what I want."

I swallow hard. "What then?"

Through gritted teeth, he answers me and delivers his final blow. "I want you to suffer."

And he's right. I would suffer. The money is meaningless to me. But Rachel? My family? They mean more than anything else in the world; they are the air I breathe, the blood in my veins, and the very beat of my heart. To lose one or both would leave a gaping hole in my life, an unbearable emptiness worse than death. Given his history and the menacing tone of his threat, I wouldn't put it past him.

Is he bluffing?

Possibly.

Am I willing to put my family's life in danger to find out?

No. No, I'm not.

I lower my head, accepting my fate.

I've lost Rachel. My love. My life. My world.

"Do we have a deal?" His question breaks through the war that's waging in my head.

I choke out my answer. "Yes." Because at the end of the day, I would do anything to protect Rachel and my family. Even if that means losing her.

A cruel, chilling grin stretches across his face, revealing teeth like yellowed shards. "Good."

He turns to leave. "I have a request," I chuff out.

He barks out a sharp scoff. "You are in no position to be making demands."

"Allow me to go to the bar to say goodbye to her. Give us tonight. I beg you." I'm desperate, my heart pounding in my chest, and I can't believe I am asking this man for a favor, but I need this more than anything. She needs to know what her uncle just did to me. To us. And she needs to hear it from me, face to face. Maybe, just maybe, my parting gift to her will be knowledge. The knowledge she needs to cut this man out of her life for good.

He lets out a deep sigh, not happy with this idea; I can tell.

But he loves his niece.

"You have one hour." With that, he hits the button on the garage door opener, and it once again ascends to the top. "Finish it."

Dread settles in my gut because I have no idea what this final command means. The men with no weapons (that are visible anyway) follow Dex out of my garage. I'm watching them go, their retreating footsteps fading, as big guy number two approaches. He removes the sledgehammer from his shoulder and winds up as if he's about to hit a home run. I shield my face with my hands, anticipating the blow I know is coming when...

BAM!!

A jarring crack echoes through the room as the sledgehammer slams into the rail, making my head whip towards the table. Big guy number one pulls a knife from his jacket, the glint of steel flashing in the dim light, and slices the blue felt tabletop, a sickening rip slicing through the air.

They deliver blow after blow to my most loved material possession. The destruction is instantaneous. With each devastating swing of the hammer, the wood of all four rails splinters into two, showering the ground with a flurry of tiny, sharp pieces of wood.

Stunned, I struggle to catch my breath, overwhelmed by the scene unfolding before me. I'm grateful it's not me they are destroying, but I also understand the message they are sending.

The hammer's next sharp blow connects with the legs. The slate table top hits the ground at an angle, the pictures scattering across the floor.

With a finality that makes my heart sink, they stop, pivot, and walk out of my garage, leaving destruction in their wake. Big guy number one stops, his large hand engulfing the garage door opener, ready to press it. "One hour." His meaty finger jabs the button.

The door shuts.

On not just my garage, but my life.

26

It's Only Us and the Stars

Rachel & Johnny

Rachel

*B*ang! Bang! Bang!

   The loud pounding on the locked bar door causes me to jump out of my skin; I quickly hang my apron on the hook.

   "Rachel! It's Johnny. Open the door!"

   His voice is frantic and breathless, with a sense of urgency I have never heard from him before. An icy wave of fear and dread washes over me.

   Three hours ago, during the finals, my chest swelled with pride as Johnny refused to throw the match, defying my uncle's demands; his quiet strength speaks volumes as to the type of man he is. And it's one reason I love him so much.

   His integrity.

   After that last shot, he ran straight to me as the roar of the crowd rang out in my ears. I felt a surge of pride unlike any I'd known. We partied as a group, then Johnny left, while the bar was put back together, with a promise to come back and pick me up so we could celebrate alone.

But now, he's banging on the door as if he's being chased by zombies. Which is not what I expected when he returned.

Something's not right.

I round the bar just as another wave of desperate pounding begins.

"Geez, Johnny. I'm coming!" As fast as my aching hip will take me, I rush to the door, unlock it, and swing it open. There stands my man, his arm resting on the door frame, his eyes shrouded in fear, a manila envelope held high in his trembling hands.

"Your uncle is one sick son of a—"

"Whoa, whoa, whoa. What is going on?" He whizzes past me, tossing the folder on the bar. I shut the door and lock it.

"Take a look." With a pained grimace, Johnny paces the dance floor frantically, clutching his side. Intently, I watch him as my hand tremors and I grab the envelope, open it, and pull out dozens of photographs.

My stomach drops.

Picture after picture of Johnny's family. Mallory arriving at school, Laura leaving work, Johnny and Scott on the job, Johnny and me on a date, Johnny and me in his truck watching the stars, Mallory playing outside in what should be the safety of her backyard, Jake playing video games with his buddies, a photo taken through the window of Scott and Laura's.

As if this isn't bad enough, pages of our private text conversations smack me in the face. I zero in on one.

> Johnny: Is Fire and Embers ok?

> Rachel: Sounds perfect. What time?

> Johnny: Scott and Laura will meet us at 6.

> Johnny: Can't wait to see you, my love

That's why Dexter and Drew were at the restaurant that night. He intercepted our private messages.

I want to vomit.

As I flip to the last photo, a wave of nausea washes over me, and I grip my stomach. It's from yesterday. Us kissing on his front porch. And written across the picture are five ominous words:

You know what to do.

A dizzying sensation overcomes me as the room spins, blurring my vision. I blink once, then twice. And even though I know the answer to the question I'm about to ask, I muster enough courage anyway. "Johnny, how did you get these?"

With a sigh, he stops pacing, and the tension builds on his shoulders as he approaches. "Your uncle and a few of his buddies paid me a visit as soon as I got home. They handed me those." He runs his hands through his hair and tugs at it in frustration, then lets out a huff. "He gave me a warning with instructions." I've never heard Johnny's voice so raw and full of pain.

My stomach bottoms out.

I rub my elbow. "What kind of warning?" I'm having a hard time focusing as my world collapses around me.

His eyes meet mine, brimmed with fear, sadness, and unease. He opens his mouth to speak, then shuts it again, the words stopping on his tongue. Words he can't say. "I have to end things with you. Never see or speak to you again, or he will come after my family."

I stand motionless as the revelation floats in the air, weightless yet heavy with its meaning. And when it falls, the ground beneath me crumbles with its weight. Taking me and my new promising life with it.

This can't be happening.

My brain short-circuits and my throat tightens, making it hard to breathe. The question I want to ask remains cramped, unable to escape. It breaks free. "What did you say?"

"I lunged for him, but before I could act, one of his guys took a baseball bat to my stomach." He lifts his shirt, wincing. The skin on his perfect abs is red and welted.

"Oh, God!" I rush over, my hand hovering before my fingertips graze the burning, red skin; he hisses in pain, pulling away. He grabs onto my upper arm with purpose, his fingers digging in with surprising strength. Hot tears brim, blurring my vision.

With agonizing slowness, he pivots, his back stiff and tense, revealing another long welt running across his back. "They started the conversation with this."

The tears that were threatening to flow spill over my cheeks. Gingerly, I run my fingertips over his red, inflamed flesh. I shake my head as the denial of our situation takes over. "No. I'll talk to him. He wouldn't go that far. There is no way—"

"Rachel," Johnny pleads as he turns. His hand, calloused yet tender as it always is, cups my face. I search his expression, desperate for any flicker of hope or a silent understanding in his downcast eyes that we can make it through this. Any sign, no matter how subtle, that this isn't our reality.

But there's none.

Only defeat.

And sorrow.

"He's been stalking my family for months. And us ... since we met." He pauses to collect his thoughts. The anguish on his face is so profound that it physically touches me as our gazes remain locked. "He had Mallory followed. Sweet, innocent Mallory." With a sharp twist, I pull away, turning my back and stepping away, needing space. If anything happened to that amazing little human, well, the thought makes my insides queasy. Hot tears brim in his eyes as he continues, his breaths hitches. "Do you really want to take that chance?"

His footsteps, distinct against the quiet, grow closer as Johnny approaches, the rhythm pounding in my ears. He wraps his arms around my waist, his grasp firm. My fingers trace the lines of his forearms while my head falls back on his chest. He sighs in my ear. "I didn't bring it, but he also gave me a flash drive. It's full of falsified documents implicating me in his little gambling ring and tax fraud."

Stop! Just stop talking! Why does it keep getting worse?

The words are soft, but the meaning is hard and life-ending. "It would ruin me and everything Scott and I built together. I would lose my family, you, and my life would be destroyed." More tears, silent, unending tears. "I don't care about me," he confesses. "But I do care about Mallory, my family. And you."

I spin around, my arms flying around his neck, and bury my head in his chest, the rhythm of his heart somehow comforting. His chin rests on my head as we stand in the middle of the dance floor, in an empty bar, clinging to each other and the life we imagined. A life that's slipping away, second by second, the chilling awareness heavy in the air. A sense of time running out.

"How long would we have to be apart?" I choke out through strangled sobs.

"I don't know, my love," he whispers. Muted sniffles follow his uncertain words.

He's crying.

"I can't do it. I can't live without you."

Suddenly, my reality, once full of promise, is now full of dread.

Johnny

I have to let Rachel go.

For my family's protection. And for hers.

My fingers dug into her back, and I hold her so tight, terrified of crushing her.

Suddenly, she lifts her head as her eyes widen with an idea. "We can see each other in secret! I mean, that's an option, right?"

My heart bottoms out with the false hope she's grabbing at.

"No one has to know. We could meet outside of town."

She pulls away and paces frantically, her arms flailing, a torrent of words pouring from her mouth.

I watch.

Stare.

"I'll get my own place." She nods in agreement with her own idea as she chews on her finger. "Yep, that could work. Micah will cover for us, and I'm sure Scott and Laura will, too. It could be like our secret hideaway where it will just be us."

She runs over to me. I stand motionless.

"Or better yet ... we could leave."

Every muscle in my body is tense, rigid, and screaming in protest. My girl, desperate and reaching for any solution, is grasping at straws. Trying to come up with how we can make this work. With a slow, deliberate step, she returns, her hands settling on my chest, her face filled with desperate hope. "Let's just get out of here. Far away from all of this." A single tear falls over her lashes and lands on her flushed cheek, her eyes searching, hoping. "Say we can make this work. Don't leave me," she strains.

My own tears spill over, fast and hard. I've never cried this much in my whole life. Not even when my dad died.

With a deep inhale, I pull my hands from my sides and take hold of her wrists, the warmth of her skin seeping through mine. "Rachel, I don't want to," I whisper.

"Then don't!" she shouts as she jerks away from me. "We can do this, Johnny—"

"Rachel please..." I plead.

"He doesn't get to win! He can't do this." She continues to step backward, her eyes wild as she chokes out her words through sobs. "We can leave! Start over! This can't be the end. It can't—"

"Rachel, STOP!" Her eyes widen in shock at my sharp outburst, a gasp eluding her lips as she flinches away. She's never heard me raise my voice before. But I need to get her attention.

Coughing nervously and trying to regain my composure, I place my hands on my hips. "You saw the pictures. Nothing escapes his notice." I lift my shirt. "You saw my body." I point to my abdomen. "This was a warning, Rachel. We know what he is capable of. He told me that I was allowed to come and say goodbye to you tonight. Do you honestly think he won't be watching our every move after tonight to make sure we aren't together? I mean, forget about you, me, Scott, and Laura. We are adults and have lived our lives. Fulfilling lives. But Mallory and Jake? What if, to prove his point, he takes his vengeance out on them?"

The question hangs in the air, its weight forcing me to avoid her stare. "Are you truly willing to take that risk? Because I'm not."

Minutes tick by, each second sharpening the details of our new reality becoming clear. With a twist of my body, I ask, my voice a little unsure. "Are you?" The truth lives in that question. The answer circles us. I watch as Rachel stands, sobs. She squeezes her eyes shut ... and she shakes her head.

My body tenses, a searing heat blooming in my chest as if I'm holding a live grenade. And Dexter pulled the pin.

"AAAAHHH!" The scream is primal, full of sadness, fear, and anger. Storming over to the bar stools, I pick one up and chuck it, straining my already beaten body. Pain zips straight to my core. Rachel's hands shoot to her mouth as she yelps out. Leather and metal soar through the air, landing on the floor with a thud, then skids to a stop next to one of the pool tables.

We stand on either side of the dance floor, Rachel's sobs and my heavy breathing the only sound in this bar.

I scrub a hand down my face and motion for her to come to me. She runs over, and I grab her by the back of the head, pulling her to me. We collide in a hug, holding, squeezing, crying. At this moment—our last—she is warm, real, and mine. I focus on her. The way her hair is like silk in my fingers. Her breath seeping into my soul as she cries. How her body molds to mine, perfectly, snapping into place like a puzzle piece.

We always fit.

I won't let my mind go beyond the right now, to what I hold dear. Contemplating a future without her is like a betrayal to my heart and soul. It stings, bites, and chaffs in places I didn't even know it could.

We fuse our foreheads together, holding still. "Rachel—"

"No, no." She cants her head left and right, as if this is the most painful thing in the world. "Don't say it. Please don't say it."

"As much as I love you, I have to let you go."

Her eyes snap shut. "I know. I hate this ... but I know," seconds pass, minutes, an eternity. "I thought we would be together forever."

So did I.

"Sometimes forever can be shorter than we want it to be."

The vast emptiness of the bar amplifies her cries, her sobs a raw, visceral sound that cuts through the quiet as I hold her.

Dexter's.

The bar I love to hate. The bar that brought me *her.* The bar that's taking *her.*

She tears her head away from my chest, and her big brown eyes that I love so much meet mine, red, swollen, bloodshot.

Empty.

God, I'm going to miss those eyes.

"Are you going to tell Scott and Laura?" she asks.

I shake my head. "I don't know what I'm—"

"Blame me," she blurts out.

"What? No Rachel, I can't do that." No way. I won't.

She nods while swiping a tear away from the corner of my eye with her thumb. "Yes, you can. Tell them I worried too much about the age difference and that I felt our relationship was moving too fast. It's believable since those were my hang-ups in the beginning."

I say nothing, mulling it over.

"It has to be this way. Scott can't know."

My gut reactions is ... no.

But she's right. If I told Scott that Dexter threatened his family, well, I don't want to think about what his reaction would be. One thing I know ... his actions would probably land him in a lot of trouble. Life-altering trouble. And I can't do that to him or his family.

I've always been completely open and honest with Scott, hiding nothing.

Except now.

Plus, he knows me. He knows my tells. I am going to have to be very convincing for him to believe this lie. But I'll do it. For her.

"Okay," I agree. Even though I don't want to. Her shoulders sag in relief.

I glance at my watch, and the time, 11:50, is glaring at me, taunting me. Because that means I only have ten minutes left with her. My heart drops because all I want is to curl up into this moment. Live it. Breathe it.

Forever.

But I can't.

Palming the back of her head, I pull her in. I kiss her. Hard. While also tugging her to me, deepening our hold.

We break apart, and my lips wobble, trying to speak. "One last dance?"

She nods as I sweep my thumb over her bottom lip. "Okay." Releasing her arms from my body, she makes her way to the jukebox.

Our hands still intertwined yet recoiling with each step. Neither of us wanting to let go.

We reach out, our fingertips grazing until the very last moment.

She presses in some buttons, and Joni Mitchell's "Both Sides Now" fills the air. I extend my palm out and open, and she takes it. With a playful spin, a light chuckle escapes her lips, a sound as sweet as summer berries, lightening the heavy mood and moment.

This song is one of Rachel's favorites. We have listened to Joni on repeat when we would close the bar. Something else that will soon be a distant memory. The song is five minutes and forty-five seconds long, which is the remaining time I have left with my love.

And I plan on savoring every single millisecond I have her in my arms.

I weave my fingers through hers, then nestle our joined hands close to my chest. My other hand presses gently onto her lower back, tugging her to me until her curves melt into me. She places her head on my chest, and our feet sway to the music. No words are spoken. There's no point. All either of us wants is to bask in this moment.

Our entire relationship plays on a loop in my mind. The first time I saw her tending bar. How we spent that night under the stars and kissed for the first time. Our first real kiss in her house after I washed her hair. When I took her to register for nursing school. How, after every tournament win, she would run into my arms, making me feel like the most important man in the whole world.

I would die for this woman. Walk through fire for her. My life means nothing without her in it.

But both of us know what we need to do. To ensure my family's safety, we willingly make this sacrifice, no matter the cost.

And the cost is too much. Too expensive. It's bankrupting my soul.

Her tears, hot and salty, soak through my shirt as soft, heartbroken sobs never-ending. Overcome with emotion, a single tear rips from my eye, slides down my cheek, and lands in her soft brown hair. The rest of the world falls away as we plunge ourselves into this last moment together. She hooks her arm over my shoulder, and I shiver as her fingers graze the nape of my neck.

The power of her touch.

I don't know how to live without it.

Five minutes and forty-five seconds comes and goes way too fast because, before we know it, the last note fades, leaving nothing in its wake. Neither of us lets go. Our feet stop moving, and we stand holding each other.

"Rachel," I whisper. "I should probably go."

She pulls away from my chest and lifts her eyes to meet mine. The depth of emotion crashes over me like a tsunami, pulling me under. We walk hand in hand to the door slowly, and within seconds we are standing at the entrance. I take her face in my hands and lean in. Our lips brush as they did that first night in my truck. The memory pinches in my chest as the kiss deepens with a breathless urgency, perfectly matching the intensity of the moment.

We break apart, both of us panting, our chests heaving and our hearts pounding.

"I love you. So much." Her declaration? Breathy and sad.

"I love you too."

My hand reaches for the door handle, ready to leave. "Promise me something." Her words burst forth, pleading as her grip shoots out to stop mine.

"Anything."

The pained look in her eye tells me I will not like this.

"If happiness knocks on your door," she says, swallowing hard as she composes herself, "if a new relationship comes knocking, promise me you'll answer."

I gulp. Hard. She grabs my face with her hands. "Listen to me," she pleads. We stare.

"Who knows how long we will be apart. You deserve love and happiness, Johnny. So if it comes, take it. I would understand."

And she would. Somehow, some way, she would find out, and it may hurt, but she would be happy for me. Because that's who she is. The possibility, though?

Impossible.

"I can't promise that," I answer. Confusion flickers in her eyes, replacing the sadness.

I continue. "I've already answered it. And you were on the other side. My last shot at love." Taking her hand in mine, I bring it to my mouth, planting a soft kiss on her palm before laying it against my chest. My heart thump-thump-thumps against her hand. She smiles sadly. "You are right here, Rachel. But I need you to make me a promise."

"Anything."

Her hand remains on my chest, a comforting weight I don't want to let go of. "Remember us always lying under the stars. Remember when it was just us and the universe. Let that memory take hold, and don't let it go. Let it propel you forward as you do the big and hard things. Promise me."

"I promise. It's only us and the stars." One last time, I lean forward, and our lips connect. It's soft, sweet, and slow.

It's goodbye.

I walk out into the night with Rachel's sobs trailing behind me, and the door shuts.

Before I get into the truck, I take in this bar one last time. A bar that led me to Rachel, and a bar that ultimately became my ruin.

Suddenly, the door cracks open slightly, a sliver of light illuminating the darkness. Rachel peers out, gives me a sad grin, then recedes back into Dexter's.

We haven't shut the door completely on us.

Not yet.

27

You Are Dead to Me

Rachel

S LAM!!

The door shuts violently, shaking the pictures hanging on the walls and causing Dexter to jerk out of his chair, his hand flying to his heart.

"Rachel?" he asks after he gets his breathing under control. He scoots his chair out, using his hands as leverage on the armrests to heave himself out of it. "What in the world are you—"

I hold my hand up. "Don't come any closer to me." He lowers his head, understanding etched on his brows as he shoves his hands in his pockets. "How could you do this to me?" I ask, my words coming out shakier than I want them to.

I'm a hot mess. Being awake all night heartbroken and crying will do that to a person. So, no doubt my eyes are puffy and bloodshot, my skin red and blotchy.

After Johnny and I had a heartbreaking goodbye last night, and as soon as the sun rose, I got in my car and drove straight here to confront him. With no idea what to expect from this conversation.

"He's no good for you, Rachel," he replies, not even man enough to look me in the eye as he says this.

"SAYS WHO?!" I scream at the top of my lungs, causing him to flinch. The air around us ebbs and flows with anger as I stalk toward him. With each step, the rhythm of my approach echoes the thud of my heartbeat as I get closer to him. "I get to say who makes me happy and who doesn't. I say what I—"

"You get no say," he says through gritted teeth. "Do you even understand how that man cost me hundreds of thousands of dollars yesterday? I warned him." He rounds the desk to get closer to me. For the first time in thirty years, being with my uncle is scaring me. I take a step backward. "I told him what would happen if he crossed me. You should thank me. I gave you a gift."

"You are sick."

"I could make that whole family of his disappear"—he snaps his fingers—"like that. Instead, I chose you, Rachel. Don't you get it? The alternative was to lose him and that whole family that you love more than me."

Realization washes over me. "Is that what this is about? Jealousy?"

Now it's his turn to scream. "I did everything for you!! I took you and Micah in when you had NOTHING!" His eyes are wide and wild, and that's when I notice the dilated pupils and the redness. My attention flicks to his desk. White powder, a razor.

Coming in here, I was so angry and laser-focused that I missed what was right in front of me. Evidence that's blaring its horn, loud enough for me to hear and understand. Somehow, and I don't know when, my uncle's criminal activity has expanded. To drugs.

And he's partaking.

But I barrel ahead. "This isn't a contest! I can love Johnny and have him in my life and still be a niece to you. Why can't you see that!?"

"For months, you have been choosing him over me, your family! I took care of you! I set you up with doctors for your RA, gave you a job. I even handed you the perfect man on a platter."

My head jerks. "Who? What are you talking about?"

"DREW! I knew you would fall for him. You made it so easy, and you're so unbelievably predictable. He's your type, after all. Tall, older, handsome, and rich. I told him what to say, what to do to get you to fall for him. And it worked. But the idiot had to screw it up ... *literally* screw it up."

I can't believe what I'm hearing. My uncle orchestrated my entire relationship with Drew. A tightness builds in my chest, and the panic rises. But somehow, I push it down.

"Why? Why would you do that to me?"

"Why else? To take care of you! Drew is going to take over my empire."

Empire? He can't be serious right now? " Micah was always too weak, too into Shelby and his cooking. But Drew. Ah, Drew has all the makings. And I need for all of this"—he sweeps his arm over his office—"to stay in the family. Think of it, Rachel. We could expand. Dexter's could be a national and maybe even a global brand. A perfect house for my operation to thrive under. With Drew at the helm and you by his side, it's possible." He's in front of me now and grabs my biceps. I jump. "All of this can take care of you for the rest of your life. All Johnny can give you is—"

"Love. Johnny gives me love." He drops his grip on me as he walks away, back toward his desk. "Drew may claim to love me, but he loves himself more. Always has. And I don't care about this place, Dexter. I care about my life and what I need and want. And if you love me, like you claim to, you would see that Johnny makes me happy. I don't want anything to do with your global dreams. Count me out."

He scoffs. "That's your choice. My plan is going forward, with or without you." Standing behind his desk, he grabs a picture. I know the one. It's him, Micah, and me standing at the ocean, the water behind us. Uncle Dexter is in the middle with his arms around both of our shoulders. It was a happier time, full of love and safety. I grimace at the memory.

But now, that's all gone.

He studies it for a beat or two. His expression softens, then the anguish rolls off of him in waves.

His lip curls. "Johnny needs to pay for what he cost me. So, I'm taking from him what he loves." He shrugs as he opens his desk drawer and tosses in the frame. "Seems like a fair trade." He slams it shut. I flinch. "You and Johnny cannot see each other. Ever. And trust me, I will know if you have any contact with him. You saw the photos. I'm everywhere. If you want to keep his family safe, you know what to do."

Anger blazes in my head. "I hate you."

He plops in his chair. "That's too bad. Because I love you, and I know what's best for you. Even if you can't see it yourself."

Oh, but I'm not done. I approach the desk cautiously. "I could turn you in." His head snaps up, his eyes narrowing, and a vein throbs in his temple. "The gambling, the tax evasion. I could call the police and let them know. An investigation would start, which would lead to them finding other things, I'm sure. I'll do it."

This is it. My Hail Mary pass, my only trump card.

Then he laughs.

Actually laughs.

Shaking his head after composing himself, he points at me. "You are such a stupid little girl, you know that? Do you seriously think the cops don't know what happens at this place? Or that they aren't here participating themselves? I have them right where I want them."

"I'll go to the FBI then."

He slams his hands down on his desk. "ENOUGH!"

The outburst causes me to stumble backward. His nostrils flare, a crimson tide flooding his face as his breath hitches in his chest, a barely suppressed snarl forming on his lips.

But then, in a split second, he composes himself. "You know what, do that. Because you will see Micah hauled out of here in handcuffs right along with me."

My chest tightens at the sound of my brother's name, and I suck in a sharp breath. *Micah's involved?*

Dexter continues. "Micah made some drops for me, some runs, a few years ago when he was trying to save for an engagement ring. And I made sure he got that ring. It was nothing major, but major enough for the Feds. So, you go ahead and call whoever you want to call. But something tells me you won't do that to your brother. Am I right?" I lower my head and shake it. "And as for me?

Well, I can guarantee you I would walk away unscathed. But I can't say the same for Micah." He picks up his Mont Blanc and begins writing. "Stay away from Johnny and his family."

My God, this is far worse than I imagined. He has the cops in his back pocket, and now Micah. There is literally no way out of this.

Resignation settles in my chest with his threat. If I say anything to anyone about Dexter or his so-called empire, my brother will go away for a very long time. If I contact Johnny, Dexter harms his family.

It's all here.

Johnny stays away from me to protect his family.

I stay away from him to protect mine.

All is lost. Johnny is gone from my life.

"Will you promise not to harm the Givens family and keep Micah out of it if Johnny and I stay apart?"

He nods.

"Not good enough. Say it." He sits motionless. "I have always known you to be a man of your word in the past. If you love me, as you claim to, promise me to spare that family and Micah, and I promise you I will stay away from Johnny. Now say it!"

"I promise."

"Good. Now I will make you one last promise. I swear, from this day on, I will not speak to you ever again. You are dead to me. Nothing. A nobody. Once I walk out that door, we are no longer family, and I no longer work for you. Don't call me, don't send your lackey Drew to check on me. I am erasing you from my life. Do we have an understanding?"

He only stares at me.

"I said, do we have an understanding?"

Fully comprehending that he has lost this battle, he looks at the floorboards. His actions have cost him his niece. "If that's what you want. I understand." And he doesn't even care.

My fingers wrap around the smooth door handle. "Rachel?" I brace myself and face him one last time, the oppression of the moment heavy. "No contact."

Of course, he has to have the final word.

I swing the door open, and there, standing in the hallway, is Slick. The door clicks behind me. "Did you hear?"

He nods. "I heard everything. Come here." He waves me toward him and encases me in an embrace full of heart and empathy. I melt into his arms. Just then, Randy, Tiny, and Micah round the corner. I release my hold on Slick. "What are you guys doing here?"

"I rounded them up when I saw you charge toward the office," Micah says. "They got here a little bit ago. We were listening and ready to barge in there if needed."

My chest squeezes from the unspoken loyalty.

With a decisive turn, I move to stand in front of my brother, positioning myself between him and the OBGs. "You didn't have to do that for him. It was just a ring. We could have made something work. Shelby wouldn't have cared. She would have married you with a gumball ring."

He covers his face with both hands. "God, I know! It was so stupid of me. I'm so sorry, sis." With a gentle pull, he gathers me into his arms, the warmth of his body comforting me. "I'm so sorry I lied to you. I wanted to tell you, but I also wanted to keep you in the dark. For your safety." We pull apart. "And now, he's using it against you."

I can't be mad. There's no point. We all do dumb things when we feel we have no way out sometimes. And he's paying the price. Dexter may use this as leverage against him in the future. Or worse.

Micah and I are Dexter's only living family. I was naïve enough to think that, in a million years, he would never hurt Micah and me. And he hasn't, physically.

Emotionally, he is murdering us both.

"Please, don't beat yourself up. Dexter is doing enough of that as it is. But I quit, Micah. I'm done."

Stepping forward, he pulls me into yet another comforting hug, the warmth of his affection a welcome relief. "Me too," he muffles into my shoulder.

He releases me. "We are family." I grin, and so does he.

"And family sticks together as one," Micah and I say in unison, but we aren't the only ones. Slick, Tiny, and Randy recite it as well.

Somehow, the Oldies but Goodies have become more family to me than the poor excuse of a human on the other side of this door. And I am going to need them to get through the onslaught of sadness that is coming my way.

Thanks to Dexter, Johnny is out of my life. I will never be able to touch him again, hear him call me 'my love,' or kiss him. No more stargazing in his truck. No more hidden kisses in the kitchen or snuggles on his couch.

He's gone.

And nothing will ever be the same.

The five of us walk out of Dexter's for the last time. As we approach the door, Tiny speaks first. "Great. Now, where are we going to hang out and have a drink? That worthless piece of sh—"

"Language!" we all shout at once as we meander toward our vehicles.

He flicks his hand dismissively. "Fine. That worthless piece of *crap* has ruined Dexter's for us. What now?"

"Come to my place," Micah offers. "You guys are welcome there anytime."

Randy slides into his Jeep. "Alright then. Meet you guys there."

As I stand at my car and watch all four of them drive away, I study this bar that has been a part of my life since I was a kid. I grew up here, met incredible humans who are now my family, and it brought me Johnny. For those reasons alone, it will always hold a special place in my heart. But now, it's my past. And I'm forced to forge ahead.

To a future without Johnny.

28

Four AM

Johnny

One year since the breakup

My alarm goes off at its usual time. Four am. I've been getting up this early since my life ended a year ago.

Waking to the darkness is what I need right now. It's just me, my depression, my thoughts, and my loneliness. Granted, I have my family still. They are safe and none the wiser because of the decision Rachel and I made that day.

Dexter held true to his word. My family hasn't been touched, and I haven't noticed them being tailed or followed. I did, however, talk to Scott about installing a better security system at the house. His was outdated anyway, and I was so grateful he listened.

After I left the bar that night, I went to the liquor store, bought some Jack Daniels, and drank myself into a stupor. Something I haven't done since Daytona. I cried alone in my house and didn't sleep a wink. Also, I blocked her number. Which was the hardest thing I have ever had to do. But it's better this way. Safer.

I stumbled into work the next morning, my clothes rumpled, my hair a mess, looking like I'd been run over by a truck; the smell of stale booze and desperation clung to me. Scott noticed right away and asked what was going on. Praying that

I was convincing enough, I told Scott she ended things and proceeded to lie to my cousin for the first time in our whole lives.

He bought it.

As luck would have it, he was distracted and needed advice on how to handle a situation with Jake. Turns out Jake was feeling neglected within the family because of all the attention Mallory receives due to her special needs.

I offered the baseball tickets to Scott. The ones I got for Rachel. We made plans to go with Micah and Shelby, but instead, sitting behind home plate was Scott, Laura, Jake and myself. I told Scott that I didn't want to talk about Rachel, and he respected that. I let myself have a good time that day, but my heart was still on the dance floor at Dexter's.

The day after, I cleaned up the disaster that was my garage and started on a new pool table. I spent every free second building a table exactly like the ones at Dexter's. Somehow, I love it more than my previous one.

Because it reminds me of *her*.

Now, it's waiting for me.

After shutting my alarm off, I swing my legs off of the bed and go about my normal morning routine. It's like walking through mud. My life. Nothing feels right without Rachel by my side.

By four fifteen, I'm out in my garage, shooting pool.

It's the only place where I'm at peace.

29

Shine Bright Like the Star You Are

Rachel

Two years since the breakup

"Rachel. Josephine. Garcia."

The nursing director, Cindy, from the admissions office, calls my name as I make my way to the stage to get my diploma.

Today, I am officially a nurse.

A thunderous roar fills the air from the crowd, full of excitement. I shake hands with Cindy as she whispers to me, "I told you it would be worth it."

She's right.

As I scan the mass of people, I zero in on my brother and Shelby, who is holding my new baby niece. I can't help but smile as the OBGs clap and make a total scene.

I'm happy. Truly, I am. I never thought going to nursing school was possible for me, let alone finishing.

But a part of me is dying inside. Because the one person I need most isn't in this massive, crowded auditorium.

Johnny.

There is no doubt in my mind if he was here, he would be cheering the loudest. Maybe even wearing his red and blue uniform. With the pom-poms, of course.

One person that I'm happy isn't here is my uncle. I haven't spoken to him since our fight, nor do I plan to. We have both held true to our promises.

And I haven't stepped foot into Dexter's. Neither has Micah. Both of us have cut off all ties. A clean break. That bar is full of nothing but memories.

Memories of Johnny.

Slick, Tiny, Randy, and I, however, meet for breakfast every Sunday morning. Those three men have been my lifeline and my sanity. I love them like family. About a month ago, over pancakes and eggs, Slick slipped and called me his daughter while introducing me to an old friend he ran into.

I didn't correct him.

Even though it felt like my life ended that day two years ago, time still moves forward. And whether we like it or not, you need to move with it. So now that I've graduated, I have a job waiting for me at the local hospital and my own place. The house is small, but my favorite feature is the back deck. At night, I lie under the stars and think of Johnny. At times, I can almost sense him beside me or hear him in my ear, telling me how beautiful I am. It's as if his hand is in mine or his lips are skating over my knuckles as we talk about our future.

Almost.

I wince at the memory as I take my seat among my fellow graduates.

Another development since landing the job at the hospital is I can now afford my health insurance. With the freedom to choose my own care, I am going to be switching doctors. Hopefully, the specialists at the Cleveland Clinic can help.

Which leads me to something that's been hard to deal with. All of this stress and sadness has caused my RA to flare up. I've been struggling. So, here's to hoping a new medical facility, with its advanced technology and stellar reputation, can offer me the support I need.

"Would all the graduates please rise?" The concluding command breaks me from my thoughts. All of my classmates stand, and we switch our tassels over from right to left, then toss them in the air with reckless abandonment.

It's wonderful; a swell of accomplishment and pride washes over me. A bright spot in my otherwise sad life.

I just wish Johnny was here.

This is all because of him.

A classmate of mine and study buddy turns to talk to me. We exchange a few words, laugh at a memory, then hug, congratulating each other. Lingering in our embrace, we promise to keep in touch when a flash of a familiar silhouette comes into view over her shoulder. I release her and do a double take.

It can't be.

The figure, shrouded in the deep shadows of the dark auditorium and tucked away in an alcove leading to an exit, stands motionless. A dim light over the archway barely illuminates the edges of their form. It's a man; he's tall and leaning against the doorframe. Staring right at me.

It's Johnny.

His thumbs are in his pockets as he stands relaxed, like he doesn't have a care in the world. He lifts his fingers in a small wave. As if being here isn't putting his entire family's life in danger.

Our eyes lock. The commotion and excitement of the room fades to black and blurs around me. My heart hammers against my ribs, a frantic drumbeat in my chest.

He's here. He came.

My chin quivers, and a shaky smile crosses my face as a group of graduates brush past, obstructing my view and briefly disrupting our intense, silent gaze. I crane my neck around the sea of people.

The sea parts.

But he's gone.

Frantically, I search the room, my stomach dropping as I try to find him. But as quickly as he entered, he's gone. I rub my sternum, trying to wipe away the ache that's striking my heart.

He risked everything just to be here and watch me walk across that stage and accomplish my goal.

He still loves me. Still rooting for me. Still here for me. Even if it's at a distance.

Swallowing down the tears threatening to surface, I try to refocus, which is hard since my universe has just tilted on its axis.

After a family dinner to celebrate, I make my way home. My home.

The OBGs knew I wanted my own place. Right after I started nursing school, I was ready to move out of my brother's and into a space that would be all mine. Plus, he and Shelby were trying to have a baby. Needless to say, it got uncomfortable since they tried ... a lot.

But the OBGs also knew that I couldn't afford it because my savings were spent on my tuition. So what did they do? Randy bought a small cape cod close to my brother, flipped it, then rented it out to me with an option to own once I'm on my feet.

Not one of my rent checks has been cashed.

Those three men have been my lifeline through all of this. I have no idea how I will ever be able to repay them for their kindness.

Pulling into the driveway, I park and walk towards the front door, my footsteps echoing in the quiet night. As I fish my keys out of my purse, my foot kicks something, knocking it over. A vibrant green gift bag rests on its side, the tissue paper inside now scattered across the porch. Peering around in every direction, I try to figure out how this got here. Or better yet, who it's from.

With a slight bend, I scoop up the gift bag and shove the tissue paper back in as I step into my living room. Locking the door behind me. I peer out the window one last time, the chill glass cold against my skin, to make sure I was alone.

Curiosity is eating away at me as I sit the gift bag on the island and pull out a soft black velvet jewelry box. Peering inside, I search for a card and shake the small bag upside down.

There's nothing.

With my hands trembling, I pry the box open on its hinges. Catching the dim kitchen light is a small diamond star pendant on a gold chain. I gasp at how delicate and beautiful it is. As I remove it, the soft cardboard holding it in place loosens, and a small piece of paper falls onto the granite.

It's a note. Typed, not handwritten.

The words stare back at me.

Johnny's words.

Congratulations, love.
Now go and shine bright like the star you are.
I love you.

Without warning, a sob bursts out as my hand shoots to my mouth to contain it. So many questions swirl around in my head.

How did he know I lived here?

When did he drop this off?

Racing back over to the window, I peer out, hoping that the dark figure I saw at graduation is lurking outside. But he's not there. There's only darkness.

One question has plagued me for the last two years. Does he still love me?

After everything that happened today, the answer is obvious.

He does.

He's still with me, even though he can't be.

I take the necklace and secure it around my neck as I walk out to my deck. My favorite lounge chair awaits as I lie and stare at the stars, holding the diamond star in my hand.

"I love you too."

30

What's the Picture Of?

Johnny

Three years since the breakup

Eight thousand seven hundred and sixty hours.

Three hundred and sixty-five days.

Fifty-two weeks.

Twelve months.

Winter.

Spring.

Summer.

Fall.

Another year gone.

Without Rachel.

"Okay, so do you see the mistake you made there?" I ask my student, Brandon, standing in my garage, holding a pool cue, studying the table.

"I think so."

"Alright. What happened?"

"Too much right English?" He turns with a quizzical expression.

"Exactly. And what was the result?"

"Well, the cue ball curved more than it should have."

"Good. What else?"

"Which caused me to hit the six ball too much to the left, missing the pocket, which, in turn, didn't set up my next shot."

I slap him on the back. "Exactly! You're getting it."

"Slowly," he says with exasperation.

"It just feels that way. You have come a long way. Now, set up the shot and try again."

Brandon isn't my only student. After everything, I needed something to get my mind off of the absolute crap show that is my life. So I started offering pool lessons out of my garage. Teaching the game at Dexter's to my team ignited a spark in me. There's nothing better than watching students learn and grow as players. It's amazing.

Rachel was the one who lit this match. It was that day in the bar, when I was supposed to be teaching her, and the so-called lesson ended with her perched on the table and me kissing her.

I'd love to tell her. If only she knew.

On the day of her graduation, I knew I was taking a risk going to watch her walk across that stage. But nothing was going to stop me from going. The amount of pride I felt was unlike anything I have ever experienced.

But I paid the price. While on the job the next day, I walked out, and my truck was destroyed. Tires slashed, windows busted. It was total destruction. A small note rested on the driver's seat among the broken glass.

Next time, it will be your family.

But I had to know for sure if they were truly safe.

Scott wasn't with me, so with panic rising in my chest, I immediately called him. I needed to know if everyone was okay. I told him about the truck and then invited myself over for dinner. Thankfully, they were fine.

I wasn't. I'm still not.

Brandon arranges the table so that he can attempt the shot again, shaking me from the memory. "Oh, yeah, before I forget," he says, raising his finger. He reaches into his back pocket. "Micah told me to give this to you."

Dangling from his index finger, swaying back and forth, is an eight ball keychain. I freeze. "Micah?"

"Yeah. Didn't I tell you? Micah and I went to high school together. He was the one that told me about you."

Ten thousand questions are swirling around in my mind. "I haven't spoken to Micah in three years. How did he know I was offering lessons?"

"You know how it is." He shrugs. "Mutual friends and all that. He heard it through the grapevine. Said you were the best."

All I can do is stare at the keychain suspended from his finger. "Here." He nudges it toward me, encouraging me to take the gift I wasn't expecting.

It's from Rachel. It has to be.

With a tight smile, I take it from him and notice immediately that it has a peephole on the underside of the ball. I squint my left eye shut and raise the keychain to peer inside, my hand trembling the whole way.

The small micro picture, with its blurred edges, is of Rachel and me on my swing. She's on my lap, and her head is resting on my shoulder with my hands on her legs. Both of us grinning from ear to ear at the camera.

I remember this day, the memories of it flood my brain in vivid detail. I had a picnic at my house with my family, Micah and Shelby, plus the OBGs. Jake took the picture.

It was the day Rachel and I said 'I love you' for the first time.

"What's the picture of?" Brandon asks, breaking me from the memory.

I lower the keychain and shove it in my pocket. "It's from Dexter's. A cool shot of a rack of pool balls," I lie.

Brandon leaves when his lesson is over, both of us satisfied with his progress. When I crawl into bed, I stare at the picture until I fall asleep, whispering 'I love you' to her in my dreams.

31

Sound Good?

Johnny

Three and a half years since the breakup

"Well, the good news is, even though the wound is deep, you didn't slice a tendon. You'll need stitches, obviously, and some after-wound care, which we include in the after-visit summary. I'm going to prescribe a round of antibiotics as just a precaution. If the pain gets to be too much later on today, feel free to take some anti-inflammatories. Then, just follow up with your primary care doctor in two weeks to have the stitches removed. Sound good?"

Does that sound good? No! None of this is good!

Today, while on the job, I was helping out the carpet installers. As I was cutting through the Berber with a carpet knife, I slipped and sliced the top of my hand wide open. From the base of my thumb to my wrist.

My left hand, my bridge hand when I hold my cue.

I know better, too. I was rushing to get the job done since we were running behind, and now my minor mishap has set us back even further. Because low and behold, when you slice your hand open, there is blood. A lot of blood. All over the carpet we were installing, which now needs to be replaced.

Scott is not happy.

And how do I know this? Well, he is sitting in a blue plastic chair next to the hospital bed I'm stretched out on in the ER, arms crossed and stewing in his anger.

"Sounds good," I reply to the doctor, who looks about as old as Jake. "Quick question. I play pool. How long until I can play again since this is the hand that the stick rests on?"

"Hmm ..." He pauses, pondering. "Definitely wait until the stitches are out. Test it out and see how it feels. Since the pool cue will rub along that same area, it may be tender. If it is, I would say a month, maybe."

He said the stitches come out in two weeks. I'll be playing in two weeks, tender or not.

Sorry, Doc.

But I nod at his instructions, anyway.

"Okay, great. I'll send in our suture nurse, and we will get you patched up and out of here. Sound good?"

Still not good. With that, Doogie Howser opens the curtain, marches out into the busy ER, and slides it shut behind him.

I glance over at Scott, his ankle resting on his uncontrollably bobbing knee. "Go ahead. Get it off your chest."

"I can't believe you were that careless. Why weren't you wearing your cut-proof gloves? Do you even know the paperwork you have caused me? And now, you are out of commission for two whole weeks, and to make matters worse, the job has to be pushed back ... again." He lets out a huff. "Don't make me micromanage you."

My chest rises and falls at his tongue lashing because he's right. I rest my head against the scratchy pillow and close my eyes, crossing my feet at the ankles. "Feel better now?"

He pauses, then lets out a chuckle.

"You didn't have to come, you know," I say, eyes still closed.

"Who else is going to hold your hand while they stitch you up?"

We erupt into a fit of laughter, the sound mixing in with the ER commotion. Ride or die. Always.

Just then, the curtain flicks open, and Doctor Teenager peeks in. "So, our
suture nurse is out sick. I'm going to have to call down a surgical nurse to come
in. So, it may be a little longer of a wait. Sound good?"

Oh, my God! Why does he keep asking me that???

Send in whoever. I don't care. Just get me out of here so I can go home and
sulk.

I give him a thumbs-up.

The curtain closes again with the sound of metal against metal doing little to
calm my anxiety.

After an hour, I'm starting to get fidgety because, dear Lord, this is taking
forever. This place is swarming with workers. Why is this taking so long? Someone came in about twenty minutes ago and gave me a shot to numb my hand.
Now, Scott's scrolling through his phone, as I sit and watch the small TV up on
the wall. I don't have the energy to reach for the remote, so I'm watching ESPN
talk about how poorly Pittsburgh played the night before.

I don't care.

The obnoxious curtain sound causes me to whip my head toward the room
entrance, and my heart drops to my stomach. Because standing there with a
metal cart full of medical stuff is quite possibly the most gorgeous nurse ever.

Rachel. Wide-eyed and mouth gaping open.

She takes a step back and glances around to the other rooms, probably
checking to see if she has the right patient.

I hope she does. Please, God, say that she has the right room and no other
lunatic was dumb enough to cut his hand and need stitches. Just be me. Please.

Scott catches my attention from my peripheral, and his head is pinging back
and forth between the two of us.

She stands, blinking rapidly, sharing the same shock as me. Then, her expression softens, unlike the storm erupting in my stomach. My nerves are about to
burst out the longer we stare, my chest heaving.

Because I haven't seen Rachel since her graduation. Somehow, she has gotten
even more beautiful. Her hair is up in a messy bun with minimal makeup. As
for what she's wearing?

Scrubs. Black ones.

Rachel in scrubs is next level.

I'm dead.

My mouth has gone completely dry.

Her hand is white-knuckling the curtain as her chest rises and falls in quick breaths.

We stare.

We long.

We love.

Still.

Scott, rising from his chair, breaks us from the moment. Rachel closes the curtain and wheels the metal cart closer to the side of the bed. His eyes flick to me briefly.

From his perspective, this probably looks super awkward. As far as he knows, we broke up because Rachel was hung up on the age difference. What he doesn't know is that what he is witnessing isn't the usual tension that comes with being face-to-face with your ex for the first time in forever.

It's seeing the love of your life who you can't be with.

He's seeing two people who are being tortured.

"Rachel. Nice to see you again," he says, trying to play the role of diplomat.

She looks over at him.

I look at her.

"Hey, Scott. You, too. How's Laura and the kids?"

His eyes flick to me, probably wondering why I'm not speaking. "Um ... they're good. Jake and Mallory are living their best teenage lives."

Rachel smiles warmly. "That's good to hear. Please tell them I said hello."

"I will. Mallory asks about you all the time." I hang my head, the weight of my sadness pressing down on me because it's true. Mallory always asks about Rachel, wanting to know why we aren't together. It's torture on a whole other level. Mallory gets attached to very few people. But she was attached to Rachel.

Rachel pauses, letting this sink in. I'm sure it is hard for her to hear. She sniffles, then nods, her eyebrows pulling together. "I miss her too."

Insert the knife, twist it, and leave me dead.

Scott's expression softens, his voice kind, the way it always is when talking about his kids. "Thank you for asking about them."

With the formalities over, no one else speaks. The three of us stand here in room six, awkwardly, as the hustle and bustle of the ER whirls around us.

Scott looks at me, and I jerk my head to the right. A get-the-heck-out-of-here gesture.

He takes the hint, clapping his hands. "Okay, so I'm going to go and wait in the truck. Rachel, it was nice seeing you again." He slaps me on the shoulder. "Good luck."

Pretty sure he doesn't just mean the stitches.

Scott leaves, and then it's just us.

I miss us.

Once again, our eyes lock. I pin my gaze to her eyes, then slowly, on their own, they trail down her body. Her face lights up with a small grin, clearly pleased by the attention.

It's official. I love scrubs.

Breaking the moment, she turns and boops her name badge on the computer. "Okay, sir, sorry about the wait. My name is Rachel, and I am here to get you stitched up. Can I have your last name and date of birth?"

Her voice sounds like a song.

But a pain shoots straight to my chest. This is the first time we have spoken since that day on the dance floor, and she's being so formal.

It's probably for the best.

"Um. It's Givens. January 25, 1971." I swallow the massive lump forming in my throat. A feeble attempt to get myself under control as I watch her every movement, searing it into my brain.

After scrolling through my chart, she turns back around, head down, and puts on the gloves that rest on the metal table. "Okay, Mr. Givens, let's take a look here." As soon as she lifts my hand, she inhales sharply. My thumb grazes her knuckles, and even though I can't feel it, and she's wearing hospital gloves, I feel it.

Everywhere.

She closes her eyes and, for the briefest of moments, everything else falls away. There is no ER commotion, no beeping machines, no screaming patients down the hall.

It's just us.

Her eyes lift to mine. She skims my face as my attention drifts to the small freckle that sits on the side of her nose. Instinct takes over as I lift my other hand and gently swipe over it with my thumb, her silky velvet skin as soft as I remember. Her breath hitches at my touch. Tears pool in her eyes, tearing my heart open. We savor the moment.

Us together again.

Alone.

A voice over the intercom announces a Code Blue on the fourth floor. Someone is probably dying, but right now, I'm alive. For the first time in three and a half years.

With a shuddering breath, she blinks back the tears and refocuses back on my hand, twisting it, poking it, wiping away any blood. "So, Mr. Givens, how did you do this to yourself?"

My hand, gaping and bleeding, is the least of my concerns. "Rachel, I—"

She releases it and stands abruptly. "Before we begin, let's raise your bed and adjust your pillow some. I need you to be comfortable for this." Formal nurse Rachel returns, jarring me from the moment.

I watch as she shimmies around the small space, her hips swaying with each turn and pivot, remembering how those hips felt in my hands. Now, she's standing right by my head as she raises the back of the bed, then reaches to grab the pillow, but not before leaning in. Her face is ... so close. And she still smells like summer.

Warm breath and hushed words caress my ear. "Please, just act normal. As much as I want to, I can't. It's too dangerous. And I'm at work."

She lifts her head and our eyes lock, noses touching, lips hovering, tempting me.

Instead, I nod. As hard as it is to be near her and not pull her into this bed with me, I understand.

Just because I ended up at her place at work, our reality still exists. Dexter is still out there. A threat that's always looming large.

She preps my hand, and minutes later, she's stitching me up. We sit in silence, the moment frozen in time. But if she thinks I'm going to sit here and not talk to her, she's nuts. We can pretend to be only patient and nurse to each other while I dig for information.

Watch me.

She pokes my skin with the needle as she concentrates. "So, how long have you worked here as a nurse, Rachel?"

She doesn't look up. "I graduated from school about a year and a half ago and started here soon after."

"Do you like it?"

She flicks her eyes at mine, and a small smile dances across her lips. "I love it." She goes back to stitching. "A former boyfriend of mine pushed me to do it. And I'm so glad he did. He changed my life."

I let those three sentences sit with me for a second, filling me up. "I bet he would like to know that. Even though you aren't together anymore."

"He knows."

Yes. He. Does.

"We may not be together, but he will always be the most important person in my life," she adds with a quiver in her voice.

"Why aren't you together anymore?" I ask. And to anyone outside of this curtain who can hear us, this sounds like a normal conversation. But for us, right now, it means the world.

She sighs, stopping mid-stitch. "It's a long story, but sometimes, we catch a bad break." Her gaze lifts, and we connect. "Like in pool. You break, and the cue ball slams into the balls, and for the briefest moment, your life looks full of hope and promise. That was us. But then, the cue ball falls into the pocket, and it's over. You lose, and the possibilities are meaningless without that cue ball. That's what happened to us."

The subtle way she references one of my greatest loves resonates deeply. "So, you guys scratched on the relationship?"

She nods, finishing the stitch. "Something like that."

"But the beauty of pool is that you can always re-rack the balls and try the shot again. It doesn't have to be your last."

"I would love to play the game again someday."

"I bet he would, too."

The uncomfortableness returns, but it seems like it unlocks something inside of her. She drinks in a tight breath as the mood shifts. "I saw in your chart that you're single. Is that still accurate?" She swallows. "Is there anyone at home to help you with the after-wound care?"

I smile at her subtle probing.

Call me crazy, but I love this little dance we are doing right now. It's a little playful yet also hurts, all tied up in a neat bow. Funny how I wanted to get out of here only twenty minutes ago, but now, this ER is the only place I want to be.

I smile and answer her. "I live alone."

"So, no girlfriend to assist?" she continues her investigation while pausing mid-stitch.

My heart rate increases. "No. No girlfriend." Not since Rachel. Never if I can help it.

Her cheeks pink as she grins while keeping her head low, sewing my skin back together, clearly happy with my answer.

"Well, find someone to help and keep the wound clean and dry so it can heal properly."

"My cousin's wife Laura can help," I say, playing the part. "She's a nurse, too." But God, how I want it to be Rachel.

"Good."

With time running out and only a few more stitches to go, I need more information about her. So I probe. "How about you?"

"How about me what?" The thread glides through my flesh.

"I can't look in your chart. Are you single?"

She smiles. "Now, Mr. Givens, watch yourself. That's inappropriate for you to ask, and besides, I don't date patients." With an evil smirk, she glances up. "Yes," she mouths while shaking her head, trying to stifle her laugh.

Thank the good Lord above.

She's reached the end of thirteen stitches, knotting the thread, which means our time is almost over. Who knew cutting my hand would lead to the best thirty minutes of my whole life in the past three years? This whole encounter has me swaying and feeling unsteady.

She cleans and wraps my hand with such tenderness and ease while spouting off the instructions on what she just did, so I can wrap it at home.

I heard none of it. All I watched was her lips moving.

Lips I haven't kissed in three and a half years. But seeing her in her element, it's as if she has been a nurse for decades. This is what she was meant to do. Meant to be.

She's a star. My north star.

I soak in her every move as she tidies up her metal cart, tossing bloody gauze into the trash. She turns and weeds through some papers resting on the sink, clicking her pen and writing some notes.

"Alright, Mr. Givens, you are all done." She hands me a bundle of stapled papers. "Here is your after-visit summary that has all of your wound care instructions."

"Is your phone number on it?"

She snorts out a laugh. "You don't give up, do you?"

"I'll never give up."

Never. It may take months or years. But I'll never give up on us.

I'm sure returning with the same response would sound unprofessional, so she smiles and mouths, "Me too."

Stepping forward, I take the papers from her, and our hands graze. She doesn't let go. I don't either. Our eyes catch and seize. The air in the room crackles and sparks. We aren't in the ER. We are somewhere else entirely. Somewhere together. Somewhere Dexter isn't a threat.

"Any questions?" she asks, her voice quivering because our time is almost up.

Any questions? Yes, I have a million questions. But the one I really had, I got my answer to.

She's still single. For now. Who knows how long we will have to remain apart? She said she wouldn't give up, but what if some hot doctor here caught her eye, and that will be that? My life will be over.

Who am I kidding? It already is. My self-confidence is in tatters. She just told me she isn't giving up, but let's face it. Rachel in scrubs will turn any man's head.

"No. No questions. Thank you, though." I lift my newly stitched hand. "For this." And so much more.

Hot pressure burns behind my eyes, but I hold it back. She gives me a tight, sad smile. "You're welcome. Take care, Mr. Givens."

She turns to leave, wheeling the tray with her. Grabbing the curtain, she pulls it open, exposing us to the outside world, snapping us back into reality. She turns, only allowing her gaze to latch with mine for half a heartbeat before walking out and disappearing into the ER chaos.

I exhale and grip the papers in my hand as I walk down the hallway, but not before looking back one last time. She's standing at the elevators. The doors open as she steps in with about five other people. She turns, looks up, and sees me. We stand in a wordless stare, full of happiness at seeing each other and sorrow because now it's over.

I wave. She smiles. The doors close.

With my head down, I make my way out into the parking lot, the whole encounter playing on a loop in my head. How is it possible? How was that moment the best and saddest of my whole life?

I reach Scott's truck and open the door, sliding in, as I struggle to buckle my seatbelt with only one hand. He's quiet, watching me intently, smiling like a fool.

"What?" I ask.

"So, how did *that* go?" He starts the engine, shifts into gear, and pulls out of the parking lot.

"Well, I got thirteen stitches, and when this numbing medication wears off, I am going to be in a lot of pain. And crabby."

"Oh, come on. You know what I mean."

Pretending to be unbothered, I flip through the stapled stack of papers while we wait at a red light. "It was fine."

He huffs out a puff of laughter. "Ooookay, keep telling yourself that. You two still love each other. That much was obvious."

I ignore him, trying not to give anything away. I flip to the last page, and my heart stops dead. There, in her perfect handwriting, is a note.

I miss you. Everyday all day.

I sigh. "I miss her." The admission spills out after reading her identical confession.

"Hmmm ... well, if it's meant to be, it will work out. She'll come around. You'll see." He grins. "Sound good?"

His joke lightens my sour mood, but only slightly. Turning, I look out the window as the hospital sails past us, wishing I was still in there with her.

Yeah, Scott. That sounds good.

32

Do You Need the Room?

Johnny

I burst through the emergency room doors, the harsh fluorescent lights momentarily blinding me as I spot Scott pacing the waiting room floor, his face etched with worry. "Scott!" I call out, my voice echoing through the crowd. He turns, charging toward me, his eyes wide and wild.

"Johnny."

"Where is she? How is she? What's going on?" The questions come out in rapid succession.

"I'm still waiting. I don't know anything." He heads in the direction of the hard plastic chairs, and we both sit. The smell of sickness clings to the air of the busy ER. The same ER I was in just a week prior when Rachel stitched me up. Scott's despair weighs heavy as I put my hand on his shoulder; his head is bowed low, elbows on his knees, hands clenching and twisting.

While resting at home, binge-watching yet another TV show while I'm off work for my hand, I got the call from Scott that Laura was in an accident while leaving work. My stomach bottomed out. Not just for Scott but for Laura as well. She's like a sister to me. I can't even imagine if she—I shake the possibility from my head. "Do they know what happened?"

He nods, still staring at the stained floor. "The officer over there"—he glances to the registration desk—"said that it looks like the brakes went out in her car.

Which makes zero sense. We just had it looked at last week. You know, the annual check-up I always have her get because I'm so anal about her car being safe."

I turn to regard the cop; his eyes, narrow slits of ice, tear into me, and a prickling sensation spreads across my skin as a chill travels down my spine.

Scott turns his whole body and looks around. "What is taking so long?" Irritation laces his tone. "They said that I could go back with her, but that was like an hour ago. I'm going out of my damn mind. I just need to be with her." With determination, he stands, but I pull him back down into the chair. Mad Scott is the last thing that poor registration woman needs while she's trying to do her job.

"You sit. Let me ask her. Plus, I want to talk to the cop. Did you ask about her car? Like where they took it?"

"No." He runs his hands through his hair. "God, I can't even think straight right now."

On shaking legs and a stomach full of knots, I stand. "Stay here. I'll go over and try to get some answers."

He looks up at me, a faint, tight smile on his lips. "Thanks, man."

"SCOTT GIVENS!" Scott bolts out of his chair as both of our heads whip around to a nurse standing in front of industrial-size doors wide open. A few groans echo out from the other patients, frustrated it's not their name being called.

He practically runs over to her. "That's me."

She greets us with a warm smile. "Mr. Givens, your wife is doing fine. You can join her now, and the doctor would like to talk to you as well." It's almost as if ten years of stress leaves his body as he sags in relief and lets out a huge sigh. "Would you follow me?"

Scott turns to me, his eyes questioning, and I nudge my head toward the big open doors. "Go be with your wife. I'll wait here. Come out and let me know what's going on, though."

With a strong grip, he pulls me into a bear hug, his hand slapping my back with a resounding thud. "Thanks, Johnny."

"She's okay now," I reassure him as we break apart.

Scott and the nurse disappear through the doors as they close automatically so he can be with the love of his life.

But I have a feeling what happened to Laura has to do with mine and the stitches she gave me last week. And with how that cop is staring at me, I know I'm right.

Does Dexter have the cops in his back pocket also?

With a pounding heart, I head in his direction, and the moment I reach him, he turns and strides down the ER hallway.

I follow.

Past chairs filled with sick patients, past the coffee and vending machines, and through another set of double doors. He turns right, nodding to a few people as we continue our descent into the hospital. We eventually stop at an office with a plaque on the door that reads CHARGE NURSE.

He knocks. A second or two passes, then the door opens. A woman who looks to be maybe in her sixties stands in front of us wearing scrubs that are too small and crocs on her feet.

"Hey, Aunt Helen," the cop greets her as the biggest, goofiest grin spreads across her face. He's probably her favorite nephew.

"Hi, pumpkin. Do you need the room, Jason?"

Cop man Jason nods. Aunt Helen arches up onto her tip-toes as he leans down, kissing him on the cheek. "Take your time. I'll see you on Sunday for dinner. You bringing your famous corn casserole?"

"Of course!"

"And what about that special friend of yours?" sweet Aunt Helen asks with a wink.

"Penny will be there."

She claps her hands together. "Yay! I can't wait to meet her!"

Seriously! My patience is hanging on by a thread, and these two are going about their family business like it's nothing.

And would someone please warn Penny to stay away from this guy?

With their dinner plans firmly in place, she steps around us, out into the chaos.

Jason and I walk into the typical office, dread coursing through me with each step. A messy desk, filing cabinets, a chair on wheels, a coat rack with a purse and jacket hanging off of it. It's all here, closing in on me. Jason shuts the door and blocks it.

I'm trapped.

He turns, a slow, deliberate movement, while crossing his arms over his chest. "Dexter warned you."

Rage shoots up my body as I step forward, invading his personal space, my eyes locking on his, the tension in the air palpable. "Was it you? Did you mess with her brakes?" Spit flies from my mouth as his hand rests on his gun. Ready.

We are nose-to-nose now, his breath ghosting against my skin. But I need to remind myself.

He's a cop.

We are in a hospital.

Dexter is still in control.

I'm royally screwed.

Jason chuckles under his breath. "Laura was lucky. It could have been significantly worse. Dexter thought you needed another warning. I guess destroying your truck wasn't enough."

I hold up my bandaged hand. "We didn't plan it!" My words are strained, strangled with fear. "I came to get care. She just so happened to be working. I didn't even know she worked here. She was doing her job!"

It's pretty obvious sweet Aunt Helen is indeed the charge nurse here. Her little pumpkin is a dirty cop on Dexter's payroll, and he uses her for information on patients and also keeps an eye on Rachel.

The whole thing makes me sick.

More than likely, Helen saw her treat me when I was a patient in the ER that day and reported back to Jason. He then told Dexter. They probably sliced the break line while Laura was working.

Laura's fortunate.

It could have been so much worse.

The thought of Mallory and Jake losing their mom or Scott losing his wife is sending me into an internal tale spin. My dinner churns in my stomach as my sight blurs, but my reality is still front and center.

When will this end?

Jason reaches behind him, holding onto the door handle. "Dexter won't be so kind next time. Instead of coming to see your family in the ER, you will be called to the morgue to ID them. It's your choice."

The door swings open, and I'm all alone in Aunt Helen's office.

Laura could have died because I got hurt and Rachel had to do her job and stitch me up. How does this whole situation keep getting worse? But more importantly, who has to die for it to stop?

Taking a moment to steady my breathing, I return to the ER, just as Scott appears, his eyes quickly searching the waiting room for me.

"Scott!" I call out.

He turns, a determined look on his face, and heads in my direction. "I couldn't find you. I thought you left."

"Sorry, I went to the restroom, and then I tried to find that cop but lost him." More lies. "How's Laura?"

"The doctor said that she will have to be admitted for observation, but it just looks like a bad concussion with some bruised ribs and a broken collarbone from the seatbelt and airbag. She's shaken up and worried about the kids, of course. I'm going to stay overnight with her." He glances at me; tears brim his eyes as the shock slowly wears off. "Can you take Jake and Mallory for the night?"

"Of course. Whatever you need," I reply. I nudge my head toward the double doors. "Go be with your wife. I'll take care of the kids."

"Okay. I'll call in about an hour to talk to them." I nod as he quickly turns on his heels, heading back to Laura.

Each step to the parking lot is a struggle, the weight of my sadness pressing down on me, the air hung heavy and still.

Facing a life destined to be forever without Rachel.

33

AFTER LOCAL MAN DISAPPEARS IN MIAMI, EVIDENCE INDICATES "FOUL PLAY," OFFICIALS SAY

By Emily Kelley

Authorities are investigating the disappearance of a local man, 44-year-old Drew Jenkins of Warren, Ohio. Mr. Jenkins was last seen in a rented BMW convertible, later found abandoned in an upscale Miami, Florida, neighborhood. Law enforcement initially said Jenkins went missing under "suspicious" circumstances. As the investigation progressed, Miami-Dade Police Department revealed that evidence suggests there was foul play.

"Based on the information obtained from the victim's vehicle, our investigators believe there was evidence to indicate foul play," the Florida State Bereau of Investigation wrote in a Facebook post on Wednesday afternoon. As of this report, no arrests have been made.

The state investigative bureau on Sunday announced it would open a probe into the man's disappearance, at the request of the Miami-Dade Sheriff's Office, whose jurisdiction includes the suburban neighborhood where Jenkins' rental car was discovered.

Miami Highway Patrol issued an Endangered Missing Advisory for Jenkins, on behalf of the Warren Sheriff's Department, on Saturday, once family noted Jenkins never returned home from a planned vacation to the Sunshine State. That alert deemed Jenkins to be "at-risk," although few details have been shared publicly about the events leading up to his disappearance.

Jenkins was traveling on vacation with friends before he vanished. According to the missing persons report, on the night of the 15th, Jenkins was scheduled to "attend a meeting with colleagues," which he never showed for. He was last seen on surveillance footage leaving a Whole Foods Market at approximately 7:52 pm. This is the last known sighting of Jenkins. His vehicle was discovered three days later along the side of the road in the suburban neighborhood. The local residents noticed the abandoned vehicle and reported it to authorities.

Miami-Dade have released images of Jenkins, along with a written description. Jenkins is 6 feet, 2 inches tall, bald, with blue eyes. He was last seen wearing a blue short-sleeved shirt, denim shorts, and sandals, according to the alert. He also has several tattoos, one of which is the Chinese symbol for love with the name 'Rachel' tattooed on the left side of his chest.

Florida State investigators said they are working with local law enforcement to find Jenkins. They have asked anyone with information about the man's whereabouts to contact the bureau.

CBN News contacted both the Ohio and Florida Bureau of Investigation for more information about the man's disappearance and the missing persons case but did not receive an immediate reply.

34

Ginger Ale and Lorna Doones

Rachel

Four years since the breakup

The cool metal of the needle pierces my skin, a brief, sharp pain as the nurse inserts the IV, followed by the dull ache of the catheter. I wince.

"Sorry," she apologizes as her lips form a tight line while taping it in place.

"It's okay," I reassure her. "I'm used to it at this point."

She finishes setting me up for my monthly infusion. A treatment that has helped my RA far better than anything the doctor back home could do for me. Transferring my care to the Cleveland Clinic was the best decision I ever made for my health. Although there is no simple fix for my RA, these infusions have given me my life back. Literally. My pain has decreased, my joints are less stiff, and my quality of life has returned.

The nurse double-checks everything as I get comfortable in the chair. Reclining back, readying myself for the next two hours.

"I'll be back in a little while to see how you're doing. Do you need anything? Some Ginger Ale and Lorna Doones?" she asks with a wicked grin because she knows what I like.

"Oh, you know it."

As she scurries off to get my treats and tend to the other patients, I scooch down in the recliner, adjust the blanket over my legs, and settle in. With a tap, I open the news app on my phone to get caught up on the local happenings.

Recently, the local news cycle has been dominated by one grim and upsetting report in particular that hits far too close to home, leaving me uneasy.

Because that's how I found out about Drew.

No, we weren't friends, and I haven't spoken to him since the finals. However, at one time, he was a big part of my life. He was someone I dated, got engaged to, loved, and the man who broke my heart. But that doesn't mean I wanted anything bad to happen to him. Not even a little bit. I knew deep down the longer he had a relationship with my uncle, the more likely this was going to happen.

When the news first broke, I called his mother. She and I were close when Drew and I were together, so calling her felt natural. Like checking in on an old friend. She's distraught and shocked, which is to be expected.

But none of this surprises me.

Because, like every other person my uncle did business with, he's vanished without a trace, leaving only unanswered questions.

And I guarantee no one will ever find him.

And the tattoo? He never had that when we were together, and I have no clue when he got it. Honestly, it's kinda sad. Perhaps if he was that devoted to me when we were together, things may have been different.

But I don't like to think about it. Because that version of my story doesn't include Johnny.

Two different thoughts plague me with this whole situation. One, if Johnny had thrown that match, he would have been in my uncle's debt for life. Drew's fate could have been Johnny's.

And two, on some weird level, I'm grateful to my uncle. He didn't harm Johnny after winning. Yes, he's not in my life, but it could have been so much worse.

At least I know he is alive and out there. We sacrificed our future, but he's safe. His family is safe. I'm safe.

That's all that matters.

Of course, every thought I have always circles back to Johnny and our sacrifice. As usual, a boulder full of lead forms in my stomach when I think about how he's not in my life.

Six months ago, during a rather slow day in the OR, I got a call from the ER saying that their suture nurse called off and that they needed a hand. Craving a much-needed break, I volunteered. When I arrived, all I was told was that it was the patient in bed six, and it was a hand laceration. Opening that curtain and seeing him lying there shook me. I never thought I would see him at my job.

Small world indeed.

He looked incredible, obviously. Sounded even better. But we couldn't. Not yet, and not in my place of work. But the thirty minutes I spent with him, even though it was sad and emotional, was exhilarating.

Other than my grad ceremony, the necklace, and the keychain, there has been zero contact. It's too risky. I even changed my phone number and blocked his number in case there was any temptation to contact me.

And I have missed him every day.

Every. Single. Day.

Resting my hand on my stomach, I attempt to force back the tears that are right there.

With a sigh, I pick up my phone again, the cool glass smooth against my fingertip as I scroll until I locate the news report I was digging for. I've been following a story about a rehab facility that's being built in the area. The closest office to offer physical therapy for those with RA is an hour away. Our community needs this, so I'm eager to learn about the progress.

```
Today, officials held a groundbreaking
event for a new nonprofit medical facil-
ity planning to cater to the needs of
those with physical disabilities in the
valley. The facility assists patients un-
dergoing treatment for stroke, traumatic
```

brain injury, and amputations, as well as individuals requiring support with their overall movement. For example, those who may suffer from certain auto-immune diseases, such as rheumatoid arthritis.

"Our patients have some sort of mobile decline, meaning they can't walk as well as they'd like to," explains Dr. Michael Rossi, VP of Operations. "They can't take care of themselves, dress themselves, tie their shoes, brush their teeth. Things that you and I take for granted are difficult for these patients. So it's our goal here to give them some quality of life back. We hope to be able to provide that for them."

As reported earlier, there was resistance from local politicians regarding the implementation of this facility in the community, with the cost being the biggest factor. Johnny Givens from Givens Construction, the company overseeing the build, speaks out for the first time about how he was instrumental in fighting through the red tape. "There is a heavy need for this type of facility in our community," Mr. Givens recently

```
commented. "For me, it's personal. When
you have loved ones who can't receive the
basic medical care they need because of
something as fixable as distance. Well,
let's make it happen. Whatever it takes.
I will forever fight for these ones.
Especially those I love."
```

```
The $15-million facility is being paid
for through a real estate investment
trust. Stewart-Miller Trust is financing
the building. According to Mr. Givens,
construction is expected to be completed
by late summer.
```

My breath catches as those pesky tears I pushed back just moments ago are now resurfacing. Immediately, my hand shoots to my necklace.

I can't believe he did this. It's been four years, and he is still fighting for me. Through the article and his actions, he is sending me a declaration of his love.

If he could, I know he would be sitting next to me right now. Getting me through this with his usual bravado and jokes. Making me and the whole staff laugh along the way.

The distance has me in a constant chokehold. Still, even after four years, he's telling me he cares and is waiting.

As I clutch the star, a single tear lands on my hand, eliciting a small smile at the thought.

I'm waiting as well.

I'll wait forever.

35

A Waste of Words to the Man Upstairs

Johnny

Five years after the breakup

"And as always, our Fox 6 team was first to arrive. Our own Dana Wilhelm is on the scene. What are you seeing right now, Dana?"

"Thanks, Brett. Currently, I am standing across the street from the popular bar and pool hall, Dexter's, here on the south side. It was inside that, at approximately two o'clock this afternoon, the owner and local businessman Dexter Smith was found shot to death in his office. One of the bar employees, who wishes to remain anonymous, discovered the body. The employee was questioned by the authorities but has been cleared as a suspect. In addition, local authorities are telling me that there were no signs of forced entry and that the gun used in the murder was registered to Mr. Smith. However, it doesn't appear to be a self-inflicted gunshot wound, given the point of entry and how many shots were fired. We are also being told that the perpetrators cleaned out the office where Mr. Smith was found. One of the employees informed authorities that there was a computer, a laptop, and an iPad in the office. However, all of those items are missing, as well as Mr. Smith's personal cell phone. It appears that the assailants cleaned out every drawer and filing cabinet. In addition, police chief Henderson is telling me that Mr. Smith was heavily involved in a local, very lucrative illegal gambling ring. There have also been reports of suspicious drug

activity being conducted here at the bar. The FBI, as well as state and local authorities, have

been investigating these and other claims in hopes of finding enough evidence to arrest Mr.

Smith. The bar housed pool tournaments, and Mr. Smith was the president of the Billiards

and Pool Association, a local pool league. All in all, it appears that the investigators have

a lot to unpack here. As always, stay tuned for the latest updates on this complicated case

as it unfolds. For Fox 6 News, I'm Dana Wilhelm. Back to you in the studio, Brett."

Numb with shock, I sit on the couch, my elbows resting on my knees as I stare at the TV, the weatherman now telling me about how it's going to rain tomorrow. Lowering my head, I run my fingers through my hair, the silent scream of my inner turmoil echoing in my ears.

Dexter is dead.

More than likely murdered by someone he pissed off. None of which surprises me.

I hate to say good riddance, but....

I shoot off the couch, and my mind becomes a car on a racetrack, speeding through a million thoughts all at once.

Rachel's face immediately pops into my head. *How is she? Where is she? Does she have people around her for support? Thank GOD she didn't discover the body!*

And the poor employee. They shouldn't have seen that. I can't imagine how traumatic that must have been.

In the end, regardless of how Micah and Rachel felt about him, he did raise them. He provided for them. I'm sure there was some love there, even if his actions tainted it. So this whole situation has to be so difficult.

As I pace the living room, the sudden buzz of my cell phone from the kitchen counter punctuates the rhythmic thump-thump-thump of my own footsteps. I know, even before I reach it, exactly who it is.

Scott's name flashes across the screen. I swipe to answer.

"Hey, man."

"Did you watch the news?"

"I did." I sit on the couch again and remind myself that Scott doesn't know the whole truth. And he never will.

"I mean, we both knew that man was up to no good, but God. It had to have been pretty bad to motivate someone to do this." I hum in the phone in response, the pit in my stomach growing with each passing second. "Do you think you'll call Rachel?" he asks.

Hearing Rachel's name perks me up. "No, and I don't know if I will." It's the truth. At least not yet. Not until I know for certain that it's safe.

"It might not be a bad idea. You guys were pretty serious, and she might appreciate the condolences."

I sigh into the phone and once again remind myself that he doesn't know. "I'll probably wait. Maybe I'll go to the funeral if they have one."

"I'm sure she would like that. Micah as well."

We both are silent for a beat. What else is there to say?

Scott speaks first. "Alright, I better let you go. I'll see you in the morning."

"For that inspection on the plaza?"

"Yep. Later, man."

Silence falls after we disconnect, and a chaotic storm of questions floods my mind, each one a heavy, suffocating downpour.

Should I contact her?

He's dead, but is it safe to be together?

How long should I wait?

Or will she contact me?

Does she still want to be with me?

Because God knows, I ache to be with her. If she knocked on my door right now, I would scoop her up in my arms, kiss her to high heaven, and never let her go again. These past five years have been hell without her in my life.

I hate all this uncertainty. So, I do the one thing that I do best. The one thing that clears my mind above all else. I grab my cue and head into the garage, ready to take my frustrations out on fifteen pool balls.

I'm leaning against a large oak tree in Spring Lake Cemetery. It's a bright and warm sunny day. Even the weather's happy about what has happened.

From a distance, I watch them lower Dexter into the ground. I'm far enough away that I can't make out the minister's words. Besides, it would all be false platitudes about the evil man. My focus, however, is only on one person.

Rachel.

She's sitting in the first row of folded chairs next to her brother and some other people I don't recognize. She's stoic, her back is ramrod straight, with oversized sunglasses covering her gorgeous brown eyes. Behind her are the Oldies but Goodies. Slick has his hand resting on her shoulder. I love that she has them as a source of comfort and strength.

No one is wearing black, and I wonder if that was intentional. Rachel is stunning in a green dress that hits at her knees. This is the first time I have laid eyes on her since that day in the ER. I don't know how it's possible, but she has gotten even more beautiful with time.

A prayer is offered (a waste of words to the man upstairs if you ask me), and one by one, people form a line, grab a handful of dirt, and toss it into the ground. Micah starts, Rachel follows.

After it's over, I watch the mourners stand around chit-chatting. A war is raging inside my head because I know I should leave. Being here is probably not the best idea. But I am trying to will her to look in my direction. More than anything, I need her to know I was here.

Just like at her graduation.

Tiny glances around the cemetery and does a double-take when he sees me. He subtly nods.

I return it.

With rapt attention, I watch as he makes his way to Rachel. Without drawing too much attention, he casually places his hand on her back and whispers in her ear.

She pivots around.

Our eyes connect.

My heart stops.

A huge gulp of air lodges in my throat. We stand there in a wordless stare, full of emotion and love. With a small wave and her soft smile, we share a silent acknowledgment. Then she wipes at her cheek, turns, and heads to the row of cars parked along the narrow road of the cemetery with her brother and sister-in-law.

The encounter was brief.

But it was everything.

With a heavy heart, I walk to my truck, glancing one last time in her direction, but she's nowhere. Climbing into the driver's seat is a herculean feat because, more than anything, I want to run to her. As I sit here, my resolve is hanging by a thread, my self-control in shambles.

But deep down, I know she needs to take the lead in this. I'm not on the inside.

She is.

So I will be patient and wait.

I start the car, and when I do, my phone vibrates from the middle console.

With shaking hands from the adrenaline rush because of a ten-second stare, I grab my phone and read the text.

> Unknown number: Soon, my love. But not yet.

It's her!

Frantically, I search the row of parked cars, and there she is, the window down in a black Mercedes, watching me. The sun illuminating her face makes it all that more beautiful.

I love you, she mouths.

I love you too, I mouth back.

Then, the window goes up, and the car drives off.

I have no clue what her definition of soon is because it's been three months, and I have yet to hear from her. These last ninety days have crawled by, each one heavier than the last, unlike the blur of the past five years. My phone never leaves my side, and I'm always home unless I have something important to do. Like go to the grocery store because I'm out of food.

Which is where I am now.

Being fifty years old is doing a number on my digestion, so I'm trying to decide what kind of yogurt to buy when a flash of familiar brown hair catches my eye.

Turning, I look, and there, standing and studying the shredded cheese, is Rachel.

She's wearing her usual casual style. Tight jeans and a red V-neck form-fitting t-shirt. Adorable white-painted toenails peek from her sandals, and her hair is in a messy bun.

It's so Rachel. And she's perfect.

I avert my gaze, taking deep breaths to regain my composure. Looking back, she's still there with a bag of shredded cheddar, studying the nutritional label.

With a heart full of hope and nerves, I grip the handle of my grocery basket and head in her direction.

36

We Wouldn't Want to Make Her Blush

Rachel & Johnny

Rachel

"You know, they say that the way to a man's heart is through his stomach."

His smooth voice cuts through the air, causing me to jump. He's here, just a few feet away, in the dairy aisle, his presence radiating warmth and confidence, as it always has. The only man I gave my heart to.

Johnny Givens. Paralyzed by shock, my fingers drop the bag of cheese, and it hits the floor with thud. "Hey ... hey." I'm within feet of the only man I have ever loved, and I look like *this*.

First, in my scrubs at the hospital, and now today, looking like a bum.

What are the odds?

It can't get any worse. I'm just a lonely woman standing in the dairy section, shopping for cheese, wearing no makeup, hair a mess, and jeans I haven't washed in a week. I'm not even sure I put deodorant on this morning, and I'm almost positive these are the same underwear I wore yesterday.

Sexy.

His lips curl into an amused smile, which leads to a joyous laugh, the kind that makes my insides tingle—something I longed to hear again. And his voice. I miss hearing my name from his lips. "Hey, Rachel."

And there it is. *God, that sounded amazing!*

Without an ounce of grace or beauty, I bend over to pick up the cheese but drop it again since I can't stop shaking. I pick it up as my eyes track him, and I drink in the man standing in front of me for the first time in five years. He's wearing his usual jeans, hugging his tree-trunk legs.

I gulp.

My body bursts to life as my scrutiny of him continues to trace upwards. I take in the tight shirt he wears so well, it should be a crime. Muscles stacked on top of muscle are underneath the cotton polyester blend. Is he still as ripped as he was five years ago?

Don't be stupid, Rachel. Of course, he is.

I clutch the cheese.

Needless to say, he is aging well. When I saw him in the hospital, I was in shock, scared, and staring at his wound most of the time.

But now, I look. I *really* look. A dusting of gray is shining through his hair at his temples, and a few new lines crinkle at his eyes as he smiles at me. His lips soften, and affection replaces the hint of amusement.

We stand awkward and quiet in the dairy section of the local grocery store, neither of us saying anything. But wanting to say everything. I'm instantly drunk at the sight of him, and my mouth goes dry because he's striking. Breathtaking. And standing right in front of me.

He glances at the floor, then shuffles his feet. I don't know what to do with my hands, my arms, or my heart, so instead, I fiddle with the cheese while fumbling with what words to say.

Uneasiness crackles between us. Desperation to fill the void consumes me.

I clear my throat.

"It's great to see—"

"What have you been—"

Nervous laughter springs out as we both speak at the same time. I duck my head. "Sorry, you go."

He squints, studying me, then shifts his basket from one hand to the next. "I, um ... I was sorry to hear about Dexter."

"I wasn't." The admission tumbles from my mouth before I can catch it.

Telling the truth was always easy with Johnny.

Right after the murder and every day after, I have played the part of the grieving niece. Only a handful of people know my true feelings on the matter. My brother and sister-in-law and the OBGs. That's it.

When Micah got the call about Dexter's murder, he came to my house and told me. A wave of relief washed over me when he broke the news. Neither of us cried. Neither of us miss him. Dexter was a virtual stranger to me towards the end.

He took from me the one person I needed above everyone else. He saw me sad, crying, angry, and desperate the day after, and he never acted like he cared. Instead, his need for control and keeping up appearances was all he cared about.

His criminal empire was growing far beyond gambling. After Micah and I left the bar, rumors were all we had to go on. Talks of drugs being the most common, and considering the turn of events and Drew going missing, plus what I saw the day we fought, I believe it to be true.

For years, he had so much control over us. Yet, when we both left the bar and cut off all communication with him, he didn't so much as bat an eyelash. Money and power meant more to him than his only family. When he didn't need us anymore, he checked out.

And so did we.

But I wasn't about to test fate and contact Johnny.

Over time, the OBGs became more than just a trio of men who came to Dexter's for a nightly drink; they are our family. The solidarity Micah and I felt when they stopped going once we left meant so much to us. But obviously, they needed a new watering hole, so instead of the bar, they came to Micah's every night. I join in when I can.

But losing Johnny was the worst part. And now, out of nowhere, he's standing right next to me. My heart is fluttering, my palms are sweaty, and my head is hot with anxiety.

In my imagination, if I ever saw Johnny again, I'd be the picture of beauty, looking hot, of course. My hair and makeup would have been pristine. We'd make eye contact, then, in slow motion, I would glide toward him with stunning grace and beauty. Naturally, he would be captivated. Our reunion would have been epic and memorable. A story we would tell again and again to our grandchildren as they roll their eyes, tired of hearing it.

Instead, this is our big moment. Full of cheese and day-old underwear.

When I saw him at the funeral, it took every ounce of self-control I had to not run over to him and thrust myself into his arms. But fear gripped my soul.

And it still does.

Which is why I haven't contacted him. However, it's like the decision is being made for me because, as I buy the ingredients to make tacos on a random Tuesday, he's here.

And the fact he offered his condolences for a man he hated shows what a kind and good person he really is.

I release a puff of nervous energy while dragging my gaze to the rows of bagged cheese for self-control. "I'm sorry I haven't contacted you yet."

His face is stiff yet soft, concerned. "Why didn't you?" he asks. Our eyes collide, seizing under our mutual anticipation. "After the funeral, I thought that maybe—"

"I was afraid."

Cocking his head to the side, he steps forward as his assessment glows with a mixture of heat and affection. His closeness is doing a number on my body. The toe goosebumps return. His calloused hand gently cups my cheek, and I lean into the familiar roughness of his skin.

We touch.

I melt.

Five years float away as his fingers brush my skin, a rush of warmth like heaven.

A feather-light stroke against my cheek from his hand causes his breath to catch a silent acknowledgment of this moment. "You don't have to be afraid anymore," he whispers, his thumb rubbing lightly. "I have you. Scott, Laura, Jake, and Mallory are all safe. Dexter is gone. He can't hurt us anymore."

His lips purse into a tight smile, and he drops his hand. The heat from his touch disappears, and it's almost as if I scalded him with boiling water as he takes a step backward, and the mood shifts. Opening his mouth just a fraction, he presses his lips together, his gaze landing on the polished floor. "Or maybe that's not what you want."

Johnny has always been a man who exudes copious amounts of confidence. But now, he's a man who is doubting everything he thought he knew about us. And I can't blame him. We've been apart for five years, haven't seen each other for a year and a half. A lot can change.

But for me, nothing has changed.

Well, except for me.

I'm not the same sheepish, unsure-of-herself woman Johnny first met. I've moved on in so many ways. From the insecurities my RA inflicted on me, my deep-seated fears that I was unlovable. All of that faded and morphed into me becoming strong, independent, and resilient.

But the love I have for Johnny never budged.

Never bobbled.

Never waived.

It was strong, unshakable. Like a sail, pushing me forward against whatever high wind life threw at me. He was always there. Always present.

But after the funeral, I was afraid. Afraid that he had moved on. Or that we weren't safe, even though I knew any and all threats were gone. But also, I took these three months to get my plan in motion. One I can't wait to tell him about.

"Johnny," I plead, my fingers interlacing with his as I draw his hand to mine, imploring him to look at me. When his name tumbles from my lips, our eyes connect, a spark igniting between us. "I want that more than I have wanted anything in my whole life."

His shoulders sag with relief, and his cheeks flush, which is quite possibly the cutest thing I have ever seen. But then, his face morphs as his lips curl into an evil smirk. "I don't want our reunion to be in front of the Colby Jack."

"Or in front of that sweet old lady over there." I gesture to the elderly woman, trying to decide what kind of cottage cheese to buy.

He leans forward and exhales against my ear. "We wouldn't want to make her blush now, would we?" Every nerve ending in my body is buzzing. He pulls back, and our faces are mere inches apart, his stare holding hotly to mine, torture coiling around his features.

Why? Why am I seeing him for the first time in five years at the grocery store? Because all I want to do is hoist myself into his arms, Bachelorette style.

"Meet me under the stars? Usual spot and time?" He hesitates, searching my face. "It's going to be a clear night tonight."

He adds this in as if it will help convince me. I made up my mind the moment he spoke to me.

"I'll be there." A soft smile forms as his eyes skate over my collarbone and land on the star pendant. He reaches out and touches it, his thumb sweeping over the delicate star.

"You got it?" His voice is a mere whisper.

A low hum vibrates in my chest as his fingers, light as feathers, dance across my skin while he cradles the pendant. "I wear it every day."

He drops the star, and it lands softly against my chest. His shoulders slump with relief as a small, satisfied smile plays on his lips. "I'll see you tonight, my love." He pivots, pausing momentarily before his plump lips graze my cheek. They linger; my eyes flutter close, and I'm completely gone.

He walks away, leaving me dumbstruck with shock at the whole encounter, clutching onto a bag of Vermont Cheddar.

Johnny

I'm sitting on the bed of my truck with my feet dangling and a stomach full of nerves.

My heart hammers against my ribs, a frantic drumbeat accompanying the tremor in my hands; I've never been this nervous. I know she said she would come, but what if her anxiety got the best of her again? What if she went home, thought about it, and got scared?

However, my heart tells me what I want.

Rachel.

Forever.

As my wife, the mother of my children, and the woman I plan to grow old with. Nothing sounds better.

With a thud, I land on the ground from the truck bed, surveying everything one last time to make sure it's all in order. Our usual blow-up mattress sits in the truck, covered in blankets. The sight fills my heart with anticipation as the prospect of lying next to her here again after five years floods my brain. Next, I check the lights I have strung from the trees to the top of my truck. Everything is up and ready.

I mean, I am quadruple-checking at this point.

Next is the card table. It's covered in a white tablecloth, and resting on top are two candles flickering in the night. The final touch is a wine glass for her and a Starbucks coffee for me. A single red rose lies in the center of it all.

I step back and admire the work I pulled together quickly.

It's simple.

After all the complications that our relationship went through ... her pushing me away, us coming together in spectacular fashion, then being torn apart in the worst way.

We are due some simplicity.

A pair of headlights approaching from the distance brings me back to my reality. I watch as the car crawls forward and strain to make out the make and model. But then I realize it's been five years. She may drive something different.

All of my insides are quivering and churning as I wait. Rachel drove a Honda Civic before. Now that this vehicle gets closer, I can make out that it's a black SUV of some sort.

The SUV parks next to my truck, and the door opens.

I choke on nothing but the surrounding air.

She's breathtaking.

Oxygen whooshes out of my lungs silently as I let the moment settle.

Our eyes lock.

The universe shrinks to only this moment, frozen in place.

Her long hair falls over her shoulders in shimmering waves. Her long legs are on full display as a yellow sundress hits mid-thigh, catching the breeze. We stand

...

Breathing.

Wanting.

Loving.

She inhales sharply, turning her gaze to the ground, trying to gain composure, her chest heaving under the fabric of her dress.

But the urge to caress her, hold her, and god help me, kiss her, consumes me.

As she always has.

"Love." A tremor runs through me as I whisper my nickname for her, my voice shaking, while approaching with caution.

Suddenly, her head snaps up, and she bursts forward, running to me. With a joyous laugh, she launches herself into my arms and wraps those long legs around my waist, just like they do in those dumb dating shows she loves so much.

Not so dumb now, huh?

My hands find her waist, and with a gasp, our mouths crash in a fierce, desperate kiss, the air around us crackling with urgency. All five years tumble down into this one kiss. A fire that has lied dormant for one thousand eight hundred twenty-five days is roaring to life. Five years of built-up frustrations are being unleashed.

She recoils her legs, and I place her on her feet, all the while our lips never coming apart. Before I know it, her hands are threading through my hair, her mouth working along with mine, as if our lips never forgot the assignment.

It's crazy. Unbelievable.

The desire to touch every square inch of her body is making my hands act of their own accord. One lands on her waist while the other finds her neck. My thumb strokes down her throat, followed by my mouth. Her head tilts to the side, granting me better access. Her breath hitches, a gasp escaping her lips, causing us to break apart.

"We need to slow down," she says through pants.

No lie there.

I nod, wanting to break through all the yellow tape as my senses flicker back to life. She's right. We have time. All the time in the world now.

My fingers trace the delicate curve of her cheekbones as I press a soft, lingering kiss to her lips. As she melts into me, her gentle hum vibrates against my mouth. Her smell overpowers me, and GOD, did I miss that smell so much.

And since we were always on the same wavelength, she breaks the kiss, buries her face into my neck, and inhales. "You smell so good," she mutters. "It's new." Her lips grin against my neck.

Nuzzling her closer, I smile, my grip tightening. "It is."

"Should be illegal. You're not allowed to smell that good." I chuckle with relief. I thought of her when I picked it out.

She pulls back, her stare embedding itself back into my soul. "I missed you," she whispers.

"I missed everything," I reply softly, meaning every word.

A gentle breeze kicks up, blowing a stray hair across her face. I tuck it behind her ear, my fingers lingering for a moment, before uttering the three words I've waited so long to say again. "I love you, Rachel."

Her eyes slide shut. "I love you too." Hearing her say that was like smooth honey. I slide my palm over and then back down her spine, my thumb tracing lines through the thin fabric of her dress. Our love is open now, transparent.

"Is this it? You and me? No more obstacles?" I ask, still tracing lines, still stroking, never letting go.

She shakes her head. "None. It's you and me. Forever."

A few heartbeats later, she glances around, noticing her surroundings. With a soft sigh, she steps around me, and I take her hand in mine. "You did all of this?" she asks as she walks over to the table and grabs the rose, smelling it while never taking her eyes off of me.

I shrug, suddenly unsure. This moment is huge. Us coming together again. I could have done more. "I know it's not much, but—"

She places her hand on my chest, the gentle pressure of her touch reassuring me. "It's perfect."

With a quick turn to the table, she watches me scurry over and pull out a chair, my hand waving over its worn wooden surface. "Madam." My exaggerated English accent is awful.

Her giggle fills the air as I scoot her in, a joyful sound against the quiet.

Just like that, we are back on track.

As I pour her a glass of wine, she gestures to the coffee cup. "Some things never change, I see."

"You know me ... coffee till the day I die." I shoot her a wink as I sit and grab my cup, taking a sip of the iced brown sugar shaken espresso. A double shot, no less.

I want to be wide awake for this reunion.

With a soft thump, my cup lands on the table. I reach across, my hand outstretched in a silent invitation. She glides her hand into mine, her skin just as soft as I remember. I rub small circles with my thumb on the top of her flesh.

Even with the memory of our sexy reunion kiss lingering, a sense of foreboding settles in as I know we need to talk about everything that led up to it. "Let's rip off the band-aid and hash it all out." She nods. "What happened after I left the bar that night? With Dexter. With you. I want to know everything."

With a long, shuddering sigh that carries the weight of the past five years, she lets it all out. Anger builds in my chest as she relays how Dexter treated her the day after, choosing to never see her again. After everything, he shut her out. Unbelievable.

What a piece of sh—I guess one shouldn't speak ill of the dead. *Whatever.*

But then pride replaces anger as she tells me about her schooling and graduation, even though I was there. Next is her job, and the excitement on her face is something I hope she never loses. I saw how good she was at her job that day in the hospital, but to hear her talk about it is just plain incredible. Then relief fills my soul as she tells me about her health. About how well she is doing with her new doctors and treatment.

"I saw the news report. The one about the rehab facility." Tears fill her eyes. "You did all of that?"

"Yes." No hesitation.

"Why?"

The lump in my throat feels like a fist. I swallow it down. "You have to know I did it all for you." She chokes out a sob, barely audible above the chirping of crickets. "The fact that it was a need in the community is important, obviously, but"—I pause to compose myself—"yes, it was all for you. I wanted you to know that even though we couldn't be together, I still loved you and would always fight for you. Do you use it?" I lean forward, expecting her answer, hope rising like flood waters.

"Every two weeks."

Overcome with relief, I gently grasp her hand. "You have no idea how happy that makes me."

"Me too." A grin crests on her mouth, so bright it put the flame on the candle to shame. "Johnny, it's true that I was scared these last three months, but there was another reason that I took so long to contact you."

I tilt my head, my mind racing. With everything we have been through, nothing is off the table with us.

She reaches into the top of her sundress and pulls out a business card.

I don't know much, but I know I will not make it through this reunion unscathed if she does more stuff like *that.*

I'm toast.

With a low groan, I roll my head back. "Okay, you're not playing fair. You can't expect me to be interested in anything you have to say now."

She shrugs and laughs. What a little tease she is being. I love it.

Holding the card in place with her finger, she slides it over to me. I lift it and examine it.

The logo is of an eight ball with a fork and spoon criss-crossed behind it. The letters J-O-H-N-N-Y-S curve over the top in big, bold black letters. Taunting me.

My name.

My chest tightens. Across the bottom, it reads: Under new ownership. My eyes snap to hers, and she shrugs one shoulder while taking a sip of her wine as if to say, *What's the big deal?*

I flip it over to find the address, hours of operation, a phone number, and one more sentence. It reads: Pool lessons offered every Monday and Wednesday evenings. By appointment only.

I lift the card, holding it between my pointer and middle finger. "Rachel, what is this?"

"After Dexter died, we found out he left us the bar. The government seized everything after his death. Except the bar. He was smart enough to put it in a trust for Micah and me. I never knew. Neither did Micah. We were at least grateful to him for that. Maybe he loved us after all."

I shake my head in disbelief. "I mean, *great*, but is that what you want? To run the bar? What about nursing?"

"I want nothing to do with the bar. I mean, it will always hold special meaning for me. It brought me you." She smiles.

My body is doing its own thing at this point because I'm propelled out of my seat, rounding the table, Rachel in my sights.

After that declaration, I need this woman in my arms.

Her eyes widen as she tracks my every movement. "What are you doing?" she asks as I scoop her out of her chair before she registers what's happening. She squeals. "Johnny!"

I sit in the chair she was once occupying and gently place her in my lap. Immediately, her fingers find my hair, stroking the stands as she attempts to adjust the hem of her dress, tugging it down. My hand playfully slaps hers because … not happening. "Don't you dare." She laughs as my palm splays over the smooth skin of her thigh. "I like this better. You can continue."

"So dramatic." I tilt my mouth and smack my lips to hers in the smackiest of kisses. But I love it.

She grins and rolls her lips as she continues. "Anyway, Slick bought out forty percent. He and Micah run it now, with them being majority owners. I wanted to sell my whole share to Slick, but he refused, so ten percent of it is mine."

This doesn't surprise me one bit.

She continues. "They took out half of the pool tables and donated them to a couple of homeless shelters, then turned that half of the pool hall into a small restaurant. Micah will run that part as soon as the renovations are done."

I sweep my hand over her hair, soaking in every word. "Wow. So he will finally run his own restaurant."

"Yeah, he's pretty excited." The thought causes her to smile. "But you want to know the best part?"

I hold my breath, hanging on to her every word.

"We put in a small espresso machine." With a surge of pride, she lifts her chin, knowing how happy this will make me. "So no more lime club sodas."

My head dips, the laughter pouring out, vibrating in my chest. "I will have to come and have a cup then."

"Yes, you will."

There's a sudden heavy thickness with unspoken words as I summon the courage to ask my next question, rubbing my thumb along her tan skin. "Rachel, why is my name on that card?"

Her fingers stall in my hair, and she composes herself. "Micah didn't want it named after him, and neither did Slick. So, I suggested your name." We stare, an invisible string of emotions pulling us. "My life began in that bar the day I met you. Plus, Micah and Slick want you to offer pool lessons there if you're willing. But no pressure—"

"Yes." The answer spills out of my mouth.

"Yeah?" she asks, perking up.

I nod, then shift her so I can pull out my keys. Her keychain dangles between us. "I can't believe you got this to me."

"Micah heard it through some mutual friends that you were offering lessons in your garage. Brandon was an old high school buddy of his."

The string pulls tighter. "I was floored when he gave this to me."

She takes the eight ball, pulling it to her eye, squinting, and looking inside. "I love this picture." She lowers the keychain, and I place the keys on the table as she continues. "After this"—her fingers find the star necklace—"I had to do something. Somehow, I needed you to know that I was here. Still loving you."

"I look at it. All the time." She smiles and begins slipping, so I tug her tighter against me. "So, how is Brandon?"

"He's good," she replies, bobbing her head. "He said that he could tell you loved the game. You taught him a lot. He joined a pool league, and they went to Vegas. He won it for the team."

Pride fills my heart after hearing this. "I love that. I have been offering lessons in my garage for the last few years now. It started out to keep my mind busy, but eventually, I fell in love with it."

"Well, now, you can do it with me watching from the sidelines."

Works for me.

Anticipation builds at the thought. "You don't say?" She nods. With a tender touch, I pull her closer and press a soft kiss to her shoulder, the whisper of her breath against my ear. "Thank you," I whisper.

"You're welcome."

I continue to pepper kisses, trailing up her neck, breaking only to ask, "We never forgot each other, did we?"

"No, we didn't," she replies with a slow exhale, then giggles when I reach the ticklish spot right below her ear, the sound vibrating throughout my whole body.

I stop laughing, anxious to ask the next question. "I know that day in the hospital, you said you were single." Doubt settles around my heart. "But did you see anyone while—"

"No." With a jolt, my head whips up, the truth hitting me like a physical blow. Deliberately, her thumb reaches and skates over my bottom lip. "No," she answers again. "There has only ever been you."

My fingers sink into the softness of her hair at the back of her head. "Me neither," I confess.

Not one date, not one lingering thought of *she's cute*. Nothing. It was always only Rachel.

Her eyes darken. "Kiss me," she commands.

Without hesitation, I obey.

With a gentle pull, I bring her closer, the warmth of her body against mine as our lips meet again in a passionate kiss. On instinct, my hand squeezes her thigh, her flesh soft against my calloused skin, feeling like the silk I remember.

As if I could ever forget.

Reluctantly, I pull back, and our gazes lock. "Want to stargaze with me?"

She bites her lower lip. "Yeah."

She tries to get off of my lap, but I clamp her in place. "Let me."

Hooking one arm under her knees and the other around her waist, I stand as she lets out a yelp followed by a giggle.

Having her in my arms again ... is far better than I could have imagined. I never realized how much I missed her until this very moment. She wraps her arms around my neck. Hooded eyes meet my intense stare, filled with love and longing as I walk to the bed of my truck.

I place her on the air mattress, and she scoots back and under the blankets. With a flick of a switch, darkness falls as the lights go out. I kick off my shoes and snuggle into the bed to join her. "Come here," I whisper my plea while pulling her close, feeling the softness of her hair against my cheek as I take her in my arms. She rests her head on my chest, and in one swift motion, she slings her leg over mine. We lie quietly as I run my fingers over her arm.

Except for our breathing, there is only silence.

It's peaceful and safe.

Something we haven't felt in a long time.

Scanning the vast sky above us, she hums. "The stars are so bright tonight. It's so beautiful." But I'm not looking at the stars. Instead, I'm mesmerized by the most beautiful woman, a sight that leaves me speechless.

I can't believe she is mine. Again.

"*You* are the most beautiful thing I have ever seen."

She tilts her head, our eyes colliding. "I love you."

I take her hand and kiss her knuckles. Goosebumps erupt over her arm. "I love you too."

After that, we do little stargazing. And a lot of kissing.

Besides, we have our whole lives to look at the heavens. Right now, the only person I want to gaze at is her.

Forever. For the rest of my life.

After our non-stargazing, she rises on her elbow, resting her head in her hand, and gives me a concerned look. Her fingers rest on the cotton of my shirt. "I do have one question for you, though. It's something that has been gnawing away at me for years now."

"Anything." I'll tell this woman whatever she wants to hear as long as we never leave this truck and those goosebumps running up and down her arm as I rub it never leave.

Then, a knowing smirk appears on her face. "So, exactly what happened in Daytona all those years ago?"

Except that.

My huge billowing laugh echoes into the night.

Of course, eventually, I'll tell her about that night in Daytona.

Because we have our whole lives to tell each other our secrets.

Today, tomorrow, and forever.

Epilogue

Rachel & Johnny

Six months later

Rachel

"Well, this feels like old times, huh?" I say, wiping down the sticky bar top. The scent of booze hangs heavy in the air after a busy night while watching Johnny meticulously clean the pool tables.

He glances at me, then quickly averts his gaze as he brushes the green felt. "Yes ... um, yeah ... it does." His voice trembles, his reply shaky as he returns to brushing, the words catching in his throat. James Taylor serenades us from the jukebox.

He's nervous. And Johnny is never nervous.

Weird.

I mean, it's only a random Wednesday night, so there really is no reason for him to be so tense. I'm only here because Slick had a bartender call off, so he asked me to fill in.

And I can't say no to Slick.

I don't do this often, but I have found that the bar has become a place I like to be despite everything, especially now that the whole vibe is different. With Dexter gone, calmness and an air of fun have taken over. Plus, I love to be here on nights when Johnny teaches pool.

God, I love watching him in his element. His face lighting up like a Christmas tree when a student is catching on and making progress is absolutely amazing to witness.

The school has become so popular that we currently have a wait list for people wanting to come and pay for lessons from the great Johnny Givens. He talks about hiring another instructor, but truthfully, he likes to do it himself.

The OBGs have even started taking lessons. Slick is decent, Randy is terrible, and surprisingly enough, Tiny is really, really good. Which makes Monday nights my favorite. That's the OBGs lesson night, as we like to call it. But it's seriously more like a party.

Laura and Scott come in on Mondays from time to time as well. Mallory is dating now, so she is busy with her boyfriend, Caleb, which frees up time for them. And Laura has quickly become my best girlfriend. She is incredible.

Thinking about them all, I realize these people, with their unique quirks and strengths, are my family now. They have meant more to me than anything else.

Finally, I have the family I have always wanted.

And the man currently cleaning pool tables just fifty feet away from me. Well, he is my whole world; everything I hold dear revolves around him.

I hang my apron and walk over to my gorgeous hunk, who hasn't been himself all day. I've asked him repeatedly if he's okay, and he reassures me every time that he is.

But I know better.

As I approach him, I watch him vigorously brush the table like he's mad at it, his jaw tight. The bristles scrape loudly against the felt, so I stroke his back. "Hey, hey, slow down. You are going to rub a hole right in that felt if you aren't careful."

He stops and lowers his head while letting out a long, drawn-out sigh. "You're right. I'm sorry."

Wrapping my arms around his waist, I lean forward, resting my chin on his back. "Are you sure you're okay? I know I've asked you a million times, but..." The question lingers in the air.

With a flick of his wrist, he throws the brush onto the table, and it lands with a soft thud. He turns to me, his calloused hands gently resting on the curve of my hips. "I've never been better."

"Good," I reply against his mouth as he kisses me.

The kiss lingers far longer than planned, and I half expect him to lift me up and onto the table. Which is where I normally end up on nights like this.

I'm mildly disappointed when he breaks the kiss as I moan in frustration. With a determined stride, he walks backward, scanning the path behind him. "Hey, can you do me a favor and round up the balls for me from this table so that I can put them away?"

I give him the poutiest of pouty faces. "Sure."

He chuckles and points toward the table. "Start at the far corner pocket."

Weird, but okay.

It's on the opposite end, but I do as he asks. Reaching my hand into the pocket, I expect the smooth, cool surface of the pool balls, but something soft grazes my fingertips. I peer into the pocket and gasp.

A small black velvet box rests on top of the four, twelve, and eight balls.

With a shaking hand, I reach in, my heart pounding, and pull it out, not wanting to look because I know what is about to happen.

And I'm not sure my heart can take it.

The box creaks on its hinges, and the floor beneath my feet bottoms out. A massive, and I mean *massive,* oval-shaped diamond shines back at me, practically blinding me with its brilliance.

Holy sh—Language, Rachel!

Honestly, I'm not a jewelry girl. But I will definitely wear this!

My hand shoots up, covering my mouth as I raise my head, and there, on one knee in the center of the dance floor, is the only man who has ever held my heart.

"Rachel, I have a question to ask you," he says with his usual swagger and smirk, yet a hint of nerves peeks through.

Pretty sure I'm having a heart attack. Or maybe I'm in knee-crippling shock because I'm not sure my legs will carry me over to him, but somehow, they do, and before I know it, I'm standing right in front of him.

"Johnny." My voice shrinks to nothing.

Oh, my God, this is really happening.

Ever since that night in my living room after washing my hair, when he kissed me until I forgot where I was, I have wanted this moment.

"Rachel, you know how much I love you."

I nod as my eyes mist at the sight of him, down on one knee for me.

"So instead of repeating those eight letters to you, I want to make you some promises. Eight of them, one for each letter."

"Okay," I say with a smile, ready for his words to encompass me like a blanket.

He looks up at me, his eyes filling with tears as he begins. "Rachel, I promise to wash your hair if you can't do it yourself. I'll give you the Johnny special. A scalp and neck massage that ends with a kiss." I giggle through my tears. "I promise to somehow, someway, make you laugh every single day. How you just did." He pauses. "I promise to never let fear come in between us again." A sob sits in my chest as my attention remains on him. Always *him*.

"I promise to always dance with you, even when we are old and gray. I promise to finish that pool lesson we started the night you ended up on the pool table. I promise to watch those dumb dating shows with you. *And* we will reenact some scenes."

Tilting my head, I huff out a chuckle.

"I promise to be true to you and only you, to love you deeply, fulfill you, lifting you to heights you deserve. And last but not least, I promise to live every day of my life striving to be the best husband and man that you deserve. I'll even give Scott a run for his money."

Another peal of laughter bubbles forth.

"But that's only if you will have me." He takes the ring box from my hand and pulls out the sparkler. His trembling hand envelops mine as he slides it over my finger.

A perfect fit. Just like us.

"Rachel Garcia, will you make me the happiest man alive and become my partner and wife?"

I can't speak. I can't move. I'm hypnotized and stunned as my head answers for me. I nod.

"Yes?" he asks through laughter.

"Yes, Johnny. I will marry you."

He immediately stands and grabs me as I launch myself into his arms, laughing through my tears. He holds me close, wrapping his arms around me and peppering my face with kisses. Then our lips collide.

Sealing our lives together.

Seven years after the engagement

Johnny

The officiant asks everyone to rise, and nerves erupt in my stomach.

Is she going to go through with it?

I have no idea.

The wedding march begins, and I crane my neck so that the entryway of the aisle is in my full view. She rounds the corner, smiling just like we practiced a million times in our living room.

I release the biggest sigh of relief as her eyes meet mine.

I melt.

Our daughter Piper is the flower girl in Mallory's wedding. But nerves got the best of her right before the ceremony, even crying, saying that she didn't want to do it.

So, Rachel came and got me because, of course, she wanted her daddy.

The three-year-old currently walking towards us has me wrapped around her finger so tight, I lost circulation the day she was born.

At first, Rachel and I had a hard time conceiving. We knew we wanted kids right away. Neither of us was getting any younger, so right after our wedding, one year after I proposed, we started trying. Obviously, we were discouraged, of course, but let's face it, the trying part was fun.

After lots of tests and tears, we got no answers as to why we couldn't get pregnant. There was nothing wrong with Rachel or me. The doctors suspected that since Rachel was thirty-six, coupled with her RA, perhaps her body wasn't cooperating.

Needless to say, it was a hard, dark, and sad time.

Over time, when we finally surrendered to a life that would only be us, the double line appeared. Nine months later, another woman entered my orbit. And my heart.

Rachel needed a C-section because of some complications. The entire experience was next-level scary, but when it was over, the first cry of my daughter filled my ears, and it was the sweetest sound I had ever heard. I had the privilege of holding her first, and when the nurse placed her in my arms, I was a goner.

Sorry, fellas, but no man will ever be good enough.

You hear people talk about the love and connection they have with their kids. And you believe them, of course. You see it. But it isn't until you experience it yourself that you truly feel it. My heart became bigger that day. And it's because of the two women in my life. They make me whole.

Piper and Rachel are everything to me.

Never in a million years did I think I would become a father at fifty-four years old. Hell, some of my buddies are grandfathers. But not me—Rachel and my daughter keep me young. A tile installer at a job site just last week thought I was in my forties. I told his boss to promote him.

Redirecting my attention to my daughter, I smile as I watch her tiny, delicate hand dip into the basket, tossing flower petals on the white runner. Her white taffeta dress, with a dusty pink bow around her waist, sways as she walks. Her "wedding girl crown," as she called it, rests on top of her head, shimmering with every step.

Hands down, the cutest flower girl that has ever lived.

Piper is tall for her age, which is to be expected. Her hair is dark blonde like mine, and she has her mom's big brown eyes. And her personality? Sass for days.

Lord help me.

I'm full of pride as I watch Scott behind Piper with Mallory on his arm. Her arm is encircling his as he holds tight to her hand.

Mallory has grown into a strong, independent young woman, and I couldn't be prouder of the person she has become despite her autism. Plus, she is marrying a wonderful young man named Caleb, who treasures her and accepts her for who she is.

Something I hope for my daughter someday.

I internally roll my eyes at the thought.

I look at Scott; if I'm not mistaken, a single tear glistens and slowly rolls along his weathered cheek.

Oh, I'm going to relentlessly tease him about that; he'll never live it down!

Rachel squeezes my arm as we both watch our little angel take the last few steps. In order to persuade her to walk down the aisle and prevent a last-minute freakout, I promised Piper that she could sit with us if she made it all the way to the altar.

Making promises. I still make them with Rachel, and now I do with my daughter. All the time.

And I intend to keep every one of them.

Once she reaches us, she leaps into my arms. "Daddy! I did it!" she squeals out, earning a chuckle from everyone in the audience.

I kiss her cheek and whisper. "You did so good!"

Rachel leans in and rests her chin on my shoulder, her heels making her almost as tall as me. "Great job, baby girl," Rachel reassures her as she traces the soft, springy curls of Piper's hair.

After Scott hands Mallory over to Caleb, the officiant asks us all to take our seats. Piper sits on my lap as she arches her head to whisper in my ear. "Daddy, can I have cake at the weception?"

I look over at Rachel, and my gorgeous wife grins, nodding in agreement.

With a smile, I do what I do best.

"Of course. I promise."

His Last Shot

Playlist

- Closing Time – **Semisonic**

- Stargazing – **Myles Smith**

- Fire and Rain – **James Taylor**

- Lose Control – **Teddy Swims**

- Don't Give Up On Me – **Andy Grammer**

- To Love Someone – **Benson Boone**

- Falling Like the Stars – **James Arthur**

- Fall Into Me – **Forest Blakk**

- If You Love Me – **Forest Blakk**

- You Belong With Me (Taylor's Version) – **Taylor Swift**

- Overjoyed – **Matchbox Twenty**

- All the Ways (feat. Ray LaMontagne) – **The Secret Sisters**

- Flaws – **Calum Scott**

- First Rodeo – **Kelsea Ballerini**

- The Joker And The Queen (feat. Taylor Swift) – **Ed Sheeran**

- My Girl – **Dylan Scott**

- In Case You Didn't Know – **Brett Young**

- You Say – **Lauren Daigle**

- The Alchemy – **Taylor Swift**

- Eavesdrop – **The Civil Wars**

- Both Sides Now – **Joni Mitchell**

- Any Kind Of Life – **Lewis Capaldi**

- Time After Time – **Eva Cassidy**

- Taking You Home – **Don Henley**

- Forever After All – **Luke Combs**

Acknowledgements

Ok, so I thought that after writing three books, the acknowledgments would get shorter and easier to write. Wrong! This is still hard!

Here goes nothing!

It only feels right to start by thanking you, the reader. Whether this is the first time you have ever read one of my books, or you are familiar with my work, I owe this all to you! If you promise to keep reading, I promise to keep writing!

Next up is my family. None of this would be possible without the three of you. Brian, Jackson, and Samantha, you are *my* north star. Always.

This wonderful story is what it is because of my Alpha and Beta readers. Your ideas, critiques, and suggestions bleed throughout this entire book (I'm looking at you Delaney). I took everything you said to heart and honestly, most of the time, you are on point. I owe so much to you all!

And this leads me to, once again, thanking my editor Nevvie Gane. What can I say? You are a master at your craft. This is the fourth time we have worked together, and you still amaze me! You are stuck with me, girl!

There is an amazing piece of art included in the beginning pages of this book, painted by my brother, Daniel Evans. Daniel, I know our original plan didn't work out. But I can never thank you enough for the blood, sweat, and tears you poured into that painting. Thank you so much! Also, I need to thank you for putting up with my never-ending questions about pool leagues when I was first outlining the book. I love that dad's passion for the game is now yours. I don't say it enough, but I am *very* proud of you!

Speaking of my dad, if you noticed, I dedicated this book to him. I knew, after writing Becoming Mallory, that Johnny would have a book. But I had to give Johnny a 'thing.' And it couldn't just be construction. Then one day, while grocery shopping, it came to me. The game of pool! You see, my dad is the best pool player out there. And that's not just me, his daughter, saying that. It's the truth. Ask anyone who has played him. They can't beat him. Which is why I made Johnny such an amazing player in the book (honestly, my dad would beat Johnny in a head to head). So, not only would I have a resource at my disposal, it would be a great way to honor my dad and the game that he loves so much. So, thank you, dad!

When Johnny describes the street he grew up on, well, that was my childhood street. The Parlor was an actual bar, and, like Johnny, people leaving at two in the morning always woke me up. And also, like Johnny, I would fall asleep to my dad playing pool in his garage. As I write this, and even though he is in his seventies, more than likely, he is in his garage, at this very moment, shooting around, practicing. He truly is the best!

While outlining the book, I knew I wanted Rachel to have a chronic illness of some kind. Then while doom scrolling on Instagram, I ran across a story by a creator, sammies_booked. In the story, she stated that there isn't enough Rheumatoid Arthritis representation in fiction. If you follow Sammie on Instagram (and if you aren't, you should be!) then you know she is a Rheumatoid Arthritis warrior! I admire how vocal she is about her struggles, yet she doesn't let it stop her. Well, that was that. Rachel was going to have Rheumatoid Arthritis. I reached out to Sammie and asked her if she would be willing to help me and answer any questions. Of course, she said yes! There were so many times that I would randomly message her and ask her something. Sammie always answered right away and never shied away from telling me if I was wording something incorrectly.

So Sammie, thank you so much for your help! I truly hope that I have given a voice to those who deal with RA, like yourself. I hope you feel seen in the character of Rachel. This book wouldn't be the story that it is without your voice guiding me. I am forever grateful!

With that, until next time friends!

About the author

Elaine Evans has had a love of writing ever since she can remember. But it wasn't until she hit middle age that she turned it into a second career. His Last Shot is her third novel.

When she isn't writing or working at her day job (a medical assistant at a children's hospital), you can find Elaine pursuing her other hobbies and interests. She loves cooking, baking, photography, and, of course, reading. In the fall and winter, you will find her on Sunday's rooting for the Pittsburgh Steelers. But it's her role as wife, mother, and dog mom to her Pomeranian Vinnie, that brings her the most joy.

Elaine resides with her family in Ohio (yes, she is a Steelers fan that lives in Ohio. It's fine, really), but one day, dreams of living on the beach. Hey, maybe if this writing thing takes off, it will happen. You never know!

Elaine would love to connect with her readers! You can find her on Instagram, Facebook, and Goodreads.

instagram.com/elaineevanswrites

goodreads.com/author/show/1739279.Elaine_Evans

facebook.com/profile.php?id=61557583049180

www.ingramcontent.com/pod-product-compliance
Lightning Source LLC
Chambersburg PA
CBHW031335020726
47499CB00005B/1277